**A SAMPLING OF THE OVERWHELMING PRAISE
FOR ONE OF THE SPELLBINDING FICTION
TRIUMPHS OF OUR TIME!**

"An exceptional historical novel . . . rich in scene and mood, impressive in command of language, highly complex in characterization, delicate in refinement of motivations"

—*Kirkus Reviews*

"Rich and passionate, full of color, drama, insight"
—*Manchester Guardian*

"Combines a sensitive gift for the imaginative evocation of a distant epoch with a sense that eternal issues were being fought in those days"

—*New York Post*

"A feudal world torn by social, political and religious conflict . . . lifelike people and excellent descriptive passages . . . a richly detailed, well-plotted, substantial historical novel"

—*Chicago Booklist*

Look for these upcoming books in
THE TARN TRILOGY, available in
Popular Library editions:

DEEP ARE THE VALLEYS
THE SILENT TARN

The Tarn Trilogy · 1

HIGH ARE THE MOUNTAINS

by Hannah Closs

POPULAR LIBRARY • NEW YORK

Published by Popular Library, a unit of CBS
Publications, the Consumer Publishing Division
of CBS Inc., by arrangement with The Vanguard Press, Inc.

May, 1978

Copyright © 1959 by The Vanguard Press, Inc.

Library of Congress Catalog Card Number: 59-5091

ISBN: 0-445-04219-2

TO ALL THOSE
PLEDGED TO THE QUEST
OF LIBERATION

FOREWORD

HISTORICALLY, THIS NOVEL DEALS WITH THE EARLY THIR-
teenth century, but it reflects our own age. It is not a
chronicle and does not aim at exactitude of archaeological
and historical detail. Little is known of the intimate lives
of the characters, and the figure of Wolf of Foix, apart
from my use of some unsubstantiated anecdotes concerning his birth, a reference in the registers of the Inquisition,
and the mention of his name in a couple of battles record-
ed in chronicles, is entirely my own invention.

As to Raymond of Toulouse and Trencavel, I have tried
to recreate their characters imaginatively, to interpret what
is known of their actions, culminating, in the present story,
in the historic siege of Carcassonne. Indeed, that has been
my attitude throughout, convinced as I am that the imagination can create a more living truth than close adherence
to fragmentary facts.

For fact, moreover, is perhaps less essentially true than
legend, and the stories told by the shepherds on the Tabor
Mountain in the Pyrenees may contain the germ of a profounder reality than any annals. The ruins of Montségur
still exist, and, whether or not an esoteric cult was actually
practiced there, it was certainly a citadel of the Albigenses, and we are at last beginning to realize the immense influence that Catharism has exerted, at least indirectly, in
the mind of man through the ages. A chasm may yawn
between the dream and the actuality. The quest (whether
in its highest or most trivial aspect) is none the less real.

H.C.

Halt sunt li pui e li val tenebrus.

(La Chanson de Roland)

Know thou the One, the Soul.
It is the bridge leading to the immortal being.
(The Upanishads)

THE SILENT TARN

The Way that can be told of is not an unvarying Way.
(LAO-TSE, *The Way and Its Power*, translated by A. WALEY)

I

EVEN NOW HE DID NOT TURN, THOUGH ALL TRACE OF A path had vanished, lost in the rough scree that clothed the mountain slope before it made a last thrust to reach the height.

From somewhere invisible the trickle of water fell on his ear, but, blind and deaf to all but his purpose, he struggled on.

Above him boulder on boulder piled itself to the blunted peak. Hauling himself from rock to rock, he scrambled upward, as though all the frustrated zest of his boyhood were gathered into a desperate assault on the dense and obdurate mass.

And then suddenly, too exhausted to be conscious of anything but a dim sense of finality, he had reached the summit. Blinded by the wind, his knees and hands trembling from the strain, he flung himself under the shelter of an overhanging rock.

He had escaped; he was free. Only now did he feel certain.

For a time he lay without movement, his eyes closed, while his breath came in short, convulsive gasps and his heart pounded against his ribs. At last, as his pulses quieted, he raised himself on his knees and gazed around him.

Mountain on mountain stretched before him, wall upon wall, gashed and riven by precipitous valleys, naked but for the black strain of forest left like patches of fur on the flanks of some shorn beast.

A waste of stone . . .

He shut his eyes and opened them again, incredulous. Beyond those apparently impregnable summits, those impassable ravines, lay, they said, the arid sun-parched plateau of Spain, the luring adventures and the incredible marvels that Brother Martin was accustomed to paint in such fiery colors as though they were the snares of Satan himself. And yet they had been as nothing compared to the fantasies he himself had woven around these mountaintops, when, in hours of despondency, he had climbed the little hill beyond the monastery wall to gaze at the long, jagged ridge of blue rising against the horizon and dreamed that behind that great buttressed mass lay a realm surpassing all the wonders of the world.

The fantasies had dwindled, the wonder remained, shifting gradually, imperceptibly, from the object to the act. To climb the mountain, to reach . . . . But on the nature of the goal he had almost ceased to speculate. Only to get beyond . . . Perhaps he was even unclear as to what.

Enough that at the moment he had reached the height. Yet had he? Dumbfounded, he stared at the unending peaks, that waste of mountain and sky, an immensity measured against which all dream, all human vision seemed at one blow reduced to a pitiful nothingness. And yet amid that overwhelming sense of obliteration something seemed to rise within him exultant, gathering all else into a single consciousness of freedom and space.

He sprang to his feet and, throwing back his head, brushed the light brown hair from his forehead. His hands were bruised and grazed by the jagged stone, his tunic torn where he had caught it under the knee, but tightening his belt he clambered down from the height and set out for a narrow track he now discovered running along the farther side of the mountain ridge.

Yes, at last he was free! Almost it seemed, in his exhilaration, that the doubts and terrors of the past had been but fantasies. Beneath him the world rolled away into infinity, unreachable, lost in space. He would go striding on from pass to pass, summit to summit, till the end of time.

Forgetful of the future, oblivious of the passing hours, he tramped on. The June sun beat down upon the rock till the grayish stone shone white, incandescent, deprived of solidity. Even the wind seemed weakened under the consuming power of light.

Gradually he began to feel growing pangs of hunger

and thirst, but he passed it off. Later, perhaps, he would light on some shepherd grazing his flocks and beg a chunk of break and cheese. Maybe he might even share his fire at nightfall. But at present he gave the future little thought.

Only two days ago he had been sitting among rows of pupils at the long refectory board, while Brother Benedict in his nasal singsong drawled the lesson for the day. Almost he would have relished that platter of meat and beans, but what was a full stomach against freedom?

By now the path, descending gradually, was threading its way through high rocks. Even the distant forest was shut out. Nowhere a sign of vegetation, except here and there in the shelter of a boulder some shriveled stems of lavender, a solitary rosemary writhing in despairing prostration against the stones. On either side the boulders grew vaster and more ungainly, scarred by moss and lichen and weathered to monstrous shapes. But for the rude track, one would have thought no human foot ever trod that solitude. Only now and then the carcass of a bird, a pile of wizened excrement, told of animal life. Not a sound broke the silence.

In affected boldness he began to whistle. But even as he was about to break out in song, it died on his lips, and his feet came to an abrupt halt.

So unexpected was anything but the sight of stone in that rockbound wilderness that, as the path made a sudden dive round a projecting spur, he had almost walked straight into the tarn.

It lay before him under the wall of rock that rose from its farther brink—a well of water, dark, motionless, as though the voice of the mountain struggling for utterance in that inarticulate agony of stone was here muted to a silence so utter and profound that it brooded over the petrified solitude like a presence terrifying and unknown.

Mazed and shaken, the boy stood still, abashed, the song dead on his lips, the armor of boldness so recently donned falling from him like scales. Slowly, with uncertain feet, he strolled along the water's edge, but, awed by his echoing tread in that uncanny hush, he sank down in the lee of an overhanging rock. A heaviness seemed to sink upon him, drawing him down.

Not a ripple stirred the black mirror of water. "How deep, how deep," he murmured, as though drugged. Dead, devoid of all living things, the tarn lay at his feet—mo-

11

tionless to the rim. Silence, but for the cry of a bird swooping over the crater. Once he lifted his head. Were they real, those fawn-gray creatures that posed an instant on a narrow shelf of rock, leaped to a ledge of the mountain wall, and vanished as swiftly as they had come? Izards—the Pyrenean chamois, he thought dimly—the pride of the chase. Had he but had his bow, a javelin even; but somehow the thought seemed irrelevant, as though the ordinary values of life were melting away. Ambition, envy, the nameless yearning that had goaded him so fiercely had faded, receding to another plane familiar and yet remote. And as he gazed, tranced, on that silent depth, it seemed that, drop by drop, he was emptied of his former self and drained into the bottomless well of the lake. A strange tranquility took hold of him, a wonder deep and pervading, a peace he had never known.

How long he remained gazing at the tarn the boy never knew. Perhaps a distant shout, a stone dislodged by a footstep, had fallen vaguely on his ear, only half penetrating his consciousness, for it was another sound that at last pierced harshly through his trancelike state.

Startled to sudden alertness, he listened, for surely it had been a laugh. Actually low-pitched and stifled, in that solitude it had vibrated around the wall of rock, wounding the silence as though it bruised his own flesh. Fully awakened now, he glanced around dismayed, sure that he had been discovered, his hard-won freedom shattered at a blow. But the figure he saw standing on a spur of rock above him was that of a stranger, and if indeed a pursuer he was evidently in no hurry to catch up with his prey. For a moment, indeed, he remained immobile, regarding the scene with a skeptical curiosity that suggested perhaps less of mockery than a disenchanted registration of life's curious phenomena.

"Alas, have I disturbed the incantation?" He smiled wanly and slowly descended from the height.

Tall, clad in a hunting suit of so dark a green that it seemed almost mourning, the natural pallor of his face exaggerated by the black hair and somberness of his garb, he looked, though actually only a youth, far older, a fact accentuated by the peculiar regularity of his features and the rigidity of his limbs, which seemed, as though jointless, to be impelled by some force outside himself. Slowly approaching the boy, who, as if in instinctive self-defense,

12

had planted himself against the rocks, he halted within a few feet of him and, leaning back against a boulder, continued his curious scrutiny.

"At first, you know, I almost thought you might be part of the famous spell."

Then, as there was still no answer, he gave a little shrug. "Seems after all he's a troll and can't speak our mortal tongue. Nourished on dew and spiders, eh? Still, he looks pretty succulent." Putting out his hand he tweaked him lightly on the cheek. "Evidently I'm in luck today. First an izard, and now a pretty young changeling—good booty for a day. Ler's hope they pay a fine ransom for you." He gave a little humorless laugh. "Well, who are you, anyway? One of Lantar's brats or Perelha's, I suppose. What, playing truant?" For the boy had started at the name. "All right, don't get flustered." A look of malicious amusement curled his thin, sardonic lips. "There's still time for some fun. They're having to climb right down the chasm to haul her up—the izard, I mean. It's their own fault," he continued in the same rather weary drawl. "If only my dear cousin hadn't been in such a hurry to finish her off; but then, he never had a sense of beauty. Half a-swoon on those pretty little feet—almost as good as those Eastern dancers. . . . Never seen any, I suppose?" He smiled at the boy's confusion, registering the dreamy perplexity of the deep gray eyes, the almost vulnerable sensibility of the lips. "Brought up in a nice wholesome atmosphere, far from the world's pollution, I reckon—clean mountain air, spiced with a good dose of spiritual cant from the dear Cathars." An acrid note had suddenly crept into the flat, apathetic voice. "Don't tell me you're not a little heretic; they're all tarred with the same brush hereabouts." He laughed, but for a moment his strangely impassive features looked somehow distorted.

Heretic?—well, perhaps, the boy thought wryly, and almost smiled at the irony of the accusation but that the man's manner began to make him uneasy, and, aware that denial would only involve him in more inquiries as to his identity, he made no attempt at a contradiction.

"Silent defender of the faith, is that it?" mocked the other with a little shrug. "Still, you're not likely to suffer martyrdom up here, anyway, not yet. Well, let's have a look at the old puddle," he continued, and, rousing himself from his inertia, strolled to the water's edge.

With a growing sense of unease the boy looked about him, anxiously contemplating escape, when his companion, as if guessing his intention, turned, beckoning him to follow, and knowing that flight might only lead him into the arms of his companions, he reluctantly obeyed, an odd feeling of revulsion creeping over him at the other's proximity.

For a few moments the stranger stood looking at the water, while the old wan smile flitted over his lips.

"The Lake of Evil," he muttered; "not a bad name for it. What," he exclaimed, quizzically regarding the boy's startled face, "you didn't know? I suppose the Cathars have stuffed you with other tales. But it's a good one really," and as if lost in thought he stared at the water. "Seems long ago some filthy plague ravaged the land till the old Druids, scenting the general wickedness, got all the poor perverted souls to pile up their jewels and gold and what-not and chuck them into the lake—with fine success, it seems, for the land was delivered, though why they took the trouble to drag the stuff all the way up the cursed mountain, God alone knows. Incidentally," he added cynically, "they tell the same sort of yarn at Toulouse—about a lake that's supposed to be buried under St. Sernin's. One of the bishops took a fancy to prowling about there at night. Lusted after the gold and meant to have the thing drained maybe; anyhow, they found him dead down there. After that they bricked up the steps. There's a curse on this place, too," he paused significantly, gazing at the dark silent mirror. "See, the water's pitch black. It was green enough, they say, till they chucked in the stuff. Not a single fish has been seen in it since. Still, there's no harm in making sure." He leaned forward, peering into the bottomless depth. "Kneel down," he muttered.

Dully, as if half hypnotized by the dead, monotonous voice, the other obeyed.

"Nothing?"

After a little while, rising, the boy shook his head. As though bored, his companion had begun to dig idly at the stones with his toe.

"Well, well, we'll give the old wives credit for that part of the tale, at any rate. But they say, too," he seemed to drag out the words, "if anyone throws in a stone he'll raise the hell of a storm and find his death." He paused and, as if half forgetful of the boy, stared darkly at the lake. "As easy as that—a mere stone's throw and one could solve the great enigma. Unfortunately—" and once more that low, mirthless laugh echoed across the tarn—"it isn't the whole lake; you see, it says he'll die of the same disease that ravaged the land of old. No doubt a little fantastic elaboration of the theme, still it's not surprising—one can hardly call the place enticing."

It was true. Since the arrival of this sinister youth the tarn seemed somehow to have altered, as though a blight had been cast upon the place. Involuntarily the boy shivered.

Casually the stranger picked up a stone.

"Supposing one tried—of course, I can't vouch for the result. The story doesn't go into details. Interesting, no doubt—might provide material for our great doctors' researches. Old Arnold of Belpech keeps some striking specimens under observation down at the hospice in Toulouse."

A retching sickness mounted to the boy's throat. God, couldn't the man stop his subtle mockery, his filthy insinuations? Wildly he strove to rediscover that lost magic, his enchanted peace. Had he only dreamed it? Silent, inscrutable, the tarn gave no answer. Doubt began to gnaw at his heart, cold, insidious. Was it merely the result of the man's dark presence, or did it—could it—lie in the place itself? Horror, double-faced, clutched at him. At his side the stranger had begun to toy with the stone, silently measuring the boy's growing pallor.

"Well, shall we dare?"

But now the suavely mocking voice cut through the horror, gathering, welding all doubt, all fear, to a loathing so intense that all else was swept before it in a consuming madness of rage and hate.

With deliberate slowness the stranger had begun to raise his arm, pausing midway. "Well," he repeated. Then, slowly bending his elbow, he made as if to take aim, but before he could finish the sentence or draw his hand back for the throw, it was clutched in a vice. Reeling under the sudden impact, he saw for an instant two fevered eyes in a boy's white face close to his own, before, swaying wildly, he lost his balance and pitched crashing upon the stones.

Minutes passed before, recovering, more from shock than from hurt, he began to pick himself up.

"Bastard!" In a fury of wounded pride, the word hissed

15

through his lips. But the boy was already scrambling over the boulders and making his way blindly across the mountain ridge. Neither in his confusion saw the stone roll slowly over the rocks or heard the low, reverberant echo as of distant thunder as it rolled into the tarn.

"Bastard!" The word hurled in sheer fury struck home more poignantly than those rancorous lips ever knew, searing the solitude, echoing from rock to rock, till in the ears of the fleeing boy all the torments of his childhood seemed gathered in that familiar name, in a last triumph of mockery and scorn. Wolf—bastard of Foix. Not that the irregularity of his birth was regarded either by him or his comrades as a particular mark of shame. There were enough of his own kind in the monastery; in fact, the very name he bore might have been enough to rouse jealousy rather than disdain, for to have a drop of the blood of Foix in one's own veins was glorious in itself. But there, perhaps, was the rub. For oh, the valor, the heroism implicit in that name! What chance had he had, cooped up for years in the cloister, hunched over book and psalter, while his legitimate brothers charged at shield and quintain in the tiltyard at Foix? Sometimes he had guessed that it needed but a word from him and he might have been liberated from the monastic pale. But shyness, pride, some terror of failure, perhaps, had kept him silent. And then, in those long years of his father's imprisonment at Seo d'Urgel, the last hope had vanished, and when the count on his release had visited the monastery again the boy had stood before him tongue-tied, diffident in his proud sensibility to the point of sullenness. He could still see towering above him that magnificent and scornful head, hear the rich mocking voice asking if after all he wouldn't prefer the job of disemboweling Saracens to hooking souls out of hell? But, in face of that scathing grandiloquence, he could only stammer abashed, finding no words that could ever crystallize his own nebulous dreams, while on the arrogantly passionate countenance of the Count of Foix the proudly disguised disillusionment had hardened to cold disdain. With that, he had known well enough that he had forfeited his chance. And yet what troubled him often more deeply than the thought of what he had missed was the secret apprehension that even his father's world would not have satisfied his innermost dreams.

16

What, then, did he seek? What even did he desire? The obscurity of his feelings seemed to his groping mind to equal that of his birth till he saw in his own ambiguity the root of all his troubles and perplexities, the keynote of his whole being—doubt. Even in his most tranquil, most care-free hours it would suddenly assail him, leading him to the brink of a bottomless pit. In vain he struggled to discover the antidote, seeing how others appeared to find peace in piety or in scholastic speculation, where all such perilous errings of the spirit were at least leashed in a labyrinth of the terms of definitions or quibbling on some obscure theological point. Yet there were some, he knew, who in long sleepless nights, in days of fasting and prayer tight closed within their cells, wrestled with temptation. Them he almost envied; if only Evil wore a definite shape—lust, greed, cruelty, murder even. In despair he had tried to picture those myriad ghastly shapes that tell in a coil of horror upon St. Anthony, till, always abnormally sensitive to hideousness and disease, he had actually fallen sick.

Yet even the nightmares that haunted his fever had not exceeded his worst moments of waking dread. For what fiendish apparition could equal the horror of nothingness, the incalculable potency of things, the terrible and mysterious fact that any minute the apparent could without warning or reason change into its opposite? Where was security? Of what use were ambition and determination in such a world? In vain he sought a refuge in religion, and found but an irreconcilable gulf between Heaven and Hell. In vain he turned toward the temporal world and saw a mirage of evanescent and glittering shapes under which yawned an abyss of cruelty and lust. And yet how he yearned toward it in a fierce desire to shine resplendent in its light; while swung perpetually from one extreme to another, the fearful, agonizing urge remained—to solve the mystery, to discover, behind that apparent maze of division, a meaning, a deeper reality that could reconcile the incredible contrariness of being; his cowardice and his dream of valor, his father's splendor and his mother's ignominy. Instinctively he had apprehended that the answer lay not in some heaven beyond but in life itself, and that it was only by braving its immensity that he could find release. So it had come about that gradually his spirit's quest had become merged with the dreams that since earliest childhood he had woven around the mountain, believing

17

that behind that great wall of rock lay the end of all torment, a promised land. Even when he had outgrown those early boyish fantasies they had persisted in an unappeasable yearning for those far, immitigable heights, till they had come to be the symbol of what for him was the nearest equivalent of faith, the power of his own yearning for an absolute. Still, in his darkest hour, when in his customary diffidence he had stood before his father and hesitated to take that proffered chance, when all had seemed to crash about his ears, it alone had remained at the back of his mind, secure, till when at last he had grasped with his own hands the freedom he had feared to accept, it was to the mountain that he had fled in a last, despairing hope of salvation or ultimate defeat.

"Bastard." Blindly, the hated name still ringing in his ears, the boy sped on. Had that, then, been the mocking answer to his dreams? Taking no heed of path or direction, guided by no more than an instinctive sense of security and the fear that he was an easy target on that naked height, he had chosen the way of descent. But before long the sound of voices caused him to throw himself face downward, while with beating heart he listened to the tramp of feet, mounting behind a spur of rock, that evidently belonged, to judge by their words and a hearty curse, to men bearing a burden; but he could not catch their words nor dared he lift his head, guessing that they could be no other than the uncanny huntsman's companions. Then at last the man was real, he thought, almost with a sense of relief, for already in his fevered mind the man's mortal nature had become doubtful, and no sooner had the voices faded than he was hurrying on, bending and keeping as far as he could in the shelter of the rocks. Scrambling, leaping, tearing hands and clothes on jagged boulders, he continued his perilous descent, only to find his way impeded by chasm and torrent, so that he was forced upward again. Once he looked around expectant of pursuit, for by now the huntsmen had surely rejoined their friend, but the mountainside was bare, empty, as before, of all human life. At last, striking a rude path, he slackened his pace. His feet were weary, sweat poured from his forehead, his clothes stuck fast to his skin; but still, knowing there was nothing to do but go forward, he trudged on. Slowly it dawned on him that escape was hopeless.

18

The prey of two pursuing forces—the authorities of the monastery and his new-made enemy of the chase—sooner or later he would be hedged in. He glanced around him in despair. The sun had long passed the zenith and by now he had completely lost his bearings. He seemed, to judge by the sun, to be descending the mountain on the opposite side from which he had begun his climb. Vanished were all traces of the Ariège valley and the green wooded slopes that rose from the farther side of the riverbank. The valleys here seemed yet wilder and steeper; sometimes a turn of the path opened up a glimpse of a dark and terrifying ravine. From time to time he caught sight of a castle perched on a distant crag. Hunger began to gnaw at his vitals, till he felt sick and weak. Should he, after all, have to seek refuge in one of those mountain forts? Lantar—Perelha—the names had been on the lips of the stranger. They and the rest were his father's vassals, and after an inevitable discovery of his identity, he saw himself despatched ignominiously to the monastery, or to Foix; and now the situation was complicated by his new enemy, who might, for all he knew, be one of his father's friends, or at any rate a guest at one of those very castles. Nevertheless, measured against the growing terrors of the surrounding solitude, those human dangers began swiftly to diminish. Minute by minute the silence deepened. Around him, on every side, those remote unscalable peaks that only a little time ago had filled him with such exhilaration and freedom brooded sinister, malignant.

Hours seemed to pass. With disconcerting clarity it began to dawn on him that he might never find his way off the mountainside. He had heard of those who, losing their way in the hills, had wandered round and round on their own track, till, overtaken by night or fog, they had plunged headlong into an abyss or died of hunger and cold. The day was still bright, but with increasing unrest he watched a lozenge-shaped cloud rise and encircle a distant crag to the left. The clouds were gathering! Anxiously he quickened his footsteps. Should he call, turn back, and so run into the arms of the vengeful huntsman? But by now, he tried to persuade himself, his father might have been informed and sent out his men to seek him. He began to wish he had not taken quite so much trouble to put his pursuers off the scent. They would follow the road to

Spain. Who would look for him on that barren mountainside? He began to think with yearning of the farm where he had spent the last night, sharing a bed with the goats on the straw and refreshed by a bowl of milk and bread from the farmer's wife. Inevitably his thoughts turned to his mother. Who had she been—some serving-girl, some peasant? He had seldom given her much thought. Women had seemed almost unreal within those monastic walls, but now, stirred by the memory of the homely woman at the farm, the boy's imagination began to identify their image with a sense of comfort and warmth. Vain hope! His rest today, if he found any at all, would be a damp cavern; his food, if he reached the valley unharmed, a handful or two of berries, and to get there now he might have to traverse the belt of forest that frowned darkly beneath. What if he encountered a wolf, or even one of the bears that were said to haunt these desolate ranges? Half blind with panic, he stumbled along the track, which now began to descend in twists and turns to the ravinelike depth.

At last, far below him on the zigzag path, he seemed to detect two moving shapes. He strained his eyes. Yes, they were moving slowly toward him. In his relief the blood seemed to well anew in his veins. Shepherds? He glanced around for signs of a flock or the sound of the wooden bell the leading sheep wore round their necks. No other creatures were in sight. Were they messengers from the monastery, two of his father's men?—for it could hardly be his acquaintance of the chase. In nervous expectation his pace slackened. Now the figures had vanished behind an intervening spur. With beating heart Wolf waited for them to emerge. Minutes passed. Had he been mistaken? Was there another path leading away from here? In the despair of newly shattered hope he had ceased to care who they were, and in an agony of dread was about to shout and run wildly down the slope when the figures appeared round the bend and, seemingly unperturbed at the sight of the boy, continued their steady progress toward him.

They were an old man and his companion, and the former in particular appeared so strange and unreal on that rude mountainside that Wolf stood transfixed, and had almost let him pass, had the stranger himself not halted. Thin and frail, yet scarcely bowed, his silvery locks flowing from under the black *barreta* in shining waves

20

over his long dark robe, he stood calmly regarding the boy.

"Diaus vos benesiga."

Confusedly returning the greeting, Wolf, to hide his embarrassment, added quickly that he had lost the way.

A moment passed while the old man fixed his eyes upon him, clear as water in the pale, almost transparent face. "The Way?" he echoed. "And if I told you, you would never find it, and if you found it now you would lose it again." Then, seeing the boy's bewilderment, he added kindly: "But where are you going?"

Wolf hesitated. "To Foix," he brought out at last, clutching at anything that might seem reasonable.

"To Foix?" the stranger echoed. "Is it your home?"

"Yes—no," the hot blood rushed to Wolf's face. Somehow, before this curious old man, he felt incapable of subterfuge. "I was brought up at Bolbona, at the monastery," he attempted to explain.

"And you have friends or relatives in Foix?" Then, as the boy again hesitated: "But what brought you here?"

"I—I wanted to climb the mountain."

"The mountain?" the old man echoed.

Wolf nodded.

"Why?"

And once more the boy felt himself held by that peculiar, penetrating gaze. But he found no reply. What answer could he have given? Yet the prolonged silence seemed to weave a secret understanding between them. It was the stranger who broke it at last:

"Many, my son, have set out upon that quest, yet in their very seeking they pass it by. But you must be on your way," he added with a sudden return to the present; "though you will scarce reach Foix tonight. It is not far now to the nearest village." He turned to point to the valley. "You need only follow the path down through the forest with the sound of the torrent always in your ears, and once you come out of the gorge you will see the hamlet of Montségur. The place is too small to boast a regular inn, but at the third house you come to, no doubt they will give you lodging for the night and tomorrow put you upon your way to Foix. . . . But you have not told me your name," he added, smiling.

The boy looked down. "Wolf," he murmured.

"Wolf, Wolf of Foix," the old man repeated, dragging

21

out the words as if groping for some lost memory, and once more he cast on him that long, searching look.

Did he know? Again the crimson darkened the boy's cheek, but already the stranger was bidding him farewell. "And do not loiter," he said, "for dusk in the mountains sets in fast. God speed you, Wolf of Foix—*Diaus vos benesiga.*"

This time the boy did not answer but, without rightly knowing why, bowed his head, as at the blessing of some holy man. Then with eager thanks he set off swiftly down the hill.

For some time the stranger gazed after him; then, without addressing his companion, continued slowly on his way. But when Wolf looked back he saw the frail thin figure toiling with surprising vigor up the slope.

Long he puzzled over that strange encounter. Who was he? Who could he be? What could one so cultured, so frail, be doing among these forsaken hills? Was he some recluse inhabiting one of the castles? Montségur—suddenly the name kindled a memory in Wolf's mind. Had it not more than once been on the lips of some of the more venturesome pupils? Had not Brother Martin himself referred to it in the legends he loved to tell—Montségur, whose massive walls had first been reared aloft by the sons of the giant Geryon; Montségur, stronghold of Romans, of Goths and Franks, of dark-skinned Saracens, of Charlemagne himself? And now? Was it not said that the mighty ruin was being restored to an impregnable fortress?

One of the boys, a lad continually preoccupied with rumor and mystery, had hinted it was Perelha's fief, shared with the Count of Foix's own sister—the widowed Esclarmonde, Viscountess of Gimoez and the Isle, and she was a heretic. Was it a heretic stronghold, then, that was to rise amid these lonely gorges and crags? "Clean mountain air, spiced with a good dose of spiritual cant from the dear Cathars." As the words of the sinister huntsman flashed in his mind, the identity of the old man suddenly dawned upon him.

He must be one of the heretic priests or *bonshommes* themselves, one of the Cathari, the perfect ones. He had heard of them even at Bolbona. For heresy, the brothers lamented, was rampant in Languedoc. Count Raymond of Toulouse, libertine that he was, let them run riot in the city, delighted when the mob, roused by the *bonshommes'*

22

ascetic fervor, hurled stones and insults at Bishop Fulk and the papal legates. Even at Béziers and Carcassonne, though the Viscount Trencavel was avowedly no heretic, the Cathars, despite the Pope's warnings, were protected by nobles and burghers and allowed full freedom of speech. Only last spring an open controversy had been held at Faujeaux at which Catholics and heretics alike had been invited to defend their faith. The monks of Bolbona had been careful to keep the heretical arguments from reaching the pupils' ears, but scraps of information had leaked through.

Lucifer, not God, had created the visible universe. The Crucifix was no sacred symbol but an abomination, for how could one worship the object that had caused the agonies of Christ? Yet Christ, it seemed, had not really suffered except in semblance, for pure spirit cannot know the pain of the flesh. Paradoxical as such ideas appeared, the acceptance of a primal dualism, it seemed to Wolf, solved the enigma of an omnipotent and at the same time "loving" God having created a cruel and malignant universe; while the Cathar ritual would spare him the nausea that, as at the sight of all agony and mutilation, always overcame him when forced to gaze on the image of the crucified flesh. True, some of his companions had whispered of strange and terrible rites performed by the heretics in the depths of the Pyrenean caves, though others suggested that they had nothing to do with the Cathars at all but with pagan mysteries whose practice had lingered on since the time of the Roman legionaries.

For was not the very mountain on which he now walked, he remembered suddenly, said to be hollowed out, perforated by grottoes and caverns, labyrinthine passages, roofed with strange crystal, paved with precious stones and subterranean lakes? Was the old man really a Cathar elder or the priest of some pagan cult? Gradually, even more entangled in a web of conflicting rumor and speculation, all the wild emotions, the strange adventures he had experienced that day, the dreams he had woven through years around this mountainside, converged in an apprehension disturbing as it was vague and incredible, while once more the acrid voice ran again in his ears: "Don't tell me you're not a little heretic. They're all tarred with the same brush hereabouts." Heresy, that fearful and mysterious name. Was it then to this end that all his life had been directed? The thought spun through his overwrought brain, bewildering and confused, yet thrilling with a sense of destiny and the unknown.

So absorbed was he that he scarcely noticed he had reached the valley and had entered the gorge itself. The track had broadened but the light was failing fast, and as he stumbled on beneath the shadow of the pines it was often only the white foam of the gurgling water that reassured him of the way. When at last he gained the open, dusk had already fallen. Only the scanty lights glimmering halfway up the slope told of the small hamlet nestling in the shadow of the mountain wall. He was suddenly so tired that he hardly knew how his feet could carry him up the hill.

II

When Wolf of Foix woke the following morning it was to wonder for a moment where he was. Sleepily he rolled over, thinking he had been roused by the monastery bell, but, some unaccustomed hardness in his bed causing him to open his eyes, he found himself looking not at the familiar whitewashed wall and carved saint between the high-arched window but into a murky dimness, while instead of the clean, scoured smell of the dormitory a pungent odor filled the place. He rubbed his eyes and, remembering, sat up. But his joints were stiff from the climb, and lazily he lay back again to ponder on the adventures of the last three days.

As to the end he was not very clear, except that, arriving at last in the tiny village, he had found the house recommended by the old man, where, offered a pallet of straw and sacking in the corner, he had thrown himself down dead-beat, and must have fallen asleep at once. Evidently he had slept long and soundly, for the daylight was shining in at the half-open door and even the sound of talking had been slow to waken him. In the front half of the room, beyond the hearth, two men lounged at a table drinking, while perched on its edge a girl of thirteen or fourteen years sat thrumming a guitar. It was that which

24

had probably recalled to his half-waking sense the clanging bell, and as every now and again she struck a jarring note one of the men cursed under his breath. But the child, supremely indifferent, stubbornly continued her performance.

For a time, Wolf lay and watched, haphazardly trying to catch something of the men's conversation, but they spoke in an inaudible mutter and soon the boy's thoughts were concentrated on what his next move should be. In retrospect the whole adventure already wore almost the quality of a dream, but out of the chaos of memories the image of Montségur beckoned with fearful and irresistible compulsion. Eagerly now he sprang to his feet and, crossing to the doorway, looked out, full of expectation. The air was raw and chill and his hopes were dashed to the ground, for it soon appeared that the entire mountainside was obscured by morning mist. Dejected, he turned back. At least he might begin by having something to eat and consider a plan of action the while. He had been too weary the night before to satisfy his hunger, and in anticipation he peered into one of the pots hanging over the hearth.

"Hi, now," called one of the men, a stolid, gray-bearded fellow, to the girl with the guitar, "if you don't serve that hungry customer he'll be helping himself."

She shrugged. "We're not an inn."

But the second workman, turning slightly, swore anew: "Stop that caterwauling and leave your croon to the wake-women."

Still with deliberate slowness she slid from her perch and, crossing over to the boy, stared at him, sullen and petulant.

"Look here," he said, made bold by irritation and hunger, "I want something to eat."

Thinking he would doubtless despise the simplicity of the fare, her truculence increased: "Well," she said, "there isn't anything; mother's gone to the bread-baking."

"Over there," he pointed to the steaming cauldron.

"Oh, that," she said; "it's garlic soup; if you want, I'll bring you a bowlful."

He nodded, seating himself impatiently in a corner of the hearth.

The pungent scent of the soup as she returned with a bowl, coarse as it was, whipped his appetite.

"Bread," he muttered between ravenous gulps. Then, as she put before him a loaf and beaker of wine, feeling his hunger somewhat appeased, he thrust his hand in his pocket and drew out a handful of silver coins. For a moment he hesitated, suddenly awkward; then, wishing he could rival that grandiose and magnanimous gesture with which his father was wont to dispense alms, pushed a couple toward her. "For the night's lodging." He smiled awkwardly, attempting a careless air.

"He's got the brass all right," the second workman muttered insolently, and as he turned, Wolf caught sight of a face haggard with bitterness and toil.

At sight of the money the girl's truculence seemed to thaw a little.

"There was an accident last night up there," she jerked her head backward as though to indicate the locality, and in evident gratification she began to open up. "They've left the man at old Maent's, the herb gatherer's; his back's broken." She shrugged callously.

"And may your own belly burst in the hour of its birth pangs," snarled the voice in the background.

But with supreme indifference the child only moved a little nearer to Wolf.

"It was their best mason," she went on as a special confidence. "He used to come here sometimes; he was different from the rest, hardly drank anything, but he'd sit and draw for hours on that table there with a bit of chalk. Used to wish him to blazes, I did, scrubbing it all off. And then he marched off with the pig trough, because he liked the shape. Mother gave it him proper, but he said he'd carve her a signboard instead. Well, that's done for!" She shrugged. "But they've got to go to Pamiers to fetch another man."

"Well," Wolf laughed a little skeptically, "they're not in a hurry about it, it seems."

"They don't care," she shrugged. "They're only outsiders. They're shorthanded. They don't belong to the community," she confided. "They were leaving anyway this week—so that's why they're sending them—and good riddance," she added under her breath. "The old one isn't so bad, but he's afraid of the mountain—always seeing spooks and the rest—but the other, he's out to make trouble. They should never have taken him on. But the Countess gave orders to turn no one away."

"The Countess?"

"Of course," she pouted, as though at his stupidity, "the Countess Esclarmonde—at Pamiers."

"I'll clip your wagging tongue!" The man spat under the table and, rising clumsily, began to stretch his gaunt limbs.

The countess, Wolf was thinking excitedly; she must mean his aunt, his father's sister. Then it was true. Acting on a sudden impulse, he stopped munching his bread and leaned forward.

"I could ride to Pamiers," he said eagerly.

"The devil you could!" The mason wheeled round, but his companion, an older bearded man, touched him on the arm.

"Steady, Daniel. If he'll go, why not? It'll save us a deal of trouble, and we'll clear right out of these blessed mountains. Best make straight for Narbonne. Who are you, lad, anyway?" he asked good-humoredly.

"I'm from Foix."

"Foix?" Daniel scoffed and spat again. "One of those damned pages giving himself airs, or one of those toffs' bantlings, eh?" he laughed coarsely.

Instinctively Wolf's hand clenched and he rose from his seat.

But the old man, thrusting his companion aside, stepped forward. "Never mind him, lad, he's drunk. Page or what-not, you'll do for us if you'll be off to Pamiers and hunt up the master."

"If he doesn't run off with the horse," muttered his companion, smarting under the reproof.

"Well, if he does," the old man laughed, "they can send the bill to the Count—the girl's witness."

"And the payment *we'll* get? A score of stripes on the rump or worse," Daniel retorted.

While they argued, the boy's excitement increased to fever point. Whatever came of it, this at least was a first step. He would ride to Pamiers, messenger to the mysterious Montségur. If only, before he was tracked down, he could achieve a first feat of prowess, who knew but that the countess might even save him? Eager only that his plan shouldn't be nipped in the bud, he fumbled again in his pocket. It was his largest coin, the present of his father years ago and long treasured.

"Lend me a horse and you'll get your guarantee."

Daniel eyed the gold covetously, but the older man

frowned. "Don't be a fool, boy; the old jade you'll be getting hereabouts isn't worth it in silver."

"But where shall I find one?" Wolf cried impatient to be off.

"Nowhere," snarled Daniel. "They took the only decent nag to fetch more timber, and they won't be back till nightfall. You'll have to trot on your shanks to Lavelanet and there maybe——"

Lavelanet, thought Wolf. Wasn't it Perelha's place? He'd have to explain too much, and instead of him they'd be sending one of their men to Pamiers and he's be packed off to Foix.

"But walking's too slow," he cried.

The old man scratched his head. "True, riding would be quicker. Daniel, didn't Gino have an old roan?"

"Fell lame a week ago," grumbled the other.

The girl, who all the time had stood sucking the corner of her kerchief while she watched the transaction with growing curiosity, slowly opened her mouth.

"Arnaut down at the mill might lend his mule," she suggested.

"Then, for Christ's sake, let's be going," cried Wolf with growing irritation, and made for the door, the others following him.

The mists were beginning to lift now, and above him the mountain loomed palpably near, but the summit was still shrouded in cloud. Halfway through the village a little crowd was gathered round a hovel, which with its pots of basil wore a slightly neater air than the rest. Probably that was where they had brought the injured man, or was he dead? thought Wolf, and, overcome by his old instinctive horror of mutilation and pain, instinctively quickened his step.

"He's in there," the old man pointed a calloused, blunt-nailed hand at the door, "or was. Let's hope his soul's skipped right off to Paradise. The mason's scaffold's a mighty good jump-off, lad, to heaven or hell."

"Or to another round on this dear earth," the other jeered cynically. "Wasn't he a heretic?"

The old man shrugged and glanced at the boy. "One couldn't tell. Kept everything to himself, he did; never seemed to me he'd much use for religion at all, unless 'twas faith in his own craft."

Daniel shrugged. "Anyway, there's no help for him, or

for us either if we go his way. Dead and we're done for, each blasted one of us, smart one or idle, skilled or a fool, it's the same, and wife and brats can starve in the gutter for all they care—the mighty ones." The man's harsh-boned face seemed almost distorted with hate, and Wolf stared at him, distressed.

"But aren't there the masons' rights?" he asked.

The old man shook his head. "For the living, my son, not for the dead. Luckily for him, he'd no wife or child that I know of. Lived by himself, he did, a queer one; still, he was a damned good craftsman, and they knew it. But they'll forget it as soon. Life's like that for us, my boy, and not even one's name remembered; but one gets used to it."

Wolf did not answer, afflicted by a sudden uncomfortable sense of guilt. The old man seemed honest, the younger a coarse sort of brute, but what might he have had to go through? Suddenly an idea struck him, his face brightened.

"My father," he said, "I'll tell him. If he knows how things stand, he'll help you."

"Your father," Daniel began, scoffing.

But the other intervened: "Your father, my boy, by the look of you, will scarce care much for the likes of us."

Wounded by this rebuff to his eager partisanship, Wolf turned away, but the older man attempted a reconciliation.

"It's not only the mighty ones of this earth we should be blaming, my boy, but powers greater than they. I'd told him often, and Daniel here knows as I did, they're things it's best not to meddle with, nor names to be calling on, nor in word nor stone. From the first I said it was an unholy place, and the sooner we're quit of it the better, what with those cursed altars and that unholy lake."

As he spoke he glanced toward the mountain, and Wolf's memory flew to the silent tarn. Then there *was* truth in the huntsman's sinister tale. But at that moment they reached the mill and there was no time for further questioning.

The miller's mule was no beauty, and certainly unworthy of the importance Wolf of Foix ascribed to his mission, but in his eagerness he would have accepted any mount however wretched and, having arranged the transaction and been fully instructed as to his message to Mas-

29

ter Escot of Linars, he sprang on the beast's back and waved a last farewell.

His adventure had begun, his quest of a goal mysterious and half forbidden, but around whose magic name he was already weaving dreams more intense and glowing than all the tortured yearnings that had inspired flight.

It was not till he had left the village safely behind him that he dared turn to gaze once more at the mountain pass. Dark and menacing in the morning light, the Tabor towered above the ravine, its crown still veiled by the morning mists, but above the strip of pastureland rising from the river bed, as though torn by some convulsive shudder of the primordial mass from the rump of the mountain itself, a spur of rock stuck out, stark, impregnable, a sentinel over the abyss. Even as he watched, the mists that shrouded its height began to dissolve, disperse, and, sinking, hover like pallid wraiths over the wooded base, so that the naked peak emerging above the encircling cloud seemed to be borne on air. Sheer-cut like the narrowing buttresses of a gigantic tower, the crag soared skyward, topped at the apex by a squarer mass fused so deeply into the natural socket that it seemed hardly discernible from the rock itself.

Montségur! Instinctively he knew it could be nothing else, and even as he gazed, rapt in wonder, all the inebriation of his flight, the blind, inarticulate yearning of his fourteen years, swept toward that rocky height in an overwhelming thirst for possession and for surrender, of what and to what he scarcely knew, except that it must take the whole of himself.

III

Alas, it was anything but a dashing figure that after a number of painful vicissitudes approached Pamiers that same afternoon. The sorry condition of the mule was only matched by its obstinacy, and it was a flushed and disheveled lad, who, with reiterated prods from his sore and aching ankles, badgered his unwilling steed across the plain. But at last the towers of the city loomed nearer. Beyond the orchards that skirted the road, the castle hill rose formidable against the sky. And now he would already trace the pattern of the gardens covering the southern slopes, with their trellis of fig and wine; and breaking them here and there, as a screen against the wind, or darkening the water of a cistern, a group of cypresses black against the umber earth.

Till now, fully absorbed in his mission, he had troubled little about possible discovery; hastening through Lavelanet he had avoided the main road and felt comparatively safe from pursuit. But now, confronted by the city gates, his situation appeared more precarious. It might well be that a lookout was being held for him at the gates, though it was scarcely likely that anyone supposedly coming from Bolbona would approach the town from this direction. But the very difficulties that beset his adventure gave it an added zest. What perils was he not prepared to face for the sake of Montségur! The thought shot new energy through his weary limbs and he bullied his wretched mount for the last lap.

But his fears were unwarranted. The entry to the city was at this hour so confused by the stream of peasants and marketing women issuing from the gates that he passed unnoticed amid the motley throng. But now the mule's last dregs of patience were at an end, and neither cajoling nor kicks would get it to advance; he might have left it at the adjacent hostelry but, afraid to draw attention to himself, he slid from its back and dragged it toward a lame and one-eyed lout who seemed to do a small trade in minding beasts. "As if any soul on earth would be running off with that bag of bones," the man shouted after him, as, followed by the snigger of a group of dirty urchins, he set off up the street.

Soon he was hemmed in by decaying housefronts; the smells of the city flowed toward him with increasing virulence. His heart beat faster. Now his real adventure had begun! The diffidence he had felt a day ago was dispelled by the importance of his mission. But his exultation was quickly sobered as a jolt from a wagon laden with wine barrels almost sent him flying into the muck that overflowed the shallow gutter running down the middle of the cobbled street. At last, pushing his way through crowds of shoppers, loiterers, and gossiping women, he reached the square. The market at this time of day was all but over, the booths for the most part closed. It was behind the enclosing ring of houses that the workmen had said he would find the masons' lodge, and indeed it was the sound of hammering that gave him the clue. Following it, he was soon passing through a low archway.

He found himself in a great courtyard, at the far end of which a gigantic scaffold obscured the towers of some massive building. It was from here that the sound of hammering had come. For the rest, the place seemed almost deserted but for the slabs and pillars of stone that lay piled all around—slice, section, or segment, crystalline blocks, boulders crude and unfashioned, stretched like unwieldy torsos powdered with whitened dust.

Suddenly shut off from the familiar sounds of the street, it seemed to the boy that he had entered a new world, a world of inhuman proportions, of cube and cylinder and sphere, a world that obeyed, beneath the remorseless law of compass and of rule, a remote and incomprehensible order of its own, whose pulse was faintly heard in the reiterate beat of the hammer and the chip of the chisel on stone.

The sight of two men emerging from a door close at hand recalled him from his brooding. Deep in conversation, they had almost passed, had he not stepped in their way; Master Escot of Linars—was he here, could he speak with him? He had an urgent message to deliver. With an impatient gesture the elder of the two, a rich burgher by the look of his clothes, brushed him aside, but a sign from his companion reassured the boy that he had been heard. Nor had many minutes passed before the man returned. "Did he want Master Escot?" he asked. Well, then, he stood before him, so out with his message. "It's hands count here, not tongues," he added in a blunt yet not unfriendly voice.

Wolf, looking at the rather short and stocky figure, could not help but feel surprise, if not disappointment, so much did it differ from the imaginary architect of his dream citadel.

"There's been an accident," he struggled to be brief, "at Montségur. Guilhem of Roussillon fell from the scaffold—he's dead. They want another mason at once to take his place."

"Guilhem?" Escot's face seemed suddenly to grow older. Wolf nodded.

32

For a long moment there was silence.

"Were you there?" asked the mason at last, almost roughly.

He shook his head.

"Who sent you? Who are you?" Escot asked, puzzled by the boy's obvious refinement despite his torn and disheveled clothes.

He hesitated. "I happened to be there; they needed a messenger. I'm Wolf—of Foix." What use was there in denial? His first adventure was completed, triumphantly. Besides, for the first time he felt pride in uttering his name.

"Wolf. Wolf of Foix," the architect repeated, contracting his brows, as though he were identifying some unusual type of marble. "What, the lad there was all that fuss about—ran off from his monastery to Spain? Well, you soon found your way back," he smiled wryly. "Whatever set you marching off to Montségur?"

There was no reply, and, noticing the evident emotion of the boy's face, the architect's keen gray eyes probed it with the same precision with which they might have compassed the angle of some dizzy vault.

"Well," he said, "and what did you think of it?"

"I haven't been up—not yet." For a moment, struck by the vibrancy of the voice, Escot continued his scrutiny; then, turning abruptly, he beckoned Wolf to follow.

They passed through a doorway into a cloister flanked by arcaded columns, some smooth and polished, some turned and twisted as though the stone was flaccid and kneaded like dough, while from the carved bell of base and capital the shape of beast and bird writhed in fantastic entanglement. But the mason did not pause until they reached a large rectangular room which, in its unaccustomed lightness, reminded Wolf of the chapter house that Prior Anselm had had built a year ago in the new French manner, where the sunlight streamed in unfettered through the great panes of glass whose tracery was as fine as the veins of huge pointed leaves. But here it fell not on the old familiar faces above the monotony of the white Cistercian garb, but on a vast and heterogeneous company of princes, warriors, queens, and nobles ranged along the walls or stretched in lapidary quiescence upon the ground. There were some on whom the gaudy paint had scarcely dried, who seemed to stare at the intruders with faint supercilious mockery, others whose eyeballs wore a vacancy that matched the body still encompassed in the grayness of a shroud.

"Your ancestors," Escot pointed to the figures lying at his feet. "Asnar of Commenges." From under the helmet the hatchet face above the stiffened limbs encased in wiry draperies seemed to stare at the boy, immobile, petrified to eternal rancor, and he found himself wondering whether that look of acrid resentment had been born in defiance of death, or inspired by the long-tressed dame at his side, whose heavy nunlike wrappings seemed but the counterpart of a rigid and slightly obtuse decorum. *"Arsenda figlia Gothica Carcassonensis."*

But already the mason was drawing him over to the farther wall.

The boy stepped back almost in alarm. For a moment the figure standing there in a niche of the wall had seemed alive, as though the mailed hand only waited to tear the half-drawn sword from its scabbard and leap from its pedestal.

"Lupus Aquitaniae dux—Wolf, Duke of Aquitaine, conqueror of Roland. Liberator from the Franks."

Even to the untutored eye of the boy it was evident at a glance that here was a difference, a difference that made the other figures by comparison mere puppets, as though not only the limbs were alive under the writhing surcoat, the close-meshed mail, but the stone itself were alive, pent with the fearful stress of an unbridled spirit. Was he bound to stand on guard forever, challenging, defiant behind the great triangular shield, and never be released? But even while in fierce blind sympathy Wolf of Foix identified himself with his namesake, he was overcome with inexplicable fear—a sudden feeling that behind the challenge lay an unspeakable torment, as though the weapon the man had thrown had somehow turned back upon himself. Involuntarily he gave a little shudder.

Noticing the boy's confusion, Escot gave a gruff laugh.

"Guilhem was like that," he said. "As though he were always seeing other meanings in things. People would rate him with it sometimes, and he'd turn on them sharp—say he was only concerned with proportion, relating line and mass. It was his last piece of work," he muttered, "down here." To hide his emotion he turned abruptly away.

34

Outside in the sun-baked courtyard it was evident that Wolf's departure was expected without delay.

"One day, if you care," the mason said, "you can come again and I'll show you the plans. You'd better go up to the castle now and prove you're safe and sound," he shrugged, pointing to an arch in the far side of the courtyard. "That's about your shortest way."

He turned to go when Wolf, afraid that he had perhaps not made his message clear, hesitated.

"You will send at once to Montésgur?"

"Yes, yes!"

"I left the old mule down at the Gate of Olmes," he stammered, thinking of his promise to the miller. "Someone must ride it back, but it's just about as lame as it's obstinate!"

"It'll about match any of the fellows I have here," Escot of Linars growled bitterly, and with a curt nod turned on his heel.

Wolf watched the stocky, thick-set figure cross the courtyard and, halting under the scaffold, call to one of the masons. Then, as the man descended and the two stood talking together, dwarfed to pygmy stature under the giant structure, knowing himself forgotten, he made his way mechanically in the direction in which Master Escot had pointed.

Once through the arch he halted, undecided as to his next move. It was clear that sooner or later he must present himself and make a clean breast of his escapade. Yet the thought troubled him surprisingly little, for, moving still as under a spell to his new-won freedom, even the thought of the monastery seemed remote, unreal. Only of one thing he was sure—come what may, to that life he would never return.

He glanced up at the square towers of the castellar that crowned the hill, the massive fortress which for a century and more had been such a thorn in the flesh to the avaricious abbots of St. Anthony. Year by year they had watched it grow—defiant answer of the counts of Foix to an overweening monastic pride. For all too soon Roger II had repented the donation that had facilitated the unbridled growth of the abbey at the far end of the town and, furious, had begun to fortify the castle. So it came to pass that wedged between two rival powers—feudalism and the Church—the little village of Fredelas had developed with uncanny swiftness into the flourishing city of Pamiers.

It was an ancient Roman camp that the counts had fortified and extended stone by stone to the castellar, whose mighty keep towered above the cone-shaped rock, looking northward to Toulouse, eastward to Carcassonne, and southward over the rich valley land stretched between here and the great rampart of the Pyrenean chain.

And now? Did it not belong to his aunt, the Countess of Esclarmonde, bestowed on her by his own father as dower-house in her widowhood? Was it really behind the cyclopean walls that she had established her heretic convent, and from these crenelated towers did she gaze across the undulating slopes to the bastion of rock that sheltered her dream citadel of Montségur?

A thrill ran up his spine. Suddenly it was revealed to him that all was somehow predestined—his flight, his meeting with the elder, the accident, his role as messenger—he had been led here by some sort of providence. Triumphant excitement took hold of him. He would enter these gates not as a runaway, a miserable scapegoat, but as the predestined hero of some wonderful and mysterious quest. Drawing himself up proudly, he set out for the barbican that flanked the castle to the right.

What was she like, he wondered, as he strode up the ramp. Even the monks, he remembered, had been full of reverence for the high-born, most charitable countess, who in her widowhood had sacrificed her possessions for the good of the poor, turning her own castle into a hospice for the aged and the sick. But hadn't some whispered that she was about to be initiated in the most holy rites of the Cathars themselves, to become in fact a priestess of the faith whose citadel was to be Montségur? Here surely he could pierce its mystery, to her he might swear loyalty and fealty to its cause. Suddenly it dawned on him that he was no heretic and that he knew nothing definite about their faith. Might it at last provide an answer to the problems that his religious upbringing had failed to solve? All the tormented groping of his spirit gathered force in a new hope, a long-suppressed yearning to unburden himself. But could he? In vain he tried to visualize her. Was she a sort of saint, ethereal, unreachable, remote, or stern and imposing, unapproachable, august? Certainly she must have tremendous courage, for she was said to have defended the heretics through thick and thin in face of her husband's orthodoxy, and wasn't she to take part herself in the great conference between churchmen and heretics everyone was talking of and that, was to be held here at Pamiers quite soon? Supposing she was even something like his father?—though how that was possible he could hardly imagine. But at the thought his elation was distinctly sobered. If he should falter and stammer before her as before him! He had not even an idea how to deport himself in the presence of women, while his father had been renowned in his youth as a courtier. Ramon Drut, Ramon the enamored, they had called him, the irresistible lover, the accomplished troubadour. How many hearts had not been vanquished by his songs, if not by his valor, his beauty—even the Loba's, whom the greatest singers of the land and Peire Vidal himself had adored? He struggled to regain his bold spirits of a minute past, but the miserable truth insisted itself on his conscience. Words would fail him, words which his father could twist and turn to his fancy like a juggler's balls, letting them fly like airy darts or deadly missiles, mellowing them (one said) till their sweetness wounded more than their sting—words that with him were always fickle, deserting him at the critical moment, and which at their best produced no more than a shadow of what they tried to express.

But Master Escot, he thought, recalling his new friend, had been blunt enough of speech and yet produced such marvels. What was it he had said? "It's hands count here, not tongues." Suddenly he knew what to do. He would go back and ask the great mason to take him as apprentice. Why had he not thought of it before? His social deficiencies, his backwardness as a warrior, his shameful qualms and sensibilities would not matter here, while his father could only rejoice that at last he had found an aim. Overcome by his newborn enthusiasm, he almost yearned to feel the chisel under his hands, to wrestle with the block as he had wrestled with the mountain itself, for already in his imaginative flight he was working on the heights of Montségur.

Turning on his heel, he began to retrace his footsteps. He had almost reached the arch leading to the masons' yard when the clatter of horses' hoofs coming round the bend caused him to draw aside; but even as they reached him the foremost rider reined in his horse with an oath and, looking up, Wolf found himself gazing into his father's livid face.

"So they've found you," he cried. "Then what the devil are you doing wandering off again?"

The boy stared at him, dismayed.

"They didn't," he stammered. "I came on my own."

"On your own!" Rage brought the color flooding back to Ramon-Roger's cheeks. "Present yourself at the castle!" he shouted, and without so much as a further glance at his son, followed by his squire, he spurred toward the castle gate.

IV

A quarter of an hour later Wolf found himself within the great walls which for a short moment that day he had dreamed of entering in such triumph, but it was not as the hero of a fabulous quest but as a wretched renegade that he stood before his father in the spacious vaulted room beyond whose arched windows stretched the expanse of the plain dotted with orchard and hamlet. But to the tranquil vista spread beneath the tranquil light of the later afternoon the boy was blind, seeing only the derision of the count's arrogantly handsome face, as he turned toward him with that magnificent carriage of head and shoulder that seemed in itself to express withering disdain.

"Alas!" he mocked, while his dark and eloquent eyes held fast the pitiable image, "had you only informed us this was to be the goal of your little excursion we could have prepared a more gracious reception. As it is—what the hell is the meaning of it all?"

The boy hesitated. Where could he begin? Already the memory of his actions, that only so recently had seemed to pursue a heaven-prescribed course, was turning to chaos. He stood there silent and abashed, the very consciousness of his impotence giving his face a look of truculent sullenness.

The count, his anger trebled by his irritation, flung himself into a chair.

"A nice chase you've led us. I suppose you thought my

men in need of a little distraction and set them scouring the passes to Spain for a joke?"

With increasing impatience the count began to drum his long and shapely fingers on the table, while the other hand tugged at his pointed red-brown beard.

"Well, since your adventures were evidently of so desperate and exciting a nature as to have completely obscured your powers of memory, perhaps you can at least enlighten us as to what you are doing here?"

Wolf made a violent attempt to gather himself together: "I came with a message to Master Escot, the architect." Now, he thought, if I take the plunge and get it over. "I was going to ask him," he added, leaping every connecting link, "to take me as apprentice."

"Apprentice?" The proud, aquiline features seemed distorted by sheer incredulity. "Good God! Was it for that you actually refused the chance of a career? So that's what you think knighthood's worth?"

"Knighthood?" echoed Wolf dully.

But Ramon-Roger's amazement had given place to renewed wrath at memory of the bitter disillusionment of his last meeting with his son.

"What the devil d'you think I came for, that time after Seo d'Urgel, but to give you the chance?"

Knighthood! It seemed to Wolf that all was irretrievably lost. Now that the magic word was spoken, all his ambitions, the fluctuations they had gone through during the vicissitudes of the last days, merged suddenly in that one idea, which, though it had somehow seemed equivocal when associated with his father's predatory concepts, now shone resplendent in the radiance of Montségur. Shattered, he stared at him, pale and distraught.

Ramon-Roger groaned inwardly. Was the boy touched? He had always suspected it.

"But what on earth put the idea into your befuddled head?" he asked a trifle more gently. "Or has the good prior been infecting his dear novices with his architectural craze? I hear he's all aflame for these new-fangled French fantasies. Damned if we shan't soon be living in a tower of glass," he scoffed, his old scorn of the northerners for the moment almost getting the better of his rage.

"No," murmured Wolf; "no, it wasn't that."

"What then?"

"There was an accident in the mountains." Somehow he

could not bring the name of Montségur across his lips. "One of the masons—"

"The mountains. So you *were* there! Christ, are we ever to get at the root of this story?" Ramon-Roger settled himself back in his chair, as though resigned to a long and wearisome unraveling of the truth.

At last, in disjointed phrases, omitting his encounter with the huntsman and with much evasion of his emotions regarding Montségur, Wolf told his father the gist of the tale. And actually, as he listened to his son's adventure, the Count of Foix was not so ill-pleased. After all, though the boy's motives were completely unintelligible, and he was doubtless half mad, he'd shown some guts in tackling that mountain by himself, and evidently, as far as his role of messenger was concerned, he'd been a bit smarter than one would have expected, though naturally it would never do to admit it. Besides, the end of the tale—a mason's hireling!

"And so you came to the conclusion that the rungs of the scaffold are less arduous to climb than the ranks of chivalry! I little thought Master Escot's wooden tongue could be so persuasive," he added bitingly.

Yet suddenly that very mockery stung the boy to a defense of his new friend. "It wasn't," he retorted. "It was the things they were carving—my own ancestors!" he cried.

"Our ancestors—oh, God!" Ramon-Roger had sprung to his feet, while the laughter broke from his throat bitter and harsh. "And so at sight of his namesake, Wolf, the conqueror of the Franks, the slayer of Roland, my doughty son was inspired to take up not the sword but the chisel!"

To Wolf the silence that followed was equal to annihilation—even despair was paralyzed. How long it lasted he never knew. It was another voice that recalled him to consciousness, a woman's voice, cool and strangely musical.

"Then he really is found?" it was saying.

Was it she? His confused senses were aware of a figure coming toward him all enveloped in misty gray.

"So you are the other Wolf?" she asked. "I couldn't help hearing, but I think somehow I understand. You see, Ramon," she went on, addressing the count, who stood silent, rigid in fury and shame, "mightn't it be that he wanted so terribly to carve himself in his hero's likeness,

40

and so, feeling he couldn't do it one way, he thought maybe he'd manage it in another? Was I right?" she asked, turning again to the boy.

At last he forced himself to look up; yes, it must be she.

"You want to be like him?" she repeated.

"Yes, oh yes," it broke from him eagerly, and then he stopped, haunted by the memory of the statue. "No, not really," he stammered.

Ramon-Roger gave a harsh, mocking laugh. "Well, there you have it—from his own lips."

"But why, Wolf?" she asked gently. And yet somehow her voice sounded almost glad.

To her alone, he thought, he might have explained, but in sight of his father's disgust, and awaiting each moment a new lash from that scornful tongue, he was powerless. Seeing the stricken look on the boy's face, she did not press him, and with her strange intuition there had even begun to dawn on her an inkling of its cause.

"Master Guilhem is a great craftsman," she evaded.

"He's dead," Wolf blurted out, clutching at anything that offered escape.

"Dead?" The limpid voice sounded suddenly so torn, so wounded, that the boy could have slain himself for his clumsiness. "No, no, but it can't be true," she murmured, as though dazed.

The count cleared his throat. "I'm afraid it is. If I'd guessed. . . . It seems that this exquisitely tactful son of mine rode specially to Pamiers with the news; some mason or other had had an accident up there. It never entered my mind—"

"But not dead?" she pleaded.

He nodded. In the ensuing silence his impatience returned. Such sentiment about a mere mason was beginning to tell on his nerves. The man had certainly been a clever craftsman, though why his sister should make such a confounded fuss about him he'd never understood—a queer, crabbed fellow enough, though under her influence he had certainly seemed more tractable. For that matter, he thought ironically, as a true Cathar she should exult at his liberation from the flesh. Clearing his throat, Ramon-Roger turned toward her.

"It's cursed luck this should have happened now. It'll hold things up, no doubt." (He spoke, Wolf thought, as though men's lives ought to be dependent on his pleasure.)

"I'd better see what Escot's doing about it. He'll probably have to send to Toulouse. And there's that other matter to discuss!" He hesitated. "Do you mind, Esclarmonde, if I leave you with him a moment? He's hardly a delectable object," he shot a scornful glance at his son. "If he's too much of a clown," he added, "turn him out."

For a moment after her brother had left the room Esclarmonde of Foix stood without movement, lost in thought. Guilhem dead—and between one dawn and one sunset, one moment and the next. But was it not, after all, what he would have wished—to die in the midst of his labors, for to him joy and fullness of life came only through his art. From what ever-widening circles of vision had he been forced to return to the bondage of his self? And now—had he escaped at last? He had died, no doubt, she thought, anguished, without receiving the *consolamentum* that might have helped to release him from the cycle of rebirth. Would he be doomed to return to life on earth; was it possible that by grace of his own vision he might be freed at last to continue his journey among other stars, other realms of consciousness? Guihalbert of Castres, the Cathar bishop, she curbed herself, would frown on any such glorification of earthly genius, and, trying to push the thought from her, she turned toward Wolf.

The sight of his miserable abashment forced her mind from her own distress. "So you are the other Wolf?" she echoed, as if re-opening their conversation from the start. "I wish you'd come with another message. Still, I'm glad you've come. They were getting very anxious about you, you know. But I was forgetting," she cried, as though chiding herself for absorption in her own grief at the expense of a guest, "you've come so far!"

Feeling her gaze upon him he flushed, once again aware of his lamentable and travel-stained appearance. But she was studying not his clothes but the small spare figure, too slight for its years, the clear brow over the deep-set eyes, the sensitive yet somehow almost a little obstinate mouth. "Messengers can't look like fops," she smiled, reading his thoughts. "And have you eaten anything? Of course not! Why, you must be starving." Before he could thank her or protest, she had called to her servants, and soon there was spread before him a feast of honey cake and fruit and wine.

"We grow everything," she said, seating herself in the

window. "We've our own orchards and vineyards and apiaries. We do it all ourselves, and this year we reaped a bigger harvest of fruit than they—the monks of St. Anthony, I mean. And how angry they were! We are only women, you see. But now," she was saying, leashing her own loquacity, "you must tell me about yourself—when you've eaten," she added, and to put him at ease she helped herself to a peach.

"Only women—" he thought. Yes, he supposed now he must have imagined her almost inhuman, austere, remote, yet here she was, warm and laughing almost, and eating peaches. Well, perhaps women were always like that, he reflected between eager bites; he had known so little of them. Over the edge of the cup he gathered courage to look at her.

Within the smoke-gray folds that shrouded her from head to foot her face looked paler than it perhaps really was; it wasn't so young, either (since he had heard her voice he had forgotten that he had actually imagined her far older). And the sadness of her face seemed somehow to deepen when she smiled. He put it down to her sorrow for Guilhem, not realizing that in part it was because that smile gave to the sharpened molding of flesh and bone a wistful reflection of warmth and richness they had lost.

"Actually," she was saying, "I meant to ask your father to bring you long ago. But we were always so busy," she sighed apologetically. "Anyhow, you came yourself, and here you are. It must have been quite bewildering," she went on after a little pause; "like waking up . . . coming out of the monastery," she explained, in recognition of her own quaint habit of beginning a sentence in the middle of a thought. "I can guess a little," she went on, "because, you, I was away twenty years. Just think of it, Wolf, twenty years; it must seem a lifetime to you! And then to come home!"

She speaks, he thought, as though she's been let out of prison. Home? Why, she had come into, not out of, a convent!

Half unconsciously she had turned to the window and looked out across the plain.

"Do you know," she went on, "what I used to miss most? I think it was the mountains; one could just see them from Gascony. Before rain mostly."

She noticed that he suddenly brightened. "Why, you

43

must have seen them easily from Bolbona," she added. "It's not nearly so far."

"Yes," he stammered, "I saw them!" The thought that he could tell her thrilled her with joy. "That's why I was so keen . . ."

She smiled. "And so you ran away?"

He nodded.

"How far did you get?"

He looked at her without answering for a moment. . . . "To the top of the Tabor."

"The Tabor?" she murmured, and her thoughts seemed to wander far away. "Why, you might have got lost," she added, as if waking. Anxiety troubled her brow.

"I did," he said. And then he told her of the strange old man and how he had come to Montségur. Now, he thought, now he might tell her all.

"It must have been one of our elders," she said, "on the road to Ornolac. How lucky you found him, for if the mists had come down you might have walked over a precipice or into one of the lakes."

"Are there many," he asked, "up there? I came across one of them. They call it the Lake of Evil," he muttered, "but—" If only he dared unburden himself about the sinister huntsman.

"But it has another name, too," she smiled faintly, "the Lake of the Trout."

"The trout?" he echoed, astonished. "I didn't think there was a single fish."

She looked at him strangely. "Perhaps there aren't. There might have been once upon a time, or— Did you ever hear of the fish soul?" she added.

He glanced at her, puzzled. "In the Bible—about the fishers of men? Brother Martin—"

"Ah, yes," she said, "that too; but there's a story, a fairy tale you might call it, about the soul of the girl that was locked in a golden fish, and whatever her enemies did to her it couldn't really touch her."

And she began to tell a tale of far-off lands. Scarce taking in their meaning, he listened to the words falling from her lips, low and wistful yet with that faint unexpected hint of laughter, till subtly the lost enchantment was conjured up again, and as she spoke he seemed to see himself a golden fish lapped in those dark mysterious waters as in the music of her voice.

44

"So you see," she concluded, "perhaps a fish isn't a fish at all, or a peach a peach." She gazed bemused at the half-bitten fruit in her hand.

Had she known it, too, that fearful, inscrutable *something* that rendered a thing more or less, or anything but itself? Yet while she spoke it began to lose a little of its horror.

She saw his brows contract, the perplexed intentness that gave the too-vulnerable lips a look of sullen brooding.

"Things have such different meanings," she said with a little sigh.

Different meanings—other meanings—he pondered, why, wasn't that what Master Escot had said about the work of the dead sculptor, and once more he was confronted by that baffling image. And the old fear took hold of him again.

"A fish that isn't a fish," he echoed; "if nothing is what it seems, and a hero isn't a hero? Was that why . . . the statue, I mean?"

She paused before she answered him. "They say he won at last by treachery."

He winced as though the accusation had touched himself.

"But he freed his people," he protested.

"It was the enemy he betrayed," she answered—"if it was betrayal. He laid them a trap. But perhaps it was something else that Guilhem meant—that Wolf of Aquitaine betrayed the image that he had made of himself." But the thought of the sculptor recalled her too suddenly to her grief. "There isn't anyone to take Guilhem of Roussillon's place," she sighed.

He did not know how to break the silence, fearing to hurt her again.

"Is it true?" he asked after a little pause, "that many of them are so badly off—the masons, I mean—that when they're dead no one cares for their families and children and all that?"

Rousing herself, she looked at him sadly. "I'm afraid it is, in part. They try to help each other within the lodge. and we do what we can down here for the workers. We're only beginning, you know, Wolf, and there are so many. There's so much injustice in the world. Far more than that."

He looked up, eager, "But can't one fight it?"

45

She nodded. "But so few care."

"Oh, but we must make them. If they really knew," he gazed at her eagerly. "It would be like a Crusade," he cried, and his eyes looked suddenly bright. "And we'd be like crusaders—Templars—a real order." He stopped, breathless with excitement. An idea had suddenly struck him. "Up there," it broke from him at last, "at Montségur."

"Montségur—" She was looking at him so strangely, as though actually her gaze was directed not at him but through him, at something beyond. But in his excitement it seemed to him as if they were sharing some inexpressible secret, and in that moment pledged each other to an unspoken alliance. In his eagerness he had sprung to his feet. His face, freed from the torment of uncertainty and doubt, seemed suddenly radiant, transfigured.

"When shall we begin?" he clamored.

"Begin what?" the voice of Ramon-Roger cut in abruptly from the doorway and, coming toward them, he smiled ironically at sight of the eager boy. But Wolf, inebriated by excitement, had almost forgotten his diffidence and, remembering his promise to the workmen, began blurting out his story.

"I told them, I told them when I'd explained to you, you'd surely help—"

"Explained to me! Christ in heaven! And you presumed, to a couple of lousy workers! Good God, boy, did you run away from the cloister to preach rebellion to the mob? As though there weren't enough unrest in the land already that you want to go infecting the rabble!"

"But," Wolf's blind and passionate idealism was still arming him with desperate courage, "it wasn't *that* I meant; only to fight, to defend . . . Montségur must stand for—"

"Montségur! What the hell is Montségur to you?"

At that Esclarmonde of Foix seemed to wake from her dreaming.

"Why, Ramon," a look of pain mingled with a faint irrepressible shade of amusement flitted over her features. "First you were angry because he wasn't warrior enough and now when he's proved himself so bellicose . . . but look, he's dead tired," she said, glancing at the boy's distraught face. "Come, Wolf," she said, rising, and as he hesitated with a glance toward his father, she laid her

46

hand lightly on his shoulder. "Not now," she said softly, beckoning him to follow.

They seemed to pass through a labyrinth of corridors. "It's not much of a room," she said at last, opening the door of a little chamber in one of the turrets, "but I thought you'd like the view—look," she crossed to the window. Below them the valley of the Olmes displayed its ruddy fulness of ripening fruit, but far away, beyond the undulating ramparts of hills, the rocky mass of the Tabor rose against a bank of cloud. Side by side they stood gazing at the scene till slowly she turned. "Wolf, you don't want to go back to Bolbona, do you?"

The desperate look he fixed on her was enough.

"But you are a bit of a problem, you know," she smiled; "still, I think we can manage you. After all, we have to fight *and* build at Montségur, haven't we?"

For a moment she looked at him intently. "Sleep well," she murmured, but before he could answer or thank her she was gone.

Dazed, he stared at the closed door, till in the silence, suddenly weariness fell on him like a dead weight. Montségur. . . . In a last wave of deep, uncomprehending happiness he flung himself on the bed, and in a moment he was fast asleep.

"He'll have to go back," cried the Count of Foix, as a little later his sister re-entered the room. "He's impossible."

She did not answer at once, but, seating herself in the window seat, took up a piece of embroidery.

"No, Ramon," she said with a look of quiet determination; "he can't go back, not now."

"And why? He's proved himself useless for anything else." Moodily Ramon-Roger began pacing the floor. "One would have thought it was just his mark. Among the inmates of the almshouse he can slake his love for his fellow men to his heart's content, and if the perfume becomes too strong even for *his* nostrils, I suppose he can ring a change, hacking a few gargoyles on the chapel roof. By then perhaps he'll see what he's missed. At any rate," he laughed bitterly, "he can't say I never gave him a chance."

"A chance?"

"Well," he muttered roughly, "what did I go to Bolbona for last time? And even today. . . ."

"But don't you see, it's all or nothing with him. He can't compromise or see things in proportion, and if he thinks he might fail—"

"He gives up—a shirker."

"Oh, no—he may try a new way. Underneath he never lets go. But he's all perplexed. Life stares at him with a double face—all contradictions—and he can't make the ends meet. He's like it himself. But now I think he's seen a goal . . ."

"A goal! He's scarce capable of looking a span ahead of him."

"Yes," she smiled, "that's just it. But it doesn't prevent him from fixing his eyes on the unreachable, till he'll go blind."

"The unreachable! And you, Esclarmonde?"

She interrupted him with a sigh. "Yes, I know," she said wistfully; "but perhaps that's why I understand."

Ramon-Roger paused in his angry pacing, and for a moment, as he gazed at his sister, the arrogance of his expression seemed almost to soften, but to hide his emotion he turned on his heel.

"Well," he said gruffly, "what do you want me to do with him?"

"He must see the world."

"Hm, I suppose I can have him at Foix."

She shook her head. "He's too sensitive now."

He frowned. "You mean, of course, I ought to have had him home long ago?"

"No," she smiled reassuringly; "shut up in Seo d'Urgel, one could hardly expect—"

"But before—of course there was time enough. Philippa would have had him. I'll give her her due."

And handled that problem, thought Esclarmonde (not without a touch of playful malice), as efficiently, as dispassionately, as she handled everything else. What would he have become like then? Selfishly, she admitted, she was thankful Philippa hadn't had the chance. Now he was hers, to make up for all she had failed in toward her own son. Yet she *had* tried. Oh, not enough. What was she to blame her brother? But where there had been love. . . . Yet wasn't that the very cause? Fiercely proud as he was, he could not bring himself to admit defeat; undaunted in all else, he was desperately afraid of his own suffering. He would never admit—why, he probably did not know himself—that his chagrin, his desperate impatience with the boy, resulted but from the exorbitant demands of his love.

"No," she said, "it was probably best as it was. But now we shall have to find a way, Ramon." She turned toward him.

He had halted before the window and stood staring out into the fading distance. For a time she remained silent till, following his gaze, her eyes traveled eastward to the darkening hills. "Carcassonne," she mused, wrapped in memories. "I haven't seen young Trencavel since he was a child. He must have been younger than Wolf then—fresh as milk and apples!"

"Well, he's much like that still," he laughed a little wryly. "Fair as his uncle Raymond of Toulouse—once was. Still, he's got some of the Trencavel guts at any rate, but a cooler head."

"Like his mother's?" She smiled almost a little roguishly, remembering her brother's vain assaults against that lady's impeccable armor.

He shrugged, frowning slightly. "He's renowned at least as a very paragon of knightly virtue."

"Although his education lay in the tainted hands of heretics?" she mocked.

"Hm, even his enemies must give Bertran of Saissac credit for the job."

Esclarmonde of Foix laid down her sewing. "Well," she said after a moment's pause, "Why not send Wolf to Carcassonne?" She was prepared for that slight stiffening of his head. The old rivalry with the Trencavels, she knew, died hard.

Ramon-Roger crossed to the table and poured himself a cup of wine. "That boy at Carcassonne," he cried bitterly; "while you're about it, why not let him go the whole fling? The world. . . . Esclarmonde, didn't you say, let him loose on the world? Well then, pack him off to Toulouse."

"No," she said quietly, "not Toulouse." But she had seen that she had gained ground, and with her instinctive knowledge of her brother, she pressed the point no further.

"Is Master Escot sending for another mason?" she asked after a moment.

He nodded. "He's setting his hopes on a man young Mirepoix was talking about. Raymond of Toulouse got hold of him. Some outlandish fellow, no doubt."

She did not reply, but went on sewing blindly till the needle pricked her fingers, and with an effort she pulled herself together. "Raymond," she echoed dully, "how is he?"

The Count of Foix flung himself into a chair. "Sluggish and conciliatory as ever. Well, you can be thankful at least that he's managed to keep his papal highness at bay—for the moment. How long it can go on, heaven alone knows. Innocent isn't one to waste his breath on pastoral admonishments forever. Rainier failed, Peire and Raoul are going the same way. The Pope keeps silence and lets the legates pocket their pride. He's waiting—the eagle hovering on the wing—until, true to the Conti arms, he hurls the barbed lightning."

She put down her needle, her face troubled. "Ramon, do you think it's really coming?"

"Not yet," he muttered. "As yet he can do nothing really—alone—a few gestures, of course. Bell, book, and candle, interdict and the rest. Do you know Cîteaux's latest? He and Castelnau are traipsing the countryside in monks' habits, dragging their perfumed feet through the dust of Languedoc. I swear, old Peire will sweat enough grease to make his own pomade. Do you remember the reek of attar of roses last time he paid us a visit? Damned if he didn't offer you a phial to tempt you back from the chaste sin of heresy. And now, seeing there's no other way, they're trying to rival the Cathars in piety—true followers of the Christian life. I reckon they shower more silent curses on the little friar than they ever vented on the heretics themselves. But for him they'd never have hit on the idea!"

"The little friar?" she asked.

"Domingo something—Spaniard, of course—canon of Osma really, but humbly vowed to strict observance of the Augustinian rule, and less meekly, to the extermination of heresy."

She looked up swiftly, frowning. "The man they talked of at Montpellier?"

"Hm, he made quite a noise there."

"He began," she murmured, "with miracles. I don't know why, but I'm afraid."

"What, of the little monk? You, Esclarmonde!" He laughed aloud.

"Yes," she said; "not of Castelnau, or of the formidable

Abbot of Cîteaux; no, not even of Innocent—but of that little canon!" She tried to laugh at her own foolishness. "It's senseless, of course. I haven't even seen him."

"I shouldn't wish to. Still, the man's got such damnable cheek he might even turn up at the Conference. . . . You're set on it—still?" he frowned.

"Yes," she said quietly. "You promised, Ramon."

"Oh, I'm not trying to get out of it, but heaven knows whether it won't be more harm than good." He rose with a gesture of impatience and once more resumed his restless pacing.

She watched him, troubled. "It's a symbol, Ramon, of our liberty."

"Our liberty!" He turned, his rich voice suddenly harsh with bitterness. "Can't you see where it's leading us?"

"Whatever happens," she said quietly, "we must keep faith."

He looked at her, but her very quietude drove him to desperation. "Keep faith! To what, to whom? And ourselves? . . ." His concealed apprehensions, followed by his anxieties over the boy, had strained his nerves to breaking point. "Christ, is our land to be thrown to the winds for a pious myth? For the moment, dear Raymond may play cat-and-mouse with the Pope; but if Innocent wearies, if at last he manages to wheedle that sly fox, Philippe Auguste? Don't you see they're only waiting?" he cried, his voice vibrant with hate. "They've waited since Roncesvalles."

She shuddered. "We're not prepared," she murmured, anguished, as if thereby she could ward off disaster.

"Prepared! Heaven knows we aren't, and in the meantime we hold conferences and twaddle about love and tolerance. But once those northern jackals are let loose it won't be even our convictions we'll be fighting for—but our lives." Exhausted by his outburst, he leaned back against the column of the window, but in a second he had recovered his old poise. "Anyhow, jeer as much as they like, spite us, mock us as weaklings, decadent—and God knows if they aren't about right," he cried bitterly, "with one thing they may forget to reckon—there's still Foix."

As she gazed at him, all the violence, the frustration of her brother's life were revealed to her suddenly with overwhelming poignancy; the decadence of Toulouse, the overweening pride of the Trencavels, all the pettiness of feudal rivalry. If the south could turn to him, not Toulouse or Aragon, as leader!

"There's still Foix," he was saying, almost triumphant. "And if it comes to the worst—" he paused and looked at her searchingly; even before he spoke she seemed to know what was coming—"there are the mountains—Montségur!"

This, then, was the reality. To Esclarmonde of Foix it seemed that for the second time in her life she was watching the death of herself.

Montségur a Cathar refuge, a citadel of the spirit on earth, handed over to violence as the center of her brother's military strategy. Once, long ago, another image, more radiant, born of a singer's vision, had been shattered by her husband's jealous bigotry. Had the dream rekindled an instant by this boy's ardent enthusiasms, only been born anew to suffer a repeated annihilation?

As if re-echoing her spirit's protest, her body tautened. Beyond destruction, the threat of war that faced them, hadn't Wolf pointed to a fulfillment almost transcending all those far-off hopes?

She did not speak, but as she raised her head she seemed to Ramon-Roger of Foix transfigured, almost youthful in her passionate vision. And he cursed the years of agony that had wrapped her in a mantle of sacrifice of repudiation of the flesh, while his old jealousy of the Cathars tore at him anew; to watch her dedicated to this round of self-abnegation and toil, here in the great castle that should have been the pride of her widowhood, the tool of beggars and charlatans and driveling old men. And now, even worse, to see her growing remoter yet, drifting from him through the rigor of the vows that she had sworn to take—a ghost prisoned in a pale Cathar world of the spirit.

"Esclarmonde!" he had come nearer. In his voice was all the passionate persuasiveness of the young Ramon Drut, "Have you promised yourself—is there no way back?"

"No!" Slowly the ecstasy faded from her face. She shook her head. "Now less than ever—but I shall stand by you."

Her face even more than her words told him that all argument was vain. He turned away.

After a moment she rose and came to his side. Together they stood gazing out over the widespread land. Below them the Ariège flowed down from Foix past them to the

52

unending plain of Languedoc, but neither spoke, and perhaps, even as they gazed, past and present seemed to grow unreal as the landscape in the transcending light of the waning day.

SUMMER LIGHTNING

O Toulouso, Toulouso . . .
Toun cel, toun soulel d'or
(LA TOULOUSAINO)

I

THE JUNE SUN STREAMED DOWN UPON TOULOUSE, BATHING it in the glory of its famed gold. The whole city basked in the light that poured from the deep blue sky, gilding the crumbling marble of a ruined but ever-present antiquity, or gathering to a fierce glow in the rose-red brick of wall and tower.

Still, though his temples lay in ruins, Apollo held silent sway. The towers might incite and menace, the threat of a perpetual *memento mori* resound from angelic trumpets and the winged evangelic beasts on the churches' portals—the light denied it, so that the uncouth cyclopean front of the great basilica of St. Sernin itself seemed mitigated as through some act of grace, while terminated by its garland of little chapels, clustered about the apse like limpets stuck to the truncated tail of some vast and glowing reptile, its great rose-red body stretched contentedly in the sun.

Even the tomb of the illustrious counts of Toulouse had found its way into the open, as if, shunning the dark shadows of the crypt, its inmates had chosen to lie at rest in the embrasure of the southern porch, where still the golden light falling upon the porous stone of their sarcophagi could pierce to their dead bones, and their sightless eyes, touched by its radiance, turn to those yet sunnier territories conquered by their race.

All seemed somehow turned outward, externalized in an indolent abandonment to that lambent glory which squandered itself with such prodigal splendor, permeating even the gestures and the very voices of the inhabitants, so that it appeared natural for common speech to round itself harmoniously to the fullness of song. Song indeed was everywhere, falling drowsily to the thrumming of a guitar from an open window, springing spontaneously from the lips of some passerby, or echoing in the rich waves of laughter that broke from a group of youths passing with reckless swagger under the shadow of that staid and venerable institute of civic liberty, the Capitol. But then, speech itself in that warm, southern idiom of the Languedoc was a sonorous music, resonant, full as the waters of the Garonne that swept with careless abandon on past the city, under the great fortified and crenelated walls that indolently flaunted their own superfluity as though amused at some monstrous atavism. In a widening curve the river flowed, under the lowered bridge, past the ponderous, ungainly mass of the ancient Castel Narbones, that still through the passage of the centuries, the shifting triumph of Roman, Frank, and Goth, kept watch unmoved over the imperturbable glory of Sacra Tolosa.

Still that faint aura of something sacrosanct, inviolate, hung over the city, as when its temples were consecrate to the god of light, for who knew but that the veneration of the Latin deity was but a continuance of a tradition infinitely older, dating from an age remoter even than that which saw the Celto-Iberian tribes return from their raid on the far land of Greece, dragging the fearful and sacred booty, the Delphic treasure, to their stronghold among the surrounding hills?

II

"To THE NOBLE COUNT OF TOULOUSE:

"What pride has taken hold of thy heart, thou leper? Thou are not wrought of iron, thy body is as that of all men. Fever may invade it; stricken by leprosy or paralysis, crippled by incurable disease, the demon of madness may descend on thee. Yea, even as it befell the King of Babylon, by the power of God thou mayest be changed into a beast. And why? The illustrious King of Aragon and other mighty lords thy neighbors have sworn peace and obedience to the apostolic legates, whilst thou alone repudiatest them, warring for the sake of greed and lucre like a raven glutting itself on a carcass! Hast thou no shame that thou darest violate the oath by which thou art sworn to chase heretics from thy fief? And when our legate reproached thee for defending them, didst thou not presume to answer, a heretic or Cathar might easily prove the superiority of his belief to the Catholic faith . . . ? Tremble, thou godless wight, for thou shalt be chastised! Thou breakest the peace of the Sabbath and robbest the cloisters. To Christianity's shame thou sufferest Jews to hold public office at they hands. Our legates have excommunicated thee. We ratify their decree. But as it is our duty to convert the sinner, we command thee to do penance that thou mayest receive absolution through our mercy. Hence, for thy insults against the Church and against God cannot remain unpunished, know that we shall see thee deprived of thy possessions and incite the princes against thee as against the enemy of Christ. But the wrath of God will not rest at that. The Lord will blast thee!"

Slowly, with an air of slightly cynical amusement, Raymond VI of Toulouse laid down the parchment and settled himself more luxuriously on the cushions of the sumptuous couch. Certainly, he smiled to himself, Innocent's style was gaining in power—painfully lacking in subtlety, of course, so that now on a second reading its effect was considerably impaired. A pity, he deliberated; for, sensitive to stylistic finesse as he was, preoccupation with aesthetic values might unconsciously have led to a growing receptibility to the spiritual theme. Yet Lotario Conti prided himself on his literary taste—in the reverberant Roman tradition, naturally; one could hardly expect the sensibility of a *fin cuer leal*. Well, perhaps one was becoming too ultrarefined—so much preoocupation with soulful states. A curious paradox that the guardian of the spirit should be so obsessed in the attributes of the flesh—"Leper, carcass, disease—The Lord will blast thee." But then, it had become evident long ago that the representative of the Lamb on earth inevitably assumed the role of the thundering Jehovah. No wonder the Cathars refused to acknowledge the patriarchal Godhead.

Languidly his hand stretched out to the enameled goblet. Having sipped, he licked the point of his tongue appreciatively over his full loose lips; then, dropping his arm, let his fingers linger with instinctive delight on the gleaming tissue enveloping the fleshy form whose outline, despite his physicians' pains, was year by year achieving a more ample curve. Yet once it had been svelte as the young archers on the brocaded silk. "Stricken by paralysis"—covered with the sores of "incurable disease"? His blue eyes, their original size and brilliance long since diminished by encroaching creases of fat, gazed at the immaculate whiteness of his heavily ringed hand. "Tremble, thou godless wight, for thou shalt be chastised." Was it the sixth, the seventh warning? How much longer would Innocent content himself with bombast? One day, next time, or even this, might not the eagle swoop, the threat to his possessions become grim reality? It was evident the Pope was taking the great Gregory for his model, tireless, unappeasable in his ambition till he had brought about a new Canossa. Involuntarily Raymond gave a little shiver. But the vision of the wintery courtyard, the iron-barred threshold deep in frozen snow, had no power over the oppressive heat that encompassed him. Even the gleaming floor and the veined columns seemed to sweat, and in the shadow of the vault, a fulgent glitter from the interminable incrustations of gold and semiprecious stones recalled the sultry subterranean heat of the mines. Outside, the noonday sun of a resplendent June beat down on the parched vegetation of the courtyard, causing the rosy sandstone of the walls to glow as with inner fire, so that the scalloped shadow of the horsehoe arcading seemed clipped with tongs from the red-hot stone. Only the fountain under the black columns of the cypresses gave a last hope of coolness.

Not that Raymond himself suffered from the excessive temperature. Around his head the heavy air, stirred to perpetual movement under huge feathered fans wielded by the bronzed and glistening arms of two Moorish slaves, caressed in tender and rhythmic embrace the thinning locks of perfumed hair, golden by virtue of art if not by nature despite his fifty years. And indeed, if the heat ever troubled him at all he had readily come to ignore it for the sake of the authenticity it gave to that Eastern atmosphere that he had imported with no stint of expenditure into the rugged fortress of the ancient Castel Narbones— an atmosphere to which, though the stranger might be inclined to regard it as an affectation, he laid claim as to a natural birthright, being the heritage of his illustrious ancestor Raymond of St. Gilles, who over a hundred years ago had so gloriously founded the colony of Syrian Tripoli.

Certainly had he possessed a greater share of his forefather's energy he might long ago have embarked with an expeditionary force to support a not altogether dubious claim to that coveted realm. But Raymond of Toulouse had little left of the predatory blood that had brought his ancestor glory and an untimely end; it was easier and more salubrious to import the East into Languedoc, and with the power and wealth accumulated by a sagacious father there were few limits set to his dreams. His agents, connoisseurs in the art of living, kept him amply supplied with a variety of feminine grace that could equal any Eastern harem. The choicest Levantine wines found their way to his cellars, his table could boast the most succulent and exotic of spices and sweetmeats; added to which he could assure himself of being accompanied wherever he moved by a retinue of sages and astrologers, while the ablest physicians, both Jews and Arabs, were ever at his beck and call to counteract the licences of the flesh. What more could he desire? Without having to encounter the deserts, the fevers, the general disadvantages of the East, he could enjoy its most superb fruits.

Undoubtedly Raymond of Toulouse made little or no attempt to dissemble the fact that the acquirement of the culture of Saladin or Noureddin seemed of far more importance to him than the liberation of the Sepulcher. In vain had the Pope threatened, the legates flaunted with excommunication and interdict. What matter! He knew he could always get a couple of Cathars to absolve him at the last, and surely, he smiled cynically, if there were a grain of truth in that holy babble at all, there was more chance of entering heaven through their hands than by the anointment of some corrupt priest. Besides which (though the count was apt to suffer many tremors on account of his body), he felt far removed from leaving the world at present. Apart from a touch of dyspepsia, his health had been very fair of late; and he ran few risks, setting little score by front-line heroics in warfare, regarding with weary skepticism the antics of his foolhardy brother-in-law, Don Pedro of Aragon, caracoling about at the head of his troops playing the part of Roderigo or Arthur. Leave chivalric prowess to the poets, Raymond was wont to say.

How much more was to be achieved through a few well-planned marriages (and incidentally, divorces). By his betrothal to Joan of England that trouble with Richard had been settled more satisfactorily than by all the machinations of Bertran of Born. And presently it was certainly worth putting up with the dullness of Eleanor if that insensate quarrel with Aragon could be settled at last. Through the Christian bond of marriage how much bloodshed might be spared! Yet was it not into that very carnage that the threats of the Church were driving him? What were the skirmishes of his *routiers* for which Innocent arraigned him against the approaching holocaust?

War—the attribute of barbarians. Of course, for the most part humanity had got no further—a state of affairs, he smiled ironically, that Holy Church would be in no hurry to improve. Only too conveniently might Innocent rely on the blood lust of the feudal princes, the wild bears of the north. Doubtless they'd enjoy the fun. Philippe August (sly Capet though he was), Philippe fortunately was comparatively civilized and preferred to play the game of cat-and-mouse. And yet, slowly, surely, the storm clouds were gathering. Could the tempest still be warded off? For how long and by what sacrifice—a show of penance, a little Jew-baiting, a heretic hunt? Would the voracious appetite of the clerics, the maniacal pride of Innocent be appeased. But already his innate aestheticism, always tormented by actual spectacles of suffering, recoiled in disgust. Curious, he ruminated, how certain natures seemed to derive from the thought of persecution a gratification equivalent to that of erotic lust. For many years he had contemplated the fascinating task of compiling, completely dispassionately, a treatise on the subtle and indirect means of courting Dame Venus.

Involuntarily his mind flew to the man whose visit had been announced and to which rather reluctantly he looked forward any minute—Bernard-Jordan of the Isle, his brother-in-law to be. Frankly, he did not particularly savor that nearer relationship; he even felt something of guilt in foisting this consort on his natural sister, but at her age India of Lautrec could hardly expect to be squeamish. Jordan was young, and in his way presentable enough, certainly an improvement on that wizened old Lautrec, her former husband, and she for her part seemed content. Luckily she had learned early enough that the rules of diplomacy are of far more importance in the conjugal bed than the presence of Amor—a renunciation for which, after all, the laws of courtly love provided ample compensation. Nevertheless, he could not rid himself of a feeling of distaste. Reserved and immaculate, capable at times of an acrid though gloomy satire, there was yet something undeniably sinister about Jordan, by comparison at any rate with the vivid, sparkling, and often all too abandoned nature of the count's own entourage. Inevitably Raymond's eyes roved to the courtyard, to the handsome youth reclining in the shadow of an arch, his gleaming chestnut curls bent over the brilliantly illuminated page. Aware enough of young Mirepoix's faults; pleasure-loving, unstable as he knew him to be, obsessed in the pursuit of his own delights and the avoidance of everything that stood in their way, it was characteristic of Raymond's innate generosity to accept a thing of beauty wholeheartedly at its face value. Was it not that almost elemental grace, that brilliant wit, that exquisite aesthetic sensibility a divine gift that it would be sacrilegious to question? Marry him off to India? he reflected. It might almost have been a chance to bind him closer—and then to watch him coarsen into middle age. . . . He laughed, and the slackened contour of his full lips tightened bitterly. No, the gifts of the gods were fleeting. One must count oneself blessed to snatch uncomplaining at their brevity. But Jordan—morbid, wrapped in a mantle of gloom—had he really cared so much for that bigoted, bowelless father of his, while toward that exquisite creature, his mother, he seemed to feel almost cold resentment? Curious, the youth was definitely warped. Still, Raymond pondered, personal antipathy was a small thing in the face of matrimonial exigency. And at the moment what choice could have been more appropriate, in view of the steps he was now taking, than this scion of the ancient house of Selio, that once had given birth to the saintly bishop of Commenges and still prided itself on its bigoted piety? Had Jordan's father fondly imagined that he had inherited the good bishop's proselytizing gift, and could crush the incipient demon in his lovely wife just as the saintly Bernard had led the legendary dragon to the altar steps? Would not his ghost turn in his grave to see her now, Cathar abbess, avenging her faith in a surfeit of self-abnegation for the years lost in patient endurance of her bonds: avenging a forbidden faith or herself? He wondered, recalling her image.

Esclarmonde of Foix, so lovely, yet remote—less in pride than in a strange indefinite elusiveness, as though the very sympathy she showed for the weaknesses of men rendered her at once intangible, inviolate, the creature of another world—yet of the Cathars? He paused. Out of the mists of memory there rose before him the image of a girl entering the massive, somber hall of Foix to welcome him, her liege lord, and pledge him in the crystal cup she bore in her hands. A vision of the Grail. For a minute the whole of his life had hung in the balance. If his soul could have been saved from perdition it would have been then. Even so for Christendom? he pondered wryly. At any rate he had not failed to acknowledge his debt—and she had appeared to appreciate the gift. Once more he wondered what had become of that singer he had sent her in token, with his strange tales of an Eastern Grail. Heaven alone knew where the man came from—some wandering bastard probably, born of the Crusades. What was his name— Kyot? No one appeared to have seen him since. Some talk of his wandering off to the north. At the time he had taken no note, his mind occupied with other things. Later, however, when the subject had begun to intrigue him again, he had been unable to trace him. Had that old bigot, her husband, had some hand in his disappearance after all? . . . Grail or chalice, he went on musing, cauldron or life-spending fount—how that concept had penetrated into all religions. Spear and cup—the primordial urge, blood sacrifice, the mystery of fecundity—Attis, Cybele, Adonis, Astarte. Why, here on this very soil, under these columned porticoes, what feet had trodden, and to what strange rites, what fearful sacrifice? For where the Holy Ghost now breathed, in the hands of the officiating priest, the doves of Aphrodite had fed from vestal hands; through these streets was dragged in jubilation the treasure of Delphi, while on the mountain heights the Berbers built their altars to Belissena and the Iberian Baal.

Oh, Innocent, he laughed, oh, Lotario Conti, what avails you all your learning against the demon instinct of the flesh? Or did he know it too well, know that under the crypts of Toulouse, in the crumbling ruins of Arles, of Orange and Saint-Rémy, the pagan ghost breathed an incantation before which the dour prelate's prayer faded to a mere whisper, while on summer nights on the mountain slopes, or amid the marshy stretches of the Camargue, the flocks and the great drifting herds of the bulls were goaded to madness by a music that never fell from the pipes of mortal men? Older far than all Manichaean and Gnostic mysticism was the voice of the dark gods. Ah, was the Church's inexorable pursuit of heresy but the frenzied realization of its impotence against a deadlier power which, if it were not crushed at the root, might one day rise again and overthrow the whole edifice of the Church? In the Italian lands under the giant structure of Roman power it had been held in leash and silenced; but here, where south and west and east met in such strange confluence, it had still not been utterly quelled but might rise, incalculable, like the subterranean streams of the land, undermining, disruptive, breaking out in a thousand disguised and fantastic forms. Extermination of that power meant extermination of the land! Suddenly it seemed to dawn on him with an almost preternatural clarity of vision. The Church's onslaught against heresy, the threat to his own realm, was but the symptom of a far deeper urge, the ceaseless conflict with a Power whose unfathomable mystery Innocent in his amazing intuition at least divined. While seeing himself the God-chosen instrument in an ultimate gigantomachy, he vented thereon his whole prodigious energy to the final triumph of the Church of which not Peter, not Christ himself, but he, Lotario Conti, was the predestined savior.

The heart of Raymond of Toulouse stopped beating. As if suspended on that breathless noon, time seemed to cease, the feathered plumes pause in their rhythmic beat, while in the courtyard the plashing jet congealed to crystal and for one instant, in the burning silence of the solstice, the soul of the aging Epicurean felt upon it the dark wing of destiny. Was it his fate to stand against this superman, this incarnation of the warring archangel upon earth, as champion of that paganism from which he himself had fled into the gentler arms of an Eastern Nirvana? Was he called upon now, in vengeance for the hours in which he had dallied with it so wantonly, that in retribution he should bear the onslaught of the northern hordes with their barbaric appetite, the jealous thirst for a wine untasted, the more enticing because as yet but known by hearsay? Should they drain to the dregs the cup from which he had only sipped, preferring always the bouquet to the full draught? Were they to grasp what he no longer had the vitality to uphold, that they, the young, virile, should inherit what once in like measure his own Gothic forefather had won from decay? But how much would be destroyed, trampled underfoot, lost, the perfected bloom of a civilization regained with such infinite pains. Perfidious Franks! Somewhere at the root of him the old resentment stirred. Was there still a drop of the old blood in his atrophied veins that had prevailed in the face of Clovis when Alaric fell? Involuntarily he glanced down at the flaccid limbs veiled by the rich brocaded silk. Could they yet be roused to action, rise from their couch of sloth at the clarion call of his land? Which of the others had loved it, apprehended the depth of its mystery, as he? Would they flock to his banner, stand united behind him, forget their rivalries—Béarn, Montpellier, Commenges, Trencavel and his hidalgo arrogance, or that old predatory mountain breed, the Foix? Well, he pondered, with a return of his accustomed cynicism, was he now even now preparing to knit the last to him by subtle cords—so subtle that they might give in any direction he pleased? Compromise! Ah, there was no denying it, the old feline game, diplomacy. What noonday madness had almost befallen him?—invincible warrior, scion of the puissant house of St. Gilles, defender of the south, champion of a mythic gigantomachy—he, the weary machinator in an effete civilization, the unwilling controversialist amid the sordid rivalry of ecclesiastic and temporal powers. He laughed bitterly and aloud, so that the vacant apathetic gaze of the slaves found a brief focus point, the rhythmic monotony of the waving fans was broken, and in the blazing courtyard the fretful plashing of the jet grew audible once more. Time and its irrelevancies had resumed their course, demanding not philosophic speculation or intuitive vision, but action, immediate and irretrievable, and dragging the protagonist in the ever-tightening meshes of its net to an inevitable doom. Wearily, the old hedonist put out his heavily jeweled hand and sipped once more from the goblet. Then, arranging himself on the cushions with an air of majestic indolence, he prepared to receive the guest whose arrival was at that moment announced by the appearance of his page.

LOST PEACE

Pace non trovo, e non ho da far guerra;
Et emo e spero, ed ardo, e son un ghiaccio;
E volo sopra 'l cielo, e giaccio in terra ...
In questo stato son, Donna, per vui.

(FRANCESCO PETRARCA)

I

CARCASSONNE—A MONTH OR TWO AFTER THOSE LAST VIRU-
lent denunciations had fallen from the papal throne—the
slopes and meadows beneath the ancient Gothic fortress
were gay with revelry.

Actually, festivities on so large and lavish a scale were
comparative rarities there, and daily existence in that
many-towered and embattled city maintained a certain
reserve and feudal dignity that caused the citizens of
Toulouse and Narbonne to shrug lightly.

It was no longer as in the days of old Raimon Trencavel or Roger Taillefer, when Alazais had held her courts
of love and played off poor Arnaut of Mareuil against Aragon's king.

Young Trencavel, they laughed—though he could do
things superbly well if he chose, as at the present moment,
for instance—had a flair for the simple life. Came, no
doubt, from being dosed as a boy with all that heretic jargon. though they hadn't managed, for all that, to convert
him to the faith. Besides, he was obsessed by athletics—of
a pleasantly aesthetic variety certainly, reminiscent of the
antique—racing, wrestling, javelin-throwing and the rest;
armor reduced to a minimum. Not much of that heavy-
weight stuff they indulged in in the north, though those
beef-eating barons had better think twice before they
scoffed that the knighthood of Languedoc had grown so
used to handling their tender lute strings they couldn't

keep a grip on steel. Still, it was all a bit virtuous and edifying.

The occasion was, therefore, one to rouse much excitement, expecially among the younger squires, and it was with feelings of disgust and bitter disappointment that Wolf of Foix and one of his comrades found themselves despatched, in the midst of the festivities, to escort a couple of pompous and elderly councillors halfway along the road to Narbonne. For, by quiet determination, Esclarmonde of Foix had succeeded in her plan and for a couple of months now Wolf had been enrolled among the squires of Raimon-Roger Trencavel, Viscount of Béziers and Carcassonne.

The process of transformation was naturally fraught with pain and travail, and often enough, despairing of ever catching up with his companions both in physical attainments and in worldy wisdom, he had fallen into a succession of poses in which puppyish pretensions to the bravura of a young tough were strangely mingled with the role of the *ingénu*, which with the cunning of the sensitive he would even purposely exaggerate as a safeguard against those dreaded assaults on his hidden self. And so, under a hardier mask, he still remained, inwardly, bewildered, uncertain. For though his companions had delighted in making sidelong attacks on his innocence, forever hinting at the dark mysteries of what they termed Life, they seemed determined, as by some conspiracy, to keep him from its ultimate secrets—a campaign dictated perhaps not only by cubbish sadism and the instinctive knowledge that fuller revelation would mean an end of their insinuating game, but (to give some, at any rate, their due) by an unconscious, almost superstitious awe of the boy's integrity, a lot that had he been ill-favored, sickly, or weak-spirited would never have been his. As it was, though a constant target for their teasing, bullying, and even petting, he would somehow still evade them, withheld, with or against his will, in that secret, inviolate sanctuary of his being which he could not or would not surrender. And yet at times he would be assailed by an overwhelming desire to spend himself in a feverish self-abandonment that caused him to throw into his puppyish wrestlings with his companions a passionate fierceness that amazed and disquieted them, and left him, after a transitory orgy of violence in which for one brief moment the anguish of human separateness was extinguished, emptier than ever, so that he was thrown back upon his own isolation as a fish upon the shore.

It was evening by the time they returned and, urging their horses through the crowds of revelers loitering around the gates of the city, at last clattered into the castle courtyard; for the hundredth time that day young Villemur showered curses on the head of old Saissac. A few minutes later Wolf, having begged and bullied a grudging servant to prepare him a belated bath, reflected, a trifle more philosophically under the influence of those reviving waters, that he was about right. It was old Longshanks all over to send one off on some futile errand at the last moment. As if the wretched consuls couldn't have found their way by themselves! Show respect for the representatives of that ancient civic institution? He'd just been out to spoil their fun. Part of his system of discipline, no doubt, a little exercise in restraint—*temperantia, modestia,* and the rest. Cicero be damned. "Driveling old burghers," Villemur had raged. "If at least they'd had the decency to stay to the end. Pressure of duties? All they were after was to rub in their confounded independence, mumbling all that legal jargon to make one feel small." Still, it had been something of a revenge to see the old worthies' faces when one of the reputedly brainless esquires had come out pat with that bit of Latin. Even the scornful Villemur had had to admit that the monks had proved of use for once.

Life in the monastery . . . how long ago it seemed! Bracing his muscles, he sprang from the bath. Well, even his father, he thought, mightn't be too ashamed of him now. He had half hoped, half dreaded, the count would attend the festival, so that he scarcely knew whether it was disappointment or relief to hear he had gone to Andorra with his legitimate son, Roger, to arrange the latter's marriage. Why, soon his things, he saw, dragging on his clothes, would be growing tight at the shoulder. Nevertheless he wished he were a bit taller—Roger was such a giant. But the long tunic, he consoled himself, would give him height. With keen delight he stroked down the folds of deep sapphire-blue silk embroidered with a border of silver thread. Even the exquisite Mirepoix would not be able to deny its beauty, and he thrilled a little at the memory of that elegant and superbly self-confident youth who, arriving recently for the festivals, had singled him out among the squires. He had not been blind to their jealousy. To the majority of those adolescents, the honor of being addressed by that young gallant, whose fantastic exploits had won for him a fabulous if somewhat disreputable fame, meant almost more than praise from the viscount himself. Why he should have been the recipient of such signal honors he could scarcely imagine, except that the old senhor of Mirepoix was his father's greatest vassal, the foremost of all that ancient clan, the sons of Luna, who traced their lineage back to the moon goddess and bore her crescent in their coat of arms. And then, to his great surprise, for he would never have connected so very mundane a personage with his aunt, Mirepoix had brought him greetings from the Countess Esclarmonde. For an instant, as he buckled the belt round his tunic, Wolf's hand rested on the silver clasp. It had been her parting gift—symbol, he had dreamed, of the sword he should one day bear in the name of Montségur. . . .

But if he didn't hurry. . . . Curse it! His hair was full of dust from the ride. Dragging the comb through the gold-brown waves, he was thankful at least he hadn't Villemur's perfumed ringlets to deal with. He was ready at last, and, impatient of his comrade's fastidiousness, waited no longer, but leaping down the stairs made his way along the ramparts, and affecting an abandon intended to rival the reputed rakishness of Mirepoix approached the meadows in which the festivities were being held.

But for the guards, a few henchmen, and a couple of desultory loiterers, the ramparts were deserted. Behind the castle the sound of boisterous revelry and snatches of bawdy song came from the town, where the citizens were making no less a holiday and rivaling the gaieties of the nobles in the drinking booths and in sports in the market square. But soon even the sound of that distant clamor died away beneath the increasing tide of chatter and laughter that welled up from the meadows beneath.

The southern dusk was rapidly falling as he reached them, and everywhere lights and torches were being lit. In the mixed light the world looked bodiless, the rich colors of the dresses dimmed to the sickly hues of faded tapestry, while the music seemed at that distance frayed as the haphazard plucking of some worn-out string. But soon he had drawn nearer. On a strip of sward, saved from utter desiccation by a careful system of irrigation, a score of figures were moving to and fro in the intricate pattern of a dance. Should he join them! Alas, the coveted nonchalance of Mirepoix was fast deserting him, and for a time he watched them, fascinated by the rhythmic interweaving of the figures. But what a clumsy fish Vaqueras was—those finlike movements of the short arms were unmistakable; and that idiot Raimbaut mincing about like the little monkey my lady Agnes kept hopping about in her rooms. Did he really look such a fool himself when he danced? he thought scornfully, masking his own diffidence under a mantle of cynicism. Almost he felt inclined to make an oath, here and now, that he'd never try again. Of course Villemur swore the dancing wasn't the main thing, and he and Laurac had made a long list of every nuance of pressure a hand could exert, had evolved in fact a perfect code of tactile eloquence, the attainment of which seemed to Wolf more hopeless than even the handling of the great two-handed sword itself. Besides, which of those categories could really have been applied to the emotion he felt in regard to that willowy girl in the pale-gold dress with the cornflowers in her hair? She was rather like the corn herself, he thought, or the long mountain grasses waving in the wind, and he felt a sudden angry desire to snatch her away from the corpulent noble whose wheezing breath was audible every time he passed. But already the dance had ceased and she had turned away to talk to a stranger, gabbling in that Norman jargon he could not understand. And if he had, what should he have found to say, clumsily groping for those airy nothings that came so lightly to the tongues of Villemur and Laurac? His former exhilaration already chastened a little, he drew back.

He supposed, moreover, that it was his duty to make his return known to Trencavel or old Saissac. If only he could escape "the fair Agnes," he thought, revolting against the wearisome duties that he knew, by experience, the whims of the viscountess would entail.

It was almost dark by now. Here and there torches hung from the trees or, stuck in great iron sconces in the ground, threw their fulgent light on the brocaded awnings of rich pavilions, or on a group of revelers reclining on sumptuous carpets or beneath emblazoned banners hung from the boughs of the trees. Carried by the general stream, Wolf moved on, while pages burdened with flagons of wine and platters of sweetmeats pushed past him, strange faces, illumined a moment, flashed up in frightening intimacy, or snatches of conversation hurled at him like cockroaches through the gloom.

"And Amery sent him headlong over the saddlebow . . ."

"Genuine? Well, he certainly paid enough for it—old Calonymos saw to that—he'll be adding a crystal dome to the princely mansion soon. . . ."

"You like it? My dear, they say they're wearing them still deeper at Toulouse—gave dear Fulk another theme for a moving sermon, one that he . . . well . . ." The voice trailed away in an insinuating giggle.

Bernard of Rabat, dashing past in breathless haste as though he had been despatched on some matter of life and death, cried without halting, "She wants some of those candied peaches."

Agnes, he supposed. If only he could get that behind him. Was Mirepoix about? involuntarily his pulses quickened.

A greater conglomeration of lights and laughter suggesting the proximity of the viscount, Wolf made toward them, and soon enough he caught sight of the great pavilion emblazoned with the arms of the Trencavels of Béziers and Carcassonne. There was the old senhor of Lantar, gray-bearded, venerable in that surcoat of old-world cut, and the ancient dame with that deep-throated chesty laugh; wasn't that Faïs, his father's aunt? With an amazing scorn of diplomatic tact she would probably ply him with questions as to the Count of Foix's visit to Andorra, entering into a complex discourse on the art of dynastic marriages while her sharp brown eyes, embedded in their wrinkled caverns, would scan him from top to toe finding fault with this and that. "Heavens, in my young days boys wouldn't have dared to deck themselves out like girls."

No, he didn't feel like letting that formidable lady's irony damp his pleasure at the outset, and to avoid her magpie eye he drew back out of the illumined circle. He paused a moment, hesitant, as from the shadow of some trees behind him the sound of a man's voice was borne toward him; strangely harsh and insistent after that evanescent chatter:

". . . right on the boundary of my lands. But they'll know it if they let as much as a goat over the pale. Damned if he won't soon be wishing his blessed star had led him to others' pastures."

"A globe, Guilhem—a fiery globe—give the good monk his due for a touch of orginality." Didn't that resonant laugh belong to Aimeric of Monreal, his father's friend?

"Hm, as long as it remains fixed securely in the celestial heights and doesn't start rolling over Languedoc," another voice chimed in, lower, almost foreboding against the foil of gaiety.

"It's near enough to rolling over Fanjeaux," the senhor of Durfort growled again. Wolf was sure he recognized him as the flare of a passing torch threw the dark angry face into momentary illumination. He must be talking, he thought, of that Spanish monk who had sworn to exterminate heresy and was setting up his mission house in Prouille, the man whom Esclarmonde of Foix . . .

"If only Olivier were still alive," laughed the owner of the eloquent voice, "you could have asked his advice. He was a master hand at managing abbots. That little affair at Alet, back in ninety-seven, you remember. Bertran of Saissac was regent then. The old abbot had given up the ghost and the dear monks were set on having their man as successor, much to Saissac's disgust, for which one can't blame him—the old priest was as corrupt as you can make them. Anyhow it was managed, though one can hardly think old Bertran approved of his brother's means. Olivier was always a wild one, but that beat everything hollow. . . . Raked out the corpse and set it up, dressed in vestments and all, to preside over the chapter. Christ, if the holy brethren weren't soon persuaded not to dispute my lord regent's wishes!"

A little shudder ran up Wolf's spine, and instinctively he turned toward the light. Contrasted with that macabre anecdote, the gaudy figures moving beneath the torches' glow seemed suddenly unreal.

"What, have you seen a ghost?" One of the figures had detached itself from the crowd of revelers and, catching sight of him as he passed, clutched him, laughing, by the arm. With a jerk the phantasmagoric scene switched back into focus.

"Sicard!"

"So you did get back in time—where's Villemur?"

Wolf shrugged. "Still arranging his curls maybe."

"For Alys?" Sicard of Durban laughed. "Well, if one has a husband as bald as old Uc, they're probably a consolation. Come over to us!" he hurried on impetuously.

70

"Gaucelm's going to sing presently. Savaric has challenged him to a tenson." And without waiting he had dashed on, wriggling through the crowd like an eel, regardless of the final havoc wrought on his unruly mop of thick brown locks. Wolf, doing his best to follow, found his progress impeded by a posse of servants trundling along a huge vat of wine, so that to avoid collision he was forced once more into the moving tide and inevitably drawn into the circle that had gathered in an adoring group around the queen of the festival.

Enthroned on the silken cushions of her couch, Agnes of Montpellier, Viscountess of Béziers and Carcassonne, presided over her court with an air of elegantly peevish indolence. But with consummate skill in the arrangement of the tiniest detail she had allowed, either by ruse or feminine instinct, one extraordinarily miniature foot to peep with alluring piquancy from under the scintillating tissue of her dress, while the voice that came from the pretty pouting mouth was certainly not lethargic. Like the tinkling of bits of glass, Wolf had called it, forced in his belated pagedom to listen to its inane twitterings hour by hour; though luckily Trencavel was shortening that stage of his courtly education to a minimum. Sometimes he wondered whether it was sheer adoration or innate chivalry that seemed to make the viscount blind to her vapid frivolity; but in this, as in much else, Trencavel remained a mystery, and Wolf was not the only one to ask himself whether the striking yet somewhat enigmatic countenance that he presented to the world was truly expressive of the man, or a mask. Certainly it was arresting. Framed by the deep-gold curls, and sharply molded as the profile on an antique coin, it seemed almost to belong to that of a young, though perhaps slightly disenchanted, god.

At that moment he was standing a little apart, talking to a superbly elegant young man whose gaily insouciant manner made Trencavel's laughter seem by contrast almost remote and reserved, and Wolf, catching sight of him, was overcome with confusion.

"Why, if it isn't Mirepoix!" exclaimed a voice at his ear. "Thought he was quite attached to Toulouse. Since Raymond's hobnobbing with such pious friends, things, I suppose, are getting a bit dull up there. Damned if we don't yet see the good count licking the pontifical toe."

"Not likely," the other laughed. "He'd fight shy of the

71

journey. Roman fever and the rest. Incidentally, Mirepoix always did possess a genius for ingratiating himself with both sides of a faction—"

"Or their wives." His neighbor's glance roved toward the viscountess, whose blue forget-me-not eyes lifted every few moments under their long lashes to wander in Mirepoix's direction. Indeed, so captivated were they that Wolf felt with relief that there was every chance of escaping their attention, and he was about to make another attempt to reach Sicard, whom he could see waving frantically from the distance, when he felt upon him the cold, appraising gaze of Bertran of Saissac.

Old Longshanks, as they irreverently called him, had been regent during Trencavel's minority. Impossible, thought Wolf, that their austere scholar, this upholder of rigid principles, could ever have approved a scheme as bizarre as that which Aimeric of Monreal had told of with such gusto. None the less, the wry expression of those thin lips, as Wolf reluctantly advanced, certainly suggested that he had been right in thinking Saissac would have rejoiced if they'd missed the fun. And as he tried to meet those cold, scrutinizing eyes he could not help apprehending something akin to cruelty inhabiting that stern conscientiousness and rigor, though he was well aware that, all said and done, the inexorable old man was no more exacting toward others than he was toward himself. Nevertheless it was, as usual, with a sense of relief that Wolf, after giving a brief account of their errand and being ordered to present himself with young Villemur on the morrow, found himself dismissed.

"So you have been on a little trip to Narbonne?"

At the sound of the voice with its peculiar intonation Wolf glanced up in surprise, to find himself addressed by an opulently clad stranger who had been following the conversation with some curiosity. A little reluctantly the boy explained that he had only been halfway.

"But next time, maybe, it will be the whole. Certainly you come sometimes to Béziers with the Viscount," the stranger continued, smiling. "I have a house there myself. You may have noticed it even from a distance. It has a roof, shining like gold. Ha! You are thinking, 'All is not gold that glitters,' eh?" he chuckled; "but Caravita, my young friend, deals only in the genuine."

The Caravitas of Béziers, thought Wolf. They were

bankers, Trencavel's financiers, one of the most powerful Jewish houses in Languedoc. That gilded edifice, scintillating above the crowded roofs of the ghetto, was a frequent joke among the squires.

"When you ride again on these errands of diplomacy," the old financier continued, "you must pay us a little visit. The house of Caravita is famous for its hospitality. But perhaps," he added, noticing the boy's awkward expression, "Béziers is not to your taste—nor, alas, to my daughter's. She is always deserting her father in his provincial countinghouse, running off to spend his money in Narbonne—ah! Narbonne, a city of the world." He gave a lachrymose sigh. "So, you are fond of gems?" he asked, his eyes fastening suddenly on the clasp of Wolf's belt, and drawing nearer he bent down, curious.

Involuntarily the boy stiffened. But Caravita was already so absorbed in contemplation of the chiseled buckle that Wolf was forced to suffer in silence and stare out grimly over the dark oiled ringlets bowed above his waist.

"Sassanian workmanship—you see the rider? Very old. To tell exactly is difficult, I should need my glass, but costly, certainly. It would fetch a good price." His voice, thick, deferential, grew almost cajoling.

"It isn't for sale," Wolf blurted out, and then, fearing he had been insolent to the viscount's guest, he added hastily, "It was given me by my aunt."

Caravita luckily seemed impervious to offense. "No, no, who would dream of selling—now? But it is precious—and sometime—life is at moments difficult." He smiled again.

To the boy's relief the financier was at that moment joined by another guest, a figure which in its dignity and grave dark robes afforded a strange contrast to the ornate opulence of the former.

"Our young friend," Caravita was saying, "is interested in gems." (The boot, thought Wolf, was on the other leg.) "I have told him when he comes to Béziers he must visit our house—and I was thinking, if he is sometime in Narbonne, Reuben perhaps would show him his collection."

The bearded face under the tall cylindrical hat nodded absentmindedly, but his companion turned to the boy confidentially.

"The rabbi's son has works of art that even the Viscount could scarcely buy, though he is not so much older

73

than the young squire himself. Ah, Benjamin, before I forget," he turned, drawing the rabbi aside, "I think I have done a little business—that Syrian manuscript, there is no need to worry, cousin," his voice trailed away inaudibly, while the cylindrical study in headgear inclined at a perilous angle toward the shining locks, and feeling himself agreeably superfluous Wolf bowed and withdrew.

"Can't understand," said a broad-chested noble at his elbow, glancing pointedly at the two exotic figures, "how Trencavel puts up with the breed." He made no attempt to lower his voice.

His companion shrugged. "Our incorrigible southern laxity," he laughed. "Besides, a bit of variety seasons the dish—and their money's useful."

"Hm, so it was to Richard," the other scoffed, "but it didn't stop him from a good wholesome massacre when their stench began to offend his Angevin nostrils."

"My dear Guy," came the laughing retort, "will you never remember that you're on Roman soil? With us, even the Jews are civilized."

Wolf was uncertain as to his own emotions. Out of range of touch, his new acquaintances exerted a certain fascination. And the rabbi certainly cut a more dignified figure than many of those obese, bald-faced priests. Of course, that pretentious old cousin of his had wanted to show off. Still, he'd meant to be friendly no doubt, even if to his own gain, which was more than one could say of some of these overbearing nobles. A queer breed! Yet they certainly brought wealth and luxury to the towns and to the Trencavels. Vainly he tried to picture them within the grimly feudal walls of Foix, amid the rugged mountains that gave his father, despite all his passionate abandon, a core of hardness that made him so often break out in scorn of the effeminate inhabitants of the plain. And for a moment, as the boy glanced about him, he was haunted by his father's angry foreboding. He had guessed well enough that Roger's marriage meant more than the mere advantages of feudal alliance. But in a second the specter faded, powerless amid that glittering throng and, as so often, he was telling himself that his father's fears were unfounded, when a high feminine voice cut shrilly through his reverie.

"Foix—come here, young Foix!" There was no escape. Reluctantly he obeyed that well-known summons.

"So he's quite forgotten the pretty manners we taught him." Agnes of Montpellier pouted her tiny rosebud mouth. "And if the others hadn't been more gallant than he, we should have had to starve, shouldn't we, Gogo?" she cried, plaintively addressing the tiny dog coiled in her lap.

"I've only just got back," Wolf muttered.

"Just?" she lisped. "And it was so much more important, wasn't it, to talk to a miserly old Jew than to pay his respects to his liege lady." At that moment, to his infinite relief, the singers began to tune their instruments. The dog immediately started to whimper.

"Oh dear, oh dear! Gogo doesn't like the music, does he?" Catching the animal against her, Agnes fondled and petted it. In vain the little beast only set up a long and plangent whine, till the viscountess's flower-petal face puckered petulantly. "Take him, take him away," she cried, thrusting the creature into Wolf's hands. "But you mustn't leave him," she implored, gazing at him with childish pathos; "he'll be so lonely without his mama!"

Inwardly quaking with suppressed fury, Wolf, clutching the struggling creature, marched off, and, blind with rage, almost collided with an exquisite gallant who was just approaching with evident intention of paying homage to his lovely hostess, so that the rose he twirled so daintily in his fingers was all but knocked from his hand. Wolf did not stop. With head held high and burning cheeks he strode on, furiously aware of the grimaces the merry Sicard was cutting from afar.

"The whelp's coming on," laughed someone as he passed.

"Hm, still more of the lamb than the wolf about him," muttered his companion. "Know how he got his name?" "That yarn about Ramon-Roger hunting the wolf to the doors of Salenques and the good nuns. . . ."

The boy neither saw nor heard, his spirit rankling against Agnes and all women.

Smarting with indignation and the fact that he was cheated of the singing, Wolf strode on into the darkness, for although, meeting with a familiar steward, he had soon been able to hand the wretched little dog over to his care, he dared not lurk anywhere in the neighborhood of the viscountess for fear she should upbraid him for desertion of her pet or send him on further errands to gratify her whims. He might have listened at a distance, but goaded by irritation he wandered on, past the last few scattered groups of guests, till he found himself alone on a deserted path leading down to the river.

The moon had risen. Behind, above the torch-spangled gardens, the towers of the city rose ghostlike, bodiless, between the heavy canopies of the trees. At his feet the river coiled, gleaming, serpentine, forcing a barrier between the flaunting sun of revelry and the moon-bathed plain. Silent, remote, the land spread before him, a vast carpet dotted with the pattern of olive grove and vine, neat, ordered, meticulous, yet planned, it seemed in that disembodying light, according to some strange and fearful symmetry, immeasurable, inhuman. As he watched, the scene he had just left appeared by comparison unreal, a delusion, fragments of which even now were borne toward him, frayed cobwebs torn from a glittering web in which he had become entangled, till the whole of his life at Carcassonne seemed suddenly to partake of that unreality. A deep nostalgia began to steal over him, a sense of estrangement which since the days at the monastery he had scarcely known, while the old sense of self-division took hold of him anew, and in that sudden silence, detached from the flux of his surroundings, he found himself looking back on the life of the last months and asking where it had landed him. In his fierce bid to catch up with his companions in physical accomplishments and prowess he had seemed to achieve so much—but to what end? Wtih sudden guilt it struck him that he had almost forgotten the aim. Instinctively his gaze tried to penetrate the moonlit landscape to convince itself of that thicker line of darkness between the fluctuant plain and the deep dome of the sky—Montségur! Withheld, secretly guarded in his heart, it had tended in the tumult of his present life to grow remote almost as the fantasies of his childhood, and yet it had ever remained, though less consciously, the impetus to all his fevered athletic zeal. Inevitably, his dream-image was already beginning to take on much of the robust heroic quality of his companions' predatory ambitions, tempered by Trencavel's athletic ideals, so that he saw it now rather as the invincible fortress, the symbol of southern chivalric pride only waiting to defy its enemies—an image thrown into more vivid illumination at each new blast from the papal throne, when for a brief second the south, visited by the nightmare shape of barbaric hordes, would turn restlessly in its enchanted sleep, only to sigh and slip back into lovelier dreams. But stone by stone it must be growing as the Count of Foix, seeing what none would see, drove on the workers. War! Still, against that foil of distant revelry, it seemed unreal, spectral, as, a moment since, the feast had done. But while boyishly the thought thrilled him with the sense of dark adventure, his memory flew back to that other dream of combat to which with such fervor he had sworn himself, in silent allegiance to the woman whom since his arrival in Carcassonne he had never seen.

He knew well enough that his father's ultimate consent to his sojourn in Carcassonne had been won because it removed him safely from Montségur, and he could guess that there had been a definite understanding between the count and his sister that she should exert no influence on his religious views. Trencavel was avowedly no heretic, and Ramon-Roger of Foix had rightly reckoned his son would have enough to do catching up with his chivalric training to keep his head clear of such new fantasies.

It struck him now, with a sense of guilt, how little attempt he had made to keep in touch with her at all. At first, impelled by a desire to make himself worthy of her expectations, he had determined not to visit Pamiers till he had achieved something to be proud of. Then, since news had come of the failure of the Conference, of the insults publicly showered upon her at the assembly, he had been overcome with mingled shyness and rage. For what could he do to protect her, what did he really even know of her faith? But whenever he had made up his mind to learn more about Catharism, his resolution had been immediately swamped by the demands made upon him by his new career. Roused even now by this new resolve to a sudden awareness of the present, he realized that an hour might have passed while he was wandering about lost in reverie. The music might be over, Agnes would be fretting for her pet. He could guess pretty well what lay in store for him if he deserted, and, though he was prepared to risk the consequences, the thought that Trencavel might require him convinced him that it was time he made his way back.

He had struck another path from that by which he had come, and soon he was entering a little boscage. Here and there the murmur of voices, a muffled laugh, drifted toward him from some solitary group or couple among the trees. From above he could hear the sound of a guitar. Now he was ascending a narrow flight of steps flanked by tall bushes and evergreens. As he brushed against them the air grew heavy with the scent of rosemary.

It led, he realized, to the pleasance where Agnes and her women were accustomed to spend summer days. But she was unlikely to retire there now, he considered, when she had the chance of being the center of all eyes, and he continued on his way till the steps terminated in a little terrace screened on one side by tall cypresses and shrubs of oleander.

"But surely you know, my love," laughed a familiar voice close to his ear, "sin may be forgiven a woman, never the possession of brains." He could have sworn the voice was Mirepoix's. After all, was the viscountess there?

Wolf, on the point of beating a hasty retreat, hesitated. Of course he wouldn't dare address her like that. Besides, to connect Agnes with brains!

At that moment another masculine voice cut in sardonically: "Woman, what business is it of yours to argue at such an assembly?"

Unable to master his curiosity, he rounded the bushes and found himself in the open.

In the circle of a miniature lawn, flanked by cypresses, two men were seated at a small octagonal table, gleaming marble-white in the moonlight and laden with fruit and wine. One of them, a harsh-faced youth, had tucked his hands into his sleeves and, affecting an air of mock asceticism that evidently parodied the bearing of a monk, glow-

78

ered at the group of figures reclining in the shadow of the trees. "Make haste, and return to your spindle."

"And stop illuminating the world—

> *'N'Esclarmunda vostre noms signifia*
> *Que vos donatz clardat al mon per ver.' "*

Throwing back his impudently handsome head, Peire-Roger of Mirepoix, stretched elegantly on the grass, drew his fingers over his guitar strings. In a second there flashed through Wolf's mind what they were referring to. They were parodying the impertinence of that wretched friar who at the Conference of Pamiers had dared to insult Esclarmonde of Foix in those very words: "Woman, return to your spindle."

Even while he stood confused under conflicting emotions of excitement, shyness, and a vague feeling of resentment, Mirepoix glancing up, had caught sight of him, and starting up with an exaggerated air of surprise flung out a welcoming arm.

"O *dieus*, if it isn't the little monk himself! We were lamenting," he sighed, "the execrable behavior of that scurvy friar toward your revered aunt."

Somehow, though half gratified by the young man's notice, Wolf's sense of unease increased, but while he stood hesitating, his brow puckered in a nervous frown, a heavy-boned youth lolling at the table leaned forward and, laying his arm drunkenly round his neck, drew him forcibly to the seat.

"D-don't take it to heart so, man," he hiccupped; "of course she's a j-jewel, a jewel wasted on—barbarians."

"In short," laughed the impersonator of the monk, a student to judge by his dress, "Radegonde number two—minus, alas, the excellent Fortunatus—and all owing," he sighed with mock lugubriousness, "to the pitiful decay in the fine art of pastoral *amor*."

"Christ," Mirepoix rocked himself with laughter, "to think of the fulminating Almeric taking old Venantius's line with the dear Countess. Why, with a little culture he might even have saved her from the Cathars."

"And Guihalbert's poeticized castigations of the flesh," the student concluded sardonically.

"While good old Fortunatus . . . It would have been so much more artistic, wouldn't it, darling?" yawned Mirepoix, bending over the figure that lay on the grass behind him. "A pretty offering of flowers, a few disticha."

A feeling of disgust crept over Wolf, but wedged between the dubious student and his tipsy neighbor he could only shift uneasily. For a moment there was silence. The moonlight streamed, immitigable, serene.

> *O regina potens, aurum cui et purpura vile est*
> *floribus ex parvis te veneratur amans. . . ."*

Rich-textured, burnished, the words flowed through the darkness. Unconsciously the boy ceased his struggles, hypnotized despite himself by the husky, languorous voice.

> *"Quamvis te expectet paradisi gratia florum. . ."*

"Oh, spare us, Miriam; we're not in church," growled Wolf's neighbor.

"If only, Alaman dear," the mysterious voice laughed softly, "you'd cultivate a little more brain as well as that splendid muscle. Pass us a peach."

"From learned females, Lord God deliver us!"

Stretching out an arm, Alaman of St. Gilles, taking a fruit from the dish, threw it toward her, when Mirepoix, exquisitely agile, caught it in mid-air. As he moved Wolf had a momentary glimpse of the girl's face. Yes, surely it must be a girl, though the dark curled hair hung hardly longer than a boy's upon her shoulders.

"See, the apple of the Hesperides." Gracefully Mirepoix dangled the fruit. "Shall I? Shall I not? No, my Minerva, I think I am going to keep it for Venus. With half the women turning into pedants and the rest into vestals or Cathars, what'll be left for us?"

"There's always Agnes, Peire," answered the girl. "Gogo says it doesn't matter a teeny-weeny bit if one's ever so stupid," she mimicked, "as long as one's pretty. The only trouble is," she added, laughing, "would Gogo appreciate your exquisite aesthetic fantasies? After all, Peire, I'm afraid you'll have to put up with brains."

"Sensibility, my sweet—not brains."

"Exactly," echoed the student. "Complete confusion of the premises and the functions—heart, liver, brain."

"And you're so afraid of the heart, aren't you, Hugo?"

she cut in, mocking. "Another lost soul, isn't he, Peire? No hope for salvation for those without sensibility."

"I'm quite content to be damned."

"And miss the ecstasies of the soul enraptured of beauty, purified by intellectual love? No," she laughed softly, "you can't deny, either of you, that the intellect is supreme."

"Vision of intellectual beauty, apotheosis of intellectual love," Hugo grimaced, "alias—titillation of the heart with the higher and nether regions."

"Why not? After all," Mirepoix laughed, "the richer the experience the better. Let's put it to the vote. Is woman to be worshiped for her heart, her beauty, or her brains? Well, here's my answer—All three. The perfect synthesis. Hugo, of course, reserves judgment. He refuses to worship anyway. Alaman?"

"No doubt about it. I hold with the judgment of Paris."

Miriam laughed. "You'd best be careful, Alaman. Minerva may be vengeful. Remember Paris's fate!"

"A matter of opinion," Mirepoix shrugged lightly. "One forgets too easily what he was spared. Ever thought of the aging Helen in the bed of Menelaus?"

"Good God!" groaned St. Gilles, swallowing another gulp of wine. "Well, anyhow, give me Paris's luck. Love and enjoy, for tomorrow we die."

"Or better, we love," chanted Mirepoix; " 'for tomorrow again shall love the lover, and who never loved, tomorrow shall love.' Any further comments?"

"The little monk, you've forgotten the little monk," Wolf's inebriated neighbor slapped him noisily on the back:

"Why, so we have," laughed Mirepoix, dramatically raising his hand for silence. "Let's all hear the verdict of our young and honored guest, the Wolf of Foix."

Wolf, feeling all eyes upon him, wished only that the earth would swallow him up.

"Come, out with it, Wolf-cub," cried the resilient Mirepoix. "Heart, beauty, or brains? Still a hope for you, Miriam," he laughed lightly.

Suddenly roused to defiance by their banter and an impulse of boyish chivalry, Wolf, vacillating between instinctive feeling and the irresistible desire to appear as a young blood, struggled desperately for an answer.

"Come on, then," Mirepoix urged. "Make it easier. Minerva or Venus?"

But Wolf's confusion only increased, while classical tags and Brother Martin's maxims flashed madly through his brain.

"Our ancestors," he brought out at last, in a wild attempt to defend her, and realizing at once his absurdity, "our ancestors venerated women for their wisdom."

Of course he had done for himself. All, it seemed, broke into uproarious laughter.

"Hear that, Miriam?" laughed St. Gilles, eager to avenge that former insult. "He thinks you're a sort of sibyl, as ugly as the Cumaean."

"Never mind," Mirepoix, bending over her, toyed gracefully with the girl's hair, "you're not quite a hag yet. After all, I don't know whether I shouldn't"—and he put the fruit to her lips.

She smiled in drowsy gratification, while her eyes fixed themselves, mocking, on her taunter. "I shouldn't be so cocky, Alaman. After all, you mightn't have so much to boast about, you know, if the Goths hadn't sought counsel of their wise women."

"Well done," scoffed Mirepoix. "You'd better start emulating your Gothic forebears, Alaman, in more than muscle and your yellow hair!"

"And the noble sons of Luna," St. Gilles retorted hotly, "who let their women bear the scepter instead of the spindle—a damned matriarchy." He had sprung up, suddenly sober, his heavy-boned body towering almost formidably above his rival; but in an instant Mirepoix was on his feet, his lithe, supple limbs suddenly tense.

Freed from that unwelcome embrace, Wolf clutched at the chance of escape as the two, already locked together in a first grapple, backed into the shadows. But even as he jumped to his feet a hand was laid on his sleeve. He turned, reluctant, to see the girl's eyes, inscrutable yet curiously compelling, fixed upon him.

"Which one?—Or are you going to fight them both?" she smiled, languidly amused. "It's much too hot. Hugo," she turned to the student, "I think you really ought to see they don't kill each other."

"Not much loss," the youth grunted.

"But it would be such a pity to deprive the world of a bit of beauty."

"And save it another bit of rot?" Chewing a mouthful of plums, Hugo d'Alfaro spat out the stones, then, stuffing a couple of peaches into his pocket, rose to his feet.

She stretched herself. Under the tenuous silk, her limbs seemed sinuous as a cat's. Inevitably Wolf compared Agnes's simpering movements.

"Oh, do sit down," she murmured, motioning him to her side. "It makes me tired to look at you."

Dazed, he watched Hugo disappear across the terrace. At last, still wavering, he sat down on the grass.

"Aren't you thirsty?" she murmured, stretching out a hand to fill the goblet. Her arm was bare but for the broad jeweled bracelets above elbow and wrist. Blindly he put the cup to his lips. The wine, cool at first, began to run through his veins like fire. A moment ago Mirepoix had been sitting here. But he was powerless to think. She lay there watching him, her dark eyes half hidden under their heavy lids, a face, it seemed in the moonlight, carved out of ivory and framed by the heavy veil of blue-black hair. Yes, she was beautiful, he thought, beautiful in some strange exotic way. Where did she come from—Syria, Tripoli? He wondered, and to increase his self-confidence, took a deep draught of the wine.

"You're parched—oh, not only like that," she laughed softly, as hastily he put down the cup. "You don't quite know whether you admire them or hate them, isn't that it?" she said after a little pause. "I watched you—one moment you looked just consumed with awe, and envy; another, as though you'd like to devour them. I shouldn't bother." She yawned. "Alaman must be fearfully tough and Mirepoix . . . Why not try collecting them instead? They're quite amusing really, like works of art—almost as good as my cousin's collection. We've the same tastes, you see," she explained, "only I prefer them alive."

"Alive!" he echoed, still dazed.

"And his are dead, stone dead—stone and wood, statues, paintings, you ninny," she mocked, for horror had dawned on his face. "He thinks his far more exciting, of course—the sacred vitality of form and all that. He calls mine a menagerie. It includes all sorts, as you saw, but I've never had a wolf before. Ought I to be afraid?" She laughed, that throaty infectious laugh, while her heavy eyelids lifted a little and for a moment held him fast in half-drowsy scrutiny. "Wolf?" she repeated, as though unconvinced. "Why ever did they call you that? Wolf! Oh, heavens!" For a moment she roused from her lethargy. "It's too, too marvelous. Reuben would be so jealous."

Reuben—groping, his mind suddenly found the key. Reuben—the art collection, her cousin—then was she old Caravita's daughter?

"You see," she was explaining, "he was mad because he couldn't get that statue of Wolf of Aquitaine—and now—supposing I've got the live article? But mind you live up to it and save us from the Franks!" A faint smile, enigmatic, provocative, played about her lips. "Well, you may have to, you know, if Innocent keeps to his word."

Of course she was taunting him—and he deserved it—all those absurdities he had babbled about their ancestors. She watched his perplexity, amused. "You might begin," she said, "by saving us from ourselves. We're horribly degenerate, you know, in spite of the blameless Trencavel. The Round Table gone to pieces except for a couple of dreamers out in search of the Grail, though Trencavel would probably prefer the Golden Fleece. Even so, you know, even the *Argo* ended among the stars." She laughed, gazing up at the dark, spangled tent of the sky. "It always does—the same old escape from earth."

"But why—why should it?" he asked wonderingly. He had never known women could talk like that. Esclarmonde, of course, but she was in a class apart.

"Ask the Cathars. They'd tell you probably—the rottenness of the flesh."

"But is it really?" he persisted, thinking of that talk with his aunt at Pamiers. "Mightn't it be just society that's rotten?"

"The curse of Mammon? Money at the bottom of the world's woes? Then why not go and join the Waldenses and give up lands, house, riches, everything, and live among the workers of Narbonne—the brothership business—equality on earth as before God?" She regarded him quizzically. "You'd best ask Hugo whether he'd share his room."

"Hugo?" he echoed, bewildered, wondering whether she could possibly mean that scurrilous student.

"He's studying the law," she laughed, reading his thoughts, "because he wants to refute it. He's one of the d'Alfaros. Awfully rich really, but he ran away and lives in the slums of Narbonne. It's his way of feeling superior—to his hidalgo forebears, you know."

He winced. There was no doubt as to her mockery.

"You think I'm not serious, don't you?" Raising herself on her elbow, she refilled his goblet. As she moved, the scent of sandalwood fell on the air, faint but bewildering. "It's so refreshing to find someone with a drop of faith. And you see," she went on, "fundamentally I agree. Why shouldn't everyone have the same right to happiness? The only trouble is that people don't really want to be happy!"

"Don't want to be?" he echoed.

"You don't believe me?" she paused a moment. "Well, listen," she said.

Somewhere beyond the trees, a tenor voice throbbed through the darkness, impassioned, rhapsodic, borne away on the ecstasy of its own pain, till the night seemed to exude yearning like drops of sweat:

> *"Plus trac pena d'amor*
> *De Tristan l'amador*
> *Que'n sofrit manhta dolor*
> *Per Yzeut la blonda."*

"And if he got his desire," she murmured, "it's what he'd most hate. Give us happiness and we're not content till we've destroyed it. What we're really craving is frustration."

He looked at her, uncomprehending, bewildered. But clasping one arm behind her head, she lay back further upon the cushions.

"Hugo calls it a symbol of the times, the last throes of civilization wallowing in its own agony. But why try and resist? In the end you'll have to learn to accept—or go under."

"No," he protested.

Her eyes were dark, unfathomable, with the skeptical weariness of ages. "Dreamer," she murmured. For a little while she lay watching him, silent, and once again the faint mocking smile played about her lips. "You don't approve of me," she said, subtly challenging.

Insidiously that husky voice, the scent of musk and sandalwood crept over his senses. He knew himself powerless, as under a spell, enchanted by the mystery of her voice, the distant music, a thousand indefinable sounds and scents, till the fire of the wine circling in his veins seemed to dissolve all boundaries, enweaving him in the shimmering web of the night, and he seemed to sink away, floating on endless seas—Jaufre Rudel, he thought vaguely, drifting dying to those distant shores.

"You're so different," he attempted at last.

"To Agnes?" she laughed softly. "I wonder her pages don't become misogynists for life. But shouldn't you be adoring at her little feet, deserter?" she teased.

He hesitated and, realizing suddenly how long he had dawdled, half rose.

"Well, if you must," she said; "after all, it isn't farewell forever. Don't you ever come to Béziers—or Narbonne? Béziers's is so hopelessly boring."

"I got halfway today," he stammered eagerly. So she was definitely Caravita's daughter.

"Well, when you come we'll discuss reforming the world to your heart's content. But don't say I haven't warned you." Looking at him with that strange mixture of irony and seriousness, she stretched out her hand. Before he knew what he was doing he had bent above it, impelled by some blind urge to the ritual of that very gallantry against which, under the instruction of Agnes of Montpellier, he had so fiercely rebelled; then, overcome with bashfulness, he turned swiftly and almost ran, as the student appeared in the offing.

"They're all right," Hugo called. "Just escaped a bath in the Aude."

Wolf did not hear her reply. For the rest of the evening he moved in a dream, scarcely knowing to whom he spoke, thankful only that he seemed to escape the notice of Agnes. At last, as one after another of the guests began to retire, he, too, stumbled up to his rooms, but his brain was still on fire and four hours he lay listening to the heavy breathing of his companions, while the darkness kindled with burning vistas of strange and rapturous promise.

III

Morning waking him from a brief and broken slumber, already exerted a sobering influence on those dreams. His head ached as a result of that potent wine, blurring his memory of the actual happenings of the night. And yet the sense of an experience overwhelming and deeply exciting remained, leading him, amid the boastings of his companions, to keep his own adventures a secret, and giving him a new sense of power. Indeed, his habitually shy reserve was now perhaps not entirely unmingled with a mischievous gratification that he could thereby avenge himself for their mocking superiority in the past, a vengeance the more effective as the few hints he let fall seemed to point in the direction of the notorious Mirepoix. But neither cajoling nor bullying would draw from him his secret.

Bertran of Saissac, for his part, immediately prompted by the boy's heavy-eyed pallor to a sermon on overindulgence, was too absorbed in his own rhetoric to notice Wolf's ill-concealed reactions at some reference to Narbonne. Not so Villemur, who the moment they had returned to their companions lost no time in launching a new attack.

"I've got it!" he cried gleefully. "The little monk's lost his heart in Narbonne. Sure he's just hankering for the old man to send him toddling after those consuls, or else he'll die—he'll die of love. Unless, of course, he's only itching for another chance to show off all his learning."

Sicard of Durban, who was sitting on the table mending a string of his guitar, struck a plaintive chord.

> *"This very day*
> *I die—*
> *Sweet lady, if I lose you,"*

he sang, turning up his eyes in mock languishment. "Tell us, is she pretty? You'll introduce me, won't you?" he teased. "After all, she might prefer a song to your monk's Latin."

So after an ensuing tussle with hopelessly unequal odds from which he was rescued at last by the merciful departure of the mercurial and unmalicious Sicard, in company with that whole tormenting tribe, Wolf was left once more to his own brooding and an increasing desire to put an end to his uncertainty by action. At least, it struck him with growing excitement, he might win a glimpse of Miriam Caravita from a distance. She would surely be staying in Carcassonne and taking part in the festivities yet to follow. Determined at last to discover her whereabouts, he made his way to the stables and in a roundabout way began to approach one of the grooms as to the lodgings of the old financier, only to hear that Caravita and his daughter had already departed. His hopes dashed to the ground, he was making his way back when the clatter of hoofs sounded from the further yard, and the next moment Peire-Roger of Mirepoix, accompanied by a handful of youths, came dashing round the corner.

Mounted on a white arab, the light flashing on its gilded trappings, he looked even more resplendent than usual. He was wearing an emerald surcoat embroidered and fringed with ruddy gold. His head was bare, and the sun falling on the long, flying locks drew fire from the gleaming chestnut waves. Involuntarily Wolf halted, momentarily overcome by such radiance, and then his heart seemed to stop as he realized suddenly that he himself was the rival of this gay cavalier. Would Mirepoix challenge him? It flashed upon him, and in a wave of sudden pride he had drawn himself up to his full height when Peire-Roger called to him, laughing:

"What ho, so the little monk escaped safely from the Venusberg!"

The youth's impudently handsome face bore not the slightest trace of animosity, while those green-gold eyes, under the quizzically raised brows, regarded the boy with unfeigned amusement. For a moment Wolf stood gazing after them unseeing, blinded by chagrin and the sudden Icarian fall of his pride. It was clear that Mirepoix regarded him as a mere chit, one of those little pages, no doubt, with whom Agnes and her ladies held dalliance to while away the tedium of the winter day. Or did he not know? For a second hope revived, to be as instantly dismissed, for it was pretty certain that by now Mirepoix had received a highly colored version of the incident. He could imagine what fun they would reap over the new addition to the "menagerie"—another topic for her languorous cynicism. Well, let her content herself with peacocks, he thought bitterly, as the glittering cortège vanished toward the bridge; and turning about, his former purpose abandoned in angry pride, he made his way back to the castle.

The same day toward evening he was passing through the rosewalk that ran along the edge of the pleasance when the sound of tinkling laughter roused him from his brooding, and glancing up he caught sight, only a few yards away on the other side of the trellis, of the viscountess with Peire-Roger of Mirepoix. The long train of her clinging robe had evidently become entangled in a trailing brier, and dropping on one knee Peire-Roger was absorbed in the act of disengaging it from the silken folds. He seemed to be taking an inordinately long time about it but the fair Agnes apparently had no desire to hasten the process of that lingering hand.

As though he had been caught eavesdropping, Wolf halted, not daring to breathe, while contempt and fury raged within him. And yet as he stood, powerless to move, he was gripped by a curious fascination, the detail of the scene impressing itself on his mind with unnatural clarity, as though, detached from time and the surrounding world, it had attained a strange and almost fearful existence of its own, finite, remote as the trim-cut geometric flower beds, the hexagon of the porphyry fountain. And still amid the chasm of the deep green silk the while jeweled fingers groped. Half hidden in the satiny folds, guarded by its great hooked spines, velvet-petaled, the rose, creased to the secret heart, flamed crimson. *Rosa mundi.* . . . He scarcely knew that, wild and feverish, the words of the prayer half-forgotten had risen to his lips.

At last, after an eternity, the figures stirred, became once more part of the dazzling scented garden and passed —a woman leaning on the arm of a gaily-dressed cavalier, laughing and murmuring softly, to vanish behind the trellis of a bower.

As if freed from a spell, the boy tore himself from the spot. His senses overpowered by a sickening giddiness, he stumbled on. At last, scarcely knowing how he got there, he reached the meadows above the riverbank and in the shadow of an old olive tree flung himself down and buried his face in the grass.

IV

Curled with an air of graceful boredom in the window seat of her bower, Agnes of Montpellier, toying between yawns at her embroidery, suddenly gave a little cry. For a moment her sky-blue eyes stared as though horrified from her punctured finger to the drop of crimson on the piled samite in her lap; then with a long-drawn sigh, she swooned sheer away—or appeared to. Even the serving woman, as they rose to her aid, gave a little shrug of impatience, throwing each other a skeptical glance. The viscountess had shown more than her usual petulance that morning, and, used to her affections, they guessed that not much was amiss. They were surprised therefore, as they bent over her, to find that her peachlike complexion had really lost much of its bloom. When, however, a few moments later, recovering under the influence of reviving balsams, her sighs and moans gave way to a violent querulousness, their dawning sympathy was soon dispelled.

Nevertheless, to give the fair Agnes her due, her malaise was, for once, at least partly genuine, and the faintness that had overcome her at the sight of that tiny speck of blood had been but the climax of fears that had tormented her for weeks, confirming her ever-growing suspicion; for the whole time she had perfunctorily dallied with her embroidery she had been unable to rid herself of the thought that before long she would soon be working at something less romantic than a favor worn by some adorer, or even at a fancy leash for her beloved Gogo. Swaddling bands! Now, as she sucked ruefully at her wounded finger, fury overcame her, and in an anguish of self-pity she caught up the little animal, which, distressed by the commotion, was concernedly trying to lick her hands.

"And will he be jealous of a nasty, slobbering, squirming little worm that hasn't half the sense of a clever little doggy, and doesn't do anything but cry and cry all day?"

"Oh, madam!" One of the young women almost jumped from her seat, while her companions raised their heads in excited question. "Is it really true?"

But far from feeling flattered by the flutter of excitement and congratulations of which she was the center, Agnes of Montpellier's irritation was only increased. Of old Forneria, of course, one would expect it, old-fashioned matron as she was; but that these others should behave like a posse of clucking burgesses—they who were always so eagerly defending the laws of courtly and romantic love—love of which the poets sang; love that knew the thrilling torment of passion unassuaged, the tenderness of a single and last caress; love, fulfillment of which was but defilement, that profane coarseness of the marriage bed to which woman was led as to the slaughter, to have her beauty violated by the brutishness of the male!

Calling for her mirror, she hunted anxiously for signs of the ravages to which she had been subjected, but anger had brought the color back to her cheeks and the face that gazed at her from the gleaming surface was certainly less that of a misused woman than of a petulant child. Critically she surveyed the smooth milk-white neck, the slender shoulders, the small apple-round breasts that thrust themselves so cunningly against the confining silk. Soon they would swell and coarsen like those of a peasant girl, the tiny waist under the jeweled belt grow shapeless and deformed. In a fit of peevish fury she flung the mirror from her and burst into hysterical tears.

In vain they attempted to calm her, and it was only the entry of the aged Forneria who, summing up the situation, began to warn of the disastrous effects that might ensue, which at last restored her to comparative calm.

"And think of the disappointment that would mean to the Viscount," the old woman urged—advice that might only have produced the opposite of its desired effect had it not been followed by palpable threats of the havoc that might be wrought on her beauty; and at last Agnes sank back on the cushion in an attitude that purported no doubt to express, with ineffable grace, the victimization of the lamb.

"Well," she yawned after a succession of sighs, as though she were still waiting for fulfillment of an order, "isn't anyone going to read?"

Without answering, a tall, elegant young woman who almost alone among her companions had preserved a skeptical indifference to the news, put aside her work and, stretching out her hand, set a heavy book upon her knee. It was evidently her habitual task, for she showed no hesitation in finding the page, and soon even the excitement aroused by the viscountess's revelations had fallen into the background under the irresistible spell of the adventures of Sir Lancelot du Lac. Heads were raised from embroidery frames, a needle paused in mid-air, while now and again one of the girls gave a sharp sob, or the face of another was dissolved in silent tears.

But today the torment of the hapless knight who, thralled by passion, shrank not even from shame for love's

91

own sake, was powerless to gratify the vanity of the viscountess. She had often compared herself to the ravishing
and worldly woman who was destined to be Arthur's
queen, well enough aware of those covert jokes that circu-
lated about the court and of whose origin she was directly
as well as indirectly not altogether innocent, which
credited Trencavel with the emulation of the Round Table,
the fact that he was young and handsome enough only
adding to her chagrin, as did his enthusiasm for the antique; for in the romantic mind of Agnes of Montpellier,
the mania for pure athletics which he encouraged among
the younger knights and squires aroused only mockery and
ennui, and she would lose no opportunity of secretly urging them to exploits more dangerous and bizarre. Lancelot
was, after all, always forthcoming, and if not equal in
perfection to the prototype, then equally or even more
entertaining, through the variety offered by plurality.
Guinevere, however, she now reflected bitterly, though
forced to suffer boredom through her blameless spouse,
was at least spared the miseries of childbed. Considering
Trencavel had imbided so many scruples from his Cathar
tutors, why couldn't he have followed them in their tenets
regarding sex? (Agnes's fervently avowed Catholicism
could suffer curiously convenient heresies when she
chose.) Didn't they call marriage a fornication, and generation of the flesh but perpetuation of Satan's power on
earth? But, of course, what Trencavel would like was to
ride ahead of his splendid young men while women,
broad-shouldered, barefooted, like those on the Roman ruins, followed, dragging a train of infants at their heels.

"Oh, but how could she be so cruel—the queen?" the
girl's voice suddenly cut in on her ruminations.

"But she had to put her lover to the test," the reader
pursed her rather narrow lips, annoyed at the interruption.

"Is that how you're going to treat Villemur?" laughed a
plump creature whose mocking face was surrounded by an
aureole of golden ringlets.

"What the woman needed," muttered Forneria, sorting a
bundle of wools, "was a good horsewhipping."

"Heavens, did old Guilhem really beat you?" the golden
head asked mischievously. "Surely you're not quite as ancient as that?"

"One's always fifty years behind the times in the country," Alys scoffed.

"And fifty times ahead in sense," retorted the old woman, and, gathering her wools together, departed, shaking her head.

"Common sense? Oh, naturally." Alys of Nior shrugged, seeking her place in the book. "Knowing all about childbirth and babies; behaving as if one were just a cow—"

"While Villemur makes you feel so spiritual, doesn't he, darling?" the girl teased, laying her head against Alys's knees and gazing up at her with mock rapture. "Those curls—just like a seraph."

"Of course, if you favor bulls . . ." Alys mocked disdainfully. "Didn't we all see you dance with that lump of beef and brawn, St. Gilles?" And before the other could hit back she had resumed her reading.

Wearily Agnes gazed out on the garden beneath. The glory of summer flowers had vanished, but still a few belated roses drooped over arbor and trellis.

"Love is an art, not a pillage—" Who had said it? Why, surely that delightful Mirepoix. The memory caused her a new pang, for that such a fate should have befallen her just when their acquaintanceship promised a growing intimacy doubled her chagrin. Had he not hinted at the likelihood of revisiting Carcassonne in the late autumn, when Trencavel was almost sure to be away on the hunt? Still, even then, she comforted herself, if she took precautions . . . Last year Alys had managed to strap herself in so well that no one had noticed a thing till well into the seventh month. Of course, she herself was daintier-boned, but with care she might well succeed in preserving her figure past Christmas. The thought of the *divertissements* that might still await her had set her fancy spinning so fast that she felt herself almost recovered. True, Mirepoix dallied with every pretty woman, and his taste was quite bizarre. She had heard he actually kept a Negress at Narbonne— for the sake of novelty—and talked of the texture of a woman's skin (not to her, of course) as another man savors the bouquet of wine, so that feeling his hand rest, ah, so delicately, upon her, she had not been able to conquer the suspicion that he was secretly comparing her flesh with that of his ebony-skinned paramour. Nor had she altogether been taken in by his jests about Wolf of Foix and the Caravita girl. The little monk almost seduced by that exotic Jewess—it had seemed incredible. She remembered too well her own attempts to break the boy's armor. Nevertheless, still waters run deep. And she still had a score to settle from the night of the festival. So it was for *her*, she thought spitefully, he had deserted her pet. Her eyes narrowed, little creases appeared between her penciled brows, the point of her tongue ran over her lips, while her fingers stroked the lap dog's back. Suddenly she gathered the animal to her and with almost passionate vehemence whispered in its ear, "Shall we be avenged, Gogo, shall we be avenged?" Then with her old peevish impatience she turned to her women, "Fetch me the little monk. Someone fetch me Wolf of Foix."

He stood in the doorway, flushed from exertion. They had found him in the tiltyard, practicing. There had scarce been time to wipe the sweat from his face. Excuses were vain. Reason?—useless to ask. They knew it perhaps as little as he—one of her whims. But that it boded ill for him he could guess. Since his abandonment of the wretched Gogo she had treated him (actually much to his relief) with the utmost contempt, and now as he reluctantly obeyed her summons he was prepared to be met with a fresh burst of petulant invective. To his surprise he found himself greeted by one of her most coquettish smiles.

"And did we drag him away right in the midst of some mighty feat of valor? Why, see, if he doesn't still bear the marks of combat upon him!" she cried, pursing her lips in mingled disgust and delight, her love of elegance always half outweighed by the irresistible virility of mail-rust and sweat. "He isn't really fit for a lady's bower, is he?" she lisped, lifting the dog against her face. "But still, as he's so very brave, we mustn't scold him, must we? Come nearer, come nearer!" she called, as the boy still stood sullen and hesitant in the doorway. "It's no use his pretending, is it, Gogo? We know all about him, don't we, though he's too modest to come and tell us himself that he challenged young Villemur to a joust."

"It was at the spear-throwing," he retorted, his desire to refute her overriding all vanity.

"Still," she insisted, with a look of tremulous horror, "whatever it was, you nearly got killed."

He laughed, scowling. He was well enough aware of the

scorn with which she regarded Trencavel's taste in sport and of her romantic craving for bloodshed.

"But I can see it," she pointed to a dark mark on his temple, while curiously the girls craned their necks.

Angrily he brushed the hair over his forehead. "It's only a graze. Arnaut threw askew," he muttered.

"Well," she sighed, "if you *will* fight without armor." Holding up the dog, she squeezed it till it whined in pain. "You see, Gogo says he'd never be such a silly doggie and get all covered with horrid scars—unless, of course, it were at a real tournament, or for someone very, very special." From behind the animal's back, her forget-me-not eyes dropped coyly under their absurdly long lashes. "Won't you for once sing her a song instead?" And as he stood frowning, silent, "Sing something!" she repeated, in a tone of command.

"I can't sing." (She knew it well enough.) "But if you like," he clutched at a chance of escape, "I'll fetch Sicard." The hope of flight was enhanced by the thought of avenging himself on young Durban's recent teasing.

"But I don't want Sicard. He's sure to sing about peasant girls and roundelays. Still, if he can't sing," she sighed, turning to her women, "I suppose he can read. But of course he can," she tittered. "Why, Gogo, we had almost forgotten, hadn't we, that he was meant to be a monk. Come, give him a book. No, no, not that," she clapped her hands impatiently as Alys, with mocking disdain, held out the volume. "The little monk must read us a love song."

Before he could save himself, another book was thrust into his hands.

"But what, but what?" cried half a dozen voices.

"Bernard of Ventadorn," someone clamored.

"Or that dawn-song by Guiraut Borneilh."

"No, Arnaut—Arnaut of Mareuil," laughed the girl with golden ringlets; "because it was here he sang—here in this very room—the song for which the Viscount's mother banished him, all for the sake of a kiss."

They had guessed that Agnes had some deviltry up her sleeve. She cared little for poetry except to gratify her own vanity. It cost her effort enough to try even superficially to keep up the tradition of her accomplished mother-in-law, the late Alazais of Burlats. Not that Trencavel showed any special desire for her to do so; indeed, to Agnes, the aversion he showed for the whole convention of courtly love, providing as it did another example of the wearying obtuseness of her husband, was one of the chief reasons that egged her on in any pretense to literary taste.

"But if he's so warlike," the quiet brown-haired girl who had shown such compassion for Lancelot attempted to save him, "let him read Bertran—Bertran of Born."

"No, he shan't," Agnes, watching him through narrowing lids, laughed musically; "he shall read us the song of Jaufre Rudel to his far-off lady."

"So out of date," Alys of Nior sighed.

But Agnes would have her way.

Inwardly quaking, he sat down on the stool at her feet, while the curly-haired maid bent over him to find the page. Behind her, he knew, the others were giggling.

> *"As the rivulet from the fountain*
> *Limpid springs from mead and knoll,*
> *And eglantine breaks forth in flower,*
> *And high on branch the nightingale . . .*
>
> *Beloved, far beyond sea and mountain*
> *For love of you my heart makes dole . . ."*

Bravely, his eyes fixed on the page, he struggled on till he reached the third verse:

> *"Fevered I pine from hour to hour,*
> *No wonder that I needs must pale,*
> *Seeing that God was never fain*
> *To make one fairer, nor to dower*
> *Jewess or Saracene . . ."*

Hot and burning, the blood rushed to his face, but, the words choking in his throat, he made a wild effort to finish:

> *"More sharp than thorn on flower,*
> *The wound where joy is wed to pain,*
> *No solace would I crave then."*

He ceased, thrust the book aside, rose to his feet. Agnes was looking at him, her doll-like eyes wide with mock distress. " 'No solace would I crave then,' " she echoed.

"Think, Gogo, he's even too proud to want comfort. But supposing, after all, we were very kind, and begged the Viscount to let us go to Béziers quite soon?"

Her tinkling laughter echoed after him as at last, her malice evidently satisfied, he was able to flee from the room.

If it had ended there! But, whether by her design or mere coincidence, before long Trencavel announced his intention of visiting Béziers, and, though as usual he was holding no great court there, Agnes insisted on accompanying him. Rather to his surprise, for the boy certainly showed little sign of becoming an accomplished courtier, she had begged him, while there, to let her have Wolf as page. If he remained in darkness as to her motives, Wolf certainly did not. From first to last she kept him at her beck and call, leaving him scarcely a minute out of her sight. Even at night he was forced to sleep at her door. He was virtually a prisoner; but every attempt to escape, the slightest action that betrayed his unrest, would, he knew, only arouse her spite and sarcasm.

Once, riding through the city, he had caught sight, through a gap in the crowded roofs, of a glittering patch of gold. Forced as usual to ride at her heels, he pretended not to see, but Agnes, perched gracefully on her white palfrey, lifting the dog coiled in the crook of her saddle, pointed to the gilded roof with mock delight. "Look, look, Gogo, a fairy palace. Perhaps there's even a enchanted princess and no one dares ride through the fearful ghetto to rescue her from distress." Turning, she shot the boy a mocking glance, but, though his heart was hammering, he affected a stoic indifference.

Nevertheless, frustration and the thought of Miriam Caravita's proximity left him no peace, diminishing even the memory of her cynicism, while her image haunted him ever more with its mystery and allure. Should he send her a message? But what use, when he could not escape the watchfulness of Agnes? Might not Miriam herself, remembering her invitation, send for him? But if her letters were intercepted? If only he could get free, perhaps he might avail himself of her father's invitation. Once, in the hall of the castle, he passed Caravita himself, but he was not alone and too occupied with business matters to take note of him. It seemed to him that the old financier, removed from the glamor of that festive night, looked weary and drawn.

Daily he began to feel more desperate. Little enough time was left, for the viscount had no special love of the city and always did his best to curtail his visits as much as possible, limiting them for the greater part to mere administrative transactions, though he devoted himself to them and all that concerned the town with almost feverish intensity. "Cathar conscience redeeming the sins of his fathers," mocked Agnes, fretful and bored.

Then on the last evening, to his surprise, Wolf found himself free. Even then fate seemed resolutely against him, for on his way through the hall he ran into his companions, who on the least provocation would have begun to mock him concerning his mysterious romance and without doubt insist on accompanying him on his way. Dusk had fallen before he at last escaped, and by the time he had woven his way through the maze of the ghetto and arrived outside the Caravitas' house it was already dark. It was by no means so opulent a dwelling as he had been led to expect from afar, and now in the moonlight, deprived of its strident gleam, the arcaded façade seemed to wear an ancient, almost melancholy dignity. Drawing back into the shadow of a doorway, he stared up at the façade. It seemed strangely dead. A sudden feeling of unreality began to invade him. What, too, could he offer as an excuse for calling at so late an hour? But at last, in desperation, knowing it his only chance, he crossed the street and knocked at the door.

On hearing he had come from the castle the servant who opened it greeted him with oily deference, and even while he hesitated snatched the words from his lips.

Yes, Master Caravita was up at the castle himself, attending a special meeting of the council. Perhaps he had sent a message?

"No, but . . ." Feeling the ground sink away beneath his feet, Wolf blundered out that his message was really for the lady Miriam.

Into the suspicion dawning on the old man's face shot a curious look of rancor, as though he had been struck on a sore place. Did the young esquire not know that the lady Miriam was not here, that she resided almost entirely in Narbonne? If he would speak to Master Caravita, he might wait. But already, muttering vaguely, the boy had turned and disappeared in the dark.

Fool that he had been! It was clear enough now—the ridiculous goose chase he had been led. But what galled him worse even than the viscountess's malice was the realization of his own idiocy. What absurd edifice of hope he had built in these last days! Had not her father, had not Miriam Caravita herself said she was bored to death in her home? The menagerie was large enough. Had he fondly imagined that she would stay or return to Béziers for his sake?

Where he went that night, in what direction, he scarcely knew. Back through the steep narrow alleys of the ghetto, up to the fortifications, the ramparts overhanging the riverbank. Hours passed. Still he was wandering blindly through the silent streets, oblivious in his misery of a greater agony that brooded ghostly, impersonal, over the sleeping city, and as he passed unseeing beneath the towers of St. Magdalene's, his thoughts were far from the blood that had flowed down those altar steps from the heart of old Raimon Trencavel, slain by the knives of the burghers for injustice done; nor did he dream that the deadness within him but echoed faintly the silence of another dawn in which the whole male population of the city had lain dead, massacred in their sleep by the Spanish hirelings of Roger Taillefer, the old viscount's avenging son.

v

Up at the palace, Raimon-Roger Trencavel rose from the meeting. Till late that night he had sat in council, bent on getting through the business in hand, forcing his attention on every irksome detail—wearying reports on the revenue, the eternal quibbling of the councillors, friction between the castle guard and the civic militia, the perpetual tension between feudal sovereignty and the rights of the town— an endless catalogue of petty grievances and rankling jealousies.

At last the final petition was filed, conciliatory measures adopted—panaceas that could only temporarily assuage. One by one the members of the council departed. Now only Moses Caravita was left. Drugged by weariness, Trencavel watched him sort his sheaf of parchments beneath the light of the tapers. Amid the ponderous, finicking wrangling of the councillors, the old financier's perspicacity had been the one relief. But the man had aged considerably, Trencavel thought, seeing his face relax. No doubt he had his own domestic troubles. He had been devoted to his dead wife, a daughter of the great house of Calonymos in Narbonne. The old man was cut out of a patriarchal household, but he had been left childless but for one girl—a beauty, he seemed to remember, in her Eastern way. Why, incidentally, had Agnes displayed that sudden interest in her? She was hardly her line, something of a Laïs, from what he had heard.

"How's the accomplished daughter?" he smiled as Caravita collected his last sheaf.

"In Narbonne." The astute, dark eyes clouded with melancholy. "It is too quiet for her in the house of her fathers—always she is seeking the new. Art, music, poetry."

"And she can't find them in Béziers?" As he spoke a shadow passed over Trencavel's face, hovering strangely on those almost too inviolate features, and for a moment Caravita gazed searchingly at the countenance that he had known since boyhood but which seemed somehow to grow more and more incalculable.

"If the Viscount would return . . . if he would hold court at Béziers as did his sires."

Ignoring the question, Trencavel turned abruptly away. "That business with Italy," he began after a moment, "you're sure it's advisable?"

"But certainly," the financier put in hastily. "The Viscount may rest assured. I shall make inquiries—Genoa . . . perhaps also Venice. Always one must see the gold is kept fluid, convertible in case of emergency. . . . The farther spread, the more likely to return."

"Let us hope so," said Trencavel wearily. "And so may the daughter," he added, with sudden return of his evasive slightly self-mocking gaiety.

"Maybe . . . maybe," Caravita murmured, bowing his departure. "In the end all things return. There is no escaping one's roots."

For a little while after he had gone, Trencavel stood gazing abstractedly at the scrolls that still lay scattered about the table. That at least was finished. He took a deep breath, as though in infinite relief. Tomorrow they would be gone—not back to Carcassonne, even, but up into the hills. To break through the covert hot on the track of the stag—to watch the falcon shoot arrowsharp to the skies, hover, soaring poised on the wing. Tomorrow—why not start now? To start before dawn would break again on the hated city, before God-knows-what new duties might frustrate his desire; call to his squires, tear his knights from their slumbers, rouse the whole household for the sake of a whim. Still he would sometimes wake from sleep hearing, he thought, the voice of his father echoing from the great hall, cursing and shouting, the stamping hoofs in the castle yard, the clang of the portcullis as it lowered behind the troop. And then the vast hollow silence of the castle, filled only with the pounding of his heart. Whether it was excitement, awe, or terror he had not known, or had forgotten. He had not even been certain of the reason for those nocturnal disturbances, and when, a little older, he had identified them with sporadic raids on the territory of Toulouse, he had perhaps been more thrilled with excitement than anything else, an emotion only strengthened by his mother's cool and smiling disdain, as if these demonstrations of the natural brutishness of the male were too self-evident to permit even of consideration, and sighing elegantly she had returned to the far more intricate problems of the latest fashion in coiffure or a particularly tantalizing conundrum to be raised at the next court of love.

Only to be gone, to throw off the dreary weight of statesmanship, the burden of eternal compromise, the patching up of a system hopelessly outworn. His hand stretching out caught at one of the parchments, crumpling it beneath his fingers.

To swing themselves on their arabs, thunder through the gates. Already he was at the door. "Villemur, Durban, Foix!" The names were already on his lips. Why, it struck him suddenly, the boy just lately had looked peculiarly pale. Possibly he'd been overdoing things, trying to catch up with what he'd missed all these years. He'd best leave him to attend on Agnes while he went up the mountains. She seemed quite concerned about him and the necessity of imbuing him with a little courtly grace—an opinion with which the Count of Foix would doubtless agree. Well, let her have a shot at it. . . . But the interruption of his sudden impulse had already brought another memory in its train. He had almost forgotten that embassy from the clothmakers' guild he had promised to receive before his departure in the morning. Yes, and that business about the recobbling of the streets—the houses down in the eastern quarter—the wells had dried up or were poisoned. Béziers—Béziers whose welfare he had sworn himself silently to serve that day he had first understood the horror of its past, the massacre perpetrated by his father.

His hand, already in the act of drawing aside the door curtain, dropped slowly. Raising it again, he passed it across his forehead, then, stiffening, pulled open the door. Outside, he turned, not in the direction of the hall but up another flight of stairs to Agnes's bower. On the threshold a page rose, blear-eyed with sleep; but dispensing as usual with all but the most necessary service, a habit incomprehensible to most of his friends, he bade him make off to bed.

How often as a boy he had quailed to have to enter that room! "And how far has my infant prodigy proceeded along the path of chivalry today?" his mother would greet him, laughing carefully, as though afraid to crack the impeccable enamel make-up of her face; and drawing him nearer, running her fingers through his curls, her eyes sharply appraising every detail of his dress, she would put him through the customary catechism while her circle of serving-women would look on amused. Usually, one of them had been reading from some fashionable romance (he had hated them ever since), and then they would regale themselves initiating him into those mysteries of *courtoisie* without which no man, they said, could attain honor or rise above the state of a beast. Baffled and wounded in the depth of his boyish pride, he would writhe, caught in the mocking circle of those feline eyes, still at last he was able to escape and flee into the meadows or tiltyard, or the dark shadows of the armory. Only to escape from the constriction of that threefold haunting threat that followed him whichever way he turned—the famed ruthlessness of his father's the asceticism of his Cathar mentors, those women's romantic denigration of the flesh! To be free and live reborn in the strength of the body, the cold sharp cleanness of sword and steel!

Moonlight streamed through the unshuttered window. In the huge bed of state Agnes lay wrapped in sleep, almost pathetically childlike, the inseparable Gogo coiled at her feet. For a second he felt well up within him the tenderness that he knew would perish the moment she woke. Might there after all have been a way to hold it? To have allowed her entry into his being. So often he had made up his mind to attempt, to see it wither with the opening of her eyes, the first fatuous twitterings of that rosebud mouth. But his was the fault as much as hers; more so, since she was at least without pretense. While he? . . . Leaning against the column of the window, his half-ungirdled belt in his hand, he stared out over the sleeping city—at the clustered eaves wrapped in silvery tranquility. Somehow it seemed that he was gazing on something already dead. Caravita's daughter had fled to escape her death of boredom. It was for him to wake it to new life. But how without waking also those ghosts? Once more the old horror rose out of the stillness.

To wipe it clean, to erase the nightmare of those streets, the crimes of his fathers . . . to live wholly in the present—to shape Béziers anew.

But behind him the voice of Caravita sounded out of the darkness: "There is no escaping one's roots."

VI

Autumn drew to its close. Most of the time Trencavel was away hunting in the Black Mountains, while Wolf was duly left behind doubly galled under the circumstances by his enforced servitude to the fair Agnes.

Not that the viscountess continued to show her rancor. On the contrary, her vengeance temporarily appeased, she had begun to treat him with indulgence, even lavishing favors upon him, ostensibly amused by his stubborn recoil and watching with relish the obstinate hardening of those vulnerable lips. "He's so silly and obstinate, isn't he, Gogo?" she would laugh; though he's all hurt and bleeding inside."

True to his promise, Mirepoix had paid another fleeting visit to Carcassonne, and the viscountess was too absorbed in his devastating gallantries to pay much attention to Wolf. Peire-Roger's departure, however, brought a new bout of peevishness, and Wolf soon found himself the whipping boy for her gallant's promiscuousness, which she found ample opportunity of avenging in hinting at Mirepoix's intentions toward Miriam Caravita—a fact all the more bitter as Peire-Roger had insisted on treating him with a charming condescension that had obviously branded him a mere chit.

Luckily, however, there was enough to occupy Agnes besides, for during Trencavel's absence she was surrounded with a crowd of dandies and courtiers.

"Third-rate poetasters, most of them," Sicard had scoffed. "No wonder Trencavel shoos them off the scene. Of course, Mirepoix's a bit different. He belongs to the fast set in Narbonne and Toulouse, and they're awfully advanced. He's always running some sort of cult, though every month it's something different." But Wolf showed little desire to discuss Mirepoix's interests; indeed, since the summer festival he had displayed such an apparent resentment at the name that his companions came to the conclusion that they had hit on another clue to the little monk's romance. Since the incident at Béziers at bit of the truth had actually leaked out, and he was still a butt for their mockery. However, under their repeated assaults he was managing gradually to cultivate a stoic indifference.

In his wounded pride he would even try to affect a hard-boiled cynicism, and in very defiance of Mirepoix's disdainfulness make desperate attempts to convince himself of his manliness by emulating his companions in flirtations with some of the maids, escapades that caused his fellow squires to raise their eyebrows and left him with a more violent sense of futility than ever.

Often, indeed, he would blind herself to the cause of his own restlessness, attributing it rather to that general sense of unrest that brooded over Languedoc.

Still the threat of approaching disaster loomed unreal, no more than a motionless streak of cloud on the far horizon, less a menace of storm than a sultry throbbing intensification of the solstice calm that enwrapped the south.

Throughout France and Burgundy, in Flanders and across the Rhine, the Cistercian missionaries made their indefatigable way, inciting, haranguing against the deadly heresy of the Albigenses and the moral pollution of the south. From pulpit and rostrum, Arnaud-Amelric, Abbot of Cîteaux, thundered his invectives against the new Babylon, the henchmen of the Antichrist, more deadly than Saracen and Moor, while his fiery tongue evoked the terrors of hell, threatening with doom not only the heretics themselves but any who harbored and protected them in their lands. At the same time Innocent III, following up his warnings to the Count Raymond of Toulouse, had written to Philippe-Auguste, King of France, and the princes of the north, calling upon them as defenders of the faith to do all in their power to assist the Cistercians in their extermination of heresy, and, should nothing else move the blaspheming count to contrition, to humble him through the threat of their armed might.

If, in Languedoc, equanimity was ruffled for an instant, the majority—the nobility and the wealthy, at least—soon began to shrug and fall back into their old habit of *laissez faire*. After all, they argued, Philippe-Auguste was too absorbed in his perpetual strife with England to engage in any serious conflict with the south. Burgundy, of course, as the center of Cistercian power, was a very stronghold of orthodoxy. Its temporal lord, however, was hardly considered formidable. Duke Eudes III had always been fond of adventure, provided it was accompanied by not too much hardship and by sufficient glamor. Very possibly he might be persuaded by the fanatical abbot to engage in a little punitive expedition against the south, but it would doubtless turn out a harmless enough affair. He would arrange for a lavish reception in Toulouse. Raymond, naturally, would have to drain his coffers a good bit and make some promises about the heretics. There should be little difficulty, though, in coming to terms, and after a month or two's entertainment the duke would return to Burgundy well content, his pack horses richly burdened and his own person yet a shade more ample about the girth.

The Cistercian, it was true, the renowned Abbot Arnaud-Amelric of Cîteaux, was a regular fireband, and would certainly make things pretty hot for some, but luckily, people comforted themselves, one had never taken this heresy stunt too seriously. The parish priests would testify to that. Had one not always been careful to pay for plenty of masses? Besides which, many of the old padres got on well enough with the good Cathars anyway, often even dined and hobnobbed with each other quite amicably. Why couldn't those Roman bigots allow people to live side by side in tolerance and good will? After all, wasn't peace on earth what Christ had preached?

There were some certainly in Languedoc who, enervated by excess of luxury and ease, and having extracted the last nuance from every emotion, began to crave for a fiercer sensation. Bloodshed, battle, were still names that quickened the sluggish pulses, the languid heartbeat. On the whole, however, the very intensification of frivolity betrayed the nervous tremor beneath, and the more sharply the threat was apprehended, the more closely was it disguised. "Live and let live, for tomorrow we die." As yet it was only a shadowy specter grinning behind the veil of revelry and gala and song.

To Wolf it all appeared a mocking echo of his own torment. Often the strains of some troubadour singing in the great hall, the chance words of a love song drifting up from under the ramparts at night, would cause Miriam Caravita's words to come surging over him: "The trouble is, we don't *want* to be happy. What we're really craving is frustration." And once more the memory of that bewildering husky voice would set his pulses beating, rousing all the burning confusion that in his attempted bravado he thought he had overcome. From below, the plaintive voice rose and fell, and even while his boyish willfulness rebelled against the despairing lethargy of those eternal avowals of a hopeless passion, he was plunged precipitously, with the uncompromising finality of youth, into an agonized confession of their verity. There was no way out, except by the cultivation of a cynicism that enabled one to flirt gracefully with emotions as did Agnes and Mirepoix. Did it satisfy them? To all appearance it did. And Trencavel? Was he oblivious or actually careless of his wife's faithlessness? If marriage, as the troubadours sang, were a mere convention, his true feelings might be expended elsewhere, on a love which, unfulfillable, could alone sublimate desire—like that of Agnes and Mirepoix! Sickening, their image rose once more before him. The old horror of double-faced appearance clutched at him anew. It seemed to Wolf that they were all walking in a labyrinth of clandestine passions, of secret lusts and vices. Were they all then groping in chaos, tearing a moment's illusion from the darkness they could not penetrate?

How often during the last months he had tried to convince himself that the experience of that summer night had been but foolish madness and—to Miriam Caravita—the fleeting pastime of an hour. And yet he felt, with increasing disquiet, it was the gate of a hidden realm to which some hidden power mercilessly compelled, though it led past the abyss of fear that gripped him at the sight of Mirepoix and the viscountess in the pleasance. To evade it was but cowardice. Whatever it was—evil or good—it was there. And *was* it evil? Out of a white carven face, two dark and enigmatic eyes stared at him sphinxlike, eternally baffling and holding a knowledge of things terrible, maybe, yet profounder and more potent than those that had hovered a moment behind the shadowy figure of Esclarmonde. How remote that world now seemed—simple, almost childish. And yet it had seemed to offer so much. Did it perhaps still? Was it perhaps the great alternative, and did the choice lie with him? Salvation or damnation? Was there still hope for him in heresy. He determined anew to carry out his resolve to learn more of the Cathar faith.

The long-enforced habit of harboring his inmost thoughts in secret made him shy of broaching religious matters to his lighthearted companions; for as it was, his former vocation already provided a target for their wit. As for Trencavel, though he entertained the greatest respect for the heretics, doing all in his power to protect them from persecution, he did not appear to identify himself with their faith.

True, there was the old chancellor, a last survivor from the days of the heretic regency, but the thought of the bleak doctrine that would surely fall from the lips of that inveterate stoic held little attraction, and he suspected that it was the pessimistic aspect of heresy that attracted Saissac rather than any quality of faith.

Faith! How many really possessed it? The longing for it perhaps—the wild, tormented yearning of those who have lost all belief, a fierce clutching at sensation, to rescue themselves from the abyss of their own emptiness. Was that, too, but a symptom of the times, as Miriam had said—"the last throes of civilization wallowing in its own agony"?

For the majority at the court, certainly, heresy or the defense of heresy (for few seemed really to practice its tenets) appeared to mean little more than a fashionable cult, to be discarded as easily as an outworn dress. And lately, indeed, since the threats from the papal throne had become more violent, too extravagant a deviation from the orthodox habit was hardly considered recommendable, while for the more earnest-minded, defense of heresy was usually bound up with political exigency, the old tradition of a people that had ever asserted itself against the compulsion of alien force.

Earthly tyrant or God—it was the same. The stubborn independence that in the great cities had resulted in the ancient institution of civic consuls, who accepted an overlord (even the great counts of Toulouse themselves) only in name, had long been extended to their spiritual sovereign. Let the priests hold guardianship over the soul's welfare as long as they kept within the boundaries of their appointed task. But if they overstepped it they trod on ground that was not theirs. Mediators between God and man, guardians of the Spirit, was it their function to preen themselves in the light of the world's vanity, to hold courts that rivaled in splendor those of the temporal peers, to wallow in every form of luxury, corruption, and vice? The guise of poverty lately adopted by the legates at the advice of the Spanish priest Domingo was considered but a trick of the Church to beat the Cathars on their own ground, and too venal a device to be convincing. Could such men as these lead a man to the throne of God? What validity had the Sacrament in the hands of the sinful priest? Unpardonable heresy—it was the pivot of Cathar and Waldensian teaching alike. For all their differences—the ecstatic spiritualism of the one, the simple puritanism of the other—on this they agreed: the sinful priest cannot mediate between man and God.

Above all, either way, heresy meant freedom—freedom and the promise of equality for the simple artisan (and on the whole it was the humbler classes who followed in the steps of Peter Waldo of Lyons); freedom and license for the nobles and burghers who favored the modified Manichaeism of the Cathar faith. And while in the homes of every Waldensian worker no evening passed without some member reading aloud from the Gospels, tracing the written word with finger gnarled or blackened by work, in castle and urban mansion the nights were gay with the worship and practice of love. For though the Cathar elders—the perfecti or *bonshommes*—conformed, with a strictness that even their orthodox enemies did not ques-

108

tion, to a rigid asceticism, they were notoriously lenient toward their fallible brothers, the mere "believers," trusting in conversion by example rather than violence and threat; for how, they maintained, could the mystery of love be transmitted by intimidation and force—the weapons of Jehovah, the avenging God, alias Satan? For Christ was Love.

And Love was a name that awakened infinite response, as it was capable of manifold interpretation, for where did the boundaries of flesh and spirit end and begin? Their very ambiguity was manifest in the songs of the troubadours—courtly, ideal, romantic love that strove always toward the unattainable, the image that was destroyed by realization. The secrecy, the veiled allusion, the very obscurity of the style favored by so many a singer might signify or hide anything, from passion and lust to worship of the most Platonic ideal, from obsequious adulation to the fervent confession of an esoteric faith. But always yearning—to lose oneself, to throw off the burden of the individual, whether in the passionate embrace of the flesh or in a transcendent merging in the absolute—a consuming ecstasy that left no room for the personality, let alone the body.

An utter merging in the infinite! Transmutation into the Divine Spirit.

Cynics might mock. It was inconceivable, of course, but for that matter who could conceive the Resurrection, or would want to, except as an artistic fantasy (minus the smells)? And the prospect of a complete Nirvana was at any rate more enticing than sharing an orthodox heaven with one's pious but excruciably tedious acquaintances. Even hell was likely to prove more entertaining, if not altogether comfortable. True, the Cathars denied its very existence. No hell except on earth. (Quite a pleasant one, at that rate, for some people!) No doubt one would have to reckon with paying for one's sins in the next incarnation, till the balance was even—a rather wearisome journey, as even after finishing with the earth one was faced with making a tour of the stars! The process, though, might be speeded up by receiving the *consolamentum*, if only one didn't get carried off all too suddenly. Old Raymond of Toulouse was certainly wise to drag two perfecti round on his travels. Even if the blessed thing was no more convincing really than extreme unction, there seemed more chance

109

of winning salvation through the hands of the good Cathars than from those hypocritical priests.

There were disadvantages, however. If, after all, for instance, one didn't kick the bucket, the outlook of leading a semihermit existence, fasting and what not, for the rest of one's days was scarcely enticing, and once one had taken the *consolamentum* there was no escape. Cunning foxes, even the good Cathars! Had their own way of baiting their catch, and they weren't backward in pocketing a good fee either—not for themselves, of course. To give the fellows their due, they couldn't possibly do themselves more stingily, and all they took was for the community. But that, by the way, wasn't all joy either. If this stunt for throwing away one's property were to be carried too far, the consequences might prove alarming. Though holy charity was a mainstay of orthodox teaching itself, the Church at least knew how to keep it within bounds. A bit of philanthropy did no man harm, nor his estate, but this mania of the Cathars for casting one's goods to the winds was going a bit too far—for the most part female hysteria, of course; still, with women like Esclarmonde of Foix at the head of it, one couldn't take the thing too lightly.

If there were too many like her, certainly one might have to feel a bit chary about all this emancipation of women. They'd got the *bonshommes* to support them too, making light of the marriage tie and refusing to bear one's children—sinful to perpetuate the species, the flesh being the devil's. The Church, one had to admit, with its wholesome respect for the family, at least defended man's rights. No, all said and done, one must keep an open mind. There was something to be said on both sides. The best was to follow the golden mean and maintain the tradition of tolerance toward churchmen and heretics alike, and incidentally cull advantages from both.

Such, on the whole, were the impressions young Wolf of Foix had received of the general attitude toward heresy among the nobility, and though they did more if anything to strengthen than dispel his growing suspicion that a hard-boiled cynicism was the only means of getting through successfully with the vexed business of life, his innate idealism refused to accept defeat, and in the torment of his adolescent and confused emotions and desires he clutched wildly at the last hope of discovering faith.

The Church would not give it him. It was too mixed up

with memories of his anguished childhood, the hours and years he spent in a wild longing to believe, vainly struggling to reconcile the evidence of his senses and the threats of the priests with the creation of a God who was omnipotent, all-knowing, and just.

In that direction, at any rate, the faith of the Cathars seemed to hold out hope. For them, God was the infinite, the all-pervading, the creative essence of Love, from which all things had flowed and into which one day they would be gathered again—in the end, even Satan himself. For if on this last point opinion appeared divided, and a certain section of the Cathars held that the principles of good and evil were co-eternal, none identified God with the vengeful Jehovah whose priests cowed the soul with threats of eternal damnation. Enough the immense purgatory of the world, in which the sick soul of man flung itself back, groping and blind, into repeated cycles of agony and shame, till by experience and suffering it freed itself at last from the wheel of existence.

There was no gospel but that of Love, of the Spirit, which St. John had preached. In God was the true, the only light, which man, flinging off the shackles of the flesh, might retrieve again. God was the true Creator, Satan the imitator, the distorter—the artifex of a world of illusion that held the soul in thrall. But that man might free himself, at last, Christ had appeared on earth. Not born of woman (for how should Spirit become matter?) he had taken on the apparent form of flesh. Not dying (for the Spirit is eternal) he had freed man, not by redemption, not by the blood of the Eucharist, but by his teaching—by the Word through which he pointed the Way.

VII

In despair, Wolf made a new attempt to get in direct touch with the Cathars.

Carefully, and with apparent nonchalance, he tried to probe Sicard on the subject, for he knew that, in spite of that youth's complete lack of reverence for everything but song and poetry, the Durbans were adherents of the Cathar faith. Moreover, among all his companions it was to Si-

111

card if anyone that he felt drawn, though he had little chance of closer companionship, for young Durban was as evasive as he was capricious, and forever running off and hobnobbing with some troupe of errant musicians whose political tags and popular ballads he found so much more stimulating than the conventions of the court.

"Still seeking consolation for a broken heart?" Sicard had laughed, his irregular features puckering with mischievous amusement till they resembled more than usual those of a young faun. And abruptly Wolf had changed the conversation.

One winter afternoon not long after, however, Sicard, with some mysterious references to a little adventure, led him across the river to the house of a rich burgher in one of the outlying *faubourgs* of the town. At first Wolf had thought their goal must be some amorous excursion or one of those recitals that the wealthy merchants of the south were accustomed to hold in rivalry with their feudal compatriots, vying with each other to secure the most famous singers of the day. But the room they now entered scarcely seemed decked for any such entertainment. To right and left men and women of every type and station stood in rows and groups, united in hushed expectancy almost as in some place of worship, and in a flash Wolf guessed where he must be. With beating heart he followed Sicard, who, unperturbed, was making his way through those silent rows to where a grave white-bearded man made room for them among the congregation. Scarce daring to look at his companion for fear of the almost certain gleam of triumphant mischief on that elfin face, he stared stolidly ahead of him.

There was little enough in the room to suggest the symbolism of religious practice. A banqueting hall, perhaps, stripped of its customary furniture and trappings, and containing nothing that might have been expectant in an improvised church. No painting or tapestry broke the monotony of the wall, no image of saint or gilded reliquary, no altar even. Only at the far end a plain table, on which lay an open book. Though he had heard of the Cathars' simplicity, the entire absence of all imagery estranged the boy, so long accustomed to every detail of the Mass. Gazing around for some sign of a familiar symbol, he saw there was indeed no crucifix. Then perhaps they really believed that Christ, emanation of the Divine Spirit, had never suffered death, had never been born of woman, incarnate. Suddenly, in spite of the momentary relief he had felt at the absence of the tortured image, an apprehension of the full meaning of such a denial rushed in upon him. He felt forsaken and afraid. Between him and the unknown, the growing silence seemed to shift itself, palpable—not the old remembered peace of the monastery, the sleepy quiescence of the whitewashed cloister, not even the deep, well-like calm of meditation, but something remote and implacable, a silent will gathered almost physically to a hard concentrated force.

They must have been almost the last to enter, for nothing stirred in the room. So complete was the hush that a stifled cough, a shuffled foot seemed to fall outside its pale. Minute by minute it seemed to increase, weighing on him, paralyzing all thought, till it seemed he must cry out to find relief, when at last the spell was broken. The congregation had fallen on their knees. Between the bowed heads a tall dark figure was approaching the open book. Now they were rising to their feet and stood turning toward the newcomer, motionless in hushed expectancy. Here and there Wolf recognized a familiar face—the Senhor of Laurac, Alienor of Durfort, elegant even in that dark simple cloak. . . .

" 'Thou fool, that which thou sowest is not quickened except it die.' "

So sudden, so unexpected was the impact of the words that the boy started as though cut to the quick, and yet the voice that spoke them was curiously low. Peering between the heads of those in the row before him, Wolf caught sight of the speaker.

Tall and gaunt, clad in a long black robe, he stood towering motionless above the book. Somber, ghostlike in his strange rigidity, he seemed to stare before him unseeing. Whether he read or recited one could scarcely tell.

" 'There is a natural body and there is a spiritual body.' "

Low yet strangely penetrating, the words cut through the silent room. How strange they sounded in the common tongue, and yet Wolf had heard them often in those far-off days, invoked in ponderous Latin mumbled by old Father Ambrose half asleep over his desk.

Framed by the dark clinging hair, iron-gray at the high hollow temples, the face actually was that of a youngish man, but so emaciated that it had lost both the fullness

113

and resilience of youth. And yet it seemed to the boy that neither that haggard countenance nor the taut, almost skeleton, body beneath the robe wore the quality of the spiritual, but resembled rather some metal so tempered in consuming fires that it had transcended its own nature, till by sheer will all earthiness was burned away.

" 'Now this I say, brethren, that flesh and blood cannot inherit the kingdom of God, neither doth corruption inherit incorruption.' "

He paused, and turning from the book he stood a minute, looking on the congregation with eyes that seemed to pass through and beyond the object at which they gazed, and then as though addressing an invisible audience he began what was evidently the sermon. It was a tirade on the vanities of the flesh. Gradually as he spoke the voice seemed to gather momentum until, galvanized, the words shot through the room:

"What is all earthy glory but the husk that must perish, as the barren grain blown in the wind?" It cut through the silence, searing, a sultry gust sweeping over desolate plains. "For said not John the Apostle, 'Except a corn of wheat fall into the earth and die, it abideth alone. But if it die it bringeth forth much fruit'? What is the seed that quickens within the grain when the husk falls asunder like a shard? That which is born of the flesh is flesh and that which is born of the spirit is spirit, for corruption cannot inherit incorruption. How then can spirit be born of flesh? Truly spoke Paul of Tarsus, saying, 'Two bodies has man, one terrestrial, one celestial; but the glory of the celestial is one and the glory of the terrestrial is another.' "

Vibrant, the words ran through the room. Here and there a head was bowed in confusion, a face turned pale, but still the voice continued unrelenting, while as it rose triumphant the walls of the narrow room seemed to fall away, and before the eyes of the wondering boy there unfolded itself the Titan imagery of the Manichaean duality, the remorseless gigantomachy of Light and Darkness, of Satan and God. For how should God the radiant, the incorruptible, give birth to the corrupt? And, thrilling, Wolf beheld mankind no longer sprung from the loins of old Adam but fallen angels incarcerated in the demon flesh.

Once, glancing aside, he saw Sicard leaning forward, his chin cupped in his hands, his eyes lit with so eager a concentration that his quixotic face seemed suddenly transformed. Irresistibly the voice of the Cathar, harsh now as with strangled ecstasy, drew him back.

"As the light in darkness, as the seed in the brittle husk, is the spirit of man imprisoned in the mortality of the flesh. Yet that darkness in which you wander is lit with the deluding beams of a false day. For see where you stagger blinded till you faint in the fire of its consuming rays. Have you not burned and, to that burning, night only has brought release? Have you not known the bliss of embalming darkness and, waking, cursed the dawn?"

He paused, his face ashen, his eyes half closed. "Why then shrink from the night in which the glittering torches shall be extinguished, the last fires quenched, till from that ultimate darkness breaks the true morning, the only light?

"For what is man's life on earth but a thirst unslakable, and his last dream but unfulfillable desire?"

Desire . . . The word seemed to vibrate through the room, echoing against the naked walls. A harsh shuddering sigh broke from the congregation. Somewhere a woman cried aloud. Many had fallen on their knees, a richly dressed burgess had torn off her necklace and thrown it at the speaker's feet.

"Ah, God, how long have I groped in darkness!"

"See how I have lusted after the world's splendor!"

"Senhor, pray for us sinners and bring us to a good end."

Almost it seemed that the preacher swayed, but with a convulsive effort he held himself erect and stood gazing, as though unseeing, at the congregation, while the pile of jewels and gold grew at his feet.

"*Deus vos benedicat, eus fassa bon Chrestia, eus port a bona fi.*"

A long sigh rose from the little throng. Now all were on their knees: "Our Father which art in Heaven, hallowed be Thy name, Thy kingdom come, Thy will be done in earth as it is in Heaven." The words poured from those fervent lips with an urgency Wolf had never known. "Give us this day our *heavenly* bread"—confused, he paused on the unfamiliar word, till he was swept forward upon that hungry tide.

115

Outside, the westering sun mocked them with a brazen resplendence, turning the insubstantial scene into a masquerade of gaudy light. Illusion or truth? Unknowing, he plunged on past whitewashed walls, through gulfs of shadow, the road dissolving beneath his feet. "Desire. . . ."

It was Sicard who at last broke the silence. "Heavens, the man ought to be writing dawn-songs. It was almost an *alba*. And that bit about the fallen angels," he rippled on in irrepressible enthusiasm, "it's the real stuff for an epic—if anyone dared. The trouble is, of course, that Satan's bound to be the real hero. And what would the Church say to that? Even the Cathars, though Guihalbert certainly—"

"Guihalbert?" Wolf echoed, as the name, stirring some chord of memory, roused him suddenly from his stupor.

"Who else?" Sicard's impish countenance lit with glee as his joke was completed triumphantly. "The little monk's been listening to none other than the great Cathar bishop himself—Guihalbert of Castres. Better run along quick and confess."

But the jest struck on impervious ears. Guihalbert of Castres—Guihalbert from whom Escarmonde of Foix had received the *consolamentum*, "Guihalbert and his poeticized castigations of the flesh." With sickening clarity the ribald words of Mirepoix and the student rose mocking through his confused senses.

"What's up?" Sicard was saying, suddenly aware of the boy's pallor. "They probably won't frizzle you if you promise to reform. Father Benedict's pretty lenient, you know. What, you don't mean to say they've caught you already?" he teased. "Suppose I ought to have gone slow with you. Rather a strong first dose for babes. Luckily Guihalbert only turns up once in a blue moon and the rest of them are mild by comparison—all brotherly love and the Paraclete. Seems I'll have to be keeping an eye on you," and actually warmhearted as he was irresponsible, Sicard of Durban was beginning to feel conscience pricks. The boy looked awfully queer. For a moment he was almost afraid he was going to be sick, but to his relief Wolf was already pulling himself together, and taking him by the elbow, Sicard steered him along the path.

"Look here," he said, "if you really care about all that stuff you'd better come home with me next leave; our place just reeks of it. Mother's always got a Cathar in tow and my aunt's a sort of hermitess. Even my little sister swears she'll never marry. Fears, I suppose, to become the bride of Satan, suckling a lot of little demons at the breast."

Through a heaving mist the words penetrated to Wolf's consciousness. Yet behind that familiar banter Sicard's presence was suddenly reassuring. The Durbans might be his aunt's friends. After all, Mirepoix and Hugo . . . . His rising anger at the thought of their ribaldry began to clear his head.

For a while they continued their way in silence. The sinking sun of the winter afternoon fell full on the city across the river, bathing the walls and towers in its glow. In that watery, tenuous air they seemed insubstantial, half unreal, and yet charged with some strangely formidable significance. Far away from the inner city came a dull echo as of shouts or revelry. They had reached the bridge, and unconsciously the two paused and, leaning against the parapet, gazed at the burnished ramparts.

"Carcassonne the impregnable—even Charlemagne couldn't take it," exclaimed Sicard. "As for old Innocent's threats," he laughed, "imagine Philippe Auguste going a-pilgrimaging to Roland's tomb and taking Carcassonne by the way."

"But the others?" murmured Wolf out of his gloom.

"Fat Burgundy, Nevers, St. Pol? Scarcely a Roland among them, an Olivier even:

"Count Roland swings his blood-stained sword—
Well saw he how the French were losing heart,"

sang Sicard, gleeful, mocking. "Well, at any rate they were enemies worth having, and look at them now!"

"And us?" Wolf wondered himself at the sudden wave of boldness that had allowed him to utter so subversive a remark in view of the older boy's patriotic exhilaration.

Sicard gave him a swift glance. "Do you know," he said, after a moment's pause, "sometimes I almost wish they'd come—don't you?"

"Yes," Wolf muttered harshly. At that moment it seemed the best way out of the muddle. "If only . . ." Suddenly he found himself telling Sicard about his father's desperation with his countrymen.

Sicard listened, unusually earnest. "You know," he said, "really I should have been sent to Foix, but the Count was captive then in Seo d'Urgel, and as I'd begun here they thought I'd best stay. But if it comes to it, I'll be fighting under him all right. We're his vassals. Durban's different from this place, wild enough, up by the Mas d'Azil. They reckon us pretty soft down here. Of course, Trencavel himself's different—he's magnificent at the spearthrowing, isn't he? But one can't get at him, somehow. And as to the others . . ." He gazed at the slowly fading ramparts. "Do you think they were like us when Clovis marched on the south? Probably they called old Alaric decadent, touched with the Latin rot and all that. . . . I wonder," he went on, after a pause, "what songs they sang. It'll be strange if it happens, there'll be an end of love lyrics and *albas*—all war songs and the rest. The joke is we'll be having to take theirs as a pattern. One can hardly dream of bettering them, curse them!" he cried, scowling under his conflicting emotions. Moving on again, he began to hum, till unconsciously the words formed on his lips:

> *"Count Roland spurs across the plain, his hand*
> *Holds Durendal that cleaves full clean and sharp."*

In very defiance of his feelings he was almost shouting, the words. A passer-by glanced curiously at the boys, surprised perhaps at this blatant apotheosis of northern heroism, which only added to the gusto of the incorrigible Sicard.

"But where did you learn it?" asked Wolf.

"From old Arnaut. It's not quite the thing with us, of course. They tried making a more patriotic version down in Spain, pushing the honors on to the southerners for despatching Roland, but it's not a patch on the original."

For a moment the memory of Roland's murderer flashed across Wolf's mind, and dreading the inevitable pun on his own name he would have tried to change the subject, but in any case the impetuous Sicard, carried away on the tide of his unconquerable enthusiasm, was blind and deaf to all but his song. "Why can't they make things like that now? It's all so precious. All 'I—I—I,' as though there were nothing in the world but one's own blessed feelings about love—and then they're afraid to come out with it. But listen to this," and he began to chant once more that song of prowess and hard bitten comradeship, till in Wolf of Foix the torments of the last months, the restless fever of a first infatuation and disillusionment began to subside and fade into ever-greater distances.

> *"High are the mountains, and somber the valleys,*
> *Roaring the waters . . ."*

But to Wolfe it was no longer of Roncesvalles that Sicard was singing. Montségur . . .

They had left the bridge. Mounting the steep ascent to the ramparts they strode on through the dusk, caught up on the ardor of the song and the new bond of sympathy between them. The very streets seemed to lie under the spell. But for some distant shouting, the city was unusually still.

They had reached the barbican when the sound of clattering horses recalled them to the present. A company of guards were sweeping by from the inner town. At their approach the few desultory loiterers retreated quickly into the shadow of a passage or convenient arch. It was only then that the two became aware of the fact that many doors were closely barricaded and windows shuttered. Here and there a face peered, furtive and curious, through a grille. But it was not till they reached the castle that they heard the news. The papal legates Navarra and Peter of Castelnau, denouncing Raymond VI as perjurer, tyrant, and coward, had excommunicated him anew. That same evening, crossing the Rhône beyond Fourques, Castelnau had been murdered, stabbed in the back by one of Toulouse's men. There had been joyful demonstrations down in the city. One of the wandering friars trying to intervene had been attacked by the mob. Carcassonne had had its first taste of blood.

THE VANISHING SKY

For out of the north there cometh up a nation against her, which shall make her land desolate, and none shall dwell therein; they shall remove, they shall depart, both man and beast.

(JEREMIAH 1)

I

"SWORD, SWORD, LEAP FROM YOUR SHEATH! CLEANSE THE earth of the last heretic! Vengeance for the death of the Pope's legate!"

Inciting to a crusade as urgent as sanctified, as that to which Peter the Hermit had roused European chivalry for the liberation of the Holy Sepulcher, the papal summons spread through the north.

And the reward was as good. Universal indulgence and dispensation. Pardon for every crime—lust and gluttony, rape, sodomy, felony, murder even. The bait was attractive enough. And for the rest, the adventure lured. Sight of the far-famed, the glamorous south. Song, laughter, blinding color under an ever-shining Mediterranean sun.

Outside, the long hovering wraiths of a November mist blotted the marshes of Flanders from view. Languorous nights, women bare-shouldered, sloe-eyed. Was not that heathen count, Raymond of Toulouse, reputed to keep a veritable harem in his palace? Breasts tight-sheathed in gleaming gold, taut as inverted goblets. . . . Unconsciously the cup turned in a musing hand, the dregs of Rhenish wine crept over the blackened boards to filter through a cranny of the moldering walls. . . . Years ago on the Crusade—down in the ends of Acre—sin? But even that was venial. Flesh was frail—far from home. God had mercy on His soldiers who fought to free His citadel, who were ready to risk their lives that the plague of heresy be wiped from the soil.

A squall of wind, damp, ague-ridden, driving along the Seine, tore open a shudder in the hall of the royal palace. Philippe Auguste, drawing the ermine closer around his sunken chest, bent closer to the fire without interrupting his dictation to the wizened clerk:

"To the most Holy Pope Innocent III—"

He paused, gazing deeper into the embers. Burgundy, Nevers, St. Pol had taken the cross. Let them, they had not spent a lifetime in combating an implacable foe—England, ravenous, insatiable. Was he to let go what he had won with unending toil, the work of a lifetime? So, after all, it was wit, not muscle, that counted—in the end. He smiled to himself thinly, his small weak eyes narrowing to almost invisible slits.

Henry Plantagenet, Richard—father and son—he had outlived them both, and might outlive the third. Well, John Lackland had got England at last, if the barons didn't yet wrest it from him, but he should continue to lack France! He had sworn it and he would keep his word, despite the miserable body they in their Angevin arrogance had mocked, that day when Richard . . . He had been a mere whelp then, but he, Philippe Capet, would never forget. Nothing would deter him in his path, nothing let him relax his watchfulness for one moment—not even the cause of God Himself.

Let them go! Let them pin the Cross on their shoulder—no, of course it was the breast this time—the cause was closer to the heart. Not surprising—adventure without the travails of the East. A little excursion, a handful of plunder. Death for a few, wounds for more, and things would be patched up with a pretty bonfire of heretics by way of a last spectacular reward. For after all, Raymond was powerful—his lands stronger than those of Burgundy or Nevers. And the little *Île?* France—France, all that was left. And yet he held the Angevin leopard at bay. Step by step, inch by inch, he would get there still. The thin rheum-distorted fingers burrowed in the soft close fur of his robe. Only time—only time—Rex *Francorum* . . . from the Mass to the Rhône, from Picardy to Navarre, even across the dread gorges of the Pyrenees—and so far he had scarce done more than hold and consolidate that miserable remnant of his inheritance. Yet how many of those lands were still his in name. Even the south. But still, if he went warily, ever warily, biding his time. Be rash and lose all. Let them go! Let them appoint a commander, bound to him in fealty—vassal of France.

Shaking back the lank wisps of his thinning hair, he turned his head toward the patient scribe:

"It is impossible for me to levy and maintain two armies—one with which to defend myself against the English king, the other to march against the Albigenses. If my lord the Pope provides the money and the soldiers, if above all he forces the English to keep the peace, then we will see. . . ."

II

Procrastination—Philippe, the sly fox, had evaded and was likely to go on doing so, Languedoc laughed.

On the death of the legate a shudder had run through the south, a shudder that turned as soon to a wave of triumph. Liberty was not yet dead. Still, despite the overblown glory of an ancient civilization, the spirit of freedom that had given it birth flared up in the face of oppression.

In the end, Raymond VI, for all his policy of vacillation, had had enough of the legate's impudence. Whether he was himself the instigator of a plot against Castelnau, and thus guilty of the murder, none could tell. Probably one would never know. It was one of his own knights who had done the deed, on his own responsibility perhaps, in a bout of fury, to avenge those insults against his lord. Still, one couldn't blame the count's enemies for drawing the worst conclusions, seeing that he had openly enough threatened to pursue the legate to the ends of the earth. Well, the haughty old devil hadn't got very far.

"God pardon my murderer"—at any rate, he had shown a little more Christian feeling in death than in life; high time, no doubt, with Toulouse's spear sticking in his rump; anyhow he had paid for his pride and that of his fellows. One was hardly taken in by the humble mask adopted of late by the dear prelates through the zeal of Canon Domingo de Guzman. The monk himself was no doubt sincere. In spite of his complaints (he had grumbled that the heretics held his preaching of no more worth than a rotten apple) he had worn quite a following among the erring sheep, was in fact becoming rather trying, even dangerous, maybe. He had vowed to exterminate heresy and was, it seemed, attacking the problem with true Spanish fanaticism. Not content with setting himself up in Prouille (for all their boasting, the Durforts had been able to do very little about that), he was sending his representatives scouring the land to sniff out the least scent of heresy. Luckily he appeared, for the monent at least, to direct his energies toward the obscurer classes, petty landlords and peasants for the most part. Since the venerable Peire Maurand, back in the seventies, had been forced to bare his eighty-year-old carcass under the redeeming scourge, and the ire of ancient Toulouse had fallen upon the ecclesiastics, the more exalted families had been tackled more warily. Nevertheless this new method of dealing with the recalcitrant was perturbing, incompatible with one's principles of personal liberty, to say the least, let alone Christian. And the inveterate cheek of these fellows, holding out as bait a period of preliminary grace during which the whole district was invited, through the mercy of God, to voluntary confession—or denunciation, as the case might be—for naturally, to lay bare a neighbor's heresy was counted a work of Christian love, being the means of saving the soul, not to say enriching the Church's belly. A nice state of affairs where men were encouraged to inform on their enemies, servants on their masters, children on parents. No knowing where that might lead, for hell (despite the Cathars) could wear lurid colors, and even an honest man, threatened with its terrors, might commit perjury for the sake of his soul. As for the rest, there was no knowing who might not bear one a grudge—a man's conscience would soon not be his own.

Resist, protest? Innocent's threats might well turn to reality any minute now. But things couldn't go on like this. Indignation was rife, and among the believers persecution only fanned the fire.

In vain Fulk, erstwhile troubadour, now Bishop of Toulouse and zealous persecutor of heresy, pronounced new decrees, instituted more novel and crueller forms of penance and punishment. The heretics only increased. He knew it of old. Drive them from the towns and they cropped up in villages, winning new followers. Drive them from thence and they took refuge in the woods and caverns in the hills. And the godless lords of the land, taking them under their protection, laughed aloud: Toulouse the murderer mocked at the interdict; Foix, blaspheming God, harbored them in his gorges and mountain fortresses, and Trencavel refused to banish them from his lands.

"I am no heretic," the viscount had retorted in answer to the new laws, "but my people's conscience is their own. What they think of God has no bearing on their temporal allegiance"; and he had refused to deprive them of their property.

His courage aroused a wave of admiration, not least among the body of young squires.

They had always admired him, worshiped him in a way—in the tilting yard, out on the chase. Not really so much older in years, at those moments he was their comrade, their captain, and watching him hurl a spear, take the long leap, or jousting in light harness out on the fields, they were carried away with enthusiasm, till even Bertran of Saissac's dogma that the well-disciplined body was something almost divine attained meaning. It had smacked of the schoolroom and they had smiled at the double heresy that denied the Cathars as much as the Church. But with Trencavel in their midst that philosophy was unconsciously lived, and they were swept up on his own exultation.

Away from the sports field the spell was broken. In the midst of diplomatic and courtly existence he appeared to them always a little unreal, rather splendid still, but with the fire gone out—a figurehead, to be served, obeyed, but as a form, a memory only of what he had been at their games—scarcely even that. Almost between the two, man and ghost, there was no real relationship. He was lost to them, as perhaps he was lost to himself. Almost it seemed that he hated the routine of the court. He had reduced its etiquette to a minimum, yet none could have accused him of gracelessness or parsimony, any more than of priggishness or conceit, least of all toward the townsmen.

One hardly bore him malice—but was he quite human? Even his apparent friends would sometimes doubt it. Somehow, in spite of his charm, an invisible wall seemed to surround him. No one could really get near him.

Long ago, when as a child, golden-haired, with all the fair beauty of his mother's race, the blood of St. Gilles refined to an almost angelic perfection, he had ridden through the streets of Béziers at the side of his tutor un-armed, speaking with the burghers and with the meanest as if they had been of his own court, he had seemed to the townspeople a creature from another sphere. Had they really forgotten the gulf of blood that flowed between them and his paternal kin?

Wolf knew that story of murder and retribution, of how in the course of one fearful night the entire male popula-tion of a city excepting the Jews had been wiped out, and the women forced to bed with their husbands' and fathers' murderers.

Was Raimon-Roger Trencavel himself freed from the curse? Through that infiltration of the weakened blood of Toulouse, had the natural passion of his race at last been expunged in him, the unbridled violence that had never hesitated to grasp what it desired, had reaped murder through injustice, and answered murder by massacre and rape?

No doubt Alazais of Burlats, his mother, with the cir-cumspection so characteristic of the house of Toulouse, had done all in her power to guard him against a resur-gence of the paternal heritage and a belated retribution on the part of the burghers of Béziers. So sandwiched be-tween the iron guardianship of scholars and Cathars and the hardly less exacting ritual of her fashionable court—the haunt of poets and singers and the most brilliant femi-nine wit of the time—the boy had been schooled in chivalry according to the strictest rule of self-discipline and the precept of the golden mean. Forced so long to steer a path between conflicting factions, noble and bur-gher, churchman and heretic, the worlds of spirit and flesh, had he really managed to achieve detachment? Wolf, trying to make out, found himself up against a blank wall. For before him lay always the bleak precipice of Bertran of Saissac's dogmas, and he could not but suspect that in the old man's rigid self-mastery, in his very gospel of dis-interestedness, lay a shade of greater intolerance, or at least a gradual alienation from all human values. "Judge not that yourselves be not judged." With him, at any rate, that tenet seemed born less of religious conviction than of a cold divinization of reason. Since we act only according to our seeming, and to each man the world appears differ-ent, who has the right to blame another? Where, then, was the absolute? Where the standard by which one could save oneself from the abyss—good for good's sake? Better certainly than good for the sake of heaven, but what was good, since to his stoic judgment evil existed only in the imagination? Did Trencavel, Wolf wondered, manage to deny its existence? Sensitive, a little fastidious, he surely shrank from a contact with what he loathed. Did he drive himself to believe it existed only as a fantasy? Certainly, with all his enthusiasm for athletics, he could not accept the Cathars' identification of evil with the flesh. But was he really as dispassionate as he seemed? Sometimes Wolf had the impression that beneath all that grace and charm lay something hidden and almost painful.

One morning, out on the hunt, Wolf found himself riding by Trencavel's side. Spurred by his proximity, the wintry morning, the sharp crystal air, he was filled with a fierce exuberance and a desire to distinguish himself.

For a while they rode in silence, the only sound the clink of their bridles and now and then a snort as their horses pawed the wintry earth. They had just emerged from a gully opening upon a vast sweep of pasture and fallow field. Down by the banks of the Aude the gnarled stumps of the leafless vines speckled the umber soil, awaiting the rains of spring, the violent onslaught of that southern sun. Beyond it the land spread empty and wide to where, far to the north, the ridge of the Black Mountains rose threatening and dark. Silhouetted against those clear and vacant reaches, erect above the pacing horse, the figure of Raimon-Roger Trencavel wore a strange grandeur, as though in that sharp crystalline light every detail of the supple body, the beautifully poised head were chiseled against space, giving him a quality of solitariness that smote the boy with a sudden pang and, rousing a vague apprehension, filled him, he scarcely knew why, with a fierce upwelling sense of allegiance.

After a time he saw they were alone. The others seemed to have been left behind or had followed another track.

Unconsciously they slackened rein. Unfettered, the arabs sprang forward, their hoofs churning the frostbitten soil. The hunt was almost forgotten. Soon it had become a race between them. Knees gripped tight, bent a little above the flying manes, they flew foward, rising, dipping, spanning the breadth of the plain.

Amidst a stretch of heathland a clump of juniper rose darkly. By silent understanding it had become the goal.

Straining every fiber, Wolf was actually ahead when, within only a few yards of the goal, Trencavel shot past and, drawing rein, turned toward him, laughing.

"Why, you almost had me beaten. Heavens, but you've come on since you've been here."

The boy looked up, glowing with pride. For a little while they rode on at a light canter, silent.

"Your father will find a change in you, I reckon, by the time you get back to Foix."

In the midst of Wolf's elation the words struck chill. The thought of his father, the unbridgeable gulf between them, the ancestral castle that had never been his home ... Even Montségur seemed remote.

It was as though the other read his thoughts. "What, fighting shy of the barbarous mountains? I thought by what the Countess was saying you were sworn to them heart and soul. She'll be blaming me next for turning you into a sybarite of the plains and thinking she might as well have sent you to Toulouse."

Did Trencavel know? He had passed through Pamiers lately. They must have spoken together. Confusion took hold of him.

"And if you once get up there," the other continued, "God knows whether you'll ever come back to earth." Suddenly he turned to Wolf so passionately that the boy was almost startled: "The earth—" he echoed, "well—isn't she good enough?"

Setting spurs to his horse he dashed forward again as if in challenge.

The earth—thought Wolf, speeding after him. Yes, what more did one want than this? What was it Miriam had said about ending in the stars? She hadn't been here riding at his side, feeling the horse's flanks straining beneath one, outstripping time. And all was sharp and clear and present, as when Sicard sang. I'm alive, he thought exultantly. This is me, the earth is me, and the sky and the wind. It didn't make sense, perhaps, but it was truer than reason. . . .

When at last they came to a halt they were breathless. Words would have failed anyway. But for a moment Trencavel's gaze met his, almost as though it were searching, pleading for something—for confirmation, perhaps?—as if it were a matter of life and death itself.

If only Wolf could have been sure, if at least he could

have found words to speak, but even while he was struggling to find them that old look of withdrawal had come into the other's face.

At that moment a horn rang out. Not far away from the edge of woodland on their left the hunting party reappeared, silhouetted gaudily against the darkness of the naked trees.

Answering, Trencavel raised his own horn to his lips; then, waving lightly, rode to meet them. Wolf, falling a little behind, watched him, silently cursing the intrusion. Once more it was the old familiar scene, gay and colorful enough, but the rapture was gone. Suddenly all seemed separate and alien.

III

"Condemn him as heretic, then only have you the right to pass sentence upon him and to invite me, the Court's sovereign, to confiscate legitimately the domains of my feudatory."

Philippe Auguste, in the act of dictating his answer to the Pope's final indictment of Raymond of Toulouse, paused on the last word—"feudatory"; Raymond, the sixth of that name, heir of the house of St. Gilles, Count of Toulouse, Duke of Narbonne, Marquis of Provence—vassal who had never done homage, never paid allegiance, vassal of France.

Beneath the open window the Seine, sparkling in the sun of March, flowed past the Isle of La Cité. Sharp-cut as metal in that crystal light, the truncated towers of Notre Dame rose against a bright blue sky. From the trefoiled galleries, pompous and grave in their enameled robes, the hierarchy of saints and prophets looked down upon the crowd of human ants hurrying fretfully through the doors below, coldly indifferent to their salvation or doom as to the ceaseless interchange of pigeons alighting and strutting on the roof or crowning with their lime-white droppings the heads of the *chimères*.

A puff of wind sent a cloud of catkins whirling down the quays. Shivering cascades of light blew down the river, lifting a silvery wave. Gently the water heaved and lapped against the embankment, threatened the rotting remains of a half-submerged cask, chuckled, and subsided.

Stone-gray isle, anchored in the embracing Seine—*Île de France* cradled amid the shifting territories of the realm. Still they would endure when the fierce and fickle waters of the Garonne had swept over Raymond's palaces, when the Languedoc had long been swallowed up in the rippling flow of the *Languedoeuil*.

Lost in reverie, Philippe peered from the palace windows with his weak rheumy eyes, still gradually a second scene shifted, uncertain, transparent before the sharply delineated contours of the bright March landscape. And kneeling prostrate at the foot of those unshakable blunted towers, knocking upon the iron-studded door. . . . But not yet, not yet. Perhaps not even in his time—but one day they would thank him. France would thank him—Philippe the realm-maker, Philippe Auguste. He turned, sighing, and drawing the parchment to him, scanned the page. Pointing his trembling fingers at the empty space, he nodded to the scribe:

"As it is, you have not yet let it be known whether you regard the Count a confirmed heretic or not. . . ."

He had evaded again. But Innocent's patience was at an end. Let the King of France back out under cover of England's threats, he need no longer rely on him. Arnaud-Amelric, Abbot of Cîteaux, had not been idle. From province to province he had struggled on, haranguing, declaiming, inciting to God's most Holy Crusade against the Satanic heresy of the Albigenses, the iniquities and abominations of the followers of the Antichrist. From Auvergne to Normandy, from the *Île* to Champagne; from Lorraine and Flanders, even from across the Rhine, men flocked to the standard of Christ and, kneeling, took the Cross.

"Might, after all, the threat be earnest?" reflected Raymond of Toulouse, stretched at ease on his sumptuous divan. The armies of the north were gathering. Thousands armed to the teeth might not be dealt with so easily. He preferred argument carried on from the comfortable level of his couch. On that point, it was true, Burgundy might agree with him, if he offered a sufficiently sumptuous show. But those barbarous warriors, those growling Normans and Germans, would certainly understand no language but the sword. And the alternative? The legates were adamant; Fulk, the viper, implacable. To think the most holy bishop was once a troubadour and had received quite an ovation for his love songs—very mediocre, of course, except perhaps for their faultless construction. The man's whole mind worked in formulas. He should really be less hard on the infidel. Why, his very life was an algebraical problem, worked out, bit by bit, from the start. The three degrees of Amor—Love alias x neatly raised to second and third degree, step by step without a flaw. First, apprenticeship in my lady's bower. Second, ministrant of Divine Love (in its less alluring respects) to the sinner. Third, no doubt, entry as Mary's troubadour in heaven. But what was x raised to the nth degree? That was the question. Fulk of Marseilles' meticulous scheming might yet encounter some uncomfortable surprises. In the meantime, though, the man was an infernal nuisance. For the sake of getting rid of him, and the rest of the legates, a fight might really prove worth while. After all, the house of St. Gilles couldn't put up with protracted insults. The Castelnau affair, all said and done, was hardly to be regretted. Toulouse to be abused by a set of pettifogging clerics! More dignified, certainly, to take up the fight with Innocent. For a moment the memory of that summer soon returned in which he had seen himself the visionary defender in an almost mythical conflict. He smiled a little at the thought of that high-flown fantasy.

Still, the south could muster a pretty potent army if it chose. With a united front, the onslaught could be held at a civilized distance. Whatever happened, he would see to it that the streets of Sacra Tolosa would not flow in sacrificial blood. Meanwhile one could arrange a well-staged reception for my lord, Duke of Burgundy. One must make sure about his taste in wines. And did he prefer the petite high-breasted type to the Junoesque build? That little dancer from Cyrene now. . . . He must feel his way. No, things couldn't be hurried. One could still hand over a few heretics. Make the legates uncertain, keep them marking time. Besides, when it came to final terms it was good to have shown oneself capable of being reasonable. In the meantime one must prepare. Those vassals might prove cursedly obstinate to deal with. Béarn, Commenges, he could pretty well count on them both, certainly on the Lauraguais—they had had enough of zealous Domingo. Foix? He'd been waiting a lifetime to have a go at the northerners. But he'd have to keep an eye on him—he was capable of any sort of deviltry toward the clerics and might prove compromising when it came to a treaty. Luckily Jordan might act as a go-between. He was still hand in glove with the Church. After all, he had done well in his choice of a son-in-law, though he got on his nerves and it was a relief to be rid of him of late. Trencavel? . . . He paused, his thick lower lip protruding a little, while the delicate linear network engraving his well-massaged skin deepened to creases between mounds of fat. Would he start raking up that ancient feud, and with the typical arrogance of his father's claim himself Aragon's vassal, not subject to Toulouse? Why should he? After all, that foolish quarrel had worn itself out. The youth was his nephew, flesh of his own blood. Why, he had actually resembled him at his age—outwardly at least—a trifle softer in contour, no doubt. Athletics had never been his line. But inwardly?—he smiled, pondering what might have been his fate if Constance of Boulogne, his mother, immersed in her own woes and spending, poor soul, half her time in prison, hadn't left him to the tender care of bawdy old maids. But then, into what obscure depths of knowledge he had been led through that early initiation! Besides, even the threats and chastisement of a tyrannical father were preferable to the sermons of those sanctimonious old worthies with whom they had surrounded the budding Viscount of Carcassonne. The heretics had set up a perfect oligarchy during his minority. True, they hadn't managed, it seemed, to convert him to the faith. Perhaps an early acquaintance - with both sides of the religious question had opened his eyes to the humbling in each and had left him with no fetish but tolerance. Anyhow, he had ample opportunity of practicing it with that old dodderer Saissac always in the background, mouthing Seneca and his Stoic doctrines, mean of heart as the rhymesters had branded him mean of purse. Why on earth didn't Trencavel get rid of him? But then, that was perhaps what he wanted—the institution of the perfect state on a true classic basis modified on the lines of the Round Table. Though if he imagined Agnes playing the part of the virtuous Roman housewife! . . . Well, between them all they had literally encased the boy in a strait jacket of moral prejudice. He might as well have been brought up by the monks. Fanaticism of whatever kind was equally destructive, though it seemed Trencavel had managed, outwardly

131

at least, to emerge from it comparatively sane, thanks to the balance afforded by the mundane elegance of his mother's court, though the worldiness of dear Alazais had been modeled on as rigidly conventional a pattern as any moral code. Between them all the man must be a walking bundle of repressions. It would be interesting to see what curious phenomena might after all be hidden beneath. A pity, really, he hadn't taken more trouble to know him better, but Trencavel had always seemed to have an antipathy to Toulouse, and he never believed in forcing friendship. Still, they might share some sort of interest. He appeared to have taste, though of the painfully austere variety. Trying a sort of neoclassic cult with the squires. Completely wholesome, of course—moralized athletics and all that. The viscount was a paragon of chastity in spite of that little hussy Agnes. A child, they said, was, on the way—Trencavel's? He wondered. The youth would probably spend his time, if he had his choice, worshiping in the groves of Artemis. That, after all, might prove a point of contact, though Trencavel was unlikely to appreciate the goodness in all her aspects.

Definitely, he decided, his thoughts returning to the original theme, he must make sure of him. With Carcassonne behind him, even if war were inevitable, there was little to be feared.

Accordingly, letters were written and despatched by messengers to Carcassonne. The answer was given in the affirmative. Raimon-Roger Trencavel with due formalities sent his greetings to his maternal uncle, accepting his invitation to Toulouse. So Trencavel set out, determined not to let prejudice conquer reason, convincing himself of the atavistic absurdity of that ancient feud, rendered doubly insane through the blood tie; admitting to himself that Pedro of Aragon's claim to the overlordship of his lands was no more disinterested than was Raymond's, that the Spaniard's religious orthodoxy had produced more misery than his uncle's libertinism.

But the gulf was unbridgeable. As always, Toulouse roused in him that faint revulsion as though beneath the gorgeous and luxurious veneer he could detect the faint but ever-present scent of decay. The guilt, the glitter, the glimmering, disintegrating haze of that Oriental and exotic atmosphere veiling every thought and action, as it did the massive rugged structure of the old Gothic palace, gave him a kind of vertigo, through which his uncle's voice, mouthing its incredible plausibilities, fell bewilderingly on his ear. And minute by minute, in spite of every effort, he shrank back further into a hardening shell of aloofness.

Raymond watched him, his faded blue eyes quizzically narrowing in their pouches of fat, with amusement at first. Why, the youth was even more striking than he had imagined, graceful but aloof, becoming every instant more and more the intransigent god. Had he ever in his own day, he wondered, managed to produce so perfectly that effect of divine inviolateness, even with the help of the most expert of make-up? It was evidently not only a matter of feature (unconsciously his ringed finger wandered over his cheek in search of its lost contour). That had been similar enough. But then, too, it was generally the Dionysian divinity he had cultivated. Engaged, on these private ruminations he simultaneously unfolded his plan of diplomacy.

Struggling against the enervating influence of his surroundings—the glittering walls, the somnolent voice, the heavy scent—Trencavel strove to follow the thread of the count's amazing opportunism. At last, after an hour or two's argument or (more correctly) persuasive rhetoric on the part of his uncle, quivering with disgust and sickened behind that apparently unruffled mask to the point of collapse, he had risen, and with unimpeachable grace but maddeningly paradoxical intransigence refused to continue the discussion. Without further ado he had called for his horse, while Raymond cursed the old Trencavel arrogance, perverted, it seemed, to such unbearable priggishness in his young nephew. Those mythological themes, capable of such various and fascinating deviations, had not even been touched upon.

Trencavel rode hard toward Carcassonne, the meeting a failure, his conscience victorious. But was it? Still bewildered by his antipathy, he was even now unclear as to what had really transpired. Only the count's blatant opportunism remained unquestionable. Resist, make a final stand against the tyranny of the Church, its encroachment on ancient southern liberty? Set about preparations for a common front? Well and good. But in the meantime, keep the prelates at bay by handing over another lot of heretics to their mercy; cast them out from his borders; deprive them of birthright and lands? Never. He saw the trick— playing for time. And even then, if, for the sake of exigency, he had forced himself to such perfidy, what of the issue? Could Toulouse be trusted? If it came to it, would Raymond really fight, and, if so, for how long? Nevertheless, again and again as he rode, one thought persisted, tormenting, through his confusion. Had his defiance of Toulouse after all been prompted less by principle than by personal antipathy and mistrust?

But was doubt not justified for the sake of his people? Supposing Toulouse betrayed them? And yet—should he not have allowed his uncle the benefit of the doubt? Did not fantasy create its own reality? Now, he laughed bitterly to himself, he had almost forced him into betrayal. Was that perhaps what he wanted at bottom—an avowal of the old hatred, the old enmity? Was there within him some other self, something beyond his control, dark, hidden, unillumined by the grace of reason? If he was himself unsure, what right had he to judge Toulouse? Supposing after all his uncle possessed the greater sagacity, saw that by the sacrifice of the few greater misery could be spared?

But he could not. At stake were the lives of the men he revered, men threatened not by death alone but unspeakable agonies. Maybe they feared them as little as the stoics of old. Maybe they yearned for martyrdom. But still, their blood would be on his hands—"as long as one doesn't see it," Raymond had spoken quietly behind thick shapeless lips.

No! Whether Raymond was right or wrong, to join with him would mean to sacrifice forever what he had loved and striven for. If indeed Languedoc was doomed, a civilization played out, no help would ever come from joining with Toulouse. Whatever the danger from outside, the deadliest peril could only come from within. Only by keeping their own hands clean could they keep themselves from utter ruin, could the south be reborn. Through his very defiance, old hopes, broken in the incessant need of makeshift and compromise, began to rise before him. Maybe he had defied Raymond against sense and reason, had violated the principles on which he had been nurtured, which had become the mainstay of his own policy and rule—tolerance. But there were limits. At that moment tolerance appeared to him no more than a pallid ghost, masking a deeper failure. No, and again no! As he rode, something seemed to free itself within him. With fierce determination he galloped toward Carcassonne.

His qualms as to the rightness of his actions were confirmed as far as Bertran of Saissac was concerned.

"It is not possible for a man to follow what appears to you, but only what appears to himself. Therefore whatever happens, say to yourself—so it seemed to him."

The words falling from between the bearded lips of his old tutor seemed more damning than any violent reproof, and once again, as in his childhood under the impact of that withering detachment, he felt revolt surge up within him, despair of a sagacity that preached a high humanitarianism and stood remote from its realization. How often in his boyhood he had frozen beneath it. Yet when he might have rid himself of it he had not, partly perhaps because he wondered whether essentially those principles were not right, partly because imperceptibly the ice had spun a thin layer around his own self, and last but not least out of a sense of loyalty, a gratitude for what that same wisdom had given him—a vision of a golden age! For in reading the classic poets the crust of his old tutor seemed perforated, as though, confined by the leash of hexameter and pentameter, human passion had power to reach that sterilized heart. To the boy it had been an escape into an almost visionary world, as remote from the asceticism of his mentors as from the fashionable conventions of his mother, a world that he had even been able to re-create in a small measure in sport. Now, when either as a symbol of tacit disapproval or actually, as the old man avowed, on account of his failing health, Saissac retired to his family estates, his departure left Trencavel with a sense of more than personal relief or loss, as if indeed it was another and inevitable step in a process of self-liberation that filled him with exhilaration yet with bewilderment. Therewith he seemed to have effected, beyond even his own will, a complete rupture with the past. Yet he stood in the midst of a void. Which of those who surrounded him understood or really knew him? These feudal barons, companions of his sport and of the chase, what did they care for Carcassonne or Béziers? Caravita, perhaps, who had stood by his house for years and been entrusted with many a secret of state? But how could that astute speculative brain, however ready to rescue a precarious situation, really comprehend a cause that Trencavel himself admitted irrational?

True, there were enough who would applaud him

wholeheartedly; first among them the man on whom he could count above all others—old Pons, the armorer, the veteran of his fathers' wars against Toulouse. Often in his childhood he had fled from his mother's house or from under the rigor of Cathar mentorship to be regaled with Pons' store of legends of ancient heroes and feats of arms. But it was something other than the old soldier's crude defense of feudal quarrels that he needed now.

Among all those who surrounded him there was indeed scarcely one whose judgment he could completely trust. By his resolve to defend the liberty of conscience of his people he certainly won the support of the consuls, though many of them, in spite of their independence and moral scruples, showed some doubt as to the wisdom of quarreling with Count Raymond at so critical a moment. For the rest, the reaction of his vassals was varied. A good few of them, mostly tough old barons inhabiting the remoter and wilder districts, loudly approved, less on account of the principle involved than at the thought of a possible tussle with Toulouse. Even if it caused the threat of the Crusade to loom nearer, it appeared as a stimulating interruption of a monotony that was beginning to pall, and they began to dream of booty, even a fat ransom or two, for many of those northerners were said to be rich. The issue was still uncertain enough, but with a certain gusto they began to inspect their arsenals, telling stories of the good old days, of those frequent sallies against Toulouse under Roger Taillefer, while a few even remembered the great days of old Raimon Trencavel himself, and they turned to his grandson approvingly. High time the youngster indulged in something more vigorous than that bloodless gymnastic mummery of his! There was much of the true Trencavel spirit in him after all. In spite of his Cathar preceptors he had managed to show some spirit.

Others demurred. Why, the man had always prided himself on his tolerance and regarded those feuds as an outworn atavism. If this crusade did ever materialize it would be advantageous, to say the least, to stand firm with Toulouse. Raymond would pretty certainly manage to wrangle things all right with Burgundy. But there was no reckoning what he might do now out of mere pique. If he made a truce for himself, and those barbarian hordes once passed Toulouse? Carcassonne was impregnable, of course. Still, sieges were tiresome, and for those with small castles

136

to defend it was a different matter. No, for once Trencavel had been a bit too high-handed. All very well to make a show of agreement with a handful of city councillors at Béziers. Their palaces were safe enough.

Even now, however, a large number, immersed in their pleasures and the comparative security of years, could not be brought to take matters seriously. Raymond was too easygoing to worry himself about taking vengeance on his sister's son. Besides, he was sly. He would play cat-and-mouse with those skulking priests to the last; keep them dangling, and in the end, after a little skirmish perhaps, the bubble would burst.

It was the old story. Wrapped in self-complacency and self-interest, they were indifferent to everything outside it. As they had responded to the young viscount's attempts at reform they responded now, with a smile or a shrug, even toying with the idea of warfare as the unquestionable overthrow of barbarism by the civilized, involving at most a few picturesque heroics. It might be amusing, flattering to one's self-esteem (or sense of superiority)—just as Trencavel's liberal government, his enlightened concessions to the masses, his physical-regeneration stunt. To take life as a game, a pleasurable spectacle, was their privilege—the privilege of the civilized. Few troubled themselves with the thought that the game might suddenly become earnest, the alluring spectacle resolve itself into the wild dance of puppets controlled by a merciless and incalculable hand—the audience, the grinning mask of death. If any apprehended it, they pushed the thought from them, retreating yet further into a realm of glamorous illusion.

But perhaps more than anything it was that general attitude of *laissez faire* that, now he had taken the responsibility on his own shoulders—for right or wrong—seemed to provide Trencavel with the very justification he was looking for.

As to the youth of Carcassonne, they rallied round him with enthusiasm. The leader of their sports was well on the way to becoming a hero, the champion of freedom. Let him hit out hard, go his own way, and prove it with lance and sword instead of playing cat-and-mouse with Fulk and the legates. The question of autocracy became a frequent topic of debate, leading to heated discussions among Wolf's comrades. Was absolute power on behalf of the ruler after all not more beneficial to the people than the

137

dull officialdom of the consuls? Most of them, like young Villemur, sons of noble houses from the Black Mountains and remoter parts of the country, burst out in ardent avowals of feudal superiority. Others were all for the strengthening of the consular system, without which the liberty of the south stood in jeopardy. Why, wasn't it one of their chief advantages over northern barbarism? To which the first faction would retort hotly that the hide-bound bureaucracy the city councillors set up in the cities was deadlier than any tyrant's whims.

Wolf of Foix, racking his brain on the subject, could come to no definite conclusion. While his whole nature rebelled against arbitrary ruthlessness, he could not help wondering whether the consular system did not end for the most part in sensational pompousness—and how far were they really representative of the people?

Apart from that, there had never been the ridiculous cleavage between the nobles and the burghers that was supposed to exist in the north, and many of their companions on the tilting field and on the chase were sons of the more prosperous merchants and tradesmen. But it was all a matter of the same privileges and rivalry for wealth and favors, though undermined with a fashionably skeptical derision of the very system that made them possible. A bit of revolutionary antiproperty talk, clichés garnered from Catharist and Waldensian dogma, epigrammatic tags bandied for the sake of wit. It was fun enough, in hall or in the wine shops, and Wolf found himself more and more intrigued by the swirl of discussion. But where did it lead? At bottom, it all seemed much of a muchness, the continued and useless fret about a system hopelessly outworn.

THE SPIRIT AND THE EARTH

But, O, the unbroken enchantment of living Creation
Wells up in a hundred fountains. A play of forces
None can stir without wonder and adoration.
Words still melt into limits we cannot trace. . . .
      (R. M. RILKE, *Sonnets to Orpheus,* translated by
                J. B. LEISHMAN)

I

THAT SUMMER, SICARD, TRUE TO HIS PROMISE, TOOK WOLF
home to Durban, and there he found himself in the midst
of a true Cathar household. Not that the widowed Mabilia
of Durban appeared of an outspokenly pious, or at any
rate mystic, turn of mind. In so far as the world presented
to her eyes a panorama of the most pitiable waste and
confusion, she most certainly agreed that the devil's work
must be behind it; but the indefatigable war the benevo-
lent little lady waged upon chaos caused her to be absorbed so entirely in the things of this earth that little or
no room was left for speculation on the world of the
spirit.

Indeed, Wolf was surprised at first at so marked a sense
of actuality among confirmed Cathars.

Sometimes he would accompany Sicard and his mother
on their visits to the vassals and serfs, at which, with all
her customary energy, she would dedicate herself to their
welfare, completely absorbed in the task of instructing
them in better living. But there was definitely more to her
kindly bounty than the whims and self-gratification of
philanthropy. Even if a good portion of her assiduity
could be ascribed to her love of methodical management,
in home and village and at the simple social gatherings she
was always organizing there was little sign of feudal patronage, but rather a remarkable evidence of a community

of feeling, as though mistress and servant were bound together in a common aim; all of which would inspire Sicard to the skeptically indulgent remark: "Poor old Mother, Catharism's quite safe in her hands—a perpetual sort of spiritual spring-clean."

If, however, the mystic element was apparently lacking in Mabilia of Durban, it was duly compensated for in the family by her sister-in-law. Both inwardly and outwardly, Guilhelma was a striking contrast to the homely chatelaine. Tall and gaunt, and still betraying signs of a wan, cadaverous beauty, she would sometimes appear in the hall when the perfecti visited the castle or partook of a meal. Then she would sit at the table silent, her great gray eyes fixed, it seemed, on something invisible, scarce touching the food on her plate, restricting her diet more stringently than even the vegetarianism of the Cathars decreed. At other times she was seldom seen, hardly ever leaving her room in one of the remote towers of the castle, where, it seemed, she passed her days in solitary meditation, attended by an elderly maid vowed, like herself, to strictest observance of the faith. Wolf had rarely heard her speak, and the sight of the pale, gray-clad woman passing wraithlike through the house or sitting stark-eyed and silent at the board at first proved disconcerting enough.

"God knows what she broods on, cooped up in that tower, or what keeps her alive. It's all right for her, but when they get hold of them young—my little sister," Sicard frowned in genuine concern, "she's at one of those Cathar schools, you know. Of course the Catholics say they bribe them in with offers of education, and then hold them fast. As for that, what about the poor souls who're dumped in the convents because they're not pretty or rich enough to catch a husband? Besides, she wanted to go there herself. I don't know that Mother was very eager, but once Honoria gets her head set on something there's no compromise. She was always like that, even when she was a tiny little thing. Once, I remember, we had to choose between two dishes, 'bad for children to have mixtures' and all that. But she just wouldn't. Stood there and insisted she liked both equally. In the end she went without. She'd stand anything before betraying her own principles. Old Longshanks ought to have had her as pupil. I believe she was always a bit jealous of me," he laughed a little ruefully. "Really, I ought to go and have a look at her. I promised, you see, and if one doesn't live up to her expectations she takes it desperately to heart. I thought we might ride over one day."

He glanced at Wolf mischievously. "Perhaps she might even fall for you, if you talk all your Latin and philosophy, and think after all she'd found a young man with a soul. They've probably drummed into her we're all four-footed beasts. You might even try carrying her off, by persuasion if not by force—the virgin knight rescuing damsel from the wizard's tower. It's just your line," he teased, with his most elfin look. "Better than pining for the unobtainable in Narbonne." and as Wolf winced: "Honoria's quite passably pretty, you know."

So one morning they set out upon the quest, armed with bows and arrows and the lutes that Sicard at the last moment tied upon their saddles.

"They might provide the final touch. She used to be keen on music, you see, unless they've made her think it's the devil's lure."

"My singing?" scowled Wolf, reddening at the thought of his voice. "If you're thinking of that, I'm not going."

"Oh, I'll do the singing," Sicard laughed. "You can just appear in the moonlight and strike a few chords on the strings. Anyway, we'll have to be half hidden." Before Wolf could say more he was clattering out of the castle yard.

Soon they were riding up to the forest. It was still early morning, and on either side the great pines rose silent and spangled with dew. Between the trunks they sometimes got a glimpse of the water rushing beneath, while beyond, above the deep green meadow slopes, gray pinnacles fretted the clear, almost watery, limpidity of the sky. Far away, unimaginable, seemed the arid, sun-baked plain of Carcassonne.

The valley was narrowing, the road gradually winding higher across the hills. They had half descended the other side when Sicard's horse began to lame. Its shoe had loosened, and he swore impatiently: "Old Arnaut, of course. He's getting hopelessly slack, past his job really, but Mother won't sack him—she's so fearfully humane, you know. Well, now I suppose we'll have to stop at the forge. There's one at the bottom, down by the mill."

But the blacksmith, they found, was engrossed in a task

of some importance, and as they were faced with a good hour to wait, they set about exploring the valley.

"We used often to go in search of peregrines up there," Sicard pointed to a group of limestone crags. "Actually, we might have a look now. It's rather late in the season, really. Still, we might have luck."

After a short climb they found themselves amid a labyrinth of fantastic rocks carved by the action of weather and water to shapes almost bestial and semihuman. Although these hills formed no more than the outlying ranges of the Pyrenean chain and were thick with a tangle of vegetation, Wolf, reminded of his far-off adventure on the Tabor, was filled with growing excitement, and though till now their search for peregrines had proved vain, deaf to suggestions that it was time to get back to their horses he had pushed on and on. They had topped the ridge and were looking down on the other side to the woods and valleys. Suddenly from behind a rock two birds rose with a harsh scream and, wheeling, hung poised on the wing. Below, the rocks fell almost perpendicular for twenty feet, but halfway down on a ledge Wolf seemed to detect what seemed like a nest. Here the cliff was certainly unscalable, but to the right it had fallen away and shelved in a rough score to the wooded slopes in the valley beneath, and it seemed to him that from there he might be able to reach the ledge.

Behind him Sicard was gesticulating wildly, but fired by a sudden decision to get there first Wolf scrambled down over the boulders, and hanging on to rocks and bushes began to pick his way along the face of the cliff. He was now some way below the ledge, but there seemed hope, if he could get a foothold, of drawing himself up. Holding on with his hand, he had dug his foot into a crevice and was about to hoist himself up when suddenly the rock gave way, and amid a small avalanche of stones he found himself crashing downward. Luckily the gnarled roots of a bush stayed his precipitate career, and catching desperately at branches and brambles he managed to slacken speed until at last he came to rest on a shelf of grassy ground near the bottom. Dazed from the fall, a few moments passed before he moved, and it was Sicard's voice calling to him anxiously that roused him to full consciousness.

"Christ, are you hurt?"

Bewildered at finding himself alive, Wolf, beginning to

pick himself up, murmured vaguely in the negative. He seemed to remember feeling a sharp wrenching pain in his ankle as he fell. His immediate attention, however, was too focused on rubbing his bruised shoulder and wiping the blood from his face and hands to concern himself about more.

Relieved at finding him apparently comparatively unharmed, Sicard's anxiety turned to annoyance. "You might have waited, you know." By now he had reached his side and stood regarding the torn tunic, the face bruised and bleeding from the ravages of rock and brier. "It *has* rather spoiled you for your seductive role," he admitted ruefully.

At that Wolf, smarting under the double injury, made an effort to get on his feet, but at the first step he almost collapsed.

"What's up?" Sicard came forward.

But the boy was already making an angry and desperate attempt to limp on. After a few steps, however, he sank down on a rock. "It's my ankle," he muttered between clenched teeth. He had gone very white.

Kneeling down, Sicard examined the injured foot, and as he straightened it out Wolf doubled up in pain. "Doesn't look as though anything were broken," said Sicard, rising. "Still, God knows how you'll ever get to the horses. I'll have to fetch them and bring them up through the valley. But it's a long way round and, anyhow, I can't get them right up here." And as Wolf, dizzy and sick, proved incapable of future plans, Sicard began to reconnoiter. "We're nearly at the bottom," he said, returning; "if only you can get down, there's a peasant's hut just below. It's a queer sort of place, but I know the woman. Her son works down by the mill. I could leave you there while I go for the horses. Perhaps I'd better fetch her to help."

But at that Wolf made another angry attempt to get on his feet. "Come on," he muttered between gritted teeth.

So, supported by Sicard and a staff cut from a clump of hazel by the way, he struggled bravely on till at last they reached the hut in the gully.

It was a primitive enough place, and the old woman who greeted them might have aroused his suspicions at any other time, though Sicard appeared to be well acquainted with her and was utterly unconcerned about her half-familiar, half-ingratiating manner. Besides which, Wolf, faint with pain and exhaustion after the descent,

143

would by now have cared little had he even found himself among a den of thieves, and he was glad enough to sink down on the dirty-looking pallet of straw.

"I'll be as quick as I can," Sicard promised, having seen him settled. "Old Maria will probably tell you stories to pass the time."

Left to himself, Wolf lay still, too relieved at being off his feet to care about anything more. But in a few minutes the woman reappeared, and drawing a battered stool to his side began to busy herself with his foot. Through the enforced walking, however, it had swollen to such a degree that it was impossible to remove the boot.

"There's no way but for cutting it," she said, shaking her head woefully.

"Then, for God's sake, leave it—or get on with it!" cried the boy, as under the renewed agony of her tugging the cold sweat stood out on his body.

For a moment she sat gazing regretfully at the boot. "And the leather so beautiful and all." Her hands, horny and calloused, began to stroke the grained surface. "Mother of God, if his dress isn't all tattered too, and he dressed fit for a wedding. Still, it's little a man cares for his finery when he's hurt"; and fetching a knife she proceeded, with a last caress of the rich leather, to rip open the boot. But when she would have stripped off his long hose he resisted awkwardly.

"Fa-la-la! One would think he had been brought up among the holy brothers!" And as the boy, cut on the raw, would have sprung up, only to be forced back by the violence of the pain, she laughed aloud. "It's not long and you'll be learning, my lad, for all the airs you'd be giving yourselves, there's little difference between you all when you're hurt. For, king or beggar, knight or clerk, it's between a man's thighs you were all conceived, and a woman's you saw the light. Well, well. . . . But he wasn't such a coward either to have got down here on that," she muttered, laying down the shapeless and discolored foot. Then with a rude sort of tenderness she began to wipe the sweat and blood from his face: "Maybe I can make something that will ease the pain."

Rising and leaving the hut, she returned after a moment with something in a pail and, mixing a mysterious concoction, warmed it upon the hearth. "It's no use his wrinkling his nose, though maybe it isn't a perfume he'd care to be bringing into my lady's bower," she laughed as she applied the mess thickly to his ankle. "But it's better, I reckon, than many a doctor's salve."

Whatever the ingredients—and their smell was foully reminiscent of dung, as the rags with which she bound it on were all but clean—the effect was sufficiently soothing to counteract all squeamishness, and Wolf, lying back almost contentedly on that rather unsavory couch, began to take notice of his surroundings. It was a wretched hovel and bore little resemblance to the houses of the peasants he had visited with Sicard's mother; and while it struck him that Maria probably did not belong to the community, he suddenly recalled the masons at the inn at Montségur and his subsequent talks about the conditions of the workers to Esclarmonde of Foix. Remembering the enthusiastic projects he had made at the time, he was overcome with a sense of guilt, and when the woman, having busied herself with her pots, returned to his side and handed him a cup containing a steaming though none-too-attractive beverage, he thanked her with a shy sort of graciousness.

"It's not what you're used to. Still, maybe it will bring you back your strength." She looked down on him curiously, puzzled by his courtesy. "Is it the Viscount teaches you manners?" she added, laughing. "*Dieus*, but things must have changed a deal since my day." Shaking her head, she turned, and sitting down by the hearth drew a bucket of turnips toward her and began peeling them into her lap.

"The young master, of course—he was always different. Let him think you've a song or story up your sleeve and he'll give you a fair answer, whether you're beggar or prince. He's frank and free with all, though he's always having a dig at the burghers. Oh, many's the time I've heard him launching out against the old consuls." And Wolf, recalling Sicard's virulent attacks on bourgeois pomposity, joined in her laughter. "Still, times have changed," she went on, "if it's growing a common thing for a squire to give one a fair answer. It wasn't like that, I can tell you, when the young esquires of Foix used to come riding by, halloing and shouting out on the hunt. And little they cared what they trod underfoot—whether it was corn and crops or the one poor goose fattening for Michaelmas; and they catching up cockerel and sucking pig on their spears as they rode, like as they were stuck ready for roast on the

145

spit; or chasing the old sow till she all but dropped her litter by the way. For good sport they reckoned it to destroy what's a poor man's sustenance, and a lucky day it was if oneself got other than curses, though sometimes maybe 'twas a silver piece thrown over the wall for the damage done, if the Count maybe was with them. For, if the right mood was on him, he could be free and easy of purse enough—my lord of Foix."

"Foix?" echoed the boy. "Why, does he often come up here?"

"Sure, but he used to," she answered, "back in the old days, before he was married to the lady Philippa, and as soon went running off on the Crusade. And afterward too, for a little, and then it was suddenly the end. It's fifteen years or so, I reckon, since he came riding this way and I'd hear his voice echoing through the forest. Aye, a great singer he was in his time, the Count of Foix, and a great lover—Ramon Drut, Ramon the beloved, they called him. Many's the time I'd see him riding down through the woods, and I warrant it wasn't only the wolves he was chasing down to the doors of Salenques. Why, they say even the good sisters were brought to bed for love of him there. Most like they're but tales," she laughed, working swiftly and deftly with her knife. "Yet I reckon there's many a bastard of his roaming the land unknown. . . . Why, is it paining you worse?" She looked up as Wolf, catching his breath, made a sudden movement.

"No," he muttered quickly, covering his face with his arm for fear she should see the hot blood that had rushed to his cheek.

"It's the heat drawing it," she said, taking his denial for a boyish attempt at bravery. "And 'twill only do good. Aye, very likely they're but tales," she echoed, resuming her task. "But who can wonder, seeing everyone knows 'twas the devil he cared for holiness. And would he be thinking twice of the chastity of a little nun, and he not afraid of blaspheming the holy saints themselves? For sure you've heard it told how the Count of Foix challenged the Lord Himself."

And as Wolf replied with an indistinct murmur she went on, carried away by her own eloquence: "They say it was but for a quarrel he had with the friars of St. Anthony, though there were some at the time did whisper other tales, and that 'twas all for rage and grief that God

146

had robbed him of his beloved. Yet, whatever the reason, it was a bold and blasphemous stroke enough, for what does he do but, breaking into the monastery, set fire to the dormitory, and taking captive the brothers, holds them at ransom, while his men go pillaging and ransacking the church! And no end there was to that sacking and burning, and they tearing the holy images from the walls and the altar. But even that was naught to what was to come; for many's the warrior, one way and another, has pillaged chapel and church, but never I've heard before of a man so godless as set his own helmet upon the head of our Savior Himself, and spear and shield in His hand. But the Count of Foix, when he saw what was toward from the doorway, and he sitting there astride his horse, and the leaping flames behind him like the fires of hell itself—why, if he doesn't give a laugh so harsh and fierce that they thought his lungs must burst, and ripping his mailed glove from his fist hurls it at the feet of our Lord. 'Save yourself!' he cries, and setting his lance at rest, no different as though 'twere a joust, charges at Him full tilt. Aye, they're few in the land," she concluded, "for all their blaspheming ways, would dare take a like vengeance on God for the sake of their beloved."

Wolf shuddered. He had heard stories of his father's sacrilege before, but never told with such gusto as this, or so vividly interpreted in the light of the count's amorous adventures. What if even his own existence were connected with some blasphemous doings? Suspended between excitement and fear, he longed to ask more but dared not, and already old Maria was rambling on.

"Sure, there was scarce one in the land to equal him for valor, even in the old days," she was saying in a voice of genuine admiration. "Unless it might be his own mother's father, the old Raimon Trencavel himself. But pride it was that broke him in the end, though maybe 'twas the work of Toulouse as much as the burghers' vengeance that stretched him in his own blood on the altar steps of St. Magdalene's. And pride it was, akin to madness, that drove his son to vengeance, and the massacring the men of Béziers as though they were flies, and not one left alive in the city but women and children and Jews. It's ne'er been the same, they say, since. The young Viscount, I've heard, doesn't favor the city. Maybe there's too many ghosts walking about the place for him."

"But he's done a lot for the citizens," Wolf, raising himself on his elbow, sprang quickly to his defense.

She laughed. "He's not like his father or grandfather, I've heard tell. Comes of being brought up by the Cathar folk, I suppose. They say he's full of reforms and suchlike, but it's little that people care about *them* in the end; for give them a bite and they'll always want more. Aye, it's oft times I've told the young master's mother, and she giving the clothes off her back to the poor, that driveling old beggar had soon been after the other half of St. Martin's cloak if his horse hadn't carried him off in time!"

Shaking her apron, she swept the peel into the bucket on the floor. "I'm nought but an old woman, but this I've seen, my lad, far and wide, and among rich and poor alike. A man's more like to forgive you for your bad deeds than your good." Picking up the bucket, she hobbled out of the hut.

Left alone once more, Wolf mused bewildered on her lurid tales and such paradoxical evidence of rebellious rancor and deference. But his meditations were cut off before long by the arrival of Sicard.

"We'd best get home," he said, as the woman assured him there was little chance of the boy walking for at least a week. "It would probably have been pretty hopeless with Honoria anyway," he consoled him as Wolf railed at himself for having spoiled the fun.

Mounted at last, Wolf thrust his hand in his pocket. The coin he pulled out was gold, and indeed the most valuable he had, but he felt ashamed to put it back while there flashed through his mind how he had bribed the masons for the mule at Montségur. What fun, he thought, it would be to confess his identity! Would he never manage to assume his father's arrogance? Even while he imagined himself flinging the coin to the old woman with a flourish, he actually bent and almost shyly put it into her hand.

"For the damage," he laughed, reddening, as she stared incredulously at the gold. "In memory of Foix."

"Heavens, you're magnanimous!" cried Sicard as they rode off.

"Well, you see," Wolf winced, as the horse, setting out at a trot, gave a sharp twinge to his ankle, "old Maria has been telling me tales."

His injury, augmented by the strain to which it had been subjected, proved graver than they had hoped, and to his disgust Wolf found himself laid up for the greater part of his remaining stay at Durban. Still, his enforced captivity had its consolations. Sicard did his best to keep him amused, and lying in the window seat of the castle hall he could devour book on book, while a good part of the time was devoted to the study of his hitherto much-neglected guitar. Sometimes, indeed, Sicard would come back from a ride dragging with him a couple of itinerant musicians or some music-loving friends from one of the neighboring castles, and they would indulge in a competition, or argue for hours on the comparative value of a pellucid limpidity or profound obscurity of style. Then, while they conversed on artifice of form as a means of intensifying the effect of passion by its very constrictions, and one of them would embark on a far-fetched explanation of Arnaut Daniel's sestinas, Sicard would expostulate derisively.

"The *trobar clus* is done for anyway, and the *trobar ric*'s going to follow—obscurity of meaning, obscurity of style—they're all in the same boat, reducing poetry to riddles. If a song needs all these literary annotations, poets had best start making glossaries like the schoolmen."

"But an image isn't fixed," maintained a sickly-looking youth with drooping eyelids.

No, images weren't fixed, they were diabolically ambiguous, as Wolf well knew, and seeing that poetry was full of images it was surely the poet's business to suggest their disturbing and demonic quality. "If a rose, for instance, is more than a rose, or capable of becoming everything but itself under varying circumstances, yes, even at the same moment," he tried to explain—a point that immediately evoked ardent consideration.

"All the more reason," argued the irrepressible Sicard, "why the words must be simple and direct, or all their imaginative quality's killed outright, and it's just juggling with dead bones."

"Dead bones—playing at mental knucklebones," laughed a dark, wild-looking fellow who spent his winters in a monastery or Cathar hostel, as the case might be, and his summers earning a precarious living reciting his satirical and pugnacious verses in the castles of the exalted. "The whole thing's just a means of giving a damned snobbish clique a chance of rubbing in their intellectual superiority because their hearts were petrified a few hundred years ago."

"But poetry," tittered the effeminate youth in a high querulous voice, "must speak to the heart, and emotion's everything."

"Sentiment," sneered the other. "That's all they're capable of feeling."

Which roused Sicard to his usual lament that the epic was dead: "What poetry wants is to get a new infusion of communal feeling instead of wallowing in sickly private raptures"; and Wolf was inevitably reminded of Miriam's words.

Although the chatelaine of Durban regarded the caprices and poetic enthusiasms of her son and his often unruly friends with a certain concern, she had too much faith in his unconquerable humor to allow herself to be gravely disturbed by them. She had long given up all hope of exerting any constriction upon him, regarding his eccentricities as the visible retribution for her own failings, a leniency that, caused him to treat her foibles with affectionate indulgence. Perhaps, without admitting it, he was aware that his own championship of simplicity and lucidity in the field of art bore affinity to her desire for order in the practical sphere of life.

In his mischievous and good-humored attempts at teasing her, Sicard would sometimes embark on glowing accounts of their sports, as if the implied paganism of Trencavel's athletics must of necessity offend her Cathar sensibilities. But the good little lady's mania for health and hygiene so nearly equaled her moral consciousness that she listened with keen interest to her son's account of Trencavel's predilection for gymnastics.

"Yes, I am sure things are improving. I almost think I shall have to come to the festival next May. It's Sicard's last year, you see," she beamed proudly, "and then he comes home to look after the estates. But I think I must make a point of it. He assures me," she turned to Wolf, "it's much less bloodthirsty than it used to be, though these classic effects that seem to be becoming the fashion do, I'm afraid, sound very pagan. Why, I actually heard that young Mirepoix dressed himself up as Apollo, or was

150

it even a goddess?" She paused, as at Mirepoix's name Wolf colored. "Well, I'm sure I don't know. Besides," she went on, "that was at Toulouse, and they're so extreme. Still, anything is better than those murderous tournaments. It's easier for the poor horses, too. But in the north it's even worse. How they can bear that weight of iron upon them I really don't know. They say even the horses are covered in it from top to toe and come thundering down like a wall of solid steel."

"But they can only use the heavyweights," Sicard laughed, "and they're bound to be a bit slow on the move. Don't worry, Mother, we'll beat them easily with our little arabs."

She shook her head, her serenely cheerful countenance clouding with trouble. "Maybe it's all right as long as it's only sport. But if it comes to war, and some think it's almost sure to, whatever shall we do then? But they do say speed's half the battle, don't they?" She turned to Wolf for confirmation, and as he did his best to reassure her in a tone of manly authority she gave a sad little sigh. "Oh dear, if only it doesn't come to it! One can live so peaceably if one tries. Look at the villagers. They used always to be having feuds. But the *bonshommes* have done them so much good. They're really beginning to see how much they were always losing through quarreling and all that unnecessary cruelty to their beasts. Half of it's just foolishness, really, and ignorance. The Cathar schools are helping such a lot." And she gave Wolf a glowing account of heretic educational ideals and how they were setting up centers of instruction in the rural localities. "Of course there are difficulties. And many of the peasants are so obstinate, like that old Maria, living in darkness and filth as bad as the horrid mess she put on your ankle. Things *are* getting better though, year by year."

Sometimes she would speak with veneration and awe of Esclarmonde of Foix and all she was managing to do even in the face of the avaricious abbot of St. Anthony. "Of course one must be lenient toward one's enemies. Doubtless it's due to some wrong upbringing in his youth, all this false valuation of money, but in a priest it's very sad!"

And while she bustled off again to see to her duties, in house or village, Wolf was left to ruminate on the other

151

side of the question and what the brothers of St. Anthony might have to say regarding the sins of his own father.

The thought would inevitably lead back to the mystery of his own birth, but the fantasies aroused by old Maria's lurid tales were soon dispelled by his serene surroundings, besides which he had long steeped himself fatalistically in the obscurity of his maternal origin. Indeed, he was beginning to feel a certain pride in that very anonymity, in that it gave him a special right to espouse the cause of the oppressed. For in spite of Maria's skepticism regarding the mentality of the masses, his innate idealism, rekindled by the social humanitarianism of his present environment, started him off once more on wild speculations concerning a new structure of society. With this revival of his earlier faith his courage returned, and he made up his mind that on leaving Durban he would certainly pay a visit to his aunt at Pamiers. Not only was he now fortified by some factual knowledge of her faith, but he had been able more than once to talk to the Cathar elders himself.

Traveling always in couples, for they were vowed never, except in times of direst stress, to go abroad alone, they frequently visited the castle to hold a service or discuss the administration of the diocese, on which occasions they would never fail to pay Wolf a visit and inquire as to his progress, for one of them indeed was no mean physician. Sometimes they would remain a little to talk, never proselytizing, but displaying such tolerant and human understanding that Wolf often wondered that they, who denied the divine origin of the fleshly world, were so much more able than the orthodox Christians to make earthly life felicitious. What struck him particularly was that the Cathars really seemed to form a living community.

It was noticeable especially in the services that were held in the hall of the castle, and which he was therefore able to attend. Here as they all gathered together—mistress and servant, vassal, peasant, and serf—it seemed to him that barriers were really broken down, and that all present were bound together by a true unity of consciousness—something, he imagined, that must have belonged to the early Christians. For what appeared the strength of the Cathars' faith was not the promise of a hypothetical heaven but a fervent participation in the Spirit, the sharing of an experience present and vital, of which the breaking of the bread was more than a symbol. And as it passed from hand to hand it seemed to him that in that actual sharing he experienced far more poignantly the essence of Christ's being than he had ever done in receiving the Eucharist.

"I am the living bread." Indeed, it was life that was given to them, life to a whole civilization gripped in its death throes. So it had seemed to him often in his tormented meditations of the last winter, after his first harrowing experience of a Cathar service and the mystic ecstasy of Guilhalbert de Castres. Then Miriam Caravita's words had rung in his ears with all their weary seductive despair: "The last throes of civilization wallowing in its own agony."

Were they really so degenerate that they had lost the roots of a common existence? Was it only to be recovered again in an immolation of self, a complete dissolving in the Spirit?

Now Catharism seemed so different—simple, direct, and actually in practice not so alien to life at all. Yes, surely this spirit of love and brotherhood to which they aspired was what Jesus had preached. Strange that they who denied His carnal existence had come so much nearer than most churchmen to the actual practice of His word. Often it seemed, indeed, that the bewildering complexities of existence, the contradictions that haunted him, had been but phantasms, or the delusion of Satan, as they upheld. And yet, could life be divided so simply into matter and spirit?

"It is the spirit that quickeneth; the flesh profiteth nothing." In spite of the simple joyousness, in spite of that vital pervading consciousness, it was after all the keynote of the Cathar faith, made manifest in Guilhelma of Durban, in Guilhalbert of Castres. Sometimes the pale, wraithlike woman, passing through the hall, would seat herself beside him for a while. She hardly spoke, but sat with her great eyes fixed on space, or more disconcertingly upon him, and once, as though in answer to some long unspoken dialogue between them, her lips seemed to part as in a final imprecation.

"It is not enough—one can never give enough!"

Was she mad? Perhaps. And yet at the time it was as though the voice had incited him to something half forgotten, an urge to give, to spend himself to the full. But do what? For the Cathars seemed almost to offer a way and yet ...

To Wolf, compromise was impossible. If he was to accept the Cathars' faith he must accept it wholly. It wasn't enough that the elders should look with tolerance on the vices and weaknesses of the worldlings, making the best of a bad job. The new world that should arise must be revolutionized throughout, and its faith must belong to all. And did they want that? Did they want the world at all? "The earth," Trencavel had said, "isn't she enough?"

Rendered doubly impatient by his physical captivity, the memory of that ride and its exultant sense of physical exhilaration rose in him overpoweringly. But Catharism would never sanction it.

"They are not of the world even as I am not of the world."

But was the world then wholly evil? Evil certainly in corruption, in its lust for power, its tyrannies and rivalries, its chase after self-interest and gain; evil equally in its cowardice and sloth, its creeping self-abasement, the whole abject misery against which old Maria had maliciously warned.

But what if men freed themselves from their shackles? What if they managed to rise above their feudal and municipal rivalries, and created from their liberty a new faith, binding them in a brotherhood that transcended all barriers of rank or class or race? Couldn't they discover a faith that united the communal spirit of the Cathars with Trencavel's affirmation of being? Suddenly the image of Montségur took on a new reality.

In his enthusiasm to discover a plan of action he broached the subject to Sicard, who listened at first sympathetically enough.

"But how is one going to begin, unless it's through the Cathars? You've got to have some sort of organization."

"Yes," Wolf went on eagerly; "that's just it." But he had carried that image about with him as a secret obsession so long that even now he fought shy of confiding its name to Sicard. "One might found a sort of order," he attempted.

"O God! Like the Templars?—fearful snobs. It would probably turn into an aesthetic cult spiced with a lot of ritual and imitation stunts."

"Yes; but if Trencavel—he'd hate all that—if he—"

"Heavens, are you going to rake him in?"

"Well, but he's interested in—I mean, he's always bothering about the citizens of Béziers."

"It's a fetish—the old Cathars made him feel pretty sick, I reckon, about that massacre of his father's. They used to drag him about the streets when he was a mere child to make him popular with the people. Must have looked as though he'd strayed off Olympus into the slums. There's something queer about him really," Sicard went on. "In a way he's so splendid. Heavens, I wish I'd seen him defying old Toulouse. But one can't get at him. I suppose the Cathars made him so remote."

"But at sport," Wolf protested, and remembered the winter day on which he had ridden at Trencavel's side. "He's always quite different then."

"Yes, while it lasts. One thinks he's going to open up, and then it's gone again. It's as if he were afraid of letting himself go. One can't talk to him properly. We might as well be mere snippets, only fit to brag about hits at the quintain."

"Of course, you want him to try a tenson with you," Wolf mocked, feeling quietly elated at the thought that Trencavel had evidently really singled him out for special attention. "After all, he can't help it if he doesn't like poetry."

"But he does," Sicard's elfin face puckered with resentment. "Do you know," he added after a little pause, as if he were confiding an important secret, "he writes verse?"

"Does he?" His elation somewhat damped at the thought of the intimacy after all suggested by such knowledge, Wolk attempted to affect indifference. ·

"Yes," with an air half of triumph, half of derision, Sicard gave a twang to the strings of the lute lying at Wolf's side. "Latin—oh, not as lively as your wandering scholar's muck," he laughed. "The real thing."

"How do you know?" Wolf parried; while feeling vaguely excited, his mind returned to the thought of those bits of Vergil, even Catullus, Brother Martin had sometimes slipped in between parsing the Church Fathers. (Things after all hadn't been so bad at Bolbona until the old monk died.) ·

"Do you think I don't know the stuff when I see it? Old Longshanks once tried giving me a drilling, but he gave it up. He didn't like my epigrams—not classic enough. But how I found out about Trencavel—it was quite by accident. You know how he hates anyone messing about his room—the sanctum, I mean. Well, one day I was passing by when someone had left the door open. There was a hell of a wind blowing, and things were flying all over the place, so I went in, shut the window, and cleared up. Most of the stuff was all just business, copies of statutes and so on; but one of them was different. Poetry of some sort, so I had a second look at it and then I saw it was Latin."

"But how do you know it was his?" Wolf queried skeptically.

"First because it was his writing."

"Might have been a copy—"

"You might let me finish. It was a sort of elegy, and there was a Vergil lying open on the table. It looked like an imitation."

"Still doesn't prove it was his."

"But the thing is," Sicard burst out, impatient, "it was just like—well, the sort of thing he hints at when he talks about the way things were once, down here."

"Under the Romans?"

"I suppose so—or before—the Greeks or whoever they were. Anyhow, it's all dead and buried. What's the use of digging it up?"

"It's all very well for you to talk," Wolf asserted. "What about your blessed heroes?"

"Oh, that's different. They're just people—they might be real. Besides, Roland's a first-rate song—but all that stuff about a golden age! It probably never existed. They were awful tyrants, some of those Greeks."

"But one might try and make it real," Wolf murmured, lying back against the cushions. Sicard went on arguing, but he didn't really listen. A strange sort of excitement was welling within him, too unformed and tumultuous possibly to be called an idea. He wanted to get things clear and wished Sicard would stop talking. Pretending to be tired, he shut his eyes. It was quite a relief when Mabilia of Durban bustled in to see to a new dressing for his foot.

After that, Wolf seldom spoke of Trencavel. It had almost become as difficult to speak of him as of Montségur. Nor did he after all fulfill his plan to pay a visit to Pamiers, for their vacation was up before he was fit to travel, and then he had to return at full speed to Carcassonne.

At the back of Wolf's mind the emotions roused by his conversation with Sicard began to take on more definite shape. If Trencavel really cared about a golden age of the past, as Sicard made out, why shouldn't he see it as a real possibility for the future? Besides, he had proved well enough he cared for the present by his attitude toward Toulouse. If only he had spoken that day on the chase—but he had known too little then. And now in his very uncertainty the idea of broaching the subject seemed doubly difficult. Indeed, face to face with Trencavel's graciously evasive manner the whole idea seemed doubly difficult. Indeed, face to face with Trencavel's graciously evasive manner the whole idea seemed almost absurd. After all, he admitted bitterly, it had very likely been just imagination, and the poetry-writing, as Sicard suggested, a sterile academic sort of fad. At the first word he'd probably find himself laughed off as a presumptuous fool.

Certainly it seemed as though Trencavel, since the day of their ride, had retired into his natural shell of reticence.

But even if Wolf had dared speak there was little or no chance, for that autumn Trencavel was often away, apparently on some political mission or other, and even when Wolf formed one of his retinue there was little or no chance of personal contact. On one occasion Trencavel was absent from Carcassonne for a number of weeks. He had not revealed the actual purpose of his journey though it included, one gathered, a visit to Foix. Wolf, however, had not been chosen to accompany him. In a sense he was relieved. Something of the old awkwardness had always remained between him and his father, in spite of the unexpected satisfaction the Count of Foix had felt at his son's development.

Days passed. Messages came for the vassals, gifts for the viscountess. Wolf did his best to avoid her. Stirred by his growing manliness, Agnes, rankling at her failure in the past and unappeased despite her vengeance regarding Miriam Caravita, attempted new and more subtle overtures; but meeting with stoic resistance that verged almost on surliness, her ingratiating wiles soon changed to peevish rancor, and she even began to rake up old grievances against him, including his desertion of her darling Gogo at the festival more than a year ago. The insufferable little beast was still her inseparable companion on whom she lavished a devotion she certainly grudged her new-born child, and if Wolf ever met with the little Raimon it was to see him being carried far away from her chamber that she need not hear his lusty cries.

It was October, but the weather had become warmer, almost hot for the season, with something sultry and oppressive in the air; yet morning after morning broke and the sun would broil down with violent intensity, filling man and beast with restlessness and suspense.

Away to the south the line of the Pyrenees closed the horizon, heavy as lead.

To Wolf, feeling more and more the lack of daily services to Trencavel, the waiting became almost unbearable.

At last, at noon one day, a messenger arrived. The viscount's return could be expected to vespers.

Among the boys, the news aroused a sense of relief and a fresh burst of energy, so that they decided to spend the afternoon in the tiltyard, practicing some new feat of arms. The sun had vanished behind a veil of cloud, but the air grew increasingly stifling; a hot, sullen wind scudded over the ramparts, rousing a nervous fever that gave their blows something vicious and uncontrolled. And then suddenly, without warning, the rain came down, fierce, unrelenting, sweeping up from the south and blotting the mountains from view. Soon even the plain had vanished from sight.

Evening came but Trencavel had not returned. It was more than probable indeed that he would not come. By now a real gale was blowing, the rain poured down without cessation. Streams would be swollen, many of the fords doubtless impassable. He was almost sure to spend the night at a wayside inn or at the house of some vassal that lay on the road.

After the evening meal they had gathered in the hall, amusing themselves by boasting of their latest exploits and digging at each other, interrupted every now and again by Sicard who, poring over his tablets, would suddenly raise his head, worrying for a rhyme. Determined to parody the greatest virtuoso, he was trying to concoct a skittish series of seventeen-line verses on a single rhyme. They all joined in, helping, the proffered suggestions becoming every more ribald, until they too petered out in boredom, and most of them trailed off to bed. In the corner by the hearth Ville-mur was confiding his latest successes with Alys to a rak-ish young knight. At last Sicard threw down his tablets.

"Still only fifteen, curse it. Coming?" he yawned, and Wolf, who, having tried half a dozen occupations to calm his restlessness in vain had at last started mending his bowstring, hesitated, got slowly to his feet, and followed.

But sleep would not come. Outside, the wind howled and raged. He had loved it, that fierce tramontane wind that swept across the Pyrenean wall as if mocking the ease and lushness of the plains, but tonight, as he lay listening, it made him troubled and distraught. Might Trencavel af-ter all be riding through that storm? He had not cancelled his coming. Wasn't it his duty as squire to await him? He was almost about to slip once more into his clothes; but the thought that it would awaken Sicard and the others, and certainly arouse their scornful anger, stopped him, and he snuggled once more under the cover. It had turned uncomfortably cold, and the rain beating through the ill-fitting shutters even blew in sprays onto the bed. Likely enough, he persuaded himself, Trencavel was still enjoying festivities held in his honor at one of his vassals' castles where he had taken refuge on the way, hampered by a swollen ford, a broken bridge. A cold little fear began to invade him, but even as he reassured himself against such womanish forebodings it rose again in more palpable and grisly form. Was his possible host to be trusted? A poi-soned cup—a stab on the stairs? Trencavel had defied Toulouse. Before him with horrible clarity rose the fancied image of Castelnau, the lance's point plunged deep in his side. If Raymond did not stick at laying hands on the Pope's own legate, would he hesitate in regard to his feu-dal foe?

The last thought was accompanied by the sound of rending iron and a heavy thud. He started up wildly. Nothing! A shutter torn from its hinges. Beside him Sicard rolled over, muttering. After a moment, in the farther cor-ner, one of the boys began to snore.

Madness! he assured himself. Trencavel was coming from Foix. His own father might even accompany him. The possibility set him contemplating his own future. It might be that under the growing threat of war his father might even get the idea of taking him home. He wished he had forewarned the viscount and begged him to persuade his father to let him at any rate complete his term. Perhaps he would. But why should he? Did Trencavel care whether he stayed or not? Suddenly it struck him how impossible was the thought of leaving Carcassonne, or rather Trencavel's side. But that fear like the rest was absurd, one of those frenzied fantasies of which old Saissac had always warned them. He had another year before him. By that time what might not have happened?

In the act of trying every stoic precept to calm his senses he must at last have fallen into a doze, for it was from a web of tormented dreams that he was suddenly forced wide awake by the clatter of hoofs in the court below. In a moment he had sprung from his bed and was scrambling into his tunic, his only fear that the others might rouse or Villemur still be awake. But their breathing continued its unbroken monotony, and catching up a torch he was soon leaping down the spiral stairway. As he did so the thought that it might after all not be he caught him by the throat, but before it could become real the sound of Trencavel's voice, dismissing the guards, rose from below.

As usual he had dispensed with all attendance, and already he was crossing the hall to the stairs leading to his own apartments. He had mounted the first flight when, suddenly rounding the stone pier, he found himself face to face with the boy.

"Wolf!" He had stopped dead at the sight of him. "Is anything wrong?" he added anxiously, as the torchlight fell on the boy's hasty attire, the strange excited look on his face.

"No, oh no—only—I happened to hear you come."

"I'd better make you one of my bodyguard," Trencavel laughed, recovering himself.

Thrilling deeply, Wolf, lighting the way along the vast vaulted corridor, saw himself watching beside Trencavel in his tent, alone amid the sleeping armies at night.

The sight of a heavy tapestried curtain screening the arched doorway of the viscountess's bower recalled him rudely to the present. A wave of fury swept over him as he thought of the great carven bed in which Agnes was lying, her cheek resting in such apparent innocence on the white pillow, the insufferable Gogo curled at her feet. Involuntarily his feet lingered, unwilling.

Down a short flight of steps to the left a dim red glow shone through an open door. He stopped, hesitating.

"Well, if you're not too tired," Trencavel remarked at his elbow, "we might warm up a bit."

It was the room of which Sicard had spoken, a sort of sanctum in which Trencavel liked to spend many of his leisure hours. No one, indeed, would have dared disturb him there except on the most pressing business, so that even his squires had seldom had an opportunity of entering it, but in expectation of his coming that evening a fire had been lit. It had almost burned out, but a faint flicker still stirred among the smoldering embers, and as the boy threw on fresh logs the kindling flames darted high. He had fixed the torch in one of the brackets on the first holding it to the candle stuck in the metal sconce upon the table, and the strengthening light revealed a square smallish room furnished with a simplicity that amounted almost to austerity. Built into one of the towers, it belonged to the oldest part of the castle, dated in fact from the time of the Goths, and apart from hangings of heavy deep-green silk bordered with interlacings of metal thread, the walls were empty but for the glint of a few weapons; while the uncertain light playing on the rough-hewn masonry threw the jagged carving round door and window into crude relief. Nevertheless there was a certain conscious refinement in that simplicity which suggested it was the result of an almost fastidious selection rather than indifference. The detail of the few ornaments—the bronze sconce, a lion-shaped aquamanile by its side—was exquisite, while a number of scrolls and books lay half opened, as though forcedly abandoned in the middle of reading upon the simple couch.

With a little sigh of relief Trencavel, throwing off his rain-soaked cloak, spread his hands to the glow. He was wearing armor, and as Wolf, unbuckling the heavy sword belt, stripped off his surcoat, he could almost have wrung out the thin green silk in his hands.

"A hell of a night," Trencavel laughed. "Old Ademar was full of omens—owls, gibbets, and God knows what." Shaking the rain from his face, he stroked back the dark gold curls damp under the edge of his mail hood, and it seemed to the boy that his face, despite its laughter, looked strained and tired. It had lost something of its remote, untouched beauty of late; but what it had sacrificed in perfection was amply compensated by a greater vitality. The mask was somehow coming to life.

161

Struggling vainly with numbed fingers to loosen the straps of his hauberk, he resigned himself to Wolf's ministrations. "Our old tramontane's up to her tricks, all right. Maybe our friends from the north won't find it quite as comfortable down here as they imagine. That rain, I reckon, would scarce cure Philippe of his ague, of which evidently he is aware, and so prefers to sit snug at home, directing wars against John from his fireside. They say he moves armies on his chessboard."

"But not against us—hasn't he refused again?" Wolf looked up swiftly in the middle of loosening the spurs from his mailed shoes.

"To all appearances. But there are some who can play two games and more in their head at once—provided they've got the men." Divested of his armor Trencavel shivered a little, and wrapping himself in the furred robe that the boy had hung on his shoulders he sank with evident relief on the couch by the fire. "Burgundy's a good king, of course. As for a bishop, the fiery Amelric . . ." He laughed, it seemed to Wolf a little unnaturally, and his eyes looked feverishly bright.

"And the knights?"

"Still lacking—at present."

Turning toward the blaze, Trencavel desultorily watched the boy, who having poured wine into a bowl on the hearth was heating it on the fire. With studied care he sprinkled in the spices he had taken from a metal casket.

"I didn't know you were so versed in the herbal crafts," Trencavel smiled. "Thanks to the good monks, I suppose?" Then, seeing the flush mount to Wolf's cheeks, he added, laughing: "After all, even the gallant Gawaine proved himself quite a physician, besides which it's useful enough on a campaign." He paused a second. "You know where I've been?"

Wolf glanced at him, anxious, inquiring.

"Right through to Andorra, having a look at the fortifications. Innocent's Crusade, if it ever gets there, will meet with more, I guess, that it reckoned." Still his voice had that slightly forced and reckless note.

"But it won't," Wolf exclaimed eagerly. "Carcassonne's impregnable."

"The city, but they might by-pass it and make straight up the Ariège. The monks of Pamiers aren't to be trusted, and then . . ."

Before Wolf's eyes there rose a picture of the town that had witnessed the beginning of his new life, the great castellar that so proudly defied the grasping monastery of St. Anthony. If Pamiers stood in danger, then Esclarmonde and her Cathar hospice . . . "But they'd never get that far," he protested. "Toulouse—"

"Toulouse!" The word fell from Trencavel's lips with a bitter, choked sort of laugh. Wolf could not read the face gazing into the shadows. A moment passed before Trencavel, returning with an evident effort to the present, took the goblet from his hands and sipped at the steaming wine. "Well, anyhow, the vassals of Foix will stand firm. Your father has seen to that."

Wolf could imagine him, arrogant and indefatigable, taking a secret delight in dragging the Viscount of Carcassonne from crag to crag of his mountain fortress.

Gradually, as he drank, Trencavel's manner seemed to quieten.

"Roccafissada, Perelha, Lordat, Castelverdun—and the rest," he murmured, as though half to himself, his long slender fingers striking upon the golden cup as he counted the names, "they're a perfect chain. If it comes to the worst there'll be refugees flocking up there in shoals. The heretic missions will do their best, of course. They're organizing themselves in groups. Montségur is to be their center. Your aunt has put it at their disposal as the citadel of the faith. Very probably Guihalbert of Castres will be going up to consecrate it soon. The idea is that they should have their own bodyguard drawn from the nobility of the district."

He spoke almost casually now and without emphasis. In Wolf's hands the bowl from which he was about to refill his cup trembled. Perelha, Lantar, Castelverdun, Lordat— the sons of Luna and Cometa—then of course it would be Mirepoix too.

"Well, you're a Foix," Trencavel was saying, "and since you've learned a bit about chivalry by now . . ." He paused. Over the rim of the burnished cup he gazed searchingly at the boy. "It's what you've always been dreaming of, isn't it?" His lips curled to a faint smile, wistful, almost a shade ironic. "Didn't I tell you before—if once you get up there, God knows whether you'll ever come back—to earth."

In the silence, only the crackle of the flames was audible. "No, I shall come back." Wolf was surprised at the sound of his own voice coming out of the shadows.

For a moment Trencavel glanced at him, wondering, then shook his head. "The Countess, you know, told me a bit about you—only she wanted you to be quite free to find your feet. Wolf," he asked suddenly, "are you a heretic?"

A flush crept up the boy's cheeks. So Trencavel knew of his attending the meetings. "No," he murmured.

"Not that it really matters," the other continued; "hardly any of them are actual believers; but do you want to be?"

"I don't know." The answer came troubled, irresolute.

"Most of us don't," Trencavel replied, "but perhaps we long to want to be."

"Yes, in a way," Wolf attempted, not daring to look up. "They've got something we haven't."

"Faith."

"But must it be like that?"

"You mean, faith not in another world, but in this?"

Was it really happening, Wolf thought. "And yet it's so strange," he heard himself saying. "Somehow they're more alive than we are."

There was a moment's pause. Trencavel lay back, gazing blindly at the shadows cast by the flickering flames upon the vault of the ceiling. "Because they've got a common root of belief, while we—we've lost touch with our roots—even with reality. We're chasing after shadows."

"But can't we get back to it?"

"Return to the simple life—the pastoral community—living on cheese and goat's milk in wooden huts in the hills?" The old tinge of self-mockery was in his voice.

He was escaping again. Wolf made a violent effort: "If we had some common purpose, something to hold us all together—no, not looking back to the past, but forward."

Trencavel smiled a little bitterly. "We may have soon. We'll all be heretics then for them—whether we're believers or not, heretics or their protectors—spiritual libertines, equally malignant in the eyes of the Church and fit only for extermination."

Wolf, squatting cross-legged at his feet and with hands clasped round his knees, looked up at him perplexed. "But have they—up there—have they really faith in their Crusade?"

Taking a deep draught, Trencavel pushed aside the goblet. "It's easier to be unanimous in the cause of destruction than in the defense of a faith you have lost. The avenging Jehovah never lacked devotees. Perhaps the light-bringers will never be as popular as the dark avenging gods."

The boy stared into the flames dreamily. "Once upon a time, didn't they worship the sun-god on Montségur?"

"Abellio-Apollo," Trencavel murmured with half-closed eyes, "and the moon-goddess."

"Who gave birth to the sons of Luna?" Wolf echoed, still troubled by the thought of Mirepoix.

"Yes. And Cometa—all your mountain tribe—you're probably one of them yourself—true-born defender of Montségur. Didn't I tell you you'd soon be scorning this earth?" Again his voice had that note of ironic wistfulness. There was no getting past it, Wolf thought hopelessly.

For a time there was silence. Trencavel stared past him into the fire. Above the hearth the leaping flames threw into fitful illumination the frieze of riders carved on the mantelpiece. He had found it long ago half hidden among the long tangled grasses of an orchard—relic of a bygone age, lost among the debris of centuries, and bringing it home had had it built into the great rough-hewn chimney piece. Godlike youths of the strong and supple limb, the braided, filleted hair—still they rode their crisp-maned steeds, urging and leashing—toward what distant goal?

And yet could it not be here—here in the present—on this earth? Was it not their heritage, had not that people trodden this very soil, built from its rock those temples to their gods, held sports and sacrifice, been as gods themselves. Were they? he wondered, or had it been for them also a dream?

"They, too," he murmured, with a little gesture toward the frieze, "worshiped those gods. Do you like it?" he asked, as the boy, following his gaze, regarded the carving, earnest, preoccupied.

"Yes. It's as if . . ." He hesitated, trying to express what it really was that he felt.

Thrown into sharp relief by the deep-cut shadow, knit by the reiterate rhythm of those striding steeds, they rode on armed with javelin and shield, their faces resolute, upturned. "Somehow—it's as if they were riding into the morning."

Into the morning—deep down in Trencavel's own being something seemed to dawn.

"It makes one feel so strong and free," Wolf was saying, "and yet all bound together. It's like that sometimes—on the tilting field, out on the hunt—the feeling that you're part of a whole, as if you were doubly, trebly yourself, and yet part of something more."

"Part of a whole," Trencavel echoed; "part of the earth's whole rhythm. We've lost the sense of it—as if we were cut off at the roots. Perhaps that's what's really wrong. If one could re-establish a living relationship between things, between man and the seasons, between a people and their ruler. They must have had it once." Suddenly there rose before him a story told by his old nurse, long ago in his childhood. "Do you know," he said, "once upon a time the king had also to be a priest—the worker of magic—mediating between men and nature, safeguarding the seasons and the years till his powers failed and he became their sacrifice?"

"Their sacrifice?" the other echoed perplexed.

Raising himself a little on his elbow, Trencavel began to tell him the story of that ancient custom. "Kings had to die for the people," he ended.

Perhaps Wolf was struck by something strange in his voice, as though the words had a significance beyond the mere tale, for he broke out almost vehemently:

"But they must live for them first!" Eager, insistent, the words rose out of the shadowy firelit room. He had raised himself on his knees and was looking at him fixedly. "For all of them," he said; "not just us."

Now, he thought desperately, now if he missed the chance, it would be gone forever. To hide his confusion he bent over the hearth. At last, not daring to look up, "I was thinking," he began, stumbling and tentative, "it might begin up there—a new sort of community. If we founded a sort of order—not like the Cathars, but what we were talking about—an order . . ."

"Of knighthood—the knighthood of Montségur?" Trencavel tried to help.

"But bigger."

"You're very ambitious."

But now it was out, the boy was undeterred. "I mean,

166

it's got to include everybody. Everyone's got to be eligible. After all," he went on excitedly, "didn't they—the people who lived here once, before the Romans—who held the games," he nodded toward the carving—"didn't they have a sort of ideal state?"

"They dreamed of it. We've got the makeshift remnants of it anyway." He smiled a little ironically. "Our consuls—"

"But didn't the citizens have equal rights—didn't they divide the property?"

"At one time some of them tried."

"And then it went wrong—why?"

"Self-interest, jealousy, perhaps. The same thing as with us—lack of faith. Besides, there were still slaves anyway."

"But surely one could try again—better. If the Cathars do, why shouldn't we?"

Why shouldn't we?

Something was piercing to the root of Trencavel's being, tearing through a web of weariness and disillusion.

A new age, the rebirth of society. All they had spoken of tonight. A new faith that restored to men their rightful splendor in a living communion with the earth; that abandoning their chase for self-interest and power, their macabre rivalry in every form of luxury and vice, they would again tread the earth strong and beautiful, proud and free. He had dreamed of it often, only to see each new hope stifled in the demands of a conventional society he hated, in petty reforms that left the root of the evil unchanged. Who had understood?—the Cathars with their sad repudiation of the flesh, old Saissac with his bleak doctrines, poets with their fantasies perhaps? Always it had ended with the same abstractions, the same fleeting enthusiasms, the same loneliness. Was it because, after all, he had never got beyond his own privileged circle, never reached the people themselves? Would they, could they, have understood—those dark incalculable masses who had murdered his grandfather, on whom his own father had taken so terrible a revenge? He shuddered. And yet, wasn't it that which at the bottom had urged him on—redemption for the sins of his fathers?

"The people . . ." he began.

Suddenly a squall of wind sent a gust of rain hurling down the chimney. A plume of acrid smoke swept up over the lintel, obscuring the young athletes. As it cleared, the consciousness of the present swept over him, mocking those retreating dreams. To live for his people! If the Count of Foix had been right, it was something else they might demand of him soon. The business of living anyway might prove grim enough. The words half-formed died on his lips.

"War may come," he said.

Silence fell upon the room. Mechanically, to bridge over that sudden emptiness, Wolf threw fresh logs upon the fire. Then he looked up. "But couldn't that be the start?"

Still that eager light kindled the boy's face, striking home hard at Trencavel's doubt. Was that then the only way? Was the new world possible only with the complete destruction of the old? Then after all he had been right about Toulouse. In his relief he sprang up. Only then as he stood, swaying a little on his feet, was he suddenly aware of his exhaustion. But through it dawned a hope so overwhelming that as yet, in fear of being cheated, he retreated from it.

"Well, we'd better sleep while we can." Stiff and staggering a little, he moved mechanically across the room, and snatching down the torch Wolf followed.

Outside, the draught of the passage blew on them, reviving. At the door of Agnes's bower Trencavel turned, and for a moment stood gazing fixedly at the boy; then, reaching out his hand, hesitated and dropped it, suddenly afraid, so new, so strange was this invasion of his solitariness. "Only the present is ours. Besides, who knows what's going to happen on the strategical chessboard!" His voice had in it once more that hint of reckless laughter. "They haven't yet found the missing knight."

THE MISSING KNIGHT

Blow the trumpet among the nations . . . appoint a captain against her.

(JEREMIAH)

I

THE STORM THAT SWEPT RAVAGING OVER LANGUEDOC BEAT itself out against the rocky bastion of the Auvergne.

Beyond it to the north, in the pasture and cornlands of the Île, the earth lay tranquil, wrapped in a late autumnal trance. Under the thin blue haze green meadow and timbered homestead, woodland and winding stream wove to a tapestry of russet and sage and gold, in which the yellow of the cornstacks, the red of a roof glowed warm and soft as the apples drooping over the gray-green lichen-stained walls. Bathed in that glimmering radiance, the earth seemed to lie under an enchantment, as if time had ceased and that landscape of a late October day must remain forever, bodiless and without solidity—an image hung upon the eye, motionless as the poplars standing sentinel before the castle rock.

For all that there was a nip in the air—a keenness that incited to action, quickening movement and sharpening appetite; and in the great hall of Montfort l'Amaury, Simon de Montfort, rightful Earl of Leicester, consumed the meal before him with a gusto that surpassed even his customary vigor of attack, a fact that was hardly surprising, for the frame which that ample repast was intended to fill was massive, and behind him lay the best part of a day's journey on horseback.

Looking back on his history, the past months, even years, revealed a picture that presented him as seldom out of the saddle, scouring and harrying the countryside in the service of his king. While further back the theater of his activities projected an endless vista, over a series of years and as many lands, culminating in the deserts of Palestine and the Fourth Crusade. His travel, indeed, might have taken him yet farther afield had it not been for his religious fervor, which equaling his physical energy forbade him to participate in an enticing side show in Greece where the deposed Emperor Isaac Angelus was struggling to wrest his lost kingdom from the grasp of a usurping brother. The adventure had promised to be lucrative, or entertaining to say the least, but Simon had had enough of delay. Already the army, embarking at Venice, had been diverted from its sacred aim by aiding the Venetians to recapture Zara from the Magyars. The Holy Cause stood in jeopardy. "I have come to free the Holy Sepulcher," Simon had growled, adamant against bribe and entreaty, "not to patch up the quarrels of kings"; and almost alone among his peers he had set sail from Venice to join the twin branch of the crusading army that had set out from Marseilles.

But his piety had scarce found its merited reward, and certainly not proved as profitable as might that little excursion to Greece. He had returned to France even poorer perhaps than he had set out. Nor had the years that followed brought him more leisure and ease. Philippe's interminable conflict with England, added to his own restless passion for activity, had enriched him in military experience but not in pocket. Week was added to week, month to month, in lending a hand in some territorial quarrel or another, quelling this and that revolt, till the years had passed and he had spent little time on his own estates. Those in England were gone anyway, confiscated by John. But for the present, though he had sworn himself to serve his forty days on the proposed Crusade against the heretic-ridden south, he looked forward to spending his never-failing resources of energy in the ordering of his own estates. They were not particularly large or remunerative, but with care they proffered the chance of steady development. Nor had they been allowed, despite his military vicissitudes, to fall into neglect. His wife, Alys de Montmorency, had seen that, and during her husband's protracted absences had ruled vassal and serf with as energetic and exacting a hand as she did her own maids; her thrift, which revealed a veritable genius for combining quality with quantity, being indeed proverbial.

She sat there now at his side, partaking of the meal before her with as much enjoyment if not in equal measure as her husband, though to do her justice her capacity fell not so much behind his own. She spoke little, her silence dictated no more by timidity than was his by any epicureanism (his palate was singularly lacking in finesse), but rather by a mutual recognition of the necessity of giving one's full attention to the task at hand, whether it consisted in planning a maneuver, gnawing a cutlet, or supervising the combing of wool in the barn. Indeed, the complete understanding between them was based on no surrender of the female spirit but on an equilibrium of forces that nature or repeated separation had rendered completely independent, the fact that even when reunited the balance was retained being due to the clear definition of their functions. The man's place was to command—to fight or hunt as the case might be; the woman's to foster and regulate the household. In his absence she might take upon herself some of his privileges as ruler; on his return they were relinquished unequivocally. Certainly her own sphere of rule offered scope enough, for her responsibilities extended, if conceived in the full feudal sense, to the welfare of vassal and serf—the structure of that system, though apparently so arrogantly masculine, depending, in its emphasis on the family unit, almost as much on her as on him. Probably the wily woman, fully aware of her own importance, took a secret delight in the fact that by this trivial concession to men's vanity she remained in secret the true upholder of the system's stability. At any rate she was wise enough not to show it. The very atmosphere of the hall, furnished with comfort rather than ostentation and betraying a somewhat old-fashioned and conservative solidity, wore, despite the array of weapons and armorial shields over the hearth, an almost patriarchal air, while the high seat on which Simon de Montfort sat suggested that by rights it should be flanked, if not by lines of warriors, then certainly by a complete array of the members of his own household. Two long and ever-diminishing rows of offspring, ranked in strict organ-pipe formation, would certainly have appeared more at home there than any flaunting assembly of fashionable guests.

As it was, the family circle was sadly depleted. Two of his sons were training as esquires in houses far off, while his elder daughter had been destined for the vocation of a nun. (It was at the time of the Crusade and the house of Montfort had had little to spare for dowries.) She had been a plain and sickly creature anyway.

That, however, was scarcely likely to be the fate of the plump, apple-cheeked lass at Simon's side. He watched her seated there, her attention divided between her half-remembered father and the chicken bone in her hand. He would plan a good marriage for her. The child was worthy of it—a determined little wench enough, fit for the son of a king. She'd stay it, too, different from that little bawd they'd tried to palm off on Richard of England—heiress of France. Pah! He hadn't been having any—his own father's strumpet—preferred to settle his quarrels by the sword. Lost little time with women all round, for which he wasn't to blame, seeing how they played fast and loose—not Alys, of course, though with all his long absences she'd had excuse enough. Under his heavy eyebrows he glanced approvingly at his wife. She was comely enough still—a little stouter perhaps—but he could never see anything in those straight-limbed, hipless creatures that were all the fashion of late. A man must have something to catch hold of. No wonder they couldn't keep their wives in leash, slipping out of their hands like an eel, demanding that men should leave their bodies and woo their soul. Rank hypocrisy! But it was polluting the land like the plague. Of course it all came from the same source of depravity—the stinking south. One would never have thought northern women would fall for that rubbish. She wouldn't any-way—good sound stock, the Montmorencys, and the Mar-lys with them. Those boys of Bouchard's, fine strapping fellows, and as devoted to their father as to a king, though there was no nonsense about that either.

His broad, furrowed brow contracted a little. Perhaps if he'd had more chance of seeing his own lads when they were growing up it might have been the same with them. He'd taken Amery about with him wherever he could and he'd been docile enough, dutiful to the point of subservi-ence, but there was something lacking in the lad. No spark. He would have liked it better, after all, if he'd shown a bit of rebelliousness somewhere, even at the cost of a good hiding—like that three-year-old rascal upstairs. They'd have some tussles between them, he guessed. The little beggar had insisted clamorously, it seemed, on being brought down to the yard to see his father ride in across the bridge. But then—Simon recalled the incident with a certain glee—he'd be blowed if the youngster hadn't stood there stock-still and staring, and then, proceeding on his short sturdy legs to make a careful inspection of his horse and retinue, had turned away with an air of offended indifference. Recalled to join in the general ritual of welcome, he had stood firm. "But you're not my father," he had insisted, till on repeated persuasion he had pouted his lips: "But they said where Montfort moves the lion leaps—there's no lion," he cried, and turning his broad little back he had marched off in high dudgeon. Pigheaded young rascal, there was no cheating him. They'd have some spars. Simon against Simon. He chuckled to himself and washed down the last mouthful with a deep gulp of wine.

"Good stuff," he muttered, looking up at the man who stepped foward to refill his goblet. "Better than the muck we got on the campaigns, though a man's glad enough of it there. Where did it come from, Jehan?"

"Burgundy, sir. The Duke sent it. Heard you were coming home belike. Kind of an inside housewarming," he grinned, gazing admiringly at his master through twinkling peasant eyes. There was little formality between Montfort and his men—it was one of the causes of the close bond between them. No leader had been so loved and trusted by any army—trusted and feared—but he exacted as much from himself as he did from them. They knew it, and that where danger was, he'd be the first to go in.

"Burgundy!" Montfort laughed, wiping his heavy drooping mustache upon his sleeve. "Didn't know he held us in such esteem."

"And he sent us all that sugarplum," cried little Yolande excitedly, the succulent allure of the condiments proving too much of a strain on that hard-imposed ritual of silence. "Look!" Reaching across the table with an impulsiveness that won the frowning reproof of her mother, she took a candied orange from a dish, and holding it by its sugar stalk dangled it before her father's eye. "Is it really true," she asked, creasing her smooth brow, "that they grow on trees down in the south?"

"Hm," Simon growled. "Down in the hottest parts—gaudy, deluding things like the people themselves—no substance. Nothing to get your teeth into, like a good sound northern apple." Leaning forward, he took one from the dish. "You'll be spoiling that pink and white skin of yours with those sickly things," he mumbled, and then carefully, with an unexpected deftness of those great hairy hands, began to peel the apple. Slowly, inch by inch, under the unswerving action of the knife, the red-gold ribbon loosed itself and grew, gleaming, transparent, dangled and curled, an ever-growing spiral, then fell—a mottled snake coiling upon the board. He had delighted her with the feat last time he came home, but now as she watched, musing, her thoughts were far away. "I'd like to go there," she said.

"Where?" Montfort growled, but her mother was already speaking about the apple crop and the rich harvest that had almost burst the granaries this summer.

They had finished dessert and, rising, speaking the grace he never missed, even at a short snack on the battlefield, Montfort crossed to one of the deep-arched windows and looked out over the green meadows and pasturelands. "I must have a look round tomorrow. By what old Martin was saying as I rode in through the manor, you've done well, Alys," and he smiled, gazing down on his wife, who seating herself in the splayed recess had taken up her sewing. She had no special love for needlework, but idleness was to her intolerable and indeed quite unimaginable. Besides, how could one expect good work from one's maids if one shunned it oneself? Having begun, she sewed swiftly and with determination.

"It was a good year," she said. "You'll find everything in order; only down at the ford, that new tenant . . ." He listened, watching her quiet, matter-of-fact industry with gratification. That was what women should be. Give them no time for that highfalutin nonsense—nourishment of the soul—let them look to safeguarding their bodies. But it was only part of the general rot, like all this obsession with luxury and display.

"I wonder what Burgundy really wants," he muttered, his mind inevitably wandering to the lavish court of the duke.

Alys went on with her sewing. "Perhaps he wants you," she said quietly "to join him on the Crusade."

"Pah! If it ever comes to it. But till Burgundy moves his fat carcass it'll be a bit late—and the whole affair—Philippe will always get out of it. Nevers, St. Pol, and the rest? Ask me, the thing's half arranged already. A pleasant excursion to the sunny south—who wants to fight? Had

174

enough of it in the East—but it tickles their fancy to have a look in themselves before Babylon falls. If fall it does. I've taken the Cross, but I've not taken it in play. I've told Burgundy already. I'll do my forty days. I'll do more. I'll wipe Toulouse clean of every vile heretic in the place. See them burned to charcoal in the flames of their own sacrificial fires. But I'm not going to decorate his fancy army to frighten those southern milksops into a sham surrender while he sits and guzzles with Toulouse."

Alys de Montmorency looked up. Regarding her husband from under straight fair brows, her blue-gray eyes wore a look of mingled amusement and pride. Decorate, she thought, was scarcely a word a stranger would use in regard to that massive figure. The broad, thickset shoulders, the rugged, almost raw-boned head. With its mighty high-arched nose broadening a little too much at the nostril and the heavy rather protruding brows under the shaggy mane, Simon certainly had little in common with the elegant smooth-locked cavaliers who had followed in the train of Burgundy and the French king that time she had seen them at the opening of the court before her marriage, long ago; and there flashed through her mind the memory of the day she had first seen him, her future bridegroom, when her father brought him in to claim her hand—thickset even then, and when he walked, even a bit bowlegged, like those who from childhood have seldom been out of the saddle. And yet as he stood there looming above her, formidable, almost leonine in effect, her pulses had quickened. Even now . . .

"Burgundy knows what you're worth," she smiled, her teeth gleaming white and strong between long firm lips. "You'd make short work of them."

"Little valor needed for that," he mocked. "Smash their heads on their own guitars. Don't know what fighting is— the dastards. Saw enough of them in the East. But it's more than a drubbing they want," he grunted savagely.

"I believe," said Alys, biting off the end of a thread, "if you had your way you'd wipe them off the face of the earth."

He had turned again to the window, his eyes—brown or hazel, one could scarcely tell, so deep were they buried under the beetling brows—glared out over the mellow landscape. "It's all they're fit for, the swine."

She went on stitching, placid, unmoved. "You're rather

175

sweeping," she remarked without expression. "There must be some who—"

"They're all tainted," he muttered, "before they're out of their mother's womb. It's like a canker—sooner or later the rot's bound to set in."

"And so the only cure is to cut it out, even where it's not yet visible," she concluded; her voice, clear, matter-of-fact, rather loud, was incapable of mockery.

"One can't take any risks," he muttered. "The contagion'll spread. It's spread far enough already. If it's not stopped," he glanced at his little daughter, who seated on a stool over a piece of embroidery had observed her father's rough eloquence with secret curiosity—"Do you want it to get *her* too?" He laughed harshly.

Feeling herself the center of the conversation, the child looked up.

"What's to get me?" she cried, interested.

"Be quiet, child; mind your own business," Alys remarked without turning.

For little Yolande, however, now that her tremendous and almost legendary father had returned, that tone of maternal command, usually perfunctorily if not readily obeyed in the knowledge of the certain disaster it would bring to those who ignored it, had today lost much of its authority.

"But I'm not rotten and I don't catch things," she persisted. "When Amery was ill with the fever it never touched me, and when Guy and Michael had it I got it so lightly I was well in two days, and the doctor who came to see us because Guy had to be bled—"

"Hush, little girls should be seen and not heard."

"And the doctor said," she continued, breathless, "he had a head bald as an egg and when he bent down over the bed to see whether I had the right sort of spots, like Michael, but they'd nearly all gone, and I started playing a tune on it with my knuckles—"

"The pert little hussy!" Simon chuckled, inwardly rejoicing at the thought of his daughter playing tricks with Master Geoffrey. She had avenged him, he thought gleefully, for many a foul draught and filthy vomitory the old fusspot had poured into him in the days when he had been brought back all but dead to this castle, and the wound that must have killed anyone else had healed on him in five weeks.

"Now off with you, to the nursery where you belong with such babyish chatter, for a child of your age should know better," Alys began.

Pouting, Yolande looked questioningly from one to another. "Obey your mother," Simon echoed.

Under that stern implacable frown, slowly and reluctantly she began to move toward the door, but, suddenly turning, looked straight at her father, mischievous, laughing. "And he said," she cried triumphantly, "like father like daughter—the devil's own!" And before he could get her she was gone, her flaxen pigtails dancing behind her as she ran.

Simon glared after her, the muscles of his heavy face contracting with pretended rage and mirth. In the wake of her puckish glee, rancor became powerless. But he would pay back that crabbed old physician for his impudence, he swore, laughing and settling himself in the bay of the window.

"Well, Alys," he said, looking down at the close-wimpled head, "it almost looks as though our last two are going to put the rest in their pocket."

"And you too, if you're not careful."

How smooth her cheeks were, he thought, a shade less rosy perhaps, but firm and clear-cut still. Scarcely a wrinkle round the eyes, not a trace of cosmetics ruining that skin. After all, a man deserved to enjoy a bit of his wife after a life of campaigns. He'd make a long stay of it this time. As a rule there'd been scarce time enough for another lion cub to be conceived. "And the Lord shall bless him and multiply his seed." He could not deny that God had looked after him in those brief hours of respite.

"It's good to be home," he said.

"But you never stay." Her voice held neither reproach nor sorrow. "Soon I suppose you'll be going off south?"

"Doubtful," he shrugged, "if Burgundy ever moves. And he'll be back soon enough. A little booty and they're content—same old story. Saw enough of it on the Crusade."

There was a moment's pause. "Had there been more like you," she said, "I believe they'd even have won the Sepulcher. If Burgundy and Cîteaux had any sense they'd give you the command."

"Me? Wouldn't quite suit the good Duke, I fancy. My ways might prove a bit too thorough for his liking."

"The Abbot will scarcely blame you for that—he's zeal-

177

ous enough." She lifted her head from her sewing and looked at him earnestly. There was a hard, sharp light in her eyes. "If it comes to it, they ought at least to give you a position worthy of your rank; John or no John, you're rightful Earl of Leicester."

"And simple seigneur of Montfort l'Amaury."

"Your lineage," she held her point, "is as good as Philippe's."

But there was a flaw there. It could be traced at a pinch over William of Hennegau to a daughter of Charles the Bold, but also and more popularly to a bastard of Robert Capet.

"Let Burgundy find out my worth by the power of my sword stroke," he muttered. "I'm not going to fawn on that flaunting Colossus."

She gave her harsh, rather humorless laugh. "You're a bit hard on him; after all, he was a good enough soldier in his time, and he seems well inclined toward you."

Further argument, however, as she knew well enough, was vain, for Simon, despite the excellence of that wine, was pretty well proof against blandishments of that variety, and indeed a rising impatience was taking hold of him. He had come home and it almost seemed that his wife was only waiting for him to be off again. A dark suspicion began to invade him. Was *she* then also tainted by this besetting disease? He glanced up and chid himself at once for his conjecture. That clear-cut, upright head, those frank, rather hard gray eyes—ambitious, perhaps. After all, she was a Montmorency, and he'd hardly shone, except in good hard fighting. Might have got further than he had with a bit of flattery, but it wasn't his mark, and he'd never thought she yearned for courts and splendor. No, even now he'd give her her due. It was more for him than for herself. She was a proud woman surely, but blameless, and doing her part that the pride of the race should be upheld. Well, she wouldn't find him lacking either. One day he'd still get back his earldom from that scheming John. In the meantime, if it ever came to a Crusade against the cursed Albigenses, he'd do his duty and do it well, by God, if the Lord gave him a chance. Wipe their abominations from the face of the earth. His rage rose with redoubled violence, inflamed by the sense of injury he had done his wife. Blaspheming heretics! They poisoned even one's thoughts, undermining the sanctity of the family, besmirching the blessing of the marriage bed. The seed of Adam spurned as Satan's! Scarce one in that Albigensian Gomorrah, he guessed, but was born out of wedlock. Christ, if he had his way he'd force those languorous soulful bitches to be brought to bed yearly and let them scream. His eyes rested on the full, firm-bosomed woman beside him. She had suckled her last two herself. Perhaps that was why they seemed more full-blooded than the rest. Simon, the rogue, he'd have it out with him then and there. He felt like a tussle.

He rose, grunting, to his feet. "Let's have a look at that little rascal," he muttered, laughing.

II

It was three or four weeks later that a messenger arrived, despatched in haste by the venerable Abbot Gui de Vaux-Cernay, who, returning from Cîteaux via Paris, was, it appeared, the bearer of important letters to be delivered personally into Simon's hands. Montfort l'Amaury lay off his path. Might a meeting be arranged between them at one of the castles lying nearer his route?

Simon had never failed to show deference to the Church, and a grim November day saw him riding along with his usual determination between barren fields and rain-sodden copses on his way to the little stronghold of Rochefort.

At first he had tried to puzzle out what the good abbot might want. Why the mystery? He had letters—but from whom? The message had been vague. After a time, however, for he was not one to trouble about difficulties till they became realities, his mind turned to other thoughts.

The weather was dismal, the landscape on that unfriendly November day dull and monotonous, and his thoughts drifted to his own fireside, to Alys, a romp with young Simon, a draught of that rich Burgundy wine. Was the duke after all perhaps connected with these mysterious letters? Alys had suggested it, but her mind was always running away on the subject since the receipt of those presents. He had almost begun to feel surprised that he hadn't received some bothering request by now concerning

179

the marriage, very likely, between one of Burgundy's vassals and some widow on his own estates—troubling over the marriage settlement or vassalage, maybe. But nothing had materialized. Hardly likely that the Cistercian had anything to do with it. He cursed the trip all the same, though he'd make some use of it while he was here. The forests behind Rochefort were famed for the hunt.

It was afternoon when, topping the crest of the last incline, he saw, at the far end of the valley stretched at his feet, the little fortress standing somber and grim at the convergence of two wooded ridges of hill. The place looked anything but inviting, and a guest would certainly have been better received at Montfort l'Amaury. Still, it had been the prelate's own choice, and by what he said he had little time to enjoy prolonged hospitality.

The melancholy of the scene seemed intensified as he reached the level ground. Apart from the lonely fort, hardly a sign of human habitation was in sight but for the low roofs of a few farm buildings half hidden among straggling groups of alders. Except for a band of lurid primrose in the far west the sky hung dark and lowering. The wind came in sudden gusts, wildly bending the black imprecating arms of the sallows down by the stream.

It blew yet wilder on the great plain to the southeast, and the two little Cistercians, urging their reluctant nags along the rough highway, wrapped themselves tighter in their white robes.

Their conference took place in the chapel. Warmed with braziers and lit by the tapers on the altar table, it was the most hospitable place in that dreary fort; moreover, Simon de Montfort's simple piety would not have let him forgo any opportunity of receiving the formal blessing of so venerable a man as the Abbot of Vaux-Cernay. Apologies for the poverty of the reception soon proved superfluous, for it was clear at once that the Abbot Gui's business was too pressing to make him care about his surroundings. Perhaps he cared very little about them at any time. The goal was important, not the way. The soul's salvation, not its felicity.

Simon had become acquainted with him on the occasion of the Palestinian Crusade, and his straightforward efficiency had always appealed to him. But it was the face of the abbot's companion that at once arrested his attention, for it seemed to him that he had certainly met before that small undergrown figure, almost annihilated by the wide ample robes, out of which the thin scraggy neck protruded like that of a plucked bird. But the miserable body was made up for by the extraordinary vitality of the eyes. Where had he seen them last? Simon kept wondering as he felt himself fixed by their sharp piercing gaze. The mystery was soon solved as the abbot introduced him—Pierre de Vaux-Cernay, his nephew, monk of his own abbey and, of late, zealous assistant in the pious work of the most venerable Abbot of Cîteaux. At once there flashed on Simon's memory the occasion of their meeting. Surely it had been at Orleans nearly a year ago, from the rostrum erected in the cathedral square, that those sharp birdlike eyes under the receding forehead had stared down upon the crowd, while the great Arnaud-Amelric delivered his thundering tirade?

" 'For lo, I will raise and cause to come up against Babylon an assembly of great nations from the north and they shall set themselves in array against her.' "

They had flocked to his standard, baron and priest, layman and duke, in the first wild outburst of enthusiasm— that the prophecy of the Lord be fulfilled against the despoiler of His kingdom, the ravaging monster, the incestuous beast that had made her lair in the land of the Albigenses.

Simon had been among the first who had been enrolled that day, and now as he felt Pierre de Vaux-Cernay's eyes upon him he remembered how they had fixed him then, as they fixed and appraised everything, not so much in searching question but as if they automatically registered and marked their man. Was this visit, then, really connected with the Crusade? He had not long to wait for enlightenment, for the businesslike abbot soon came to the point, and drawing a packet from his voluminous robes handed it to Montfort. It contained a letter, he said, from Eudes, Duke of Burgundy. So that little matter was going to be cleared up, too, Simon smiled to himself.

A few minutes later the abbot was seated in one of the carven stalls beside a sconce of tapers and, breaking the seal of the parchment, prepared himself to read.

The day was fast beginning to fade, but in the long narrow windows behind the great stone piers the Montfort arms glowed in a last refulgence of gold and crimson. Beneath them, a little way behind the abbot, the small birdlike figure of Pierre de Vaux-Cernay had posted itself in the shadow of a giant column.

The letters commenced with the usual phrases of adulation, and the perspicacious Gui, though he made enough of the duke's recognition of Simon's prowess, knew his man too well to linger long on these time-worn and unctuous compliments. The long and short of the matter appeared to be that the duke urged Simon to give him full aid and assistance in the pious work of combating that fearful menace to God's rule on earth, the most hideous heresy of the Albigenses.

So Alys had been right after all. Burgundy wanted his help.

And to this end, the little abbot continued, it had been agreed to put forces at Montfort's disposal.

Immediately there rose in Simon something of his old truculent resistance. As he'd thought, Burgundy was going to shift the work onto him. The Cistercians had probably been badgering the duke, threatening him because of his procrastination, and to satisfy them he was going to make this show. The Church would trust him—Montfort, the man who'd refused to be sidetracked on the Palestinian Crusade. Clear. They'd let him do the fighting and then leave him high and dry.

"And his grace the Duke?" he muttered irritably.

"Will take no less a burden upon his shoulders."

A blustering laugh broke from Simon's breast. He could imagine the sort of burden that would rest in those corpulent and capacious arms.

"I have taken the Cross," he growled, "before the venerable Abbot of Cîteaux."

The blatantly insulting evasion of the duke's name was not lost on the little abbot, and something like a smile played round his close trim lips.

"The instruments of the Lord are many," he murmured, his eyes returning to the page before him.

"And that this plague be wiped from the face of the earth, the papal legate, the most venerable Abbot of Cîteaux, the Duke of Burgundy, the Counts of Nevers and St. Pol offer to Simon de Montfort, Earl of Leicester, the command of an entire force."

Simon had begun to pace up and down impatiently, but at the last words the ring of the mail-shod feet upon the tiles suddenly ceased.

"The command?" he muttered hoarsely.

"The full command." The neat fingers of Gui de Vaux-Cernay pointed out the black letters traced upon the scroll.

Through Simon's reeling brain images surged wildly—the fulfillment of his long-neglected fame. Alys's ambition, the glory of his house. But still there battled against them the stubborn independence of his race, refusing to be bribed and cajoled into a snare for the Duke of Burgundy's ease.

"I have come home to order my estates," he retorted.

Abruptly the Cistercian raised his head. "It is the estate of the Lord, Christ's kingdom on earth, that is in peril."

Had they miscalculated? Was the man after all not the zealot they had imagined? But no, his very stubbornness was the core of his strength that would keep him at the task once he was brought to undertake it, unswerving, unrelenting, till the purpose of God was fulfilled.

"It was not so you spoke that time we returned from the Crusade," he began once more. "But even the blackness of the heathen is as nothing against the vileness of those who have known God and repudiated Him. There is no sin as dark as that of heresy." Still he regarded Montfort with unperturbed assurance. Only his fingers began to play impatiently with the seal of the scroll.

"Have they not rejected baptism, spurned the Holy Communion, denied the Redemption, spat upon the Cross? Have they not exalted the Jews, condemned marriage as fornication, and, decrying the unborn child as the devil's, slain it in the womb?

"Have they not denounced justice, abolished the death penalty, and condoned lawlessness through the land, till no man's property is safe, the abbeys are robbed, the churches violated, brothels masquerade as convents, and courtesans as the brides of Christ?"

He paused, his breath failing under such unaccustomed rhetoric, but he had noticed the old fanatic look, the leonine fury dawn on Simon's face.

"The reign of Antichrist is heralded on earth. Would you stand by and see it triumph?

"Would you set yourself against God, would you spurn what He would lay in your hands?"

In his? An abyss seemed to open before Simon's eyes. Had he not sworn it? If God gave him the chance. To efface the evil, to expunge it from the face of the earth, to ravage with fire and sword till the last heretic was destroyed, till Babylon lay annihilated in ashes and dust.

Yet even now the innate realism of the man fought against the terrific fantasies of his obsession. If the work was to be done, it must be carried out to the end.

"The forces," he muttered. "They are pledged for forty days, and then—am I to depend on mercenaries?"

The little abbot rose to his feet. "There is no rock on which man can depend but God."

For a long moment there was silence but for the sound of Montfort's heavy breathing, the splutter of a candle as the grease ran down the wick.

Outside, the last rays of daylight had faded, and in the narrow lancet windows, where the arms of Montfort had glowed defiant, the leaded glass had turned black, opaque. Gigantic, the column loomed out of the shadows.

"And Babylon shall become heaps, a dwelling place for dragons, an astonishment and an hissing without an inhabitant."

Had someone spoken?

Suddenly Simon became aware of the younger monk. He stood there motionless, his hands folded in the long loose sleeves of his garment, his eyes fixed full upon him, two fiery points in a depth of darkness.

"Was it not written in the prophecies?"

The narrow, ill-shaped lips scarce seemed to move; only the eyes gleaming, devouring.

"For out of the north there cometh a nation against her which shall make her land desolate and none shall dwell therein."

Was it the voice of the little Cistercian or the thundering echo from the rostrum in the cathedral square?

"Set up a standard in the land, blow the trumpet among the nations, prepare the nations against her . . . appoint a captain against her.

"Thou art my battle-ax and weapons of war: for with thee will I break in pieces the nations, and with thee will I destroy the kingdoms."

Where was he? Around Simon the darkness flared, kindled with the fires of a world's extinction.

Blindly, floundering, he struggled back to the present, to the narrow chapel in the fortress of Rochefort.

A symbol, a sign! Still trembling on the brink of his inebriation, the soul of Simon de Montfort reached out for divine certitude. And then suddenly with a heave of his great shoulders he drew himself erect, and with unflinching determination strode up the altar steps. Flinging open the great Psalter he laid his finger upon the page.

"Read!"

It was a challenge to God himself. And for an instant, in the dim-lit chapel, the great stone columns seemed to rock, the light of the tapers darken. Or was it only the shadow of the Cistercian mounting the altar steps?

And yet perhaps even then, through the heart of the unknown, beyond the irrelevancies of time and space passed a convulsive shudder, and the cataclysm evoked by the hazard of a fanatic and truculent French baron, the machinations of a crafty Cistercian monk were but a faint dim echo of another lap in a vast and unending battle of dual powers, while nations rise and fall—*ad majorem Dei gloriam.*

"From the ninety-first psalm, the eleventh verse. 'For He shall give His angels charge over thee, to keep thee in all thy ways.' "

On the ear of Simon de Montfort the words fell not in the voice of man, but as distant thunder.

" 'Thou shalt tread upon the lion and adder: the young lion and the dragon shalt thou trample under feet.

" 'Because he hath set his love upon Me, therefore will I deliver him: I will set him on high, because he hath known My Name.' "

At the foot of the altar steps Simon de Montfort lay upon his knees. He did not see the smile on the face of the abbot, the triumphant gleam in the birdlike eyes of Pierre de Vaux-Cernay.

At last, lifting his head, he made the sign of the Cross. Then slowly, but with unshatterable certitude, he rose to his feet. He had called upon the Lord and the Lord had

185

spoken. He was no more the petty seigneur of Montfort l'Amaury, the owner of a confiscated earldom in a far-off land. He was the Knight of Christ, God's chosen vassal; and in his hands—in his—the scourge of the Lord.

THE SWORD LEAPS

Lo vescoms de Bezers no fina noit ni jorn
De sa terra establir, car mot avoit gran cor.
En tant cant lo mons dura n'a cavalier milhor,
Ni plus pros ni plus larg, plus cortes ni gensor. . . .
E sels de son païs, de cui era senhor,
No avian de lui ni regart ni temor.
Enans jogan am lui co li fos companhor. . . .
         (*La Chanson de la Croisade Albigeoise*)

I

TO LANGUEDOC, IN THE FOLLOWING YEAR, SPRING CAME
with a violent onslaught, an almost frenzied burgeoning of
leaf and flower. From the heights of the Pyrenees the
melting snows swept in roaring torrents through the
gorges, plowing deep channels in the river beds, till widening they burst, churning and frothing into the valleys. Already the knotted stumps of the vines were wreathed in
frills of emerald green. In the orchard and garden the
boughs of the peach trees reared bunches of deep-rose
blossom against distant peaks still clad with snow.

The earth was a riot of vegetation, of breaking bud and
windblown petal already outrun by the precocious forming
fruit. Seldom had the promise of harvest seemed so rich,
as if, in very defiance of the foe that threatened it, all the
fecundity of that southern earth were gathering in a last
refulgent outburst of its glory, drowning all sense of
presage in a turbulent swelling urge toward consummation.

All was in commotion, caught up in the general flux.

From village and farm the drovers led forth their flocks
in unending procession to their summer pastures in the
high hills. Herds of sheep and cattle blocked road and
ford. Here and there between that heaving mass of animal
life, the baaing and lowing, the munching of grazing

beasts, the sound of a pipe played by some shepherd taking his midday rest came, cool, remote.

Away from the foothills, along the highways fringed by chestnut and poplar, and winding to the vast hot plain, the huge yoked oxen plodded with imperturbable gravity, drawing their ponderous wagons to the distant towns.

As the land flattened, the gradient of the seasons, too, decreased. Beneath a staring canopy of azure the earth spread like a table, varied only by low ridges of rocky hill, on which each little town and hamlet, each figure traveling along the road, stood out in unrelieved brilliance, until arid and bare beneath a pall of whitened dust it sank at last to the naked level of the Mediterranean and lay consumed by the glaring light, almost indifferent to the passing of the seasons, oblivious of time and change.

Down by the coast the very air seemed withered up but for hot dry gusts that, blowing from Africa, choked more than they refreshed, sending a little shudder through the gaudy sails of the feluccas moored on the great lagoons. On the brink of the brackish marsh flamingos stalked, dipping their long necks in the ooze.

The harbor of Narbonne lay ablaze under the sun. It was past the midday hour, but many of the laborers were still lounging idly on the quays, or lying asleep stretched in the shadow of an overhanging cornice.

Following in the wake of an elderly knight, Wolf of Foix guided his horse through the stacks of merchandise that littered the quays, or, unloaded from some giant trader, were just being trundled into cellars or hoisted into the lofts of a warehouse above his head. Around him alien humanity swarmed, a tangle of dark-bronzed limbs and faces, strange voices, fragments of a foreign tongue. Hot and tired as he was from the interminable ride over the dusty plain, his weariness was soon banished by excitement, and he glanced with growing interest at the medley of human faces that swarmed about the port—merchants from Italy, Levantines perhaps, turbaned Moslems from Africa and Spain interspersed by the black shining skins of Negroes. On his rare visits to Narbonne, through which he had now and again passed on the way to Béziers, he had seen little more than the part of the city surrounding the castle, and so varied and fascinating was the spectacle that now presented itself that it was with regret he followed Sir Ademar of Limoux into the narrow streets.

Here the air was stifling. Trundling wagons laden with goods choked the way, lurching over the cobbles, tearing the scabby plaster from the walls. On the moldering steps of the doorways sharp-faced women, their hair straggling from under threadbare shawls, suckled full-grown infants; ragged children, black-haired, dark-eyed, raking and picking at the garbage that flowed down the drain in the middle of the street, rose on rickety legs, shouting and tearing at the bridles and begging for coins. Once his horse, slipping on a pile of offal, nearly threw an old man into the gutter, and Wolf, dragging it up, met two dark inscrutable eyes looking up out of thin narrow features of unexpected refinement.

"Arabs," the old knight muttered, shrugging at the boy's puzzled look. "Narbonne teems with them. Remnant of Islam's glory. Half-castes mostly. Have to thank the Franks for that. The Saracens, you know, won the place from the Goths. Held it close on forty years, till old Pepin got it by treason."

Wolf glanced back concerned, but the small dark-clad figure had already disappeared. They turned into another alley, equally sordid, yet with an attempt almost at tawdry gaiety about it. A strange pungent scent rose on the stagnant air, mingling with the rank, putrid smells. Above him, from behind a broken shutter, came the sound of a guitar, while in the opening of a brightly painted doorway two women, dressed in surprisingly garish splendor, lolled laughing. As they drew closer, the taller, a fair florid woman with yellow-dyed hair, made a slight questioning gesture, but the old knight rode on, supremely indifferent. Wolf, following behind, felt a hand laid on his sleeve. Through a cloud of heavy aromatic perfume words scarcely audible floated toward him, under the gleam of two sloe-shaped eyes. He shook his arm free. A ripple of laughter trailed after, low and vibrant, arousing vaguely disturbing emotions that he quickly strove to suppress.

All the way to Narbonne he had convinced himself that the visit was of no interest to him apart from his curiosity in the town, and that the deeper significance it would have held for him once had entirely faded. Over a year and a half had passed since the day on which he had set out for Béziers with such hopes, only to find that Miriam Caravita had fled to Narbonne. Now, he told himself, he was completely indifferent as to her whereabouts. The adventure of

189

that summer festival had retreated into so remote a past that it had ceased even to provide a topic for his teasing companions. Between it and the present lay the fullness of his friendship with Trencavel.

"Only the present is ours." The words of that autumn night had attained unhoped-for meaning.

It had begun with the pretext of strengthening the defenses. In view of the growing threat of the Crusade, Trencavel, proclaiming the necessity of a closer working relationship between the castle and the civic guard, had set about organizing the training of the whole youth of the city. Nobles or burghers, greater or less, rich or poor, powerful or humble, they were to train side by side and take part in the great sports and contests that were to be held in May. It was to be the way to a new idea of citizenship, inevitably tinged in Trencavel's mind by the thought of a golden age, of that which had been in Greece—in the land of the riders. And yet it would be their own, a future that should transcend every past.

Week by week the numbers grew larger. The meadows below the ramparts rang to the sound of steel, the shouts and laughter of young men, as, clad in his simple tunic, hair flying back on the wind, Trencavel rode at their side, their comrade, a higher embodiment of themselves. And perhaps as they raced their light arab horses bareback across the fields, hurled their lances and threw each other, limb locked in sunburned limb upon the turf, some of them had an inkling of what he meant when he spoke of a people to whom sport had been a form of religion—a people who had once lived in this very land.

Even if, for many, it was only another stunt with which to overcome a general boredom, if many wrinkled their noses at the smell of a "scullion's brat," to some it proved really an awakening. It was especially among some of the lesser citizens that Wolf had found something more than sheer enthusiasm, as though the present were indeed almost a challenge to forces long slumbering within them. One youth in particular, the son of a widow who kept a confectioner's shop in the lower city, responded to Trencavel's plans with an almost defiant pride, as though he would make clear he wasn't accepting as a gift what he considered his due. Often Wolf would stay talking in the little room at the back of the bakehouse till late into the night, while Guiraut vehemently held forth against the

privileges of the ruling classes, a rebelliousness that did
much to upset even the equanimity of his stout good-humored mother. She had been pastry cook at the castle during the regency and was a devout Cathar, but a good few
of the young men who surrounded him were Waldensians.
Trained to read the Bible in their own tongue, they were
getting at what seemed to them rock bottom, and so were
discovering for themselves that old and ever-new problem:

> "When Adam delved, and Eve span,
> Who were then the gentleman?"

Suspicious at first of Trencavel's intentions, and rankling
at what he believed the condescension of his squires (Villemur in particular was his bête noire), Guiraut had
thrown himself into the chance of training with grim earnest. Gradually, too, mollified by Wolf's bastardy, he began to show him a certain half-grudging confidence, and
Wolf's visits to the trim little shop in the lower city became fairly frequent. There was a good deal of merrymak-
ing there, too, besides heated discussions, for Mother
Martha was a generous hostess. Sometimes there was singing and dancing, not to the slow languishing measures of
the court but rollicking old country tunes that had accompanied the festivals of the seasons, or strong lilting
rhythms tapped out by craftsmen at their work.

Sicard of Durban would have been in his element, but
that winter his mother's health had suddenly failed and he
had been ordered home. Yet, although he missed him,
Wolf could not help feeling that Sicard's lighthearted
presence would have stood in the way of this new and
deeper friendship which intuitively he knew would admit
of no sharing.

Somehow Trencavel had changed. Looking back, Wolf
hardly knew in what. Perhaps it lay in the difference between an image and its reality. The mask had come alive.

Often that spring, after the exertion of the tiltyard, the
ardor of the hunt, they would lie stretched in the grass
side by side, planning their ideal city, weaving project on
project; or in dreamier mood, reading the Latin poets, in-
voke the gods who still, for all they knew, lurked in the
reeds or spied on them from out the gnarled and hollowed
trunk of some ancient olive. And yet as they eagerly dis-
cussed the rebuilding of Béziers, even Wolf scarcely real-

191

ized what ghosts were being laid in Trencavel's mind, or how far for him, lost in the splendor of some Vergilian landscape, the death-haunted world of an emasculating, self-obliterating convention had faded, while in her bower Agnes of Montpellier lay thrilling over the torments of Sir Lancelot du Lac.

If their enthusiasm was born, for one of them, of a nostalgia for the past, for the other, of a dream of the future, they were oblivious to it. Intoxicated by the seeming richness of the present, the thought of the Crusade had again become remote, a threat so continually averted that it had almost ceased to be real. And if it were, though its armies stood all but ready to march, armed to the teeth, though the missing knight had been found, was not that itself the necessary foil to an affirmation of a life so full that it laughed at death?

When Wolf, therefore, through some accident to one of the other squires, found himself allotted the task of escorting Sir Ademar of Limoux on an embassy to Narbonne, his first feeling had been one rather of annoyance, for he saw it only as an interruption of his activities at Trencavel's side; while the discovery that the old knight's mission included a visit to the house of Calonymos increased his bitterness. Though he was convinced of his indifference to the possibility of Miriam Caravita being in Narbonne, he did not want to be reminded of an event of which he was now almost ashamed. But the thought that any excuse not to accompany Sir Ademar might arouse the suspicions of Trencavel made him hold his peace. He had never been sure how much Trencavel knew of the whole matter; but whatever the case, he vowed that he should have no cause to think he still harbored an atom of his foolhardy infatuation.

Certainly he had set out for Narbonne with complete nonchalance, and if, as they neared the city, his excitement grew, he ascribed it to the marvels he expected to meet in the great harbor.

Now as a deepening unrest began to take hold of him he made angry attempts to combat it by concentrating his mind on the misery around him, forcing it to turn back to Trencavel's plans for the rebuilding of Béziers.

Sir Ademar, noticing the boy's brooding expression, laughed aloud.

"Finding the stench of the ghetto too much for you?"

Wolf looked up. In his preoccupation he had not noticed that they had entered a new quarter of the city. Actually it differed little from the former, though the inhabitants, poor as most of them were, had the appearance of greater vitality as they bustled about their affairs or stood in little groups gesticulating. Very soon, indeed, the façades of the houses grew less derelict, many wearing an almost prosperous appearance. One of the doors opened and a young woman carrying a pitcher came down the steps, quiet and unflurried, and, with scarcely a movement of her beautifully carried head or flutter of downcast eyes, passed down the street.

"The living Rebecca," smiled Ademar.

Fear began to invade the boy—fear that he would still not admit and disguised even to himself with shrugging disdain. But at that moment the alley widened and they found themselves in an open square.

Close on the left the domed towers of the Synagogue challenged the gaudy sky, rose-red, banded with slabs of creamy marble, while beyond it, emulating and outrivaling it in magnificence, the lavish façade of what in a flash the boy guessed to be the rabbi's palace flaunted its fantastic splendor before their eyes. The august house of Calonymos of Narbonne. "They're taking good care," he heard his father mocking, "to prove themselves royal, princes of the direct line of David; but for all Trencavel's patronage," he would add with a gleam of sardonic pride, "they haven't made counts of viscounts."

"They're having a bid at outdoing Raymond of Toulouse," laughed Ademar. "Must have cost old Calonymos a pain in the belly every time he had to draw out a new ducat. Well, if you like you can be having a look around at the sideshows while I discuss matters with our princely friends. I'll be at least a couple of hours."

Before he had time to think, Wolf of Foix, having helped Sir Ademar to dismount, and handing the horses over to the grooms, found himself inside the portals of that opulent mansion.

Left alone, his agitation increased, but in very defiance he dismissed all thought of beating a retreat. Soon, too, curiosity overcame his trepidation and, affecting an air of connoisseurship, he began to inspect the rich mosaics that decorated wall and ceiling. Having loitered there for a time, he proceeded desultorily to explore an arcaded cloister leading, it seemed, into a garden. Coming out of the comparative gloom, the sudden riot of color almost blinded him. He found himself in a small tiled courtyard, planted with flowering shrubs on which gigantic blossoms of waxen texture, white and glazing scarlet, gleamed as though pinned among the leathery leaves. Above, from the glaring red-brick walls, gallery on gallery of fimbriated tracery embellished with every manner of trefoil, quatrefoil, and cusp invented by the *stil ogive*, intermingling here and there with obvious inspiration from the East, rose to ever giddier and tapering heights, to be crowned at last by gilded pinnacles and domes. Even now, from one of those incredible turrets, it struck him, Miriam Caravita might be looking down on him. He looked up, nervously scanning the windows, inevitably reminded of the night on which he had stood staring up at that ancient and silent façade in the ghetto of Béziers. How much more dignity it had seemed to possess in contrast to this monstrosity! Well, if she preferred this, it had nothing to do with him. He shrugged. But the rows of windows, half shuttered against the heat, preyed on his nerves. At last, after pacing up and down the marble and tesselated pavement till the serpentine coils whirled in his brain, he wandered blindly toward an old stone fountain that stood in the center of the court and for a time stood gazing at the four crouching lions that supported the hollow well. Idly his fingers glided over the smooth weathered surfaces of stone that ran in a long unbroken curve from the head to the strong sure molding of the flanks. Somehow, amid all that garish splendor they filled him with a sense of satisfaction and peace, and it was with a sudden start that, raising his eyes, he became aware of a girl beckoning him from behind a trellis that screened the further side of the house. Hardly knowing what he did, he followed.

Passing through a vaulted vestibule, they mounted a short flight of stairs. Then, pushing aside the heavy brocaded curtains, she left him without a word.

The spacious room on whose threshold he found himself lay in semidarkness, for the shutters had been half closed to keep out the sun, and its slanting rays falling through the slats cast liquid bars of light on the exotic furnishings and hangings draping the walls.

Coiled upon a long, low couch by one of the windows that evidently looked out on the courtyard, Miriam Caravita turned lazily toward him, but at once he noticed, too dazed to know whether he felt disappointment or relief, that she was not alone.

Seated in the recess of the window behind her, a plump child with a mass of coppery hair was regarding him with blatant curiosity.

"We've been watching you for ages," she giggled, her mouth full of sugar plum.

Languorously Miriam stretched out her hand. Stiff, almost hostile, he bent above it, scarcely touching it with his lips. Drawing it back casually, she made a little movement in the direction of the younger girl: "My little cousin, Esther Calonymos."

It seemed to him that her nails, stained with henna, were dipped in gore.

"You see," she went on, laughing softly (her voice had all its old husky allure), "we were just going to bet—were you plotting to storm the harem or just admiring the lion?"

"Including or not including the setting," observed a sardonic voice in the background. Glancing round, Wolf recognized the law student he had met that night at the festival, sprawling over a book in the recess of the far window.

"Oh, Hugo," the plump, mature-bosomed child looked up protesting. "You might at least be polite about it in front of strangers. It's really rather wonderful, isn't it?" She turned to Wolf, almost commanding his approbation, and as if to ensure his allegiance made room for him by her side. Awkwardly he accepted the invitation.

"It must have been terribly difficult to build," he ventured, and was rewarded by a particularly luscious-looking sweetmeat from a richly enameled casket.

"It cost an awful lot," Esther confided eagerly.

"Luckily, or there'd be nothing to boast about," muttered the sarcastic voice.

"I'll tell Father," she retorted, pouting, "and he'll stop you coming here."

"And it would be such a pity," drawled Miriam, "when there's still a chance of improving us. You remember Hugo, don't you?" she continued, turning to Wolf. "He still sticks to us for the good of our souls, though I don't believe he thinks we've got any—imagines we're just the product of cause and effect and Divine Necessity plus a

195

series of alchemical reactions all related to the stellar spheres—mixture of Lucretius and the Arabs. He's always been obsessed with them; used to slip away from his uncle's house down to the alchemists' dens in Toledo. He's Spanish, really, pure hidalgo, though he's always doing his best to hide it. Thinks the Arabs the pick of the earth."

"So they are, for brains." Throwing aside the book, Hugo d'Alfaro swung round. That night in the moonlight Wolf had been too dazed to observe the man's face closely. Now, illumined by the bar of sunlight falling through the half-open shutter, it appeared unattractive enough, though undeniably disturbing. Possibly it was the peculiar leanness of the features and above all an habitual and perhaps largely cultivated violence of expression that gave the aquiline nose, the square bony jaw their startling aggressiveness. "Well, whom have they got to equal them?" he flashed scornfully, corrugating brows which under the careless mane of dark brown hair were singularly finely molded. "They're the best thinkers in Spain. Yet they go hounding them out like curs."

"But King Pedro's wonderfully brave," little Esther Calonymos pouted.

"On a white arab." D'Alfaro laughed harshly. "Amazing that he even tolerates their beasts. But of course one's always forgetting that Christian zeal doesn't necessarily rule out the adoption of their customs. My dear, if Aragon pockets the place, Narbonne may not prove such an Eden for the House of David. You might even wake up one day and find the princely mansion commandeered, complete with artistic embellishments, for his harem. Best kowtow to old Raymond. His tastes, after all, are all-embracing— Catholic in the best sense of the word."

"Including Jordan?" Miriam raised her heavy eyelids in skeptical question. "They were talking about him the other day."

Jordan of the Isle, Wolf wondered, his curiosity roused by the name—Esclarmonde of Foix's son? He had often tried to imagine what he was like. The vague reports he had heard didn't seem to fit in with Jordan's mother somehow. But while he was hunting for a way to approach the subject without making a fool of himself the younger girl had already begun to pelt him with questions concerning life at Carcassonne. He answered unwillingly, guardedly at first; but soon, in defiance of the enervating atmosphere that surrounded him, he was giving vent to all his enthusiasm for Trencavel and even hinting at their scheme for rebuilding Béziers.

"It almost seems," Miriam laughed, "as though before long I'll be returning to poor old Father. Béziers the city of a dream-future? One really mustn't miss being in at the start. After all, any sign that the human animal progresses—"

"Does it?" growled d'Alfaro, but Wolf was too agitated by Miriam's apparent interest to give him further notice.

"Tell me more," she was saying. Her eyes, veiled by their heavy lids, gazed at him inquiringly. Of course she was mocking, he told himself, feeling creep over him something of the old spell. Was there after all, as he had dreamed that night, something deeper behind her languorous cynicism? "Everyone has a right to happiness," the words she had spoken then returned, "the only trouble is—" But he would not accept that skepticism. Partly in very defiance, partly in a renewed hope of saving her, he began to speak ardently of Trencavel's plans, till he suddenly became aware that Esther's attention, which till now had rested wide-eyed upon his lips, was suddenly diverted to the doorway. Looking up, he saw that a head had been thrust in through the curtains and hung there as though decapitated among the folds of rich Eastern brocade.

"Oh, Reuben, do come in!" the child addressed the macabre image impulsively.

Reuben Calonymos the collector, it flashed through Wolf's mind, though certainly the face of the newcomer bore if anything more resemblance to his cousin Miriam than to that of his plump, auburn-haired sister. It was a long and peculiarly narrow face, delicately cut and of a refinement of feature almost feminine, and the quiet movements of his slender body, as, parting the curtains, he still remained standing in the doorway, seemed reminiscent of an Oriental.

"Alas, not now—too busy," his voice, low, unmoved, seemed far-off, remote.

"Oh, do stay!" Esther pleaded effusively. "We've got a visitor," she nodded in the direction of Wolf, "and he's telling us all about Carcassonne."

"Budding knight of the Table Round," d'Alfaro chimed in, laughing. "Trencavel's last hope."

Whether the slight bow that young Calonymos made in

197

his direction was born of ingrained deference or subtle irony Wolf found it impossible to tell, so restrained and evasive was the newcomer's manner. "You are fortunate," he smiled, but whether again the tone inferred a veiled envy or disparagement of his own surroundings was doubtful.

"I was down at the Capitol," he continued. "Another rumor had just drifted in. They say the Crusade's to be ready to start from Lyons at the end of June." Even now his voice remained vaguely indifferent, remote. "I must go," he repeated, and before any had time to speak, with another distant, faintly mocking bow he had withdrawn.

As the door closed behind him Esther Calonymos, staring vacantly after her brother, pursed her lips, smeared with sugar, to a significant "whew!" Wolf had jerked up at the news, but still no one spoke. With a little sigh Miriam settled herself more luxuriously on the cushions.

Suddenly d'Alfaro broke the silence with a harsh sardonic laugh. "Well, now perhaps we may begin to think a little about the reception—"

"It's probably just bluff," Esther put in, in a tone of reassuring authority, adopted from the customary optimism of her friends. "They want to force Count Raymond to get rid of all the heretics."

"Let's hope so. And if he doesn't? They'll do it for him. That ruffian of a semi-Norman they've got hold of evidently means to do things with a pretty thorough hand."

"But how can he?" retorted Esther. "He's nobody—a mere French knight."

"And rightful Earl of Leicester," d'Alfaro completed. "Unfortunately, my little snob, in his eyes you're probably less than nobody, and as far as he's concerned the only use for heretics and infidels in general is extermination."

"But the Church isn't nearly as rabid against us as against the Cathars," the child insisted. "After all, we're quite different."

D'Alfaro burst out laughing. "Because you share the same robust Judaic concepts regarding the primal mover of existence and don't despise this dear world? Good for you. Let's hope it will help to get you out of the mess. Anyway, with your amazing adaptability you'll probably manage to turn disaster to profit."

Rousing herself from her apparent inertia, Miriam Caravita regarded him, amused. "Well, isn't it more sensible than wasting all your energy rebelling against the inevitable? You're so obsessed with ideas that you despise the rock on which they're built—we're realists, that's all."

Although he knew her cynicism was directed as much against himself, Wolf, infuriated by d'Alfaro's surliness, turned toward her with an awkward attempt at chivalry: "Trencavel has promised you his support."

"Hm. While he lets the land go to ruin for the sake of a feudal atavism," d'Alfaro muttered.

"It wasn't that!" the boy retorted hotly. "Whatever happens, even if Raymond gives in, Trencavel won't."

D'Alfaro shrugged. "Well, we shall see, he might have to. It's pleasant enough to play the moral hero and leave the dirty work to another."

"He didn't!" Wolf cried.

"Well then," Hugo glanced at the boy provocatively, "why was he too damnably self-righteous to associate himself with Toulouse?"

"How could he," Wolf burst out, "with any sense of decency, of honor?"

"Honor—stone-cold, abstract honor—out of the Roman schoolbooks," d'Alfaro mocked. "What Trencavel would really like is a hegemony of noble souls setting an unimpeachable example to the gross world—purified feudalism, chivalry regenerated, free of course of the bigotry of the Church, and, unlike the dear Cathars, giving the body its due—*mens sana in corpore sano* and so on."

"He's just the opposite!" Wolf burst in. "He's going to get everyone—I mean everyone's got to have the chance—"

"Chivalry for the masses," d'Alfaro mocked. "He's having a shot at roping in the citizens, isn't he? Plato's Republic adapted to feudal privileges. A new Olympia—wrestling and races in the nude among the Roman ruins. Let's be worthy of our ancestors and all that."

"It isn't true!" Wolf sprang to his feet.

Miriam Caravita let her eyes rove over the slim figure, still not overall but lithe and strong enough. "Anyhow, it doesn't seem to have done you much harm. You look more capable of undertaking a duel than last time." The words, with their half-mocking ambiguity and stirring memories of that summer night, filled him with angry confusion.

"It's only another example," d'Alfaro went on mercilessly, "of what Miriam calls our pitiful lack of realism. Of course up there in Carcassonne, a good old feudal stronghold, it's half feasible, but down here . . ." he looked sharply at the boy. "Well, you must have seen for yourself," he motioned with his hand toward the window—"it's a bit large to tackle, what?"

Even while Wolf struggled to put up a defense, the memory of the surging streets, the squalor, the foul scents, rose overpowering—the blowsy, made-up face of the woman in the alley. . . . It was what Guiraut had hinted at.

"But we've got to begin somewhere," he pleaded, his eyes smoldering with anger.

At that moment the distant murmur of the city that now and then penetrated the window on the farther side of the room grew louder. A sound of shouting seemed to break in on their ears. Esther Calonymos, springing to her feet, ran over to the window where d'Alfaro was sitting and, jumping on the wide stone seat, threw the shutter wide open.

"There's a crowd," she cried, "making its way to the Bishop's castle."

The Calonymos mansion stood on the edge of the ghetto upon a comparative height, and from its back windows enjoyed a considerable view. Some distance away, moving in the direction of the center of the town, a stream of people was hurrying along, the figure of a monk at its head. They were constantly being joined by new adherents who, gathering eagerly around, impeded the leader's progress with cries and adjurations, even falling on their knees. But persistently freeing himself, the monk marched determinedly on. As he moved, holding on high the Cross, his red-gold tonsure flamed aureole-like in the sun.

For a moment d'Alfaro watched the procession silently and then sank back in his seat. "The zealous fraternity on the warpath again—looks like friend Domingo himself. He'll have his work cut out in Narbonne; may not find his path strewn with so many roses as in Montpellier. Still, he seems up to anything. In spite of the miracles, the man's evidently hardheaded enough. He's not been mincing his words of late and came out with it pretty plain: 'Where a blessing fails one must resort to the stick,' as the good old Spanish proverb says."

Esther Calonymos, having lost sight of the procession,

had climbed down from the window and, returning to her old place, pulled Wolf, who was standing irresolutely in the middle of the room, back to his old seat. "Reuben," she protested meditatively, "says he has the face of a saint."

"Or a fanatic—the same thing," muttered d'Alfaro.

"But," she went on, eager for a new argument, "he's supposed to be awfully courageous."

"Like Pedro?" d'Alfaro mocked.

"Wretch!" she turned on him, drawing up her stout, short-legged little body to its full height. "After all, when they attacked him upon the mountain—"

"Behold the daughter of the rabbi defending the priest of the Gentiles. So much for our enlightened civilization of the south!"

But Esther Calonymos was determined to have the last word. "He wasn't afraid of death."

"Or to send others to theirs—for the good of their souls, of course. God, if one could collect all the blood spilled in the cause of religion!"

"If only," Miriam sighed, "people wouldn't worry so much about others' salvation, the world would be a so much pleasanter place. But it's the same with everything. They're always bothering themselves about doing, instead of being content to be. The Christian shibboleth of good works. Just think of the loads of misery created in the name of charity."

"And compassion." Hugo laughed wryly. "Heavens, all I ask *in extremis* is to be spared the ministrations of the Good Samaritan."

"Poor Hugo," she murmured; "of course you'd rather let yourself bleed to death than be indebted to another living soul. But they won't let you. They're all so set on interfering. Must better the world. All this reforming business, these regenerating stunts—and if they succeeded it would be so dull. Chivalry for the people, the Waldensian community, even the 'back to nature' enthusiasts." She laughed. "Just imagine Raymond, Trencavel, Domingo reduced to the same pattern—the brute male. Why, my dear Hugo, even your enlightened anarchy. Soon freedom would pall more than tyranny itself."

"Little fear," d'Alfaro growled; "man will always be a multifarious sort of swine, but he might at least get the chance of becoming something else if he wishes. If not, let

201

the devil take him. As it is, they even begrudge a fellow the right to go to hell by his own volition. Because one happens to be born Castilian blue blood, and the rest, should one have a monopoly on life while another—"

"Oh, there he's off again," the small Jewess tittered; "it's all very well to grumble at Domingo. You ought to join the preaching friars yourself." And giving him no further attention she began to ply Wolf with more questions about life at Carcassonne, but the boy, unwilling to expose Trencavel further to d'Alfaro's cynicism, proved singularly uncommunicative. And yet, while he hated him for those sneers, the man's nihilism was exerting on him an influence strangely disturbing. A cold haunting fear began to invade him. Were, after all, the plans he was making with Trencavel no more than a dream? But at once his loyalty and hero-worship rose up fiercely to quell his doubts, and he began to feel more and more out of the picture, awkward and alone, while behind everything the presence of Miriam brooded, languid, indifferent. Lying there in the green shuttered light she seemed almost, in her clinging dress with its curious pattern of black and gold, to resemble some outlandish snake—beautiful, indolent, remote.

"Actually, Hugo," she yawned, "I think you may be having to change your tactics if you're to remain the rebel. Reforming the world's becoming almost too fashionable. Even our incorrigible Peire—"

"Peire," Esther tittered. "Oh, did you see him at the tournament—Mirepoix, I mean?" she cried, turning effusively to Wolf and, taking his gruff "no" for disappointment, rippled on in evident sympathy. "They won't let me go till I'm fourteen. He must have been too utterly marvelous, riding into the lists as defender of Artemis, all got up with the crescent moon—he's supposed to have descended from the Iberian goddess, you know. And the rest of them—the sons of Luna, just like Greeks, in nothing but tunics and armed with javelins and bows. You see," she continued proudly, "he copied those sarcophagi in Reuben's collection—Actaeon or Hippolytos or something—I've got mixed."

"In short, pageants and circuses—*Finis Latinorum*," scoffed d'Alfaro.

"Well, why not?" Miriam drawled. "After all, it's less messy and far more artistic. Dear Peire, his versatility is really amazing. What a pity the classic craze is *passé* already. But then, mythology is so gloriously adaptable—the doves of Astarte transformed into those of the Grail. He's letting Arnaut to design the crest. Mirepoix and the sons of Luna, defenders of the sanctuary—the chaste knighthood of Montségur; thinks he'll even manage to convince the dear Countess—"

She was interrupted by a shriek from Esther as Wolf, suddenly jerking round, sent the box of comfits crashing to the ground.

"Oh, never mind," the child began to defend him, moved by the distraught pallor of his face.

Wolf was on his feet staring blindly at the sweetmeats scattered over the floor. "I must go," he stammered.

"Oh, not yet," Esther pleaded. He seemed not to hear. With a vague glance toward Miriam he was making for the door. "But what upset him?" the younger girl cried as the door closed behind him.

D'Alfaro laughed. "Evidently your friend of the crescent moon."

Lying back on the cushions Miriam closed her eyes. "Hugo," she said, opening them after a little pause, "do you think he's quite disillusioned?"

D'Alfaro, stooping to pick up a stuffed date that had rolled to his feet, began mechanically to dissect the fruit. "Probably," he answered unfeelingly.

"Brute! You should have seen him that night. It was the first time," she laughed softly. "Peire was there, of course. Poor Wolf, he's horribly jealous."

Hugo d'Alfaro, picking at the extracted nut, glanced at her casually. "My dear, about you? I'm afraid I'm getting dense." He laughed callously. "I thought it was the Grail!"

II

Of course it was only a jest, Wolf persuaded himself after the first shock, one of Mirepoix's typical extravagances, as ephemeral, probably, as the rest of his fantasies. Nevertheless, the blow had struck unexpectedly deep. Wrapped up in his friendship with Trencavel, the image of Montségur had once more retreated into the background, all his energy being absorbed in the new life at Carcassonne. Yet the thought that the ubiquitous Peire-Roger was staging his cynical mummery up there, as the son of Luna, the true-born defender of the sacred rock, had stung him to the quick.

His first impulse was to beg Trencavel on his return to Carcassonne to give him leave to ride to Pamiers and pay the long-delayed visit to his aunt, but the absurdity of such a project struck him soon enough. What had he done to merit her sympathy? What attempt had he made even to keep in contact with her, while all the time evidently Mirepoix had doubtless been entwining her in his gallantries. What could he say? Accuse him of a ribaldry scarce worse than his own? For there was little doubt that Peire-Roger had already informed her of his adventure. In the exaggerated self-consciousness of his despair he saw himself for the moment as shallow and licentious as his rival, and lacking even the honesty of Mirepoix's flirtatiousness, while overcome with new pangs of unadmitted jealousy it struck him how furtive and inarticulate his feelings for Miriam had been. But he had never loved her, he scoffed. He had realized the absurdity of that night's adventure long ago, and even if he had felt a moment's uneasiness at seeing her again, the presence of her macabre beauty, her paradoxical cynicism, had soon restored him to his senses, even before she had dealt that last blow. For that matter, he strove to convince himself, what was Montségur to him anyway, since his new life with Trencavel? And now, if the Crusade really marched . . .

All the way home Ademar had been full of the news. If it was true, and the Crusade at last meant business, Raymond might even give in. Well then, they could sing small! The old knight shook his head perturbed.

"But the Viscount won't ever give in," Wolf put in eagerly. Sir Ademar nodded. Still, it would have been better in the first place, he seemed to suggest, if Trencavel had hung on to Toulouse.

At the cost of all human decency, thought Wolf angrily. Even d'Alfaro had attacked Trencavel. Well, if that was what they'd come to, ready to sell their conscience, their freedom, everything that was theirs, he could understand his father's impatience with his countrymen well enough. Only it wasn't a matter of feudal pride they'd be fighting for, but something far older, something that had belonged to the people who once, they said, had set sail from the Grecian seas and settled here. A clearness, a brightness, a freedom that had been theirs, the heroes of whom that winter Trencavel and he had read so much; something that had never died, but absorbed by the blood of those who had been here before and those who came after, had endured, beyond conquest and reconquest. It was theirs still, if they only cared. And they were going to soon, they were all going to. The sports would be a beginning, and this new sense of citizenship.

"Wrestling and racing among the Roman ruins," d'Alfaro would start mocking again. Let him! If he was so damnably critical about everything, why didn't he do something about it instead of lounging around in opulent palaces? Besides, it wasn't Rome at all, but something far older, something that Roman tyranny, Roman imperialism had petrified and tried to kill, and never had managed to completely. And now it was Rome again—the Church that would throttle what was left. For something of it was there even in Catharism, the gospel of the Spirit, the revelation received on the island of Patmos, and it was Greek heretics who long ago had brought Christianity to the Pyrenees—a religion of the people, persecuted by power.

The thought somewhat ameliorated his bitterness. After all, should he not go to Pamiers? In spite of everything there might be nothing more in that rumor than a story, a boast, one of Mirepoix's everlasting whims. Had not Esclarmonde of Foix understood as no one else, was it not she who had sent him to Carcassonne?

Angered at his former distrust, he began thinking of how he would tell her of Trencavel's plans, of all they would do if the war did not come, of all they would do afterward if it did, for it would be the beginning of a new free world. It was *that* he was going to fight for, so that she would not care whether he was a True Believer or not, and would see that there was another way for knighthood—a way of strength and vigor. Would she? He tried to recall her clearly and suddenly realized how remote she had grown, a gray-robed, misty image somehow mingled with the memory of wistful laughter. "And if a fish isn't really a fish"—wasn't that what she had said?

If he still vacillated, fate stepped in deciding. No sooner had he got back to Carcassonne than his father arrived unexpectedly from a visit to Toulouse. Raymond, seeing the Crusade at last a certainty, had sent emissaries to the Pope.

The purpose of the Count of Foix's arrival was naturally to discuss the political situation, a situation that demanded as much sanity as it did courage, and whether Trencavel possessed the former, Ramon-Roger of Foix, who never altogether approved of the break with Toulouse, strongly doubted. Vehement and arrogant, his sense of realism was nevertheless acute. To run straight into the noose because of some foolhardy ideal would be to foredoom them all to ruin, unless they could count on Aragon's support. Fight he would, and to the last, if it came to it. But there must be something tougher behind them than a pack of quasi-moral, quasi-aesthetic foibles or qualms about the burning of a few fanatics at the stake. The discussion, as Wolf gathered, had been pretty tense, though they seemed agreed at the end. For his father's truculence Wolf had been prepared, not for the fact that he had insisted on taking him home.

"Let me stay for the sports," he had pleaded. But argument was fatal with the stiff-necked count.

"Sports!" he had scoffed. "By then, maybe, you'll be tilting with something sharper than dummy spears, and with tougher opponents than the little burghers of Carcassonne."

And when, in despair, Wolf turned toward Trencavel, he answered with that strange distant look upon his face he hadn't seen for so long: "They're cancelled. We'll have to spend every bit of energy in preparing." And it had been he who had insisted he should obey his father without delay.

Wolf felt furious and hurt. Was this all their friendship meant? To be packed off in the moment of danger, when they had sworn brotherhood—to stand by each other till death?

If the Pope acquiesced in Raymond's plea, what might not be the price? Raymond might not stick at playing off Béziers and Carcassonne, but nothing, Wolf knew, would make Trencavel kowtow to Toulouse.

Yet Trencavel would not listen to his pleading. Almost he seemed distant, strained. There had hardly been time even to say farewell before Wolf found himself setting out for Foix.

Still the old awkwardness was not altogether banished between father and son. The count, though secretly well pleased with the improvement in the boy's physique, did not spare his satire in casting ridicule on Trencavel's aims, which Wolf made vain attempts to parry, but there was something about his spirited efforts that was at least an improvement on the tongue-tied diffidence that in former days had driven the count to despair. He had had a first inkling of it perhaps in the boy's absurd defense of the workers at Montségur; evidently he was tenacious enough in the pursuit of some harebrained ideal. Probably he'd been a fool to let Esclarmonde push him into sending him to Carcassonne. But what was the alternative? He shouldn't be surprised if he and Trencavel had got their heads together about this reform business. The Cathars, of course, had been squeamish about Roger Taillefer's revenge and no doubt started all these highfalutin ideas concerning the burghers of Béziers. Crazed as he was, it had damned well gone to young Trencavel's head. Stiffen their rickety legs with a little drill, wipe from the city a bit of its stench—well, if it pleased him. He'd soon find out what payment he'd get! But to risk his life for that rabble and a posse of Jews! If he were going to stand firm against the Crusade, he had argued with Trencavel, face to face, the only chance was at Carcassonne. At any rate he seemed to have grasped that. Still, pigheaded as the man proved himself in those dealings with Toulouse, he wasn't letting him run risks with his own son. Nevertheless he wondered whether he wasn't dragging the boy out of the frying pan into the fire if he was going to be carried away by this abracadabra at Montségur. He had made Esclarmonde promise not to influence him, though of course the boy would be hankering to join the guard. Evidently he'd already spun some mad fantasy around the place, that time at Pamiers, years ago. If there were going to be any nonsense about it he'd pack him off to Roger in Andorra, where he could moon over his blessed mountains till he sickened of their sight. Still, he thought, relieved, there wasn't much fear of his being infected by the mystic maggot among the members of the guard—tough mountain breed, cared not a fig for Catharism on the whole, except that it let them have their knife into Rome and the slinking priesthood. What they were concerned with was to keep those foreign devils off their soil. As for Mirepoix and his tribe, not much of saintliness there! He'd warrant he'd soon be running amok among the little Cathar nuns. A pretty contrast to this son of his. Why, he shouldn't be surprised if the boy were still virgin. Christ, when he thought of himself that age! Scarce a heart among the beauties of Languedoc he didn't break, and if now and then his own got pricked, it was soon healed by a song.

But even song nowadays was becoming forced, the old rhymes and images wearing thin. And then this craze to adumbrate everything with some mystic meaning. God, wouldn't they believe a man could get enough fun out of juggling with words themselves—good as the play of swords in a melee. Politics, maybe. Maybe Bertran had winked an eye at his *Domna composita*—soft gaze of Cembelins, locks of My Lady Anhes, white teeth of Faid-ita, slim waist of Miels-de-Ben. Doubtless he'd had his fun paying one back on the intransigent Maent and all the time had his eye on those castles. But that the chamber into which Arnaut tried to force so tortuous a path (to his uncle's chagrin) held not my lady's bed but the secret church of the Cathars, pah!!

Carried away by memories of his own youth and not without a certain delight in tickling the sensibilities of his son, Ramon-Roger of Foix had embarked eloquently on his own poetic adventures, not without gratification at the unexpected intelligence shown by Wolf. All said and done, he had evidently made some good use of his sojourn at Carcassonne, though they hadn't made a courtier of him, that was evident. The shadow of the clerk's cowl still hung on his shoulders. He shouldn't wonder if he'd make dawn-songs in Latin, though in a vocabulary less spicy than that of the renegade sons of the Church. It seemed that Tren-cavel and he had stuffed their heads full of Vergil through the winter. But as for this young Durban he was talking of—for in a bout of enthusiasm Wolf had begun to tell him of Sicard's quarrel with obscure symbolism and his conviction that poetry must be simple, direct, must appeal to—he had almost said—the people, and then, remember-ing in a flash that the word was enough to rouse a tornado of sarcasm in his father, he had stopped in time.

"He's keen on the war songs they used to sing. He's thinking of making one for us. He wants to beat their *Ro-land*."

"Let him! It's high time. And you," he laughed; "is

there a hope after all that you'll carve the name of your ancestor with a sharper blade than the chisel?"

The taunting allusion to that scene in Pamiers made the boy wince, but he parried the thrust.

"I hoped," he said, "if there'd been fighting, to win my spurs."

It was a dig for having been torn from Carcassonne.

"You? A mere cub!" his father scoffed, but he was not ill-pleased. And he glanced at the erect, lithe figure riding at his side.

Well, perhaps, after all, Esclarmonde might prove right.

The following day, after breaking their journey at the castle of the Durforts, they reached the county of Foix. Before them in the distance the towers of Pamiers rose against the sky. But the count was in a hurry to get home and only skirted the city. Suddenly rounding a bend in the road they found themselves faced by a procession of white-robed figures moving slowly toward them. Perceptibly, Ramon-Roger stiffened.

"Still at their mummery," he mocked derisively. "Of course, it's the yearly pilgrimage. Placating the God of the elements with the saint's bones, probably the rib of an old sheep. I reckon the old Thunderer thinks it a bit of a comedown after the blood of a fresh-slain ram. In pagan times they honored Him with a temple up there." He pointed toward the crest of the hill.

Slowly the monks of St. Anthony advanced, a little white-frocked band, singing and swaying under the blazing sun as they trudged on, bearing the gilded reliquary under its bobbing canopy of azure silk. Sweating beneath their load, they toiled on. The road was too narrow to pass. Dismounting, Wolf out of habitual reverence instilled in his monastic days bowed his head. A moment later he became aware that the procession had halted. Looking up, he saw his father still seated astride his horse, immobile, head held high, scathing disdain upon his lips.

The chanting had ceased. One hand upon the golden shrine, the other upheld in imprecation, the abbot of St. Anthony had turned toward him. In his heated face, flecked with pallid blotches, his eyes burned in malice and rage.

"It is evident, Count, that you show no reverence for your liege lord, the holy martyr. Well then, take heed lest in this town, of which you are master by grace of that very saint, you are deprived of every seigniorial right, and that the blessed martyr prevail so well that you are disinherited for life."

A shudder of horror ran through the group of monks. Not a quiver stirred the count's stalwart frame. Above the reddish beard his lips were curved in a little smile of withering scorn. For a moment longer his gaze transfixed the crowd of faces staring at him in timorous malice, incredulity, and fear. Then, with a swift jerk of the reins, he set spurs to his horse. The little flock dispersed before him like sheep.

Burning with shame at his own timidity, convinced all too forcibly that his own piety was little more than habit, Wolf remounted and rode after.

"So," his father mocked without turning, "I see the monk's still stuck in your marrow. Like to go crawling after them?"

A convulsed "No" broke from Wolf's lips. For a moment they rode on in silence. Then the count slackened their pace to an easy trot.

"My lord abbot is not very inventive," he laughed lightly. "Well, since he deigns to honor me with the same threats they showered on Toulouse, let's hope the answer of Foix will be more original."

III

"Know that we shall see thee deprived of thy possessions and incite the princes against thee as against the enemy of Christ. But the wrath of God will not rest at that. The Lord will blast thee."

Two years had passed since the day on which Raymond VI had pondered skeptically upon that fatal indictment from the papal throne.

The threat had become reality. Near on three hundred thousand strong the Crusade had gathered, ready to march from Lyons under the Holy Cross.

Sublimely indifferent, the sun blazed down on Languedoc, insensible to the lavish opulence of that southern soil as to the threat of its destruction.

And still its fate hung in the balance. Raymond, stricken with panic, had sent his envoys to the Pope professing his inconsolable regret for the murder of the papal legate, offering to submit in abject humility to whatever reparation the Holy Father might decree.

Breathless, Toulouse waited. Even now, under the golden aura of its sky, terror, like poverty and misery, seemed glossed over by a gilded veil. True, the fortifications of those ancient walls had been strengthened; an augmented guard paced the ramparts, troops of mercenaries marched through the city streets; and from morn till dusk young men astride their swift light arab horses charged through the gates, shouting and flashing arms, to joust in the fields of Montoulieu. In market and street, in the shadow of the Capitol, people gathered in knots. Peasants driving their oxen-drawn wagons would linger at the gates waiting for news. And yet, under the blazing sun, the face of the city, radiant, replete, seemed to deny foreboding.

Might not even now, on the very eve of disaster, the storm be averted? With Raymond's full submission, would not Innocent yet stop the Crusade? Though the hordes of the north stood ready, chafing for the signal, could not the tide be deflected from its course—to the Holy Land, for instance? The Crusaders might refuse. But to Spain, the Arabs? Hope rose almost to certainty.

But if Raymond in compensation, as was almost sure, were forced to hand over the heretics? With them, hope fed itself on few illusions. The weaker had long ago seceded. Some, in case of impending danger, had prepared for evacuation to Pamiers and the county of Foix. The majority, facing the peril grave-eyed, had planted themselves firmly behind the venerable consuls of the town, who if not always sworn believers themselves were moved by a lingering memory of Roman fortitude to defend the city's liberty.

So the weeks passed, until one day a report sped through the city—the envoys had returned. All day little crowds had gathered around the Castel Narbones while rumor ran high—a stranger had been seen to accompany the envoys—a member of the Roman Curia. The Pope had sent his legate—surely it must be to receive the count's penance. The Crusade was still to march, but make southward—for Spain. On the Saracens would fall the weight of those armed forces. Death to the Muslim!

211

A fierce sigh of relief passed from lip to lip. Almost they were shouting in joy and exultation when the doors of the palace opened. It was not Raymond, however, but the Bishop of Toulouse who appeared on the threshold.

In his troubadour days Fulk of Marseilles had prided himself on his figure. It had belonged to the convincing demonstration of a hopeless and unfulfillable passion to cultivate a befitting leanness, and to give him his due his ambition was ready to suffer all the agonies that his heart was spared. The painful asceticism, indispensable to the profession of love in its lower and mundane grades, proved, however, as Fulk in his new and pious sphere of life soon discovered, not nearly so necessary to the practice of its loftier aspects, with the result that the higher he climbed the rungs of the mystic ladder the more his person took on the traits of an undeniable earthliness. In any case, whatever had been sacrificed in the way of romantic or sartorial elegance was at the moment completely disguised by the stiff embroidered folds of his bishop's cope, and standing there at the top of the steps he managed, as usual, to produce an effect of utmost ecclesiastic dignity. As he gazed down upon the crowd, his narrow lips, long trained to model upon his middle-aged but still well-preserved countenance every shade of feeling compatible with the sorrowful but indulgent pastor of an erring flock, smiled compassionately.

Carried away by hope that had already mounted to certainty, the crowd, almost forgetful of its old antipathy for the bishop and of the ruthless efficiency with which that pastoral love was wont to officiate, were only too ready to take the smile as a sign of their own deliverance, and only slowly, as the words fell in that studied and mellifluous voice, was their import fully revealed to their bewildered senses.

Inspired by divine grace, the most Holy Father, the bishop told them, had looked with compassion on Toulouse, and had in his mercy appointed his legates to absolve the count from his most heinous sin on condition that he fulfill the terms appointed: Count Raymond must yield unconditionally seven of his castles; further, he must submit his person to whatever penance the legates thought fit to appoint.

Did the smile grow imperceptibly broader, a flicker appear in the cold gray eyes? Was there a sharpened note in

212

the unctuous voice? A little shiver of apprehension ran through the crowd.

And in token of his sincere determination to wipe the pollution of heresy from the land (a determination in which till now he had shown himself sadly reluctant), Raymond, Count of Toulouse, must swear to do all in his power to succor and support the Crusade in its pious work of exterminating the heretics.

The Crusade. . . . For a moment a hush, fearful, incredulous, had fallen on the crowd, till with realization of the truth, fierce protest broke from their lips. Maddened almost by this sudden reverse to its high-flown hopes, fear, caution, everything but their long-harbored hatred of the tyrant was forgotten, and in a wave of fury they moved forward, closing in on the steps of the palace.

Involuntarily Fulk stepped back, but the halberds of the guard were between him and the mob. And as he stood there, staring with that deprecating smile at the dawning horror and the helpless violence of the crowd of faces below, the little flicker of triumph in the steel-gray eyes was unmistakable.

He raised his hand, the soft, white, almost boneless fingers whose dexterity in plucking the lute strings had in former days so often exerted a peculiarly disturbing fascination on the recipient of his amorous plaints. The gesture, beautifully studied, and calling forth, like all his actions, a heightened attention through its slight ambiguity, seemed to express as much a blessing as a hidden threat.

Appalled now at the thought of what might come, the crowd stood hushed, expectant, while quietly, with studied crescendo, the bishop began his old invectives.

In vain had he warned, in vain had he sacrificed his own weal to save them from perdition. But they had not heard. Blind and deaf though they were, as they had ever been, one day, to the sound of rending trumpets their ears would be opened, their eyes to the leaping of flames. But as they recked so little of the hour of divine judgment, let them be judged on earth, that they who mocked at everlasting fire might quail before the lightning of the avenging sword, the flames licking around the stake. He paused, looking down on the crowd. Today no laughter, no mockery, broke from those scared faces. When he resumed his speech his voice had regained its unctuous calm.

But the mercy of the Lord was infinite. Even now He held out the blessing of His grace to the penitent, in sadly belated recognition of which Count Raymond, realizing at last the enormity of his crimes and the hideous sins of his people, had agreed to take on himself the burden of full and profound repentance and, submitting to the will of the Pope, as represented to him by his legates, would join himself in furthering the progress of the Crusade and the destruction of the Antichrist on earth.

He ceased. Yet was it only triumph that agitated his usually suave voice, or also secret chagrin? The crowd scarce heard or cared. Stupor had descended on that sea of faces. Slowly but shatteringly the significance dawned upon them. A few incipient roars of protest dwindled into silence. Fulk had vanished. Stupefied, they began to disperse.

Raymond had agreed, had acquiesced in the Crusade. Raymond had betrayed them. And then, at the instigation perhaps of some astuter brain, suddenly the reaction set in. Raymond would never let the brunt of the Crusade fall upon his own dominions. Promising everything (he was sly), he would deflect its course southward. The earlier rumors of the day might not prove so false after all. The Crusade would progress, not to Spain, maybe, but to the Aude. The Viscount of Béziers and Carcassonne had refused Toulouse vassalage often enough in the past, prided themselves on seceding to Aragon. Maybe Trencavel was Raymond's nephew, but had he not left his uncle nicely in the lurch when Toulouse had sought to make a common front against the foe? Then the danger might have been averted. On Trencavel's head fall the blame! Let him pay for his arrogance!

The very discovery of a whipping boy acted as a ventilator to the suspense of the last hours and weeks. Soon the remaining fears, even the speculations as to what action Raymond would be forced to take against the heretics, began to fade in the all-consuming wave of relief. The immediate disaster was averted. Sacra Tolosa, for the moment at any rate, was saved. The thoughts of few turned toward the central figure of the drama. If the fate of Count Raymond himself occupied the mind of anyone, it was that of Bishop Fulk.

Even as he turned his back with supreme disdain upon the fluctuating mob beneath, the mask of hypocrisy fell from him and an irrefutable sense of disappointment beset him afresh. Raymond was going to cheat him even now. In apparent cowardice, seemingly weak, incalculable as water, the count might yet manage to wrest Toulouse from its deserved fate and thus from the sacrosanct and chastening power of its bishop. If he were not careful, the machinations of years might even now prove vain, and he would miss the goal. Yet he was not shattered at the thought.

To the cool, rational mind of Fulk of Marseilles even failure was but a fact, the result of a definite cause, and as such to be considered and investigated with all the powers of reason. Later, in the fastness of his library, he set himself to the task with characteristic energy. His success in life was indeed perhaps largely due to his power to measure his defeats as dispassionately as his victories, till by a series of precise calculations the damage was repaired. Perhaps those far-off and despised days spent in his father's countinghouse had been of value after all, and the merchant of Marseilles would have marveled at the amazing ability with which his son had put those first lessons in calculation to an ever more idealistic and unworldly use. Thus with every possible device of courtly worship he had pursued the lady Aladais from defeat to defeat, until he had come to the conclusion that his failure lay not in his means, but in the object of his aim still retaining too much earthliness for the application of his pure mathematical speculation. He had not aimed high enough but, characteristically refusing to consider any experience profitless, he in no way regretted that mundane apprenticeship.

Now too, despite momentary failure, he looked toward the goal undeterred. Already he saw the way clearly. Raymond, Raymond alone, the all-powerful Count of Toulouse, was worthy of his persecution. Pursue him, destroy his power, and the fall of the rest was inevitable. Why should he waste time on the heretic rabble? He had allowed himself to be sidetracked, too concerned with the salvation of his erring flock. He smiled to himself, less out of hypocrisy now, it must be admitted, than in relief at recognizing the flaw. His fault, he realized, lay in his inclination to steep himself so thoroughly in every role that he stood in peril of deviating from the central theme. Luckily the propelling force of his zeal was so strong that it had always succeeded in restoring the necessary equilibrium, and, by a process rivaled only by the consummate logic of Gothic cathedral construction, the thousand exquisitely perfected details were absorbed into the soaring edifice of his consuming ambition—to the glory of God and the Holy Virgin.

Involuntarily his eyes lifted to the exquisite little shrine glimmering in the light of the tall tapers. He had at first been drawn to this particular statue of the Virgin because her remote tantalizing smile, the charming mannerism with which her two delicate fingers held the brocaded cloak, had reminded him of the lady Aladais of Marseilles, and he was unaware that, in the course of the years in which the statue had consoled him for his fleshly loss, his memory of that sentient form had passed imperceptibly into the painted image of stone until to his worshiping eyes the two were identical. Indeed, his loss had found more than ample compensation. Never had the wife of Lord Barral in her most condescending mood gratified so completely the vanity of the man as the Queen of Heaven, who with such intangible yet ineffable grace proved never weary of accepting—symbolically—each new tribute to the infinite and ever-growing love of his own ego.

O blessed and insatiable craving of the heart! Holiness of a passion unfulfillable! From the school of courtly love to the threshold of the Empyrean!

With a gesture of fervent and adoring humility, that if it lacked the litheness with which he had thrown himself at the feet of the lady Aladais was compensated by a greater passion, Fulk of Marseilles sank upon his *prie-dieu* and, with eyes feasting upon the image of chaste and divine beauty, turned his mind to the systematic humiliation of Raymond of Toulouse.

IV

There was perhaps only one other person in the city of Toulouse in whom the humiliation of the count had aroused an interest of anything like the same intensity, and in deference to the towering edifice of speculation to which the subject gave rise in the intelligence of the bishop it must be admitted that the influence it exerted on that

216

other mind was singularly circumscribed. Its outstanding feature was indeed not the scope of the images it evoked but their very limitation.

As, in the week following Raymond's acceptance of the Pope's decree, Jordan of the Isle, leaving the Castel Narbones, made his way along the riverbank in the direction of the Daurade, it was scarcely surprising that his attention, though sufficiently occupied with his own action in regard to the Crusade, should revert unconsciously to the subject of his brother-in-law's prospective penance: upon the steps of St. Gilles—stripped to the waist—to subject himself in all humility to the redeeming scourge, that in the agony of the flesh the soul might be purified. But the image of suffering which thus intruded on the urgent consideration of Jordan's affairs was not born of sympathy in any accepted sense of the word. Indeed, the more it took hold of his mind the more was it marked by its impersonality.

He walked slowly, oblivious of his surroundings. Around him the gardens leaning to the riverbank hung heavy with a scented riot of blossom. From beyond the crumbling wall, topped by dark cypresses, the sound of the cicadas came, harsh and monotonous, while now and then, through the interlacing of a wrought-iron gateway, the view opened on the old cemetery of the counts, where behind the arcaded cloister, half obscured by ancient fig trees, labyrinthine and knotty-armed, the red-brick towers of the Daurade glowed in the evening sun. The whole atmosphere was vibrant, enveloped in liquid continuity of light.

Suspended between that living scene and the eyes of Jordan of the Isle the image persisted, isolated, fragmentary. Indeed, at that moment it was expressive not so much of actual but of potential suffering, and the deadly fascination it exerted lay not in the fact but in its imminence. And yet, by some horrible paradox, the image was incapable of development. Replete in itself, every detail drawn with a sharpness that surpassed anything in the visible scene, it remained motionless, fixed, incapable of change.

How long that visitation persisted was uncertain, perhaps only for a few seconds, for in the mind of Jordan, suspended beyond the sphere of time and place, it was immeasurable in all but intensity.

Suddenly the image snapped, shattered by the sound of his name. Coming swiftly toward him with his characteristically graceful swagger, a flaunting enough symbol of the temporal, Peire-Roger of Mirepoix gaily waved a white-gloved hand.

"*Dieus*, one would almost think you'd been doomed to the stake already. Thought they'd at least spare you. Any new developments? I suppose you've come from the castle." He glanced toward the towers peering between the trees.

Recalled to this sudden realization of the present, Jordan muttered vaguely in the affirmative, uncertain as to whether the interruption of his visions was a relief or an intrusion.

"I'm just off to pay a little visit down by the west gate," Mirepoix laughed. "Thought I must say a last good-by to the dear girls. Coming?"

With a noncommittal shrug Jordan strolled on at Mirepoix's side. They made a strange contrast—the one with his free abandoned gait, brilliant and volatile, his gay, slightly supercilious countenance with the mobile lips curving so easily to mocking laughter, framed by the glistening locks of chestnut hair; the other reserved to the point of haughtiness and moving with a peculiar apathy which, added to his pallor and the cold passivity of the features, produced the effect of a strange lack of vitality.

"Well, how's Raymond bearing up?" Mirepoix asked, his curved eyebrows rising at a yet more quizzical angle.

"Tolerably, thanks to his physicians. He's pretty well doped."

"Good for him! So he's cheating the legates of two-thirds of the penance, the agonies of the imagination usually exceeding the actuality." And as the other gave a faint, rather unpleasant laugh, "It's definite, then? Let's hope they give him less of a buffeting than they did old Peire Maurand."

On Jordan's impassive countenance a little muscle began to twitch. And yet curiously, now that the subject was open to discussion, the image had lost its clarity.

Oblivious of the tortuous writhings of his companion's mind, Mirepoix strode on, his hand toying with the jeweled sword at his hip.

"Queer to think of old Raymond embarking on the role

218

of the martyr, unless possibly it's the Dionysian sacrifice. Well, having cultivated the divine so long, he had to expect, I suppose, that the gods would be jealous—or the avenging Jehovah, as you will," he added lightly. "I'm always forgetting you follow in the steps of your saintly ancestor. After all," his emerald eyes flashed an amused glance at his companion, "it *is* a bit difficult to keep one's bearings. What with your brother-in-law a confirmed pagan and your dear mother— Incidentally, what line are you taking?"

Jordan's manner seemed to grow yet more rigid. "I have never had any connection with my mother's religious activities."

Mirepoix laughed gaily. "No one questions it." It was more likely, he considered, they questioned the existence of any biological connection between Esclarmonde of Foix and her son. "Nevertheless," he mocked, knowing Jordan's horror of his mother's heresy and delighting to pull his leg, "you're such a dark horse—your amorous excursions, for instance, were always so exquisitely discreet—that if one were to judge you accordingly . . ."

He could not help feeling a certain delight in his attack on Jordan's circuitous approaches to the realm of love, approaches that had too often wearied and even repelled his own extravagant sense of gallantry. But by the other's obvious uneasiness it was evident that he had not missed his mark, and, incapable of prolonged malice, he turned toward him reassuringly. "My dear man, your orthodoxy is doubtless beyond question. As for me, considering this holy Crusade threatens even the freedom of the imagination, it behooves me surely to march with the glorious resistance. License, after all, is preferable to security, isn't it?" He shot a challenging glance at his companion.

Jordan's narrow lips contracted. "It seems you have managed pretty well to get security into the bargain—as one of the chosen guardians of Montségur."

"Defender of the holy citadel," Mirepoix completed, blissfully ignoring the other's venom. With a sudden dramatic gesture, snatching the snow-white cloak from his arm, he threw it round his shoulders, pirouetting slowly in a circle that his companion might take in the full magnificence of the beautifully sculptured folds, the silver wings of the dove embroidered upon the shoulder, and as

Jordan's face darkened, incapable of restraining his resilience, he continued irrepressibly: "Don't you approve? After all, one's got to do something to brighten things up a bit up there, or one would die of sheer boredom. The Cathar gospel of Love adapted to chivalric needs—the knighthood of the Holy Grail—well, isn't it superbly apt?"

"Superbly." Jordan's customary pallor seemed suddenly to have increased. "I presume—my mother—has shown her appreciation."

"Well, of course," Mirepoix tossed his gleaming locks, "one must expect her approach to be somewhat different. Still, with her exquisite sense of beauty, it would be a crime not to do things well. The Cathars are bound to make things pretty grim. She'll look on me as her aesthetic adviser." He laughed. "And, as Raymond would say, the Grail is capable of so many interpretations. Besides, the other aspect will doubtless be adequately provided by your little cousin."

"My cousin?"

"The Wolfling of Foix, one of the old man's bastards. Of course it's rather difficult to keep up to date, but at least this one managed to draw a bit of attention to himself. Ran off from a monastery, where his superfluity had been stowed safely away. You must have heard?"

"Vaguely."

"Old Foix wasn't too pleased about it. Actually, I believe, it was your mother persuaded him to pack the boy off to Carcassonne to be versed in the rules of chivalry."

"As prospective candidate for the knighthood of the Grail?"

Mirepoix laughed. "Really, you know, you might leave me the credit for my Mont Salvat.

"Well, of course," Mirepoix ran on, unruffled by the strange look on the other's face, "in a way I owe it to him. But that's half the joke. You see, he was such an innocent that Miriam Caravita called him Sir Galahad, and by chance it fitted in so completely with what your mother had told me about him. I'd just been at Pamiers and paid my respects. She seemed quite concerned about him; told me to give him her love and the rest. I was just off to Trencavel's festival. It seems when he ran away from his monastery he got lost up on the Tabor somewhere near the lake."

220

Involuntarily Jordan had halted. "When?" he muttered.

"Oh, a couple of years ago. And then one of the Cathars put him on his way to Montségur. It seems he was absolutely enchanted. Must have thought he had landed at Mont Salvat. So you see . . ."

But Jordan was indifferent to the question of Mirepoix's originality. For a moment he continued to walk on, silent. "What is he like?" he asked at last, with a vain attempt to be casual.

"Well, rather charming." Peire-Roger, sensing the other's jealousy, took an amused delight in the answer. "All eager and vulnerable—at least when I saw him. A bit broody, perhaps. Then Miriam came on the scene. He was completely shattered evidently. First love of course, and all that. Quite inconsolable till he became so thick with Trencavel."

"Trencavel?" Jordan echoed, half absent-mindedly. "He seems very impressionable."

"They're quite inseparable, I hear," Mirepoix ran on; "obsessed in this regeneration stunt. But now old Foix, I gather, has carried his son off home. Well, the boy at least will be able to console himself with his dream citadel. Soon, I suppose, I'll be meeting him up there. It might be rather amusing, really."

They had almost reached the western gate when Jordan halted. "I think after all I'll return. I'm not feeling exactly up to the mark. Besides, I have to see Fulk tonight."

Mirepoix, glancing at him, was struck by the man's deathly pallor.

"Alas, the poor girls will be desolate," he heaved a mocking sigh, but, actually relieved, he tried no persuasion. "Of course, for you it isn't so urgent, but I really ought to bid them farewell. After all," he laughed, "in case it comes to the worst, I must see there's someone to pray for my heroic soul. Besides, they deserve a glimpse of me in all my glory. The poor things must have yearned for their spiritual brothers so long. Too bad never to have provided the masculine counterpart."

But Jordan of the Isle was already oblivious of the light-hearted figure waving a last farewell, his white cloak blown out on the breeze. As he made his way back to the city even the thought of Raymond's agonies was far. Obsessed in its dark broodings, his memory had plunged back into a yawning pit; among the seething miasmata of

221

suspicion and doubt that had haunted him since childhood. And for the first time it seemed that the void that encompassed him was beginning to fill at last, not with love or tenderness, but at least with its opposite, the terrible and devastating passion of a hatred so fierce that it gathered all the figments haunting his tormented brain to one positive image—the face of a boy, eager, too sensitive-lipped, brooding above a mountain tarn.

CROSSWAYS

Forest water lost itself in virgin sand, and hail
Drove before the wind upon the pools. . . . To think
How, obsessed as fishers up of gold or shell,
I, the fool, had not a thought to pause and drink!
(ARTHUR RIMBAUD, translated by N. CAMERON)

I

SO LITTLE HAD CHANGED!

Closing her eyes and letting her fingers stray over the carved arms of the chair, as though she must confirm by sense of touch what her eyes could scarcely believe, Esclarmonde of Foix sat for a moment without movement, absorbing the old familiar atmosphere of the room. Twenty-five years had passed since she had left her ancestral home. She had never been here since. Even when those long years of her Gascon exile had ended, and she might have returned, she had settled straight away in the castellar of Pamiers that was to be the seat of her widowhood. Perhaps because at the time her brother had still been absent, a prisoner in Seo D'Urgel, and she had always dreamed that it was he who should bring her home to the place in which they had passed their inseparable childhood; perhaps because she had half feared that the sight of things never forgotten—things so familiar and pregnant still with a thousand memories and dreams— might have power to shake her in the resolve she had made. Now they held no menace, and today for once she would allow herself this luxury of remembrance. Tomorrow it would be impossible, and all her thought, her energy would be absorbed again in the exigencies of the moment, at the council of the vassals of Foix, at which she was to be present as co-owner with Ramon Perelha of the mightiest of the mountain fortresses—Montségur.

For everything was drawing on to an immense, incredible fulfillment. The image that had haunted her for years was to become a reality, not as she had dreamed, but with anguish and terror in its wake, the last hope perhaps of their faith, their liberty.

As if to catch breath before a realization too overwhelming, she closed her eyes, breathing in that faint, well-remembered fragrance of long-lost things.

How still it was after these last weeks of constant planning and organization, struggling to keep in touch with the disseminated members of the Cathar church, trying to regulate the ever-increasing flow of refugees. And since her arrival in Foix last night there had been so much to discuss, so much to overcome, while Ramon-Roger, as of old, fired up in resentment against her faith. It had almost been a relief when at noon he had ridden out to supervise some improvements in the fortifications of his castle, Montgaillard, and she was left to enjoy this last quietude.

The Crusade had marched. Close on three hundred thousand strong, it had descended the Rhône, stood encamped before Montpellier. From Bordeaux a second army was pouring down on the Carcassais. War, persecution, and death—almost they seemed impossible here amid the quietness of half-forgotten things rewon. Peace of a summer afternoon, coolness in the shadow of the thick ancient walls, and from below the rushing of the Ariège. Always it had been there, so familiar that it had not been heard, till afterward in the silence at Selio she had found herself listening for it in vain. Even at Pamiers it had not been the same as here, where it still muttered with the savagery of its mountain source in that ceaseless interlocution with the castle rock, which looked as though it had been hurled down from those heights by one of the giants in a rage. At least that was what they had pretended then, she and her brother, when they were children together here at Foix. And when he got into one of his furies (which were frequent) it was all explained and excused—between them, at least. The blood of the old Titan breed had come to life in him again.

Certainly young Ramon-Roger had been the very devil, the terror of peasant and serf, harrying the flocks and setting fire to the cornstacks. She could see him still, as, down in the meadow beyond the river, he goaded the bulls, caring more about the loss of his beloved arab than his own gored shoulder. Not even the merciless chastisements of their stiff-necked, obdurate father had availed to break his spirit. No one could tame him, unless it was she. But then, she was part of the story, she, the nymph of light who alone could assuage the terrible fires in the heart of the giant's son by blinding him with the cool shimmer of her hair—she, Esclarmonde. But there had been that other day on which the old Cathar bishop Nicetas, who had come all the way from the East to preside at the synod of Caraman, had stopped, seeing her at play, and laying his hand on her head had asked her name. "Esclarmonde—the light of the world," he had echoed, looking at her long with his dark, penetrating eyes. "But it is harder sometimes," he had added, "to keep the light burning amid our own darkness."

At the time she had not understood. But later . . . It had been incredibly hard, and at times she had been sure almost that the light had gone out. Yet a little spark must have remained somewhere, for it would suddenly flicker up again at the thousand and one tiny, meaningless things that made life. For they were unending, always cropping up again and again and where one least expected them. Perhaps, after all, it wasn't the fierce exultant joys that counted for most in the end. At least it seemed possible to think that now. Was it only age, renunciation, excape? Things—she had always been devoted to them, so that Guihalbert of Castres had had to warn her often about the illusion of appearance. But if in them, too, the light was there, imprisoned in matter as the soul in the flesh?

Her eyes, returning to the room, lay a moment on the empty fireplace round which they had gathered so often in winter, while Ramon-Roger had stared fiercely into the fire planning some new escapade, till he had sprung up with a song on his lips and flung from the room. Or, over against the wall, the huge carved chests of blackened oak from which she had taken the best linen on festive days or when important guests had been expected at the castle; and though it was day the great candlesticks had been lit because the heavy vaulted hall, her mother had said, looked fitter for a prison than a banquet. She could see her sitting there now, in her cold proud beauty with that faintly derisive smile on her lips, thinking, no doubt, of the brilliant and luxurious courts of her father, Raimon Trencavel, at Béziers and Carcassonne. In that mingled light the flames of the tapers had glimmered so small and lost that everything had seemed unreal, and ordinary things had changed their customary face. How many had sat in the high place—dukes and princes and even kings, for Foix lay on the road leading over the pass to Spain. Alfonso of Aragon, Raymond the fifth of Toulouse—how many rivals had helped to polish the griffins on that ancient oak? Once it had been the present Raymond himself. Raymond. . . .

For a moment her mind returned to the thought that had occupied her so often during the past days, but the other image was stronger, clear as though it had been yesterday. She had entered the hall and seen him sitting there, young and indolently magnificent, leaning back in that very chair, the almost classic head framed by the golden locks, its beauty already marred by debauchery. And then that startled surprise, the strange expression that for a moment had illumined his face, mingling so unexpectedly with its irredeemable sensuality as, standing before him, she pledged him in the cup her ancestor had brought home from the first Crusade; and, gazing still, he had murmured something about the Grail.

She had not thought more of it then, had quite forgotten it. But Raymond, it seemed, had not forgotten, and later in her exile at Selio . . . It had been just a whim, of course, but so characteristic of his epicurean gallantry, still to have remembered after all those years. A whim, a cup, mere chance—and yet holding so much fatality! Else would he ever have come—Kyot, the singer with his strange stories from the East, "sent by Count Raymond of Toulouse in token of a vision once beheld at Foix"? And as he sang, the barren rock, the glaring light of Gascony were forgotten, while imperceptibly that mysterious citadel amid the Asian wilderness became one, in her nostalgia, with the ruined fortress of her Pyrenean home—Montségur. She had never forgotten the time she saw it first, once when, as a child, they had stayed at the Perelhas and her brother had been full of tales of the giant Geryon who had built it—the race from which he had sprung. Though there were other tales, of the altar on the crest of that fantastic rock and at Lavelanet—altars built to the god and goddess of light. But as she listened, waking as from a long wintry sleep, she had begun to see it peopled with the images of the singer's tale, real with the reality of a vision imaginatively shared—shared and as suddenly shattered. And still in the silence that followed it had lived on, suffering that gentle transmutation into an image fulfillable in time and space—a citadel of Cathar knighthood, guarding, against the dense obduracy of the world, the radiance of the Spirit, the temple of the Paraclete.

Yet it had been long before she had actually believed in the possibility of its realization; even when, dying, her father had left her as heritage, in co-seigniory with Perelha, the lands of Montségur. A symbol, the memorial of a dream—what chance was there of it becoming more, hemmed in as she was by the ruthless bigotry of her husband, the insurmountable alienation of a sickly boy? And then at last she had found herself free.

Incredulous still, she had first spoken to Ramon Perelha of rebuilding the ruined fortress. Little was said, and of that dream nothing. Enough that on the horizon the clouds were gathering, the threat to heresy growing day by day. To the earnest, singlehearted warrior, himself a heretic, the prospect of a Cathar stronghold and this chance of strengthening his own domains had been welcome enough, while the Count of Foix, her brother, cynical though he was toward any form of mystic idealism, orthodox or heterodox alike, had been well content with the idea of fortifying so strategic a point. If anyone, it had been Guihalbert of Castres who evaded, afraid of the too-tangible symbol.

Perhaps even then she had questioned the possibility of its actuality. The dream was inviolate. Perelha in the meantime had started rebuilding. As for herself, she had enough to do solving a problem actual enough—the foundation of the Cathar hospice at Pamiers. For her way had become clear—to dedicate herself entirely to the faith that had become her life. There was nothing to hold her back. Jordan, her son, had drifted away in cynical indifference. He had not even shown the resentment she had expected in view of this triumphant revolt against her dead husband's orthodoxy, nothing more than the old silent mockery with its perpetual unspoken accusation of renunciation and escape. He had always been like that since infancy, grudging her every sign of joy (for joy existed still, cropping up quite unexpectedly in little things—the dappled shade of leaves in the wind, the bloom on a grape, children's laughter at play), and the sight of her pleasure would fill him with a violent resent-

ment—would it had been at least to fits of passionate jealousy. But he would only draw away, sullen, following her
with his dark, opaque, unchildlike eyes, or later with that
cold close-lipped smile that seemed to mock her slightest
delight, as though he would force her to confess, to bring
her to her knees to compel her to admit her secret anguish.

It had been like a secret battle between them, but she
had never given in. Yet to Jordan, perhaps, her retirement
to Pamiers appeared a confession of her guilt, as though
she sought oblivion and expiation in self-imposed stricture
and good works.

There in the hospice, confronted by a misery that
seemed to put her own torment in the shade, and reprov-
ing herself for past egotism, she had dedicated herself to
the tangible sufferings of those before her with such earnest that the dream-image of Montségur had faded into a
plane remoter than ever.

Yet it had triumphed.

Was it she who had pursued the image, or the image
her? Did the dream at last create its own reality, or did a
secret power, a potentiality, lie in the thing itself, which it
was given one, through some mysterious power of sympathy or affinity, to bring out, till the spirit imprisoned in
matter was freed by the realization of thought? But abstract thinking had always defeated her. Perhaps that
monk at the fatal conference at Pamiers had been right after all: "Woman, return to your spindle." And even
Guihalbert of Castres—she smiled wistfully, always unable
to blind herself to her own failings—Guihalbert with his
uncompromising absolute, his relentless cleavage of spirit
and flesh, would he ever have approved such a thought?
Yet somehow it seemed to her that old Bishop Gauceli
would have understood, and she remembered the day in
her girlhood before she had been borne off to Selio in
marriage, and how she had heard him preach that even
into the veil of illusion which Satan had spun around the
soul the spiritual might be enwoven so cunningly that in
our desire to pierce through the husk we might too easily
tear asunder those delicate fibers and lose the essence.
However it might be, the image had triumphed. For then
Wolf had come.

Wolf with his own dream, eager, burning, vulnerable,
and for a moment the dream had sprung up so sharp, so

228

unbelievably near, that it seemed she had but to stretch
out her hand. Yet afraid of dragging him into her own fatality, perhaps even jealous a little of her dream, she had
held back. There was so much, besides, to make her. It
was difficult enough at the time to keep her brother from
sending him back to the monastery, while any discussion
of Montségur, recalling as it did his son's rebellious fantasies and adding, moreover, to his inherent impatience
with mysticism, would only have fanned the fire. So she
had prevailed on Ramon to send the boy to Carcassonne,
and but for a message or two in these two years had kept
silence. Of her own story she had told him nothing. But it
was as well; by now it seemed to her that there was something bigger behind it than herself. If it were destined for
this thing to fulfill itself, it would.

Since then the fate of Montségur had developed with an
almost amazing rapidity—Innocent's threats, the murder
of Castelnau, the arming of the Crusade, and now the terror that so long had seemed a nightmare stood palpable
upon the threshold. She shuddered as though awakening.
Guihalbert had hesitated no longer, grateful enough now
for this stronghold amid peril. She tried to quell that little
feeling of triumph that would always rise at the thought,
unable to stifle a faint regret that the consecration of
Montségur could not be at the hands of old Bishop Gauceli—as if it weren't enough that it should be at all!
Montségur! Legendary citadel of an esoteric religion,
dream-image of a love unconfessed, it had become real
enough as a refuge, the last, perhaps, from persecution
and terror.

Yet it had all come about through her, through a cup
that still perhaps lay there in a great iron-banded chest,
wrapped in its covering of brocaded silk, emerald as in
that tale, she mused, though in Kyot's song it hadn't been
a cup but a stone—a jewel—yet still the Grail, and with
the same properties—that ever-spending font. . . . But
once more in the brooding quietness her consciousness was
drawn back from the pure idea to the tangible ghosts of
the past.

Once more she saw herself, cup in hand, standing before Raymond, the young Count of Toulouse. By now that
indolently graceful figure, even then too soft in contour,
must have grown flaccid; the voluptuous head, already a
little depraved, would be robbed of everything but vicious-

ness and a shrewd perspicacity. What chance, what fate had swayed his life from sensuousness to corruption, from unprincipled curiosity to betrayal, as hers was destined by that cup? Chance? Was it not all the working out of that fate which man prepared for himself in this or in some former life, in that perpetual reincarnation of his own sinning and redemption? Yet how often the threads crossed, entangled. At every movement one was blindly deciding not only one's own but another's fate. What right, then, had one to censure, to blame? If one did, it must be the principle surely, not the man. Yet even so, through no more than a word spoken or left unsaid, some tiny gesture seen so often and yet suddenly imbued with such significance, all was altered, the pattern broken, a life wrecked, a nation sent to its doom.

Toulouse had given in. At least the blood of many would be spared, but how many others would not escape from terror and torture, from the stake—the avalanche that was sweeping over Languedoc?

And Trencavel? What choice was left to him? Certainly he had stood out against Raymond's expediency. Hadn't her brother himself mocked him idealist, statue-blind—Icarus, who in his fall would drag them all in the dust. But Toulouse and the Crusade were different things, and if Trencavel gave in. . . . Three hundred thousand strong they stood before Montpellier. Who had reckoned on that except her brother perhaps? And he was realist enough to know that unless they could hold out at Carcassonne the only hope was to win over Aragon—Pedro, crowned king of the Pope! Horror swept over her again. For what, she thought in despair, could be the outcome of victory bought with bargain and intrigue, bloodshed and massacre, except new misery and revenge? Would not wrongs violently redressed inevitably give birth to new reprisals? Could anything be born from destruction without being tainted itself? Ah, was there no escape from that ceaseless round of hate and crime and vengeance; must it always be man's way, ruthless in his lust for power, intransigent in his idealism; impatient, burning to destroy? Why, even Wolf. . . .

For there he was, chafing and restless because he had been torn from the scene of danger. She had known it the moment she had seen him last night. There had hardly been time to talk.

He will have changed, she had prepared herself so long.

Had he? Or was it only a mask with which he guarded himself as he stood there before her, a little taller and so much stronger than she had imagined. He had shut himself up. But of course—it was so long since they had met. So much must lie between them—a youth's shame, perhaps, for the memory of a childish enthusiasm; or fear that she might expect an avowal of her faith, might try even to hold him back from fighting, fear above all that she would stand between him and his friend? She had been ready for it. That Ramon had dragged him home had hit him hard. He was sworn to Trencavel in more than allegiance. That they had become closely bound to each other was certain from the little he had said, which was not to be wondered at. She recalled the day two years ago on which Trencavel, passing through Pamiers, had visited the castellar. She had been unable to rid herself of the feeling that, despite his grace and gaiety, there was a quality of sadness within him, and she had been filled with sorrow, less because he was lost to the Cathars than that he was, it somehow seemed, lost to himself. He is not here, she had thought, he is forcing himself. He is like one walking, talking, in a world that to him is dead.

"He is working for the future," Wolf had retorted last night in answer to some scornful remark of Ramon's concerning Trencavel's reforms. Was he? What made her ask, what invaded her once more with some nameless, inexpressible fear? Perhaps it was all imagination, perhaps Trencavel was changed, perhaps in this friendship between the two he had found himself. Then wasn't it the very hope of a future for them all, for Montségur?

The sound of horses' hoofs woke her from her brooding. Could it be Wolf? So soon returned? Why, yes. The shadow had moved across the meadow to the foot of the bridge. The afternoon was drawing in. She had had no illusions about his readiness to remain at Foix instead of accompanying his father to Montgaillard, only to be near at hand, waiting, always restless for news. Was he after all afraid, in spite of what he said, that Trencavel would give in? He had ridden out with some message to the manor and she had given word that on his return she would speak with him. And they would talk, of Carcassonne, of Trencavel at first, till the foolish barriers that had grown between them would fall and all came naturally—Foix, Montségur, the guard. Even the last, she thought wistfully, was a compromise between herself and her brother, between the Cathar faith with its creed of passive resistance and the world. For she knew well enough that the mountain barons would brook no heretic eyrie in their midst without a grim enough defense to make it unpalatable to the enemy. The guard would be militant enough—but for the sake of defense, not aggression. Yet did not that very compromise re-create her dream? Once more there rose before her the image of that warrior order in the stranger's song—"like an order," Wolf had said, springing to his feet that day in Pamiers long ago. But no, she had pushed that from her.

Nonetheless, hearing steps upon the stair, she turned toward the door with such eagerness that the serving-maid who appeared on the threshold took for granted that the countess was expecting her visitor, and, mumbling her announcement, drew aside.

She has never welcomed me with that look, thought Jordan of the Isle, advancing toward her. He did not miss the sudden freezing of joyous expectancy on her face before, with an effort, that welcoming smile was resumed.

He bent to kiss her hand.

It is surely with evil tidings he has come, she thought—to frustrate me, now at the last.

"You were scarce expecting me." Raising his head, he regarded her with that acrid, too well-remembered smile.

"You come so seldom, Jordan," she guarded herself.

It must be three years since I saw her last. She has aged, he thought, now that the light had died from her face. She is thinner, from fasting. His eyes lay upon her hands, lined, roughened, it seemed, by work. She is castigating herself with labors of love.

"You have ridden far?" His face was scarcely less pallid than usual, but beads of perspiration stood out on his brow.

He sank upon the window seat. "I hoped to find you in time, understanding—" he paused, regarding her fixedly. "You may imagine, I had no special wish to scale the mountains."

She stiffened imperceptibly, hardening in face of danger. But she would take no step to meet him.

"You are alone," he said, glancing round the room as though he looked for something.

"Why, yes. Ramon has ridden to Montgaillard. He will be back by nightfall."

"With his sons?"

"Roger's in Andorra."

"Preparing the last defense? He may have need of it. And the other—Trencavel's squireling, isn't he? The news might be of special interest to him."

"News!" she caught her breath. "Of the Viscount?"

"I happened to be at Montpellier. Trencavel was there. As your son, it behooved me, I thought, to warn you before—"

"He has given in?" Her voice was toneless. She did not look at him.

That was a moment's pause. "No," he answered. "He came to Montpellier to discuss terms. They were not to his liking. He refused them."

Now as the news fell from her son's scathing lips she felt almost a sense of infinite relief, beyond all wisdom or conviction, beyond all thought of what might come.

"I am glad," he remarked, watching her with his strange opaque gaze, "that his resolution appears to meet with your approval. The situation, however, is, to say the least, serious. And your religion, I have always understood," he smiled skeptically, "condemns bloodshed."

How long had she known that searing cynicism, that ruthless undermining of all belief. At once her faith reasserted itself. "Yes," she answered, "but not courage."

Before her quiet gaze his eyes dropped.

"And you, Jordan?" she continued. "Is Raymond perhaps calling on your support?"

For once the blood darkened the habitual pallor of his face. He drew himself up rigid. "My blood," he muttered, "is older than that of Toulouse. I have no mind to betray it to the Capet."

He rose, then turning to the window, gazed out on the great amphitheater of hills. Was this pride of race, she thought sadly, the only thing in which he had a remnant of faith?

"With his enlightened views Raymond is hardly like to expect me to declare war on my own kith and kin. The more so," he smiled thinly, "as I fancy he has long harbored a profound reverence for you."

He paused. His fingers, curiously long, almost clawlike, began to draw on the leaded pane. "Believing that . . .

hm . . . active resistance is abhorrent to your creed, I came to offer you my protection."

She gazed at him, incredulous. "You mean . . ." she began.

"If you are ready to dissociate yourself from this project of Montségur . . . I am not, as you may know, without influence. The Jordans were always staunch Catholics. Even now, Bishop Fulk might be constrained to shut an eye. It would be necessary, of course, to disband the hospice at Pamiers."

She had half risen from her chair. Her spirit transcending the wan, worn flesh seemed to give it an almost terrifying radiance. "If you have come for that—nothing will make me betray my faith."

Was it like that she had greeted his father, he wondered, when he had wooed her in this very hall, and at the command of the old Count of Foix she had been forced to follow? If only she had confronted *him* like that from the first, given him at least her hate. But she had condoned, defended him since childhood, as though she took his sins, his baseness, his every vileness upon herself, till he was goaded to madness. Only at some cruelty done to the heretics had he seen, sometimes at Selio, that steely glimmer in her look.

"Well, as you wish," he muttered, rankling in the knowledge that, though he cynically denied it, telling himself it was only her humiliation he desired, his action had been prompted by something more. "Arnaud-Amelric's solicitude for the soul's salvation is likely to prove very ardent. The legate's extortions at St. Gilles were doubtless mild by comparison."

"You were there?" She shuddered.

"Yes." He gave an uncanny laugh. "It was insufferably hot."

In a flash memory returned. She saw, as though she were there, the great flight of steps between the flanking lions, glaring white in the sun. So it had been when long ago as a child she witnessed at her father's side the glorious pageantry of the house of St. Gilles and Toulouse. And she had grown so tired standing there in the great procession jammed in the door, till all of a sudden, on the sculptured plinth of the column at her side, she caught sight of young David vanquishing a Goliath clad in armor like huge fishes' scales. Had Raymond, she wondered, in the very hour of his shame, found solace in the fact that the foliage crowning those columns, the togaed gravity of those apostles and saints, still breathed something of an antiquity he loved; and as he lay, his coarsened lips pressed to the holy relics, did he smile, thinking perhaps that he, like them, was only playing a part in a vast and fantastic masquerade?

Once more, for a second, the ghost seemed to hover in the high seat, the depraved but beautiful head turn toward her in half-skeptical wonder.

"At last," Jordan's passionless voice was saying, "Master Thedise, throwing his stole over the Count's neck, dragged him to the altar, while in his hand the flail . . ."

Could it be his, that servile, creeping form, the obese, the pampered flesh sweating in agony?

"The crowd was so dense they had to let him out secretly through the crypt. . . ."

In her ears were the cries of the mob, rapacious in curiosity and lust.

"By a curious irony, his only means of escape lay past the tomb of the murdered legate. . . ."

But she had almost ceased to listen to the flat, insinuating voice that systematically seemed to deny all hope of alleviation from evil.

A step had sounded on the stair. Even as she turned toward the door it opened. He came toward her a little hesitant; upon his face, breaking through the awkwardness and reserve, that wild expectant plea for news, deepening to anxiety and fear as he saw the wan look on her face. It was evident that he did not know.

"Oh, Wolf," she began, in her relief rejoicing that she could tell him. But the consciousness of Jordan's presence intruded again.

At the same moment, hidden till then by the recess of the window, Jordan turned.

"My son," she murmured.

A little cry fell from Wolf's lips. But the other's face wore almost an ingratiating smile. "I fancy we have met before. I found him up on the Tabor—by the lake. It must be three or four years ago. I was staying at Lordat for the hunting. I almost took him for a water sprite," he laughed softly, turning to his mother. "Of course, had I had the least idea—but I only discovered his identity the other day, by mere chance."

Esclarmonde, aware of the boy's pallor, was looking at him perturbed. "Why, Wolf, you never told me. . . ."

He did not answer.

Jordan had sunk back onto the window seat. "It seems he had an adventurous journey," he continued. "If he had only been more articulate I might have spared him his perilous quest, erring about the mountains in search of Mont Salvat."

As he spoke his gaze shifted to his mother, but Esclarmonde, concerned at the boy's embarrassment, scarce heard. Aware moreover that Jordan, unlikely as he was to depart, might probably forestall her with news of Trencavel, she turned to Wolf.

"News has come," she began.

He made a sudden movement, his hand caught at his belt.

"Wolf—the Viscount is resisting."

His hand dropped. He stood facing her, wild and eager, breathing deep.

"He came to Montpellier," Jordan put in, "to ask for terms. He refused them."

"You were there with him?" Wolf cried, everything else forgotten.

"Yes, I was there. He sends you greetings," he added, his eyes resting on him curiously.

"He expects me," Wolf broke out eagerly; "he expects me to come."

Jordan made a little shrugging gesture. "I fancy that the decision rests with your father. Foix was never vassal to Carcassonne."

The blood deepened on Wolf's face as his father's sarcasms rang again in his ears. "But Trencavel's going to fight," he cried. "I'm his squire." Impulsively he turned to Esclarmonde. "Father *must* let me go. I'd better go at once and meet him."

He had waited only for this. She had known it well enough and cheated herself with hopes. But even if Ramon, as was probable, refused to let him go, Wolf would beg her to play the part of mediator on his behalf. If she could have spoken first, if Jordan had not come?

"Wolf," her eyes were fixed on his, deep and searching, "I was going to speak to you—about the guard."

For a moment he seemed to hesitate. Then his face hardened. "There are enough without me."

Jordan of the Isle looked up. "What, defenders of the holy citadel? A perfect galaxy—all the sons of the Comet and the Moon."

Wolf stiffened, and then suddenly, before she could speak, with hardly a mumbled excuse or word of farewell, he had turned and left the room.

Esclarmonde had almost risen. To lose him before they had even spoken—to lose him perhaps forever. And yet— what good could come of force? Through himself alone could he find the Way.

Jordan, leaning back in the window, smiled thinly. "I trust all the defenders of your citadel aren't as fickle as he. Still, if Galahad deserts, I suppose you may still bank on Gawaine. Incidentally," he continued with studied casualness, "I gather Mirepoix is staging one of his grand effects."

"Mirepoix?" she echoed, vaguely surprised.

Was she shamming? He was never sure. Never in his life had he been sure. But possibly Mirepoix hadn't yet revealed his own plans. "Perhaps it's a secret I wasn't meant to divulge. He's always afraid of spoiling the novelty, only this time I fancy," he watched her between narrowed lids, "it's more in the nature of a revival."

Absent-minded, she evaded his probing, still gazing blindly at the closed door. So this was what had come of the evening which she had expected so much.

A little later Jordan of the Isle, arriving at the stables, found Wolf, who had already led out his horse, in the act of tieing his helmet onto the saddle.

"You seem very sure of your powers of persuasion," he laughed.

The boy, uncertain, did not look up.

"I came to tell you," Jordan continued, "I didn't blurt it out all at once for fear of alarming the old lady. When I left yesterday they were marching on Béziers."

Wolf swung round so suddenly that the horse reared. It was Jordan who caught it by the bridle.

"Is he—is Trencavel there?"

"Hardly. Anyhow, there's little time to waste. I'd advise you to defy parental authority and make straight for Carcassonne, but they'd probably drag you back. I was thinking, if you like I'd tackle the old man myself. I rather fancy my powers of persuasion might be more effective."

Mistrustful, but ready to clutch at anything in his desperation, Wolf gazed at him distraught. "You mean you'll come with me?"

"Better than that. I'll ride to meet him with the news myself and explain. In the meantime you'll be well on your way. I don't think there's much fear of his calling you back."

Filled with sudden apprehension, Wolf turned toward him. "What are you going to say?"

Jordan's fingers played idly with the bridle. "It rather depends on the circumstances. However, I've an idea." He regarded Wolf quizzically. "I fancy the Count isn't very keen on a son of his indulging in all this hocus-pocus at Montségur. After all, it *is* rather nebulous, isn't it, after your experiences in neopaganism at Carcassonne?" His eyes were fixed on Wolf, burrowing, searching, as though he would strip him bare.

With a sudden movement Wolf had swung himself into the saddle, clutching his spear.

"You look very formidable," Jordan laughed. "Well, tell Trencavel I hope he's grateful for my sending him what he was afraid to ask for himself."

II

Setting spurs to his horse, Wolf dashed through the barbican. With luck, by dawn at latest, he should reach Carcassonne. Turning once, he saw Jordan still standing there immobile, gazing after him.

Jordan of the Isle—the sinister huntsman of the Tabor. Still it seemed incredible. Esclarmonde's son! Yet for all he knew, it flashed over him bitterly, thinking of Mirepoix, Jordan might have reason enough to make him a cynic concerning his mother's faith. That day up on the mountain he'd doubtless behaved like a fool, and the man must surely bear him a grudge. He was still amazed at his amiability, and yet he was unable to rid himself of a sense of distrust. Glancing back once more, he saw that the figure had disappeared. Well, whatever his motives, Jordan had given him this chance. Even if he did not keep his promise he had at least a good start. Nothing mattered if only he could reach Carcassonne.

Surely Trencavel must know he would come, would come at the first asking, despite his father, despite everything. Suddenly he remembered that autumn night when he had said, without knowing rightly why, "I shall come back." There were things one just knew without reason. Had Trencavel thought he was afraid? It was he who had insisted on his going when his father arrived to fetch him away. After all, he had the right to claim him, his squire. Carcassonne was not Foix's vassal. Of course he might have been apprehensive of a rupture with his ally. Had Jordan not said Trencavel should thank him for sending him what he was afraid to ask for himself? A sudden fear clutched at his heart. Was that perhaps what Jordan was after? But why? As far as he knew there was no enmity between him and Trencavel. The old feeling of distrust would not leave him. Should he after all have gone and pleaded with his father himself? But Jordan's quiet gibe had not proved unwarranted. His own powers of persuasion, he knew, were scarce likely to have proved effective. And even if they had, would it not have been too late? Even now—if, after all, he thought in sudden fear, Trencavel should have gone to defend Béziers. By now, if Jordan were right, the Crusade might have surrounded it. Three hundred thousand men! He would never get through.

Wasn't Trencavel always thinking of Béziers—the new Béziers they would build? But that was still all in the clouds, while Carcassonne was real—the beginning of their new world.

No, he couldn't be there. His father, all the barons, had stipulated for a defense at Carcassonne—Carcassonne that had defied Charlemagne for seven years till he had lifted the siege, and only on his way back from Spain had the towers of the city inclined themselves of their own accord before the great emperor. So the legend said. But today they would defend it even better than in the tale, if not for seven years, which was unthinkable. Besides, they had far more formidable weapons now. Armed with crossbow and arbalest, and stationed at the machines, they would hurl missile on missile at the treating foe and ride out to assault on assault.

Suddenly he recalled the evening on which, returning

from that first Cathar meeting, he had gazed with Sicard on those menacing towers (Sicard, who wouldn't be there after all, but defending Durban or riding to battle in the ranks of Foix), and Sicard had said, "I wonder whether they called us decadent when Alaric fell."

But they weren't decadent, as those cursed French and Burgundians would soon have to agree when they saw the youth of Carcassonne sally out against them and learned that the citizens were as good swordsmen as their barons and lords. If only there had been more time, if the sports had been held as they planned; but at least they'd had their training. D'Alfaro, of course, would jeer, but it wasn't the past they looked at but toward the future. Laying his spear at rest, he spurred at the imaginary foe.

Dusk was falling. To the left the towers of the castellar at Pamiers rose dark against the failing light. From one of them, years ago, he and Esclarmonde of Foix had looked out on the distant mountains. "We'll have to fight and build, shan't we, at Montségur?" Again a little stab of jealous pain shot through him. Montségur—an aging woman's whimsy, the means of placating a troublesome boy's foolhardy dreams. Thank heaven, there hadn't been a chance of having that talk. If she thought he was going to be one of her bodyguard just to please her vanity she was mistaken. "A whole galaxy—all the sons of Cometa and Luna." Of course—Peire-Roger. Well, let them play at their masquerade. Almost he wished, as he rode through Mirepoix, that he would run into Peire-Roger himself.

Actually, now he came to think of it, he couldn't remember whether Jordan had really mentioned him, but whether he had or not it was pretty clear at what he had been hinting. There was something so strained, though, in the relations between him and his mother. Of course it was the difference in religion, but somehow it seemed more. Disconcertingly, the more he tried to recall him, the more unprepossessing did the figure of Jordan become, till the old revulsion filled him anew, while that of Esclarmonde seemed somehow to regain much of the mystery and loveliness which once more he had not been able to deny. After all, might it have been better if he had spoken to her? Returning from the manor this afternoon he had set his mind on doing so, but he pushed from him doubt and regret. "It's all rather nebulous, isn't it, compared with your neopaganism at Carcassonne?" Of course that, too, was the old mockery, like d'Alfaro's, but more horrible and insidious. Again he heard that flat, insinuating voice. Well, they should both see! All that mattered was that he should get there. But still the mountains loomed in the gathering darkness close at his back.

It was quite dark now. Fixing his eyes on the faint boundary of the road, he goaded on his flagging horse. Beneath him he could feel its flanks wet with sweat. It might have been better, he reflected, to have changed horses at Mirepoix. Now he must get on to Fanjeaux. There, at least, he could get certain news.

He was meeting with few travelers now. Earlier there had been enough, but he had not dared delay for fear that he might yet be pursued. Now they grew fewer and fewer. A belated peasant driving home his beast, a couple of merchants plodding along the road. Soon even they had sought refuge for the night. He might have halted at an inn himself, but the chance of getting a mount worth while was poor, and one could never be sure of robbers not lurking about such dens. Once he came abreast of a company of soldiers bound in the same direction as he, but their sobriety was dubious enough, and followed by their coarse jests he pushed on ahead, only to doubt the wisdom of his action, for in the darkness he was uncertain of the way. He would have given much for almost any sort of companion now. Once a rider, hard-pressed as he, came dashing toward him. A messenger perhaps? But even as he would have shouted to him the other had torn past, and his voice was carried away on the wind.

At last, however, he reached Fanjeaux. Lights still burned at the inn, but to his urgent demand for a fresh mount the sleepy stableboy made scant reply. Every horse in the place, it seemed, was taken.

Impatient, Wolf made his way into the tavern. The room was full of confusion, crowded with armed men deep in their cups. Thrusting his way through their midst he made straight for the landlord, who was bustling about replenishing goblet and plate.

"A horse?" he replied, his fat face harassed and perspiring. "Might as well ask the archangel himself to lend you his wings. There's not one miserable jade in Fanjeaux, I reckon, hasn't been commandeered"; and he brushed the boy aside in order to serve his impatient guests.

"But I must," Wolf insisted.

"Must? There's no musts in war," the host called over his shoulder as he poured wine into a soldier's cup.

"Except being marched to your death," growled a dark-faced man in the background.

Desperately Wolf turned again to the landlord: "But the Viscount's waiting. I'm his squire."

"His squire? Think he can't get on without one of his nancyboys to hold his stirrup for him?" mocked a voice at his elbow, and as he turned on the man angrily, another, red-faced, his breath acrid with wine, thrust his face between.

"You'll not be finding yourself at one of your swell tournaments," the mercenary laughed. "Well, anyway, what's all the hurry about? It's too late in the day for you or anyone to be arming your lord and master for the fray."

"Too late?" Wolf echoed. An icy, paralyzing fear crept over him. He clutched at the table.

"Well, done's done for, isn't it? And now he's shut himself up in his fortress. . . ."

In his relief Wolf scarcely realized the taunt.

"Even by one of their blessed miracles themselves," the man continued, "they're scarce likely to reach Carcassonne by tomorrow. They've enough on their hands clearing up Béziers."

"What, hasn't he heard?" Leaning back, the mercenary gazed skeptically at the horrified boy. "News just came in. The Crusade broke in this morning. Now I guess they're having their fling."

"But," stammered Wolf, unbelieving, "it was bound to hold out—at least a fortnight!" he cried, blindly echoing his father's words.

"A fortnight?—everyone thought a month at least. And there it is—puff!" the man spat out.

"And not through the hand of my lords and barons even," the other laughed.

"Even?" the first man echoed. "Even? Is it ever they do the real fighting?"

"Long live the mercenaries!" The shout went up in drunken chorus. "Long live the *ribauds!*"

In despair Wolf had turned and torn himself from the room. Outside in the darkness he leaned against the doorway, giddy and dazed.

A hand was laid on his arm. He found himself looking into the face of an old ostler he had seen sometimes when stopping here on the hunt with Trencavel.

"No good?" he muttered. "The boy told me." Wolf shook his head. Beckoning, the old man led him across the stable and, opening the door, pointed to a strong if stocky beast.

"Well," he smiled slyly, "it's hardly a fair exchange, but it'll serve."

"Whose is it?" Wolf asked eagerly.

"The captain's. Don't be a fool, boy. The man's got the better bargain. Besides, he's in no hurry. Waiting till the Crusade gets nearer, I reckon, to see whether he can reap more profit from the other side—the swine!"

While they saddled the beast the old man told him the news, brought but now by a messenger from Carcassonne. The hard-pressed rider, thought Wolf.

Arriving at Béziers, the crusaders, it seemed, had pitched their tents outside the city, intending to gather strength for the attack. This morning the citizens, in a fit of foolhardy bravura, had burst out of the town, to impede the enemy in making his preparations and setting up his machines. Soon, indeed, the camp was in confusion. When, however, the skirmishers were drawing back to the town, a pack of *ribauds*, followed by the mercenaries, dashed after them through the gates. Before they could be closed the crusaders had forced their way into the city.

"And the Viscount?" Wolf murmured, appalled.

"Safe, thank God, at Carcassonne, where he belongs," the old man answered. "They say at first he was set on defending Béziers. But God knows whether even if he'd been there things had gone different. Anyway, I reckon the Trencavels have sacrificed enough blood to the rabble of Béziers to have need to lose more to the *ribauds*. Still," he added half grudgingly, "they were the first—those burghers—to stand against the Crusade, though their old traitor of a bishop had come to make them give in. But they won't be the last," he muttered, clenching his fist while his face turned involuntarily to the hills above Fanjeaux. "Better to have your body torn piecemeal in battle than your soul stripped bare by those scavenging monks."

Again Wolf rode through the night.

The moon had risen. Bathed in that soft spectral light,

the hills lay silent, insubstantial. Nothing broke the stillness but the reiterate beat of the horse's hoofs echoing through the night, till even Wolf's fevered mind was lulled in its monotony. Remote and unreal seemed all thought of war. Nonetheless, far nearer than the scene of conflict and death, close at hand beyond the dark splash of wooded shadow enveloping the monastery of Prouille, another battle was being waged of which only the chill shaft piercing the barren cell was aware, yet passionless ignored, casting its pallid light upon those blank white walls, carving with stony indifference the figure prostrate on its knees.

In this hour that should have been his triumph, Domingo de Guzman, former Canon of Osma, leader of the mission against heresy, stared at defeat. Often enough he had failed before man and it had only goaded him to new effort. Now, he asked himself in despair, had he failed before God? Had the travail of years, the weariness, the sacrifice been for nothing?

Years ago, crossing the border from Spain, he had been caught in a storm, and as the clouds had lifted and he had beheld above him those icy peaks, it had seemed to him that God's love was a thing luminous, remote, intransigent as those snows, from which, by an infinite and miraculous act of grace, illumination would fall on man's darkness.

From that day he had seen himself leading the erring soul upward, out of those hellish gorges, through the mists that rose from those subterranean waters poisoning the mind with their miasmata, undermining the rock of faith, till at last, reaching the height of the pass, it should behold the wonder of divine grace.

It was the way of endurance he had chosen. He had seen himself as the mountain shepherd leading, gathering the errant flock, and he had been forced to drive and bully with the cudgel of a muleteer. He had dreamed of penetrating the heart with the gentleness of love, the light of divine reason, and he had ended with knife and lancet, probing in spiritual wounds more putrid with foulness than any suppurating flesh. For he had seen at last that only by knowledge of the soul could it be healed, by a process of infinite inquiry, of slow dissection, by the unraveling of the subtle snares that enwove it, till, fleeing from subterfuge, it stood naked before itself, craving the grace that it had forfeited and yet might regain. That despite blindness and hardening of the heart such grace might still be man's he had travailed ceaselessly, and he had failed.

His eyes lifted to the figure suspended in the patch of moonlight on the wall, rigid, outstretched, not in agony or in *rigor mortis*, but in silent triumph. How often in the past had he prayed and derived new strength from that glorious conquest of the flesh. Yet tonight that very triumph seemed to wear a quality mocking, pitiless, remote.

Had he not proved rigorous enough? Had he shown pity where he should have chastised? Not a single soul had he let pass through his hands untried. Defying failure, defying despair, he had trudged on by tortuous paths. Had God, then, wearied where he had not? Condemning only when all persuasion had failed, he had dreamed of leading men to the goal not by violence but by illumination. For help in that alone had he prayed, and God had answered with an avalanche.

Out of his hands, from off his shoulders, would He take the burden at which he had never complained? In the flash of His lightning, wither and blast where he had sought to save, that after massacre and annihilation and death His grace might illumine the desert plains?

Slowly, inexorably, the truth began to dawn. Had he in pride deemed himself more than God's instrument? Had he believed that grace could come from himself?

Alone, wrapped in darkness, the soul of Domingo de Guzman wrestled with despair.

THE RIDERS OF THE MORNING

Nobody knows you. No. But I sing of you.
For posterity I sing of your profile and grace.
Of the signal maturity of your understanding.
Of your appetite for death and the taste of its mouth.
Of the sadness of your once valiant gaiety.

(FEDERICO GARCIA LORCA,
translated by J.L. GILL and STEPHEN SPENDER)

I

THERE WAS STILL SANITY IN ACTION.

At Carcassonne, all that same afternoon and evening since news had come of the fall of Béziers, Trencavel had gone on preparing feverishly for the siege, wandering from post to post, ordering this, revising that, on a repeated tour of inspection. How soon the Crusade would arrive before the city, God alone knew; in all likelihood within a few days, for Narbonne would doubtless proffer its surrender.

Double the guard at the northeast. Down by the tower of the treasury the wall needed reinforcing. Ademar felt chary about that bastion in Graveillande. Best have a look himself.

The garrison, at any rate, were eager enough. After the first shock at the news, it seemed as though the men were relieved, impatient only for the combat, as if they had almost feared that Béziers might have robbed them of the first glory of victory. Now it would be theirs.

"Let them come," they cried lustily. "Let them pitch their tents under the ramparts of Carcassonne and see if their psalm-singing can outrival the sword strokes of Charlemagne." If *he* could not take the city, who could? But this time, they swore, there'd be no magnanimous recognition of the enemy—that ranting firebrand of a Cistercian, that semi-English ruffian Montfort, that Burgundian glutton. "They'll see no blessed towers bending before *them.* They'll be finding themselves hanging on them instead."

Carcassonne was impregnable. That was enough for them. But Béziers?

He had known it from the first, it seemed to him now. Months ago, when Toulouse had sent his peace messengers to the Pope, and the Count of Foix had arrived to discuss strategic plans. Then he had still dreamed wildly of open battle.

"God in heaven!" Ramon-Roger had cried. "The only hope against armies of that size is to wear them out."

Where? The surrender of Montpellier, a Catholic stronghold, was a foregone conclusion. Béziers would be the first on the line of march to offer resistance.

Béziers? Little hope, the count demurred. What fool would hang out there if he'd got Carcassonne? Before long Béziers might be forced to capitulate. Ringed around by that host, withdrawal would be impossible. Languedoc would be done for once and for all. Christ, did he think he was going to ally himself with a simpleton? But, he continued to argue, if Toulouse gave in, the Crusade, banking on general lack of resistance, would not reckon on having to tackle Carcassonne. Once get them there, and he could hold them till they sickened and he could make his own terms.

It had all sounded plausible enough. At the worst, Béziers might have to be sacrificed for the time, but tolerable terms might be got, and soon enough it would be won back. Had he reckoned on the influence of Agnes's kin, the Montpelliers? Now it all seemed pure madness.

The Crusade had marched, had poured down the Rhône, arrived at Montpellier. And then the old horror had laid hold of him again. Pocketing his pride, he had ridden to meet it, only one thought in his mind. Somehow he must save Béziers. Only not there, slaughter and death. Enough the massacre of that night! As he rode, the specters he had at last thought laid that spring pursued him like hounds.

His proposal had been received with derision and scorn. The Abbot of Cîteaux was implacable. Béziers, he'd heard, was a stronghold of heresy. Did the viscount imagine an army of well-nigh three hundred thousand had come to parley? Unconditional surrender of the viscount and all his lands, or nothing.

Silent, he had refused. At dawn he reached Béziers, had bidden the citizens arm to the defense. And they had turned to him with alacrity, with pride. Had they dreamed that he would stay to protect them? Had he himself really believed that without him their lot would be easier, and they would yet be spared by the promised overtures of their old bishop, Reginald of Montpeyroux? Now, it seemed to him, he had only pushed on their shoulders the burden that he had refused.

"Waste yourself on a pack of burghers!" the senhor of Cab-Aret had mocked. "Soon enough they'll be forcing you to capitulate; hand you over as hostage, for all you know. They'll talk big enough till the danger's there." Had he after all never conquered the horror, the distrust?

And now it was they who stood firm, repudiated their bishop, refused to betray their faith. So the messenger had said, the only one, it seemed, who had escaped in the general confusion as the *ribauds* pressed through the gates.

Only not think! Go on blindly, stick to the thing in hand. Now he was sitting in council with the barons. "If they attack from the east," one of them was saying, "we'll get them hard under fire of the arbalesters. They might push up toward Graveillande, but they'll stick. The city's closed with a ring of iron."

But there at Béziers they had ridden out. He could see them. God, would he always see them—mocking, shouting, hurling their javelins, harrying the camp while it slept at dawn, and the French, panicstricken, scarce breeched, scurried hither and thither, grasping for their weapons in vain, and then that end? But they would avenge them, they, the youth of Carcassonne who had ridden together, practiced arms, listened to the songs, they who were beginning the new order that Béziers, too, was to have had, that they should still have when they had conquered.

Now Ademar was holding forth, perturbed about the stream of fugitives pouring into the city.

"The town won't hold them," he protested. "They'll starve, and we with them."

"Not one of my subjects shall be refused protection," Trencavel retorted.

Leave them to the mercy of the *ribauds*? The scum of the cities, the dregs of Burgundy and France? Thieves,

248

murderers, lechers, dragged from the gutters of Paris, the dens and cellars under the Seine? Even now, out there beyond the falling darkness, let loose in an orgy of looting and murder and rape, among the streets and alleys that, one by one, he had planned to rebuild. And he had quailed at those Spanish mercenaries, the tools of his father's vengeance; for twenty years had tortured himself with the thought of redeeming the horror of that night, till at last he had seen a chance through Wolf. (Thank God, after all he was not here.) For all the good it had brought them or himself he might as well have gone the way of his fathers—warred and harried, despoiled as it pleased him, played fast and loose with Toulouse. Toulouse—after all, was that the root of his failure? Yet even now, he wondered, face to face with Raymond again would he act differently? Had not his uncle's action proved his fears justified, or was he but enjoying a just revenge? Well, let them share the burden of the crime. Out there, host and guide of the Crusade, Raymond, Count of Toulouse, was witnessing the despoiling of Béziers. "As long as one doesn't see," Raymond had mumbled between his lips. But if one had eyes, eyes of the imagination, of the fevered brain that could never be closed?

Dusk fell. In the deepening light the walls of the city, bristling with their machicoulis and galleries, catapults and machines, frowned formidable yet almost triumphant, as though after long misuse the ancient fort had come once more into its own and the music and revelry that had long masked its grim earnest were but an irrelevance vanished with the departure of the court.

That same afternoon Agnes of Montpellier, with her infant son and her women, had set out under escort of the lord of Durfort to seek safety in his castle, and thence if necessary in the county of Foix. Now she was gone, even her memory seemed unreal. Standing there on the ramparts, watching the long cortege dwindle moment by moment until it was a mere speck on the dusty road, he had felt neither regret nor relief, but a sense that she had never been.

So that at least was over, the endless masquerade, the courteous tolerance of a convention he loathed and hated. What right had he to blame her? The life that he would have offered was to her a mockery; hers the accredited

249

ideal of the world of which poets sang. And though she might never reach beyond its outward frippery, who knew but that it held a truth before which he had fled—already as a child, to the freedom of the meadows—the liberation of the body's strength.

The August night hung heavy, suffocating with heat. Sleep?—the mere word sounded like mockery.

He had meant to have a word with Pons about the new mangonel. Perhaps the old man might yet be awake. Yet as he made his way to the armory he was urged less by the necessity of discussing business than the instinct of old habit.

The torchlight still shimmered through the half-open door. Thrusting it open, he stood in the place where he had so often taken refuge in childhood, imbibing Pons' store of heroic tales or later delighting in his consummate knowledge of weapons.

Seated on a chest under the torch, the veteran was evidently engaged in repairing the hilt of a sword. For a moment, indeed, as if he were unaware of the intrusion, he continued his work unruffled, so absorbed, even now in the hour of crisis, in the task in hand that when he looked up his manner had the matter-of-fact simplicity of an everyday occurrence.

"A real beauty, eh?" he smiled proudly, holding up the weapon. "I warrant she scarce thought, down in her dark earthy grave, old Pons would be giving her a new lease of life; and better-tempered steel, surely, than she knew before. But it isn't the first time, I reckon, she'll have a cut at those cursed devils—Frenchies or Franks, they've scarce changed their hide."

Trencavel gave it a cursory glance, the short, narrow hilt of corded gold set with its deep-red stones. It seemed familiar, one of those weapons perhaps unearthed from time to time from the graves of the Goths. But, preoccupied, he proceeded straightway to the preparation for the siege.

Tenderly the armorer slipped the sword into its scabbard and laid it on the chest.

"All's well," he replied in answer to the viscount's question. "As for your mangonel, Escot's got some harebrained notions up his sleeve; but give him his due, he's about hit the mark this time."

For a while they went on talking about the stores of armaments, inspecting the great stacks of pikes and lances, halberds and shields. Restlessly, Trencavel wandered about the room. Pons, aware enough of his state, took no notice. The fate of Béziers was weighing on him badly, he guessed. Trencavel pride, God bless it! Leave him in peace. If he wanted to speak he'd come out with it.

So it was almost as in the old days. How often, as a tiny little fellow, the boy had found his way in here and, squatting down on a pile of weapons, had watched him at work? Even then, though the child would never admit it, Pons had felt the cruel conflict beneath that dumb, proud reserve. But after a while, watching him at work and listening to his yarns, Trencavel would always brighten, so that it seemed the armory had become for him a sort of haven, or with increasing years a refuge from the affairs of state. Even after he'd grown to manhood he would drop in for a chat, but in the last year those visits had become ever rarer—at least alone, for he'd never appear but he'd be dragging in tow that little esquire of his, and there'd be no time for peaceful gossip, with his head full of craven plans for the training of those lousy citizens. "And wouldn't Pons take them in hand?" Bakers' and maltsters' sons, and they not knowing a spear's head from a pothook!

Trencavel had flung himself onto a bundle of skins that covered a rough pallet.

"Take a nap," the armorer grunted. "Sleep sound before battle. Not as comfortable a bed as your squire would be making you, eh? But I guess you slept there more than once in the old days," he added, unable to resist a dig at the boy who month by month had come more and more between them. "But there's little lost, I reckon, in a squire who runs off the moment he scents danger in the air."

"He didn't," Trencavel retorted, terse and harsh.

"Hm. At any rate he let himself be carried off."

"I sent him."

He knew it of old—that tense, sheathed tone. No good hiding things from old Pons. It galled the man hard, he guessed, to be browbeaten by a Foix. "Put him out of your head," he advised roughly. "God knows what you all see in him. Why, while he was here of late even that walking corpse, Jordan of the Isle, seemed mighty interested in the youngster."

"Jordan?" Trencavel echoed, startled. "Why, what did he want?"

The old man shrugged. "Nothing, belike. Just happened to drop in about some readjustment to his gorget, and while I was fixing it he starts yarning in that death's-head voice of his about Foix and the rest. Never seems to have met the boy, though he's his own bastard cousin." . . . Then, aggravated by the other's silence, he burst out roughly: "Well, if you wanted him, why the deuce did you let him go?" He could afford to be generous, now the old relationship was restored. "Sure you've the right to claim what's your own and let the old Count go to blazes. When did a Trencavel ever kowtow to a Foix?"

But the viscount had sprung once more to his feet and resumed his restless prowl. At last he halted, gazing at the stacks of weapons. "They say the crusaders are more heavily armed than we."

The armorer laughed harshly. "But you can't say I haven't warned you often enough. Wasn't it old Pons taught you to use the great double-hander and ride in with mace and ax? But you were always for litheness and speed. Pretty enough sporting in the fields, but when it comes to charging in earnest against a phalanx of iron . . ." As he spoke, anger surged over the old soldier's heart, only heightened by his own impotence to help. Why couldn't they have left the boy alone to go the way of his sires instead of plastering him with learning and their namby-pamby doctrines till he'd even trussed up fighting with all that picturesque trumpery? "Well, even now it's not too late."

There was silence. Between them one thought— Béziers—the shame that could not be spoken. Trencavel in his restless pacing had halted by the chest. Half unconsciously, his hand stretched out, clutched at the sword.

"Pons," convulsively his fingers tightened round the hilt till the knuckles stood out bone-white on the long slender hand, "do you think—I was afraid?" The words, dragged out at first, ended almost in a challenge and were accepted as such.

"You!" The old man laughed scornfully. "You're a Trencavel!"

A Trencavel. Was he?

For once, without qualm of conscience, to take the straight, the simple way—violence repaid by violence, blood by blood, from past to present, from generation to generation. He had half turned when suddenly the sound of running feet rang along the pavement, shouts echoed from below. Swinging round, the sword still in his hand, he tore open the door.

Outside, the night hung breathless and sultry, seemingly unchanged but for those cries and hurrying men. In a moment he, too, following in their wake, was running toward the northeastern rampart.

Fire! The word reached his ear, hoarse, inarticulate. In a second his mind had leaped to the impossible—the crusaders, treason—they were surrounded—so that when he reached the parapet the sight that met his gaze seemed so remote that for a second he could hardly grasp its full significance, but stood among the gasping crowd, his eyes fixed like theirs on the distant darkness that far to the northeast appeared stained with a ruddy glow.

Béziers. . . .

Massacre, plunder, torture, death at the stake—of these even he had thought, not of this. No, it was impossible—a nightmare—he was fevered. Reeling, he leaned against the parapet and shut his eyes. But when he opened them again, the glow was still there, only deeper. Minute by minute it seemed to grow, now narrowing, now widening, now gathering to a new intensity. Someone pushed through the crowd. Peire-Roger of Cab-Aret stood at his side.

"French devils—Christ, but they'll pay for this."

Around him voices were clamoring, raucous, urgent. Threats, curses, the very vengeance he had invoked himself a moment ago rang in his ears, nightmarish, hollow.

Béziers—the city of the future.

Nero had burned Rome for the beauty of the spectacle, or, as some said, to purge the old fever-ridden city. Why not? The strangled laughter rose to his throat. Béziers, that he had dreamed of building anew, that the ghosts of horror haunting those streets should be allayed at last.

"No water."

"The drought's dried up the wells."

"The river?"

"Cut off, you fool!"

The words, fragmentary, meaningless, hung on the sultry air. Now the fire appeared even to abate a little, as though sucked down into a smoldering well, when all of a sudden a brighter glow kindled to the left, suffusing the sky with crimson and gold. The curtain of the night glimmered translucent.

Faubourg and city wiped clean, purged at last of their blood, their ghosts—from the castle keep to the altar steps of St. Magdalene. Then suddenly it struck home—St. Magdalene's, St. Nazaire—thousands, the messenger had said, were seeking refuge in the churches.

"The people," he gasped. "In the churches . . ."

"Frenchmen's piety," a voice mocked.

"God strangle them—and the most holy Abbot of Cîteaux!" Peire-Roger of Cab-Aret's sword rang hard on the stone.

"They'll strangle *themselves*," muttered Ademar of Limoux.

Desperate, Trencavel gazed from one to another. "God, are we to stand here and watch?"

Ademar shook his aged head. "We have to now, but when they come . . ."

Unhearing, Trencavel stared past him, aghast. "The people," he kept on crying. "The people—they're trapped."

A hand shook him roughly by the arm. "You don't know." In the reflected glow, the furrowed face of the old armorer gleamed dark and savage. "They may have got out. And if not," his voice had suddenly a strange ring, "Raimon Trencavel will be doubly avenged."

With a stifled cry, Trencavel pushed him from him, and thrusting through the crowd tore himself free.

II

Far away to the northeast, on a little hummock of ground raised above the flatness of the plain that surrounded Béziers, a group of men stood watching the same spectacle. Withdrawn a little from the host of tents that covered the level ground, they enjoyed an almost unbroken view of the burning city.

Around them, in the reflected glare of the fire, the huge camp glimmered fantastic, row on row of pavilions retreating into the night, flashing up here and there as the leaping flames threw into fitful illumination the flickering tongues of the pennons, the gaudy armorial bearings emblazoned on banner and shield. Between them groups of figures moved fretfully hither and thither, running forward gesticulating as troops of horsemen rode in with a new pack of loot; carts, wagons were unloaded, or driven once more toward the gates of the town to disappear in the turmoil that eddied around the fosse. Above it the ramparts of the city rose black and threatening against the sea of flames.

Every now and then clouds of smoke swept down over the walls, obscuring the medley of figures and filling the air with showers of ash and soot. Suddenly, among the black mass of buildings not yet engulfed in the fire, a tongue of flame shot up like a pillar of gleaming oil.

Clearing his throat, the most imposing among the little group of spectators and, to judge by the wealth and splendor of his dress, the most important, turned to the white-robed ecclesiastic at his side. "I must offer my congratulations. The reality almost lives up to the imagery evoked by Your Reverence's inimitable eloquence."

Without turning, the Cistercian continued to gaze into the raging fires. "God acts through His prophecies," he answered abruptly.

A secret smile played about the other's coarse but not ungenerous lips. "Yet surely to the glory and advancement of His Church. If the zeal of His agents continues so indefatigable, it may be that she's cheated of her rights."

The Abbot of Cîteaux turned swiftly. In the lurid light his sharp-graven features appeared haggard, cavernous. "I have explained to your grace from the first, the Crusade did not march to enrich itself but to pay back the stolen dues of the Lord."

A deep laugh broke from the Duke of Burgundy's chest. "Let us hope the Lord is too magnanimous to note that a goodly part of the debt has already strayed into the pockets of the *ribauds*. It might be perspicacious to curb the assiduousness of your divine tax collectors, not to say an act of mercy. Our knighthood has scarcely marched through this intolerable dust and heat to set on high the king of harlots."

"The knighthood of Burgundy and France," the abbot retorted, "is already defending its rights." His glance wandered toward the swirling masses at the foot of the ramparts, from which every now and then a mass of figures would reel back under the charge of a group of horsemen. "It is only to be hoped they do not forget those of the Lord."

The duke shrugged his heavy shoulders. "I fancy Your Reverence has seen to it that God's rights are duly safeguarded as far as our friend Montfort is concerned. Your admirable cousin, Bouchard," he turned laughing to the figure of a knight who stood grave and preoccupied on his further side, "is, I am sure, completely convinced of his divine mission."

At that moment the flames which for a moment seemed to have abated somewhat sprang up with redoubled vigor, steadily advancing toward a larger building that till now had stood silhouetted tall and black against the fiery furnace. Now, it, too, sprang into life and being, its dense mass perforated by dancing stars of light as though all of a sudden the windows had been lit for some great festival. Minutes passed, the walls began to glow. Only the tower still stood black, unassailable, while the tongues of flame licked and withdrew in playful courtship, then suddenly leaped forward. For a moment more the tower stood as if exultant, locked in that fiery embrace, then in abandonment seemed to lean forward, totter and fall crashing into the heart of the blaze.

The heat had grown suffocating. Now wreaths of smoke swept forward, penetrating even to the little hill.

"'And I will kindle a fire in his cities, and it shall devour all round about him.'" On the lips of the Cistercian the prophecy of Jeremiah rose in an exultant prayer.

The figure of a rider broke from the demolished gates of the city and, lost for a minute amid the drifting smoke and melee, came spurring toward the group of watchers on the hill. Springing from his horse, he bowed before the abbot. The scent of smoke hung heavy about him. Beneath the helmet his face, bathed in sweat, was smeared with grime. "It has become a massacre. Nothing will hold them. The citizens have flocked to the churches to seek refuge. Thousands have gathered in Saint-Nazaire." He paused, hesitant. "But these *ribauds*—they have not even respect for the house of God."

As though scarce hearing, Arnaud-Amelric, Abbot of Cîteaux, continued to stare into the flaming ruins.

"My lord, if you command it," the man continued, "the Magdalene might yet be spared."

Bouchard de Marly stepped forward. "Your Reverence has surely not forgotten—not only heretics but Catholics have taken refuge there."

Arnaud-Amelric turned. In the glare of the conflagration the pupils of his eyes shone dark, dilated.

"Burn them all. God will find His own."

III

All fires burn out at last.

Upon the ramparts of Carcassonne, through the unending hours of that night, Trencavel held vigil.

The glare had faded from the sky. Only the horizon still smoldered with a dull, ferruginous glow.

Down in the suburbs the cries of excitement and panic had ebbed to a dull broken mutter, interspersed with desultory shouts or snatches of conversation from the watch.

Now and again from afar came the lowing of a beast, answered by a raucous bellow from under the ramparts below, where the fleeing peasants had encamped waiting for the city gates to open at morn.

A breath of wind stirred round the parapet, bearing with it a faint odor, real or imagined, of ash and smoke. In the east, almost imperceptibly, a pallid streak began to shift itself between earth and sky.

He shuddered, dragging himself upright. His arm, wedged against the parapet, was stiff and numb. Only then did he realize that he was still clutching the sword. Mechanically he changed it to his other hand. His fingers closed over the coiled hilt, the grotesque animal heads.

Once long ago, perhaps on these very walls in the hands of another of his own blood, it had cried aloud for vengeance.

But for them too, even in shame, in defeat, one honor remained—even there in the hopeless rout when Alaric fell. "There is no escaping one's roots"—who had said it? Old Caravita long ago—or Pons? The strangled laughter rose in his throat. For what, then, that anguished struggle—father against son, son against father? The songs sang of that, too. In the end the curse returned on itself.

There was no freeing oneself but freely to face the inevitable.

257

Drawing the sword a little from its scabbard, he ran his finger along the blade, then with a sudden movement thrust it back into the sheath.

Turning, he descended the steps of the tower and, unheeding the guard's salute, passed along the ramparts.

Outside the door of Agnes's bower a young page lay sprawling asleep, eyes closed, mouth agape. No need to disturb him, even to step over him. It seemed to him that he would never have to enter it again.

Turning aside, he passed along the low-vaulted gallery and pushed open the door at the end. The room lay in darkness.

Groping his way to the table, he lit the candle. Only a stump remained. It would suffice. Since Wolf's departure he had let no one wait on him here. Blankly, his gaze wandered over the room, over scrolls and parchments strewn over table and chests—books studied and read together in the leisure hours of those months—here by the wintry hearth, and then out on the meadows, down by the Aude. The long rides, the breathless gallops over the hills—a vision of the future imaginatively shared, a fullness of being of which, before, he had ceased to dream. Friendship—but the anguish rose in him choking. Comradeship, brotherhood—sworn and defended to the death. So it had been for those whose sword he held—and for those others who dwelt in the land of the riders. Yet he had shrunk and drawn back, pretending it strength. If he had not, might even this have been averted? Useless to ask. Yet Wolf would ask, and what was left for him to remember but shame—today; but tomorrow? . . . If that at least could be retrieved—the last betrayal wiped clean by the sword.

He turned to the table, drew one òf the books toward him.

Between the pages lay a loose leaf of parchment, half-covered with writing, often erased. He had begun it so often. At first it had been a letter, then when it failed, a poem, till words proved useless. Now they, too, were not needed. He made no attempt to read them. Holding the page to the flame he watched the parchment scorch and shrivel, then, crumbling, scatter—mere wisps of ash over the book.

The pain of the flame singeing his fingers recalled him to the present. For a moment longer he stood staring un-

seeing at the open page while the torment of Gallus transmitted itself to his own anguish:

"... But now with mad passion the war-god relentless
Binds me in bondage....
You far from home (O let me not really believe it) ...
Look upon Alpine snows."

Pushing the book from him, he sank down on the edge
of the couch and buried his face in his hands.

Perhaps he had even slept. The candle had burned out
but a chill uncertain light hovered in the room. Had something stirred? With a start he jerked to his elbow. Framed
in the doorway, motionless as though carved in stone, the
figure of a youth carrying helmet and lance—once long
ago among the ruins of the old Roman cemetery at Toulouse. He was dreaming. But no! The figure moved, was
coming toward him.

"Wolf—"

"But I told you I would come back," he was saying,
"that night—don't you remember?" He was at his side, his
hands in his.

In the shadows, the carven riders over the hearth rode
on, oblivious.

IV

For twelve days Carcassonne watched and waited.

Narbonne, terrorstricken at the thought of sharing the
fate of Béziers, had surrendered. The news of the massacre had filled the country with horror. The population of
a city wiped out. Scarce a single survivor, nor man, nor
woman, nor child, but for the Jews who had fled in time
to Narbonne or followed on the heels of the viscount to
Carcassonne.

Wherever the Crusade marched, its distant appearance,
even the unproved rumor of its coming, was enough to
cause the surrender of castle and town. Far and wide, village, farm, and homestead were ransacked, horses dragged
from the stables, cattle slaughtered, the new-cut corn torn
from the stacks.

A second army, marching from Bordeaux, was pouring from the northwest. Puy-la-Roque had fallen.

Wedged in between the two forces, the Carcassais went up in flames. Day and night new fires darted up all over the countryside. Columns of smoke rose from the piles of faggots as numbers of heretics were led to the stake. Roads and lanes were blocked with swarms of men, women, and children, driving before them cattle and beasts, dragging on wagons, handcarts, asses and mules, whatever they could rescue of their miserable possessions. Day by day more refugees poured into the city, bringing with them fantastic rumors and tales—wherever the crusaders encamped water flowed in plenty, springs long sealed through the drought gushed forth anew. Arrows and spears that hit them full in the chest failed to wound. A column of fire had been seen to descend on a group of riders killed in an ambush. The dead bodies of the crusaders were found without exception outstretched in the shape of a cross. One day a crowd of peasants arrived panicstricken at the city gates. They had been bringing in the harvest. Suddenly the stubble had appeared crimson, as though soaked in blood. Women wailed and shook their heads, prophesying. In ancient days, before the sacrilege of Sacra Tolosa, the paving stones of the city had sweated blood.

Relentless, the vast procession of the Crusade advanced, and what had not already fled under the vanguard of chivalry became the almost certain victim of the mercenaries and *ribauds*, the pack of truaux and adventurers following in their train. Dragged from the gutters of Paris, the harbor dens and brothels of Bordeaux, they swarmed over the land—thieves and vagabonds, charlatans and knaves, gypsies and mummers, wandering scholars and unfrocked priests redeemed from sin by pious pilgrimage in the shadow of the Cross.

At the head of the macabre cavalcade, Raymond, Count of Toulouse, from the cushioned comfort of his litter, directed the crusading forces as humble guide and host through the lands of his nephew, the Viscount of Béziers and Carcassonne.

On the first Sunday in August the Crusade appeared before the city. Wolf of Foix, who had been taking turns with Trencavel to watch with the guard on the keep, was the first to see the tiny cloud growing above the endless stretch of road to the east. By the time, leaping down the steps and along the rampart, he had returned with Trencavel, there was no doubt about the cavalcade advancing beneath that mighty forest of spears. All the afternoon it continued to pour out over the fields—a never-ending stream of men and arms, of banners, pennons, and steel, flashing and shimmering beneath the ever-growing pall of dust, while tents were pitched, banners hoisted, and across the walls of the city rolled the thunder of wagons and machines, the trampling and neighing of horses, the raucous shouting of men.

Hard-faced and silent, Trencavel gazed down on the gathering forces, and Wolf, standing at his side, guessed his thoughts; knew that he, too, had dreamed of attack and challenge, the fierce sally in which they would ride out, the youth of the city, to glory or death. Ever since the spearhead of the Crusade had been sighted, they had gathered round him, bearing with them weapons and shields, clamoring for action.

Guiraut had been among the crowd. His face dark and fanatical, he had come up behind Wolf. "So you're back after all? We thought you'd hopped it."

Wolf swung round, but stiffled his anger. After all, it was true he'd gone off without a word.

"Shut up. We're going to fight."

But Guiraut's black eyes smoldered. "If he sticks it."

"He'll stick it to the last—mind you do," Wolf retorted fiercely.

"What do you take me for?" Angrily the youth's hands twisted the ax in his belt. "Though if you think I care a damn for your bloody Viscount you're mistaken," he scoffed, turning away deliberately from the sight of Trencavel, his face and surcoat smeared with oil and grime, helping in the repair of one of the mangonels. "But if *they* get us," he jerked his elbow out over the ramparts, "there's an end to every right we possess, let alone what we ought to get."

"You're—we're going to get them. He's fighting for it—and you know it. We're going to attack."

But at the council of barons half an hour later Trencavel rose to his feet. "We must attack," he cried vehemently; "attack before they've encamped, four hundred of us—the best horsemen—drive confusion into their ranks."

261

"Heavens, are you mad?" the old senhor of Cab-Aret broke in furiously. "Wasn't Béziers enough?"

Not until the third day did the enemy attack. Since dawn there had been commotion in the crusaders' camp. From the walls of the city they had watched as horses were led out, and rank upon rank, it appeared, was drawn up in formation. But for the last half hour the noise had abated. Suddenly, from the other side of the river, came the sound of low chanting, swelling as voice on voice joined in:

"Veni creator spiritus. . . ."

Beneath a rolling chorus the forest of spears began to move, headed by a little procession of figures in fluttering white.

*"Accende lumen sensibus
Infunde amorem cordibus. . . ."*

Steadily the host advanced behind the symbol of the Cross. But now the spears pressed forward, divided, swallowed up the group of singing monks.

"Hostem repellas longius. . . ."

The words were no longer audible, lost in the thunder of the hoofs, as, closed in formation, a glittering phalanx of iron, splashed with the gaudy hues of surcoat and banner, of flying pennon and emblazoned shield, the Crusade tore down on the city. A moment later, to the watchers on the tower, they were obscured under the black rain of their own arrows.

Did they fall short? Was the armor of the foe impenetrable? Still, incredibly, through shower upon shower they advanced, column on column, unbroken as though not one fell in their midst.

Within an hour the river was crossed. By nightfall, after ten hours' struggle, the suburb of Graveillande lay in the crusaders' hands.

The following day, inebriated by their success, they stormed the suburb of St. Vincent, but the tide seemed to have turned. Under a deluge of shots, of stones and rocks hurled from the catapults, the crusaders faltered. A rain of molten fire cleared the vanguard from the rampart. Tottering, blinded by a hail of burning pitch, men reeled backward, hurled from the scaling ladders, the moving towers and bridges thrown too confidently against the city walls.

The crusaders began to withdraw. Suddenly, out of their ranks, a rider spurred back toward the ramparts and, careless of the flying barbs, pressed forward, hard under the walls. Bending, he lifted one of the injured knights and laid him across his saddle. Then, slinging his shield across his back, dashed once more toward the host.

In vain the arrows of the besieged pursued him, grazed his helmet, glanced from hauberk and shield, till the great lion rampant upon the escutcheon had grown invisible among the lines of the retiring host.

"Montfort," the rumor spread round the walls. "Simon de Montfort, one of the commanders."

"The devil take him!" someone swore.

"The devil owns him already," cursed another. "The man's invulnerable."

The battle was resumed. The besiegers brought up new columns, more formidable engines. The besieged answered them with redoubled fortitude and tenacity. But ever and again more ladders were thrust against the rampart, new battering-rams brought up. Under tunnels of timber hoarding, sappers crawled forward, trying to undermine the walls. But always the breaches were filled, the masonry repaired, the tunnels blocked or smoked out. In the fosse the piles of dead and wounded mounted till it was impossible to carry them away.

At this juncture Pedro II, King of Aragon, accompanied by a flamboyant cortege, arrived before the city. Famed for his Catholicism, he had five years previously sworn himself to the task of suppressing heresy, upon which, journeying to Rome, he had been crowned by the hands of his holiness the Pope with a chaplet of unleavened bread and, laying on the altar of St. Peter the royal insignia, had received in return a symbolic sword, added to the coveted title of Alferez, or standard-bearer of the Church.

Arriving at the camp, the Spaniard proceeded to the pavilion of his brother-in-law, Raymond of Toulouse, which, thanks to the usual perspicacity shown by the count, had been auspiciously placed on the far side of the river in the shade of a dense copse and so enjoyed, at least for the greater part of the day, shelter from the ravages of the blazing sun.

Having dined with Raymond and partaken of his excellent wines, Don Pedro remounted his bay and, accompanied by three chosen companions, rode toward the town.

At the gates he was met by the viscount, whom the heralds had informed of the king's arrival.

To Trencavel, coming straight from the fighting on the ramparts, the immaculate, almost flaunting elegance of the Spaniard seemed at that moment almost a parody, and as he escorted the king to the castle there flashed ironically across his mind that this was the overlord he had automatically chosen in his repudiation of Toulouse.

That Don Pedro had come banking on Trencavel's recognition of the suzerainty was evident, though so far he had indulged only in protestations of sympathy mingled with mild rebuke, as though the viscount indeed held him responsible for the disaster.

"But can you blame me?" Stretching himself elegantly in his chair, his jeweled hand twirled the goblet of wine before him. "Have I not warned you often enough to rid yourself of these heretic fools and their crazy beliefs? Now that they have brought you to such a pass, you may at last see your folly. . . . You surely cannot hope to attack," he continued, after reviewing the situation. He was aware of the fiercely controlled twitching of Trencavel's lips, and to give him his due, on that point at least, felt genuine sympathy. In his own love of dramatic and heroic effect on the field of battle, the tedium involved through a long-drawn-out siege seemed intolerable enough.

Things were evidently weighing heavily upon the youth. He recalled the image of earlier years—that brilliant grace on the sports field, that remote evasive charm—an exiled Apollo, someone had called him. It must have been at the time of Raymond's wedding. Probably it was the count himself. But today the disenchanted god wore undeniably human scars.

"I understand," he continued, while his eye roved from the face stained with rust and grime to the blemished surcoat, "that you put much confidence in the defenses of the city. If it were not crammed full of refuges, of women and children, I should say that you might still harbor some cause for hope. As it is . . ." He leaned back. His fingers toyed gracefully with his beard. "I fear but one alternative confronts you—starve or turn them out."

Trencavel's face darkened. "They are under my protection," he answered shortly.

Don Pedro shrugged. "My dear Viscount, your magnanimity, though praiseworthy, is hardly politic."

"They are my people."

So the youth was really as crazed as they made out? "In that case," returned the Spaniard, yawning gracefully, "I can only advise you to come to terms with the Crusade. Much as I feel for you in your predicament, I am confident that it would in any case be the best course."

Trencavel stiffened, but the king continued ingratiatingly: "In memory of your father's loyalty to my house you may rest assured that I shall do all in my power to assist in any mediation. After all, however black the present, the future might hold the chance of an effective revenge. It would hardly be to Aragon's advantage to allow these barbarians to become all too strong. With a possible coalition of the whole south, the chances are . . ." He paused, and sipping at the goblet of wine, smiled subtly.

An hour later Don Pedro was sitting once more in the crusaders' camp, this time engaged in earnest discussion with the leading nobles, the papal legate, and the Abbot of Cîteaux. When at last, after futile argument, he rode again toward the city gate he was in no good humor. The terms he had at last wrung from the intransigent churchmen were scarcely likely to please this fanatical youth.

He was not mistaken. The evening was drawing in and, anxious to return to the camp before dusk, the king, instead of proceeding to the castle, had withdrawn with the viscount into one of the towers on the ramparts.

Silent, rigid, his back pressed against the rugged masonry of those ancient walls, Trencavel stood waiting while the Spaniard prevaricated. But Pedro's plausibility was unable to gloss the inexorability of those terms:

"That through the grace of Arnaud-Amelric, most venerable Abbot of Cîteaux, the papal legate, and the lords of Burgundy and France . . . Raimon-Roger Trencavel, Viscount of Carcassonne, be permitted to leave the city, accompanied by twelve vassals of his choice, on the understanding that the town, its inhabitants, and all who should find themselves therein be handed over unconditionally to the Crusade."

For a moment Trencavel gazed at him incredulously. The silence was broken only by the sound of his hard-drawn breath, till suddenly laughter tore from his throat.

"And they think I would accept? Rather would I take my own life or be flayed alive—before I abandon the least of my people."

Beyond the deathly pallor, the passionate disdain, there was something in the youth's face that the Spaniard could not understand. Was it exultation? He did not know. Moved, despite chagrin at the failure of his plans, Pedro's eyes lowered. It was then that he caught sight of the sword hanging at Trencavel's hip. In a flash he remembered where he had seen its like—in the treasury of his home, among the royal insignia, the torques and weapons, the great dangling crowns of the Visigoths. Mocking, his gaze rested on the short corded hilt set with its deep-red stones. Irritation and fury swept over him.

"Mother of God! Wasn't it enough that *they* should have gone under for a mad faith, or are you bent on repeating . . ." He ceased abruptly. For a second, in the failing light, the figure of the man before him had looked suddenly strange and alien, the ancient walls . . . Was he seeing ghosts? Recovering himself, he laughed impatiently and with a graceful shrug turned to the door.

On the following morning, from the outskirts of the camp, Raymond of Toulouse, seated in the opening of his pavilion, watched the departure of Don Pedro of Aragon.

It was with regret that his somewhat shortsighted eyes soon failed to decipher the details of that magnificent cavalcade.

During the last twenty-four hours he had become once more convinced of the truth that beauty has power to assuage even the bitterest tribulations. During the king's visit to his tent he had felt positively refreshed, not alone on account of its politic significance, but from the mere relief at feeling the proximity of a civilized being. No one could realize what tortures he endured in the presence of these Burgundian barbarians. Their crudity even transcended his expectations, for in most instances their proximity was rendered unendurable through their very stench. Involuntarily, as though the memory had become palpable, he drew out a little phial and sniffed the fragrant essence.

Of course one must make allowances for the campaign, but after a day's battling one would think a bath might have been considered refreshing, if not imperative. There was the excuse, it is true, of a shortage of water, but had they not securely appropriated the Aude? No, he felt more deeply confirmed on his suspicions that in their homes these blustering barons showed as much disdain for water as on the campaign, and he recalled the horror of the little Byzantine princess who, foisted as consort on the Salian emperor, had caused her German waiting-woman to gaze in blank dismay at her petition for a daily bath.

As to their conversation, was there any subject on which they could discourse apart from butchery—if not of the battle, then of the hunting field? And even the duke had proved indescribably boring after a few hours. The same coarse jokes, the same lack of finesse in regard to wine or women, only a trifle more grandiose, a shade more grandiloquent than the rest. But all of them, if it came to it, would be better entertained by a juggler than a poet. There were the French, it was true, preening themselves with their acquired Latin culture, but Nevers' perpetual quarrels with Burgundy were becoming unendurably tedious, while the supercilious arrogance of St. Pol grew more intolerable day by day. In the end he had to fall back on the prelates. Arnaud-Amelric, of course, was impossible. Fanaticism inevitably destroyed every chance of those subtle digressions that make conversation a delight. He looked forward nevertheless to an evening in company with that learned Benedictine who recently had betrayed so unexpectedly intelligent an interest in Saint Saturnin, the patron saint of Toulouse, so that it had been quite a pleasure to despatch a messenger to the Castel Narbones to fetch, from among the rare treasures of his library, the little volume in which was described so vividly the curious life of the saint's namesake, that other Saturnin, the Gnostic philosopher, whom Irenius in his list of heretics classes with no less a personage than Simon Magus himself.

There might even be possibilities, he went on thinking, of deriving some moments' entertainment from that little friar of Prouille, for it was evident that, though obsessed in the task of combating heresy, he was at least genuinely interested in its source, and in pursuing those hidden and labyrinthine streams there was no telling what mysteries might not be unveiled, or to what unknown regions they might lead. So it appeared, for instance, that the pious brother, in his zeal to investigate the problem of reincarnation and migration of souls, was already occupying himself with that extraordinary personality, Apollonius of Tyana, who, versed in the faculties of the Neoplatonic Pythagorean school, had journeyed to India in the footsteps of the master, and imposing on himself a four-years' silence, necessary to ultimate initiation, purported to achieve that detachment from material things which renders possible a communication with the dead.

He started, torn from his ruminations by the sound of augmented tumult in the distance. He had taken care that his tent should be pitched on a site that afforded not only comparative protection from the heat but was placed as far as possible from the probable scene of battle. From here, therefore, the walls of the city most persistently under attack were hidden from sight, and of the activities proceeding beneath the unassailable portions of the ramparts before him his myopic vision received only a blurred image. Every now and then, it is true, within the limits of the nearer plane, fresh reinforcements of men and arms would wind over the track below, a blare of trumpets herald the assault of a fresh company of chivalry, while between returning groups of riders, or wagons bearing the wounded, a dark speck moving across the meadows would suddenly fade mysteriously from view, shot down, maybe, by some invisible bolt.

The momentary commotion had faded. The air was filled again with the customary shouts, the distant clash of arms, the grinding and clatter of machines, the thousand varied noises of the camp. Raymond gave a little sigh of relief. No signs of any spectacular happenings, no evidence of panic or sound of jubilation. It was in all probability but another of those vainly repeated attempts to storm the inner fortifications. Each time he had felt an unconquerable dread, less from the consequences that might arise from the city's fall than from a more immediate and irrational fear. Why? The guilt was not his, but Trencavel's, his doom that of the avenging nemesis. Still, the youth's image haunted him, standing there in the Castel Narbones, proud, intransigent as a young god. Between that day and this lay the whole depth and disaster of Languedoc's debacle and his own humiliation. Nevertheless, above and beyond all thought of a justified revenge, the instinctive aesthete recoiled in horror. The shattered limbs, the head beautiful as a god's dragged in the dust—Hector on the walls of Troy unredeemed by Apolline grace. And where was Achilles?—Nevers, Burgundy, St. Pol, or that ruffian, perhaps, Montfort?

Suddenly the full significance of the image swept over him, illumined in the tragic and symbolic light of a dying civilization, of which in the noonday madness of one summer day so long ago he had dreamed himself the savior.

So, after all, the burden had fallen on his shoulders. For still, with endless care, the ruins might be pieced together; Toulouse, the heart, be saved. The path was uncertain yet, seemingly almost impossible. Before him, no doubt, a further surfeit of suffering, boredom, humiliation, apparent defeat. It appeared, however, that they could be endured, even that scene in the church of Saint Gilles, so gratifying to the mob forever craving to wallow in the objectified image of its own agony. All that was necessary was detachment. The sublimation of the martyr was one way— the Cathars had evidently achieved it. Where that failed, intelligence and the Orient between them had at least provided a means of producing that state of ecstatic anaesthesia artificially. He had often found himself speculating on the nature of those hashish-inspired illusions under which the devotees of the Old Man of the Mountains had carried out his incredible behests. He had never experimented far. For all his affected Orientalism, the cold cool light of reason had remained his ultimate guide. Even now it might prove the saving grace. With infinite care the situation might yet be saved, Languedoc retrieved from utter ruin.

He had not blinded himself as to Pedro's designs. But after the humiliating abasement of the past months, in the midst of the crudities that surrounded him, the subtle game of diplomacy had acted almost as an elixir, and though it might be some time before he himself were drawn into the center once again, still, from his present vantage point he was able to watch the spinning of the threads. Cîteaux was implacable, Fulk a very demon; even so, behind all, as a last resort, stood Rome. With Innocent, reasonable conversation might be possible. It was unlikely, too, that he would take the massacre of Béziers so lightly. In the meantime the crusaders were becoming restless.

They were ready to prolong their *quadraginta* for the sake of loot that should compensate for the treasures lost by the wholesale destruction of Béziers, but they had not reckoned with a protracted siege, least of all with Carcassonne. Nevers was itching to return to France, Burgundy had not recovered from his disappointment at having to forgo those imagined entertainments at Toulouse. Even if Carcassonne fell, which of them would be ready to take on the responsibility entailed by a usurpation of Trencavel's lands? To anyone with sense they must appear less of an asset than a liability. The visit of Aragon had been exquisitely timed. Although the king had shown himself so devoted in carrying out his duty toward the Church, his presence had acted as a salutary reminder of his claim on Trencavel's lands and of a potent force beyond the Pyrenean border, the possibility even now of a coalition of the south—Aragon, Foix, Toulouse. The policy of years, Raymond pondered, had, in spite of all, repaid itself in full. Through connubial sagacity, the man who was traditionally his rival might prove his ally in the hour of greatest need. Civilization might be saved for Europe, and after all it would be he whom the world would thank, Raymond the Sixth of Toulouse, reduced though he be at present to the status of an exalted courier to this barbaric and preposterous circus.

Drowsily he gazed out over the plain, past the kaleidoscope of gaudy emblazonings and glittering steel to the towered city rising from the groves of cypress and vine against the cloudless blue of the sky. An ironic melancholy descended upon him. Yes, reason might yet conquer, and Apollo shed on this land his luminous grace, but what might the dark gods, implacable and never assuaged, demand as sacrifice?

v

On the walls the fighting continued unabated. But still the inner ring held firm. In the fosse the piles of dead and wounded mounted day by day.

The crusaders began to grow impatient. They had taken the Cross believing in an easy entry into the fabulous city of Toulouse, and they had found themselves instead at Béziers, cheated of half the plunder by the *ribauds*. True, the incredible ease with which the city had fallen had filled them with confidence as to the capitulation of Carcassonne. Now it almost seemed that its legendary invincibility might prove true.

White, incandescent, the southern sun beat down on steel and harness, on hauberk and padded mail.

"Nothing against the oven of Palestine," Montfort cried, as again and again he drove his men to a vain assault.

Ceaselessly the white-robed figure of the Cistercians moved through the camp, under the walls, succoring the wounded, egging on the flagging troops.

"God is with us, soldiers of Christ!" cried the Abbot of Cîteaux. "Behold a new miracle. God, the Lord of the elements, has summoned them to His aid. We have water, for the Aude is ours, but up there in that nest of heretics the wells are running dry, for God has forbidden the clouds to succor the sinner."

Morning after morning the sun, mounting to the same canopy of glaring blue, broiled down on the city. On the ramparts the scorching stone threw back the heat like a furnace. Behind the timbered galleries of the machicoulis the stifling air, mixed with the smell of blood and sweat, the fumes of pitch and molten lead, grew suffocating. In the city itself one could hardly breathe. Choked to overflowing with refugees, the narrow streets were fetid with the foulness of herded humanity and beast. Even in the shadow of the cathedral the air smelled sickly sour, from the stench of offal and cattle slaughtered in the square. Still, there was meat as, desperate from hunger, the townsmen threw themselves on the herds of the fugitive peasants—meat, while day by day bread grew more scarce, prices had become fantastic. Some grumbled at the crowd of refugees, some threw the blame on the Jews. Misers and usurers, wasn't it they alone who had fled from Béziers in time, to suck the blood of honest Christians?

In vain Trencavel had opened his own granaries, stipulated for the equal rationing of the food; it seemed swallowed up before it had reached half round. If some demurred that up at the castle they still ate game off golden platters, they were soon silenced. The viscount, they defended fiercely, had little time to eat anything. Day in, day out, he was up on the ramparts, taking his turn

271

with arbalest and catapult; manning the giant mangonels, hoisting stones and boulders with his own hands. Even at night, it was said, he scarcely rested, but helped in the repair of each threatened breach or shared the duties of the guard.

The halls of the castle, that once had echoed to the sound of revelry and song, were filled with the moans of the wounded and dying. In and out of these rows of bleeding and pain-racked men the dark-robed figures of the Cathar elders passed, side by side with the cowled monks, setting limbs broken and shattered by flying missiles, bathing and binding the torn and lacerated flesh, or, where no hope was left, bringing the solace of the *consolamentum* and the last unction. Religious prejudice, that in Languedoc even in the old days had been less common than indifference and tolerance, was almost forgotten.

But soon the work of tending the wounded became almost small against the task of succoring the citizens. If food was still obtainable in some sort, water was growing scarcer day by day. Half the wells were useless, the Aude held fast by the foe. Day after day men gazed up at the sky and still no fleck of cloud broke the azure.

In the streets, vessels of a questionable liquid were hawked from door to door. On the carcasses and unwashed hides of the slaughtered cattle the flies bred in black and iridescent heaps.

Dysentery broke out in the city. Within a few days the contagion had spread with alarming rapidity. On the ramparts men collapsed at their posts, mown down not by the crusaders' bolts but by the insidious disease.

In the city itself, wrecks of humanity, skeleton-thin, dragged themselves through the streets, dropped in the gutters. Still living, man witnessed the spectacle of his own putrefaction.

"Well, do you still proclaim the glory of the body?" one of the nobles addressed the viscount, mocking.

"Yes," Trencavel answered between tightening lips. "In what it *could* be."

Among the reeking hovels the Cathars, moving unwearying from pallet to pallet, gave different consolation as they laid their hands on bodies writhing in agony.

"For we that are in this tabernacle do groan being burdened, not for that we would be unclothed, but clothed upon, that mortality might be swallowed up.

"For we know that if our earthly house of this tabernacle were dissolved, we have a building of God, an house
not made with hands, eternal in the heavens."

One afternoon a deputation from the camp appeared
beneath the walls of the city. In the name of the Abbot of
Cîteaux, the lords and barons of Burgundy and France,
the Crusade offered to the Viscount of Carcassonne and a
chosen bodyguard of knights safe conduct and return, to
discuss terms of an armistice in the pavilion of the lord
Count of Nevers.

It was arranged that the answer should be given at
dawn.

This, then, thought Trencavel, was to be that glorious
and desperate sally, that last storm. Had he perhaps still
gone on believing in it even yesterday? Time had lost its
value. One had gone on from hour to hour, from day to
day.

"Only the present is ours." It had lain on his lips, bitter
and yearning, that autumn night nearly a year ago. Since
then, how many meanings it had attained in that first up-
surging of their vision of the future. And yet again, even
on the night of the ruin of Béziers, in that very hour in
which the resolve so sternly made had been snatched out
of his hands, or at least so altered in aspect that, in one
second, death could be changed into life, the agony of
emptiness into a fulness of being unbelievable.

After the fevered agony, the fierce resolve of that night,
what had seemed so incredible at first was the simplicity of
it all—that there had been no need for justification, that to
Wolf all that had been, that might have been, Béziers itself, had no validity for him against the present, that
unless they were here now in Carcassonne the cause itself
would be dead. To fight side by side for this thing to
which they had sworn themselves—this had been a necessity to which all had led. And for a time they had been
carried away on that faith, had gone on dreaming perhaps
of that hazardous sally, of victory or an heroic end.

That, too, had been rejected. In these last weeks he had
seen well enough why. With valor and sheer bravery he
had credited these men around him. What he had seen was
greater—endurance. Racked with fever and thirst, they

273

had gone on till they dropped at their posts, or, borne away pierced by arrows and bleeding, often on the morrow, before even the day, the hour was out, they had returned; and, what was harder to defy than wounds, they had conquered sheer weariness.

It was something so different he had promised them once, riding out there on the meadows—a splendor of living, a splendor of death. But they seemed to bear him no grudge. Whether they had really understood his goal or not, in this present they were together—even the least of them.

"For all of them, not just for us," Wolf had said that autumn night long ago. That was what counted.

Still, in their wretchedness, their squalor, they won a sort of nobility. "Do you still proclaim the glory of the body?" one of the nobles had mocked, and he would still answer, "Yes."

Maybe it was another faith than his that gave them strength, and yet this thing that was happening was on earth. Whether it lead to ultimate transcendence or be the faint distorted image of the process in the absolute, the way of achievement lay *here*—that only was certain. That to every man was given the chance to find it in what way he would, through the spirit or the flesh or the fusion of both—for this freedom they were fighting, to this freedom he had been leading them, that they should more fully *live*. As long as there was life, it was life he had to defend, even in defeat.

Slowly he had paced up and down the floor of his room. Still absorbed in his brooding, he paused before the empty hearth. His eyes rested on the frieze.

"Kings must die for the people." "But they must live for them first." After all, it had been but a dream.

Had he then always known inwardly what must be his way? The massacres of his fathers, Toulouse, Béziers—they were all links in a chain and he had forged them himself. But what right had he to drag in the rest, even Wolf? Of that nightmare past, what had even he really understood? Wolf's way was in the future, and he must go to it unhindered. Perhaps, after all, he might conquer where he himself had failed. What could one know—even of oneself? Life or death, he thought suddenly, victory or defeat—after all, was it only an heroic gesture, throwing down the gauntlet to fate?

274

One could only take on oneself the readiness. To become one with one's fate. Who had said it? Yet it was one's own, one's own only. There was no breaking down that ultimate solitariness.

He had made up his mind.

When, later, he went to meet the barons in council to decide on a reply to the Crusade, he knew what the answer must be.

Throughout the late hours of that night Wolf had held watch on one of the eastern towers of the castle. Still it was the same as every other night. The starry, almost moonless darkness above the plain perforated by the flickering lights of the camp, and down in the city below, the deeper glow of the aromatic fires that had been lit to stop the contagion. . . . The monotonous tread of the guards—pausing, halting, straining their ear for the sound of sappers in the fosse below; the distant noise of the forge, the rumble of wagons as they rolled through the streets collecting their latest toll of dead. The same, and yet interminable as never before, as though it must push away the dawn that was to be different from all others. That it *would* be different was incredible—that it would be, somehow or other, an end to these weeks. The other end had seemed possible, the wild assault, desperate, perhaps even hopeless, the heroism that would end with death in Trencavel's arms, even though at moments he had been shamefully, mortally afraid.

That first day, after Graveillande had fallen and the crusaders had tried to take St. Vincent by storm, a boulder from their mangonels had burst through the wooden hoarding, and through a rain of arrows he had seen Guilhem of Rabat, or what one moment since had been he, a heap of mangled flesh at his feet. Even while he retched in sickness he was grabbed by the arm and drawn back to cover.

"Think we don't all feel it to start with?" an old archer clapped him on the back. "Better it gets you there than in the pants," and he had thrust the crossbow into his hands, till, fixing his eyes on the dancing wavering target, he had set bolt on bolt to the string and at last his vision cleared, his hands stopped trembling. Mercifully Trencavel hadn't been present. After that it had been easier, and the flaunting, flattering image of heroism had returned.

275

Now the last chance was over. They had come to a dead end. Yet even now Trencavel would make no peace that was not just, he knew. And there was hope, for the Crusade was weary. Most of them (their forty days up) were clamoring to return. Only a last hope of booty held them, and they could still scrounge enough from the castles on their way home.

Trencavel would make no peace that was not just to his people—but to himself? Fear that had haunted him all these hours began to invade him again, mounting out of the darkness, fear of what he scarcely knew. There was no talk, no thought of danger. Safe conduct there and back under the protection of his own knights. Why, it was not even submission, but a parley about a possible truce. Later, when they had water, it would be different. Aragon had hinted about possibilities in the future, Aragon had persuaded Trencavel to try and come to terms. But what if they were the same again? But they couldn't be. They'd seen themselves the Viscount of Béziers, and Carcassonne couldn't be mocked at like that. Besides, it was different. They were impatient now themselves. But what would they demand of the heretics?

His thoughts flew back to what he had seen of them during the past weeks and, seeing, had known his own dreams of valor feeble and puerile. What had he done to prove himself? And now! If only he could have had a chance, even tonight. But here, pinned down to his duty, here where no danger was likely to come . . . If only he could go with him. He had pleaded and Trencavel had answered: "The stipulation was a bodyguard of knights."

Faint and pallid, dawn began to break in the east. Footsteps sounded on the stairs beneath. He swung round, not daring to hope. A hand was laid on his shoulder.

"We're ready," Trencavel said.

Silently Wolf looked up at him in a last wild hope of expectancy, but the other turned aside his head.

Together they paced the platform of the tower.

Why, thought Trencavel, this futile prolongation, that choked, that forced itself between them, almost alienating? To cover it, he began to talk—talk that was but evasion, till that, too, died away and they stood silent, side by side.

In the east, far out beyond the stricken city, the sky was growing white. Somewhere below, horses were being taken out. As though, slowly, his thoughts came back from far away, Trencavel stirred.

"The riders—do you remember?—and you said: 'As if they were riding into the morning.' "

No answer was needed. It was enough, that slight lifting of the boy's head. Let him not speak. Let it end here. Silence could not destroy what could never be spoken. Yet one thing could be done, and quickly. Time that had seemed like a weight was too short now.

"Kneel."

Blindly, Wolf obeyed. Blind and mazed, it seemed to him that Trencavel was fumbling with his belt, then something struck his shoulder. Words clear but senseless as in a dream rang in his ears. As he rose, gathered into the other's embrace, something fell heavily at his hip. Only when at last Trencavel's arms fell away from him did realization sweep in, overwhelming, exultant.

"Now—now I can come."

"No."

It cut in incomprehensible, till slowly the word attained meaning and on Wolf's face the radiance suddenly broke and withered.

Only cruelty could help. "Are you going to keep faith?" But it had achieved its object. The boy had stiffened.

"Always—to go on—like the riders. That's all that matters. Besides," suddenly he was laughing, "long before sunset I'll be back. Is it too long to wait for your spurs?"

It was the old wistful gaiety he knew so well, but Wolf, choking back the strangling hardness in his throat, scarce heard.

Then suddenly, from far behind in the enemy camp, a fanfare rang out, harsh and shrill. Instinctively Trencavel turned.

He was going—

"Your sword." Stifled and hoarse, the words broke from Wolf's throat, but his hands clasped rather than loosened the belt.

"We ride unarmed—keep it—guard it well—till I come."

Now he had lifted his hand in a little gesture of farewell. Now he was running down the steps. For a moment the parapet hid him, then once more he appeared. Surely, surely he must turn. Somewhere a spear struck hard on stone in salute. Only a moment ago he had been there, striding along the ramparts in the dawn.

A first ray of sunlight crept over the parapet and, glinting on the mesh of mail, kindled the vinous fires in the jeweled hilt of a sword. Above it a boy's contorted face still stared, blind, uncomprehending, at the black shadow of an empty archway.

THE SACRIFICE

O legati fraus pia. O pietas fraudulenta!
(VAUX-CERNAY: *Historia Albigensium*)

I

NOTHING WAS LEFT BUT TO WAIT.

The sun rose higher, mounted to the meridian, broiled with the same intensity on the stricken city, throwing into yet more mocking brilliance the panoplied splendor of the crusaders' camp. But toward noon, for the first time, a streak of cloud appeared on the horizon, remained there without moving. If it had come yesterday would Trencavel have waited, banked on a last hope? For even now rain was no certainty. The line might swell before nightfall, hover there for days, or it might vanish, a mocking ghost.

The shadows shortened, but still Wolf, returning always to watch from the keep, could see no change in the camp. No definite movement. No sign of sudden excitement broke the shifting kaleidoscope of heraldic glory. In vain he strained his eyes trying to detect the escutcheons of the Count of Nevers, pick out among that sea of pavilions the tent from which the familiar figure must issue at last. In the end, his head swimming under the glare, he gave it up, and descended once more to the ramparts.

Hostilities, at least for the duration of the negotiations, had ceased. A sense of brooding inactivity hung over everything. Wearily the guards slouched at their posts. Here and there little knots of men sprawled in the shadow of the walls, rising now and again to cast a desultory glance through the machicolations. Sometimes, for a second, a tense mutter broke the sullen apathy, to fade again into the same listless murmur. Faces, many familiar enough, stared at him vacantly, mumbled a word as he passed; resentment, relief, or whatever emotion they felt swallowed in that suffocating inertia. As long as they had still been engaged in action, though day by day victory had grown remoter, there had remained, though not even consciously considered, the certainty of some outcome. Now that it stood before them it seemed to have lost all reality. Even the thought of the future on which none, after the fate of Béziers, held out hope, failed to rouse actual terror. With the relaxation of the will the spirit grew supine. Only the flesh asserted itself, reducing everything to a single craving that looked no further than the hope of physical relief—water.

Wandering on, he reached the hall. From the rows of rude straw pallets that covered the floor the stench of blood and putrefying flesh mounted to the stone vault, thick with flies and mosquitoes. Here and there, between the sound of dull, restless moaning, the low mutter of Cathar elder or of monk, a cry would suddenly jerk out, hoarse and inhuman.

He was passing on swiftly, dreading the spectacle of human agony, when among a group of the less seriously wounded a young man, sprawling half-clothed over the bed of one of his companions, turned toward him, looking up from a game of dice:

"Any news?"

His right arm hung in a sling and his face looked haggard and unshaven; even so, Villemur had not lost his customary swagger. "Heavens!" he returned carelessly to Wolf's distraught "No." "You look as though the steel had run through your liver. Give him time, man. They're probably feasting him. Only let's hope he remembers *us* and brings along a few titbits—a nice little capon, or what do you say to a peacock off Nevers' own plate?"

"Better a slice of Burgundy's own rump," grunted his neighbor.

"Too tough."

"Make it a wager, boys," Villemur tossed the dice in his sound hand. "There'll be something worth eating before nightfall."

"Eating—let him eat his own sh-t," cursed a voice from one of the further beds, "if he doesn't bring back the Aude. I reckon a man doesn't care what he gets to guzzle when there's no drop of water left for a dressing, and the blood caked to his thigh like dung to the flank of a cow."

"Not to say the stench," Villemur grimaced. "Wolfling, do us a favor and go scrounging round in fair Agnes's bower and see whether she hasn't left us some attar of roses."

"Or lilies—sweet lilies of chastity, eh?" echoed the man on whose bed he was leaning.

"Ask Wolf—you've had such close experience, haven't you?" Villemur turned to him provokingly. "She tried so very hard to ensnare the little monk. Anyhow, you've had a bit of respite lately. What, acting as faithful sword- and shield-bearer?" he rippled on, his gaze resting on the weapon hanging at Wolf's side. "Afraid of losing it?"

To have answered then and there with the obvious retort—triumphant vengeance for years of bullying. Villemur, three years his senior, was desperately ambitious, he knew, to win his spurs. He'd get them, no doubt, after this. In his reckless way he'd been brave enough. Wolf had been almost jealous of his wound. And the others, this crowd of fevered, pain-racked men. . . . Before he had found an answer his triumph was drowned in a miserable sense of shame. If only he could have done something, do something even now, before they heard.

"I'm due on watch," he said quickly, and was already passing on. Technically it was a lie. But what else was there but watching—watching?

"Don't forget the perfume," Villemur called after him. "Lilies, roses, violets—anything, as long as it's strong."

Near the further door, where they had instituted a sort of dressing station, a crowd of wounded had filed up for treatment. Among them Wolf recognized one of Guiraut's companions. The man, whose forehead was roughly bandaged, stared at him, sullen and resentful, and Wolf remembered uncomfortably that he still hadn't inquired further about Guiraut. He'd been hurt, he heard, while the crusaders were trying a new escalade, but he had never had a moment to look him up.

"How is he—Guiraut?" he approached the soldier.

"Bad," he answered grimly, but before Wolf could inquire further he was led away.

The bitter, resentful look that he had given him left Wolf no peace. What must the man think of him mooning around, evidently unscathed, for no doubt he believed he'd neglected Guiraut, thought himself too grand to trouble further about him. "All very fine to play at comradeship as long as it was a matter of big words, but when it came to it"—he could guess how they talked—and Guiraut

281

doubting, or not letting himself believe, for he'd caught the look of grudging admiration on the young carpenter's face as he watched Trencavel working on the machines.

"I told you so," Wolf had triumphed after Trencavel had refused Pedro's overtures while Guiraut, scowling, answered, "We haven't got to the end." And what might he be thinking now? Might he even imagine Trencavel had betrayed them, was trying to save his skin? The thought was unbearable. He was convinced that he ought to see Guiraut at once. But how could he? Trencavel might return at any moment and if he were not there to welcome him . . . But augmented now by this new fear, waiting became intolerable. If he slipped down to the town and had only a word with Guiraut . . . In any case he could hear the signal of Trencavel's return and could rush back. After all, it was for the Cause. If Guiraut doubted, and he hadn't attempted to see him, in a way it would be his own fault.

Running through the courtyard and slipping through one of the posterns, he was soon hurrying along the narrow streets of the city. Here the sense of brooding apathy was worse. Most of the windows were shuttered and barred. But for a few scattered groups of men or women talking in a low mutter, a voice rising suddenly in hysterical argument, the city seemed dead. Here and there an emaciated figure tottered along the cobbles or leaned against the wall, staring opaquely out of a cadaverous countenance at the improbable image of the still healthy. Scarcely a house in which the sickness did not rage, in which death had not taken toll of those whom the missiles of war had spared. Every now and again a door would open to let out the long-robed figures of two elders going on their consoling mission from house to house. Sometimes, in the narrower alleys, the passing of a wagon heeling over with its grim burden caused him to retreat into an open archway. It must have been the same for the last week—the lumbering wagons, the haggard, ashen faces; but then they had been blindly accepted, obliterated by the fighting on the walls. Now only did it strike him in its full horror. Suddenly in the silent alley it seemed to him that he was walking through a city of the dead.

And then all at once he was standing outside the front of the little bakery, so familiar after those nightmare streets, and so absurdly trim. The shop shutters were closed but one of the windows of the dwelling house was ajar. With beating heart he knocked at the door.

Ages seemed to pass before the sound of steps sounded behind and the door was slowly opened.

"O *dieus*, the young senhor!"

The next moment he was drawn within. "And I've been wondering all this time," Mother Martha was saying, almost embracing him, the respect and pride she had felt at the comradeship between the young nobleman and her son overruled by anxiety and emotion.

"Guiraut—how is he?" he inquired hurriedly, feeling a new pang of shame at his neglect.

She shook her head. He noticed then that her round and usually so jovial face had grown wan and furrowed.

"They never thought he could live, but it was as though he were determined against God's will." A frightened, despairing look had come into her face. "He refused the *bonshommes*," she stopped, clutching hold of his arm and staring up at him imploringly, as though all this time she had been waiting for his coming, expecting that he, at least, would condone her sin. "And I was glad," she whispered, "though it was wickedness. I couldn't bear to think of him going or, worse, that if he recovered they'd take him from me. But now—when he finds out that he's—" The tears began to flow down her gray cheeks. Still clinging to his arm she led him toward the back room.

Involuntarily Wolf stood still, hesitating before what might face him. "Is he . . . ?" he began, and ceased, aware that his tardiness would seem worse than ever if he did not even know what ailed him.

"He hasn't the fever," she said hurriedly, noticing his hesitance and afraid that after all he might go. "We were spared that."

"I'm used to it," he laughed harshly. "There's enough of it up at the castle."

"O *dieus, dieus*—there too!" she echoed plaintively, but her own troubles were too great for her to take in more. "To think it was our own men did it," she went on, as if at least it was a relief to pour out her own woes. "They didn't know, of course, that he'd got through, and it growing dark. He was bent on cutting through those devils' ladders from beneath, and well he might have. He was that handy with lathe and saw—after all, it was his trade," a note of pride welled even through her tears. "But he was too late in pulling back and, as those miscreants came scaling up, the burning pitch went raining down over him and all."

There was silence. "Can I see him?" Wolf heard himself saying at last. But she was already leading the way across the little courtyard to the room behind the bakehouse where they had often talked and argued and sung till late at night.

"And now," she was saying, "if it's all in vain. It's *that* he cannot bear, not just for himself but for the others. He was that set on the Cause, though I've always said they were reaching above themselves and no good would come of it in the end. And sure," she went on, "it isn't right either to blame it on the poor Viscount if now he's. . . ." But they were already at the door, and bracing himself, he pushed it open.

The light filtered so weakly through the half-closed shutters that at first he could see almost nothing.

"The young senhor," she began, "the young senhor from the castle—he's come to see you." Then, after a moment's hesitation, she was gone.

On the bed something seemed to move. He crossed the floor. Now his eyes, accustomed to the dimness, made out a deeper whiteness on the white pillow. After all, it was a head, but so swathed in bandages that the little segment of darkness between them might have been anything.

"Guiraut—"

There was no answer.

Steeling himself at last to look closer, he found a hand, bare, rough, suddenly so familiar after the terror of that anonymity that he grasped it, as much to reassure himself as in emotion.

Weakly it struggled to free itself but he held fast.

"So he's gone to give in?" The words came scarcely articulate, little more than a raucous whisper.

"No," Wolf heard himself answer. "No, he hasn't. They invited him to discuss terms. He'll never—"

"If he thought we couldn't take it," the toneless voice interrupted, "you can tell him from me—"

"But he knows," Wolf persisted. "He was up there on the walls—always—till the very last. He would have gone on to the end, but something had to be left—"

"Left?" The hand jerked itself free. "Of course there's something left for you—Foix, Andorra, and for the others,

Limoux, Fanjeaux, Cab-Aret—something to rescue, some cursed bit of property." In its bitterness the whisper seemed to gather strength.

"It wasn't that—the city—"

"You needn't tell me. They're dying like rats. But it wasn't they who're giving up. It's the fever did it—the slinking bastard." He was quiet for a moment. "I reckon it doesn't much matter how it gets one, one way or another," he continued, "as long as it gets you straight. Arnaud was done for straightway, and then Guilhem—a halberd got him in the side—afterward he went too." There was a pause. And then something horribly like a laugh. "We'd made a pact, we two, that whatever happened we'd not take the *consolamentum* for fear if, after all, we recovered they wouldn't let us go on fighting."

So that was what his mother had meant, saying he had refused the *bonshommes*.

"But we might just as well—both of us." Once more came that mocking specter of a laugh.

"Stop it, Guiraut—for God's sake!"

But the throttled jerking movement within the linen swathings went on. " 'Victory or death'—it sounds good—if you get there. But who does? He hasn't, has he, for all your talking. Go on, you can have it back on me easy. Well, have you ever thought what it would be like? I know what you're thinking—my face." His voice rose to a shrill whisper. "Don't you understand, even that won't matter, because I shan't—see."

Vainly in the terrible silence that followed Wolf struggled to reach out to him, but the youth's hand remained hostile, withdrawn.

"I'm a coward," he said roughly.

"You—Guiraut?"

"And I talked about taking it. I've managed to keep bottled up till now. I guessed, but I didn't want to frighten her. And then I got the *bonshommes* alone. They put me off, and said it was uncertain, but yesterday—I know and she knows and neither of us will speak."

He saw them—the old woman—the stricken youth, like two children playing a macabre game of blindman's buff.

"Now that I've got it out," the voice continued more quietly, "it's easier. At the worst, I suppose the Cathars will look after her. But I'd promised her she shouldn't live

285

on anyone's bounty—not theirs, not your bloody Viscount's."

"But, Guiraut," Wolf pleaded, "it wouldn't be that. It isn't as it used to be. We're all in it together."

'He's giving up.'

"He isn't. Christ! don't you see? It's so that we can go on. We've got to . . . somewhere, somehow—at Foix, in the mountains. It doesn't matter where as long as we carry on—as long as there's someone who cares. He said so himself. 'To go on'—that's all that matters."

The wounded youth made an effort to turn. "You're carrying on—swear it. You can. After all, you're not a Cathar."

"God knows it's truth, Guiraut."

"All right." For a little while there was silence. The figure on the bed lay very still. "I guess it's time you hopped it," and when Wolf hesitated, "Clear out," he said roughly.

It was the old Guiraut. Wolf got to his feet. "I'll be back later." He hesitated; then, grasping his hand, he was gone.

II

In spite of the haunting horror of that image, Wolf, as he made his way back through the desolate streets, felt almost calm, as if that oath, silently made at daybreak, ratified now before Guiraut, had allayed his worst and almost unconscious fears. Whatever happened, they would go on. The certainty within him became so great that his very doubts regarding the negotiations faded. All *must* be well or Trencavel would certainly be back by now. The terms would be such that, somehow or other, they could begin again. So great was the faith within him that even the deathly silence of the town seemed changed and imbued with a grave calm reflected in the deep clarity of the sky. On the far horizon beneath the declining sun the air was washed with gold. The line of cloud had vanished, but even the frustrated hope of rain made no difference. The agony of the city was ending. The Cause must go on. So rapt was he in that certainty that the sound of a horn suddenly echoing from the castle keep came only as the triumphant confirmation of his thoughts. The next moment he was bounding forward jubilantly up the ramp leading to the inner walls of the castle.

As he entered the courtyard from the postern the portcullis was already lifted, and he rushed forward to meet the horseman whom he could already hear clattering over the bridge. The next instant a rider had emerged from the shadow of the archway—it was old Ademar of Limoux.

He has sent him ahead, thought Wolf, conquering his momentary disappointment, to tell us all is well. But at the same moment his blood seemed to congeal.

Slowly, as though he moved in invisible shackles, Ademar rode forward into the courtyard, and not even when he reached the center, encircled by the fast-gathering throng, did he seem rightly aware of his surroundings, till Wolf, tearing himself from his paralysis of fear, pushed forward to take his horse. Then, silent still, as though unable to rouse himself from his stupor, Ademar loosened the reins and, dismounting, regardless of the anxious faces around him, turned toward the senhor of Cab-Aret who had thrust his way through the crowd.

"It was basest treachery—a fiendish plot."

"But he—the Viscount?" The words struggled voiceless on Wolf's lips.

Cab-Aret brushed him aside. "Christ in heaven! What's happened?"

"Prisoners, all of us," Ademar muttered. "They let me go—as the oldest, perhaps—and most worthless to them." In his emotion he stumbled. Supported by Cab-Aret and Wolf, he slowly climbed the steps.

Up in the council chamber he revived a little. Even so, he was unclear as to what had actually happened. Almost immediately on their arrival, Trencavel, it appeared, had been separated from his following. At first it had scarcely awakened their suspicion. He had been treated with every mark of honor and their own reception had seemed frank and friendly enough. They had, indeed, been feted with a veritable banquet, surprising, perhaps, at so early an hour, but plausible enough in the light of courtesy toward those ostensibly half-starved by the siege, and it was not until the long-protracted meal was at last over that some of them approaching the Count of Nevers' tent found themselves intercepted by affable excuses. "The Viscount was still closeted in secret session with the chiefs of the

Crusade." But as the hours passed, and still there was no end, they had become more and more restless. Determined at any rate to take their stand outside his pavilion and await him, they had found their way actually barred. The smile was still on the crusaders' faces but it was now unmistakably one of cold triumph. "The Viscount," one of them mocked, "was evidently so relieved at escaping from the besieged city that he had decided to prolong his stay." "For how long?" Guilhem of Rabastes had asked coldly. He was answered by a shrug. Infuriated, Guilhem made a step forward, but the Frenchman had drawn his sword. Unarmed, they found themselves encircled. In a moment all was confusion. Some of them tried to rush the ring. Young Ramon of Laurac flew at the taunter's throat. A crusader felled him by a blow under the eyes. Another ran his sword through Guilhem's arm. Two or three of them had fallen. The rest, finding themselves in shackles, had been dragged back to the tent.

Another hour must have passed. At last a crusader had come in, a man of some importance, it appeared, vaguely familiar, and then he recognized the lion rampant on his surcoat and the livery of his squire—Montfort. He stood there, feet planted apart, leaning on his great two-handed sword, regarding them from under his beetling brows as though they were rats. Then, at a sign, they had been led off. Guilhem, faint with loss of blood, had stumbled. "Sick at the thought you'll no longer be able to twang your lute strings?" Montfort had laughed roughly. "Leave the graybeard!" he had pointed at Ademar himself.

Again he had been left. After an age the flap of the tent had lifted once more. He had been ready for the worst, but instead his chains had been loosened. With beating heart he had been led to Nevers' pavilion. Within, he found himself face to face with the leaders of the Crusade. Seated at the side of the papal legate, Arnaud-Amelric of Cîteaux presided, Montfort posted as bodyguard close behind his chair. In the background, turned away a little, Nevers, evidently ill at ease, muttered something to St. Pol. Burgundy, stout and rubicund, toyed with his mastiff. Nowhere a sign of Trencavel. It had been decided, the Abbot of Cîteaux had begun, that, in view of the treaty having been drawn up with the viscount's entire consent, Sir Ademar, as the most venerable of his vassals, should himself bear to the city the terms of the capitulation. Tomorrow, at dawn, the city was to be handed over in total surrender to the Crusade. "With the will of the Viscount?" he had queried doubtfully, and asked to see him. "Through the will of God," the Cistercian answered. Vainly Ademar had expostulated against the violation of the truce, the rights of safe-conduct. "Rights?" Montfort had broken out. "Was it for them, perfidious heretics and sinners against the Lord, to presume on rights?" But he was silenced by the uplifted hand of the legate. "Nevertheless," the abbot continued stonily, "in so far as it was maintained that the Viscount himself was no heretic, and seeing that God had vouchsafed him the grace of beholding the sinfulness of his own laxity, the most holy Crusade had magnanimously granted his plea that the citizens of Carcassonne should go free, on condition that they depart from the city tomorrow at sunrise, leaving all their goods and chattels behind them, and go empty-handed, unarmed, clad in no more than breeches and shirt. The lives of all are spared." Ademar concluded his story brokenly.

"And Trencavel's?" Wolf cried wildly.

"He remains as hostage."

"Hostage?" Cab-Aret jeered. "Maybe he offered himself. He's equal to it."

"God knows," Ademar lifted his face from his hands. "They forced him to it, no doubt. Threatened him with a repetition of Béziers. He was unarmed, as we."

"They twisted him easily enough, I reckon."

But Wolf had sprung forward, white-faced and trembling. "He wanted to attack, but you didn't let him—and now—now—"

"Silence!" thundered Cab-Aret. "Get out of here." But despite his rage he was too immersed in the problem at hand to give further attention to the boy, and Wolf, backing against the wall, was still able to remain within earshot.

"We were lost anyhow," Ademar commented tonelessly. "No water, and then the fever. Now at least those who are left have their lives. The prisoners, all but Trencavel, are to be freed on the safe delivery of the city."

"And he?" Cab-Aret laughed hoarsely. "Maybe they even demand a ransom."

"He's more use to them as hostage for the moment—pledge for his lands."

Impatiently Cab-Aret wheeled round and strode toward

289

the doorway. "Christ! Of all the bunglers! If I'd been there! Treat them for what they are—brutes, ruffians, thieves—and pay them back with their own coin."

Wearily the old man rose to his feet to follow, pausing as Wolf, pale and wild-eyed, moved toward him. His eye rested on the sword. "He told me as we rode out. 'Ademar,' he said—why, I think he was laughing—'see that we don't forget his spurs.'" Shaking his head, he turned away.

III

There was no alternative. Thought of further resistance now was hopeless. The death roll had reached a terrifying height. Water was all but nonexistent. Within a few days they would be forced to surrender and then the Crusade would doubtless not show them even this promised mercy. Whether, in view of their perfidy, even that was genuine might be questioned, but it presented the only chance. The property of many now in Carcassonne lay outside the city. Possibly there was still something to rescue. At the worst they could flee to Foix and Andorra and hold out among the mountains. In the meantime they could treat with the Crusade for Trencavel's release, whereas dead, or attempting a useless resistance, they could achieve nothing. Who knew, moreover, what they would do to him in revenge? It was decided, therefore, that all who could would leave the city at dawn. Cab-Aret would retire to his fortress in the Black Mountains. Others, reputed Catholics, try once more for reconciliation through the Montpelliers. The Jews, finally, who had followed Trencavel from Béziers, would join their relatives in Narbonne.

Regarding his own fate Wolf was almost indifferent. It was taken for granted, of course, that he would return to Foix. He harbored no illusions as to the reception he was likely to receive and the invective that would pour from his father's lips against Trencavel. It would not even help, he reflected bitterly, that he had won his spurs. If only now, of all times, he could prove himself. Feverishly he had wandered about the castle carrying messages, obeying this and that behest, where in any case action was useless. Cab-Aret and Ademar had shut themselves up in private consultation with Caravita. He guessed that it might concern the possibility of concealing part, at least, of the treasure in one of the subterranean vaults.

In the end he wandered up to the battlements and stared down into the gathering darkness. Only a few hours ago he had stood here with Trencavel. Suddenly, in the silence, he re-lived that moment with such intensity that only now did it seem revealed in all its unbearable fullness. And he had stood dumb. Yet it had been like an oath between them—to go on—like the riders. Had Trencavel known—already then? To go on—in Foix—with his father—perhaps at least he could force him to fight. But it seemed so infinitely far away, while down on the darkening plain, even now. . . . O God, what had they done, what were they doing to him? Mad fantasies crowded through his brain. To slip through the camp under cover of night; to fell the guards and loosening his shackles flee with him through the night. Then gathering a great force at Foix they would pour down from the mountains and give open battle at last. For that they had been trained, for speed and action, and skill of arms under the open skies, not to be suffocated, parched with fever and thirst between the hoardings of the reeking city.

Inevitably his thoughts returned to Guiraut. Somehow or other he must be got away, but if, as he had gathered, he were too ill to move? He had already approached Ademar about him, but he had been too harassed to give him attention. There were enough sick and wounded among the knighthood who would have to be left behind, let alone this carpenter's apprentice. But he was one of the New Guard, Wolf had persisted ardently. "Would to God Trencavel hadn't mixed himself up with all that burgher riffraff," the old man had replied, and if *he* showed no sympathy, what could one expect of Cab-Aret and the others? But the thought of saving Guiraut gave Wolf no peace. To leave him in the lurch after what had passed between them appeared the betrayal of the Cause itself—and now, wasn't *he* responsible? Was that what Trencavel had meant? Turning, he hastily descended the steps of the tower, determined to go and see Guiraut at once. At the bottom he was just making his way to the courtyard when he heard himself called by name.

He stopped, startled by a familiar huskiness in the voice, and, turning slowly, found himself face to face with

Miriam Caravita. Vaguely he had heard that she was in Carcassonne with her father, but amid the horrors of the last weeks he had not let the thought trouble or even interest him, till indeed it was quite forgotten.

"I've been hunting for you everywhere. Is it such a shock," she smiled, "or didn't you really know I was here?"

"I wasn't sure," he began lamely. "And then—"

"Of course. You were too busy. I wasn't going to intrude on your heroic exploits."

He winced. "I've got to go into the town," he said quickly. "Something's got to be done."

She looked at his white, distraught face. "We're all in the same boat. Can't I help?"

"No." He felt her gaze, dark and searching, upon his. "It's nothing—one of us—a friend of mine," he evaded.

"You'd better come and tell me about it," she said earnestly.

He hesitated. After all, it was a chance.

"Not here." Lightly touching his arm, she beckoned him to follow.

"I haven't much time."

But already she was leading the way along the passage. At the end she unlocked the door. It was a room, he knew, used by Caravita as a kind of office, small, circular, barely furnished except for a few heavy chests against the wall, a table strewn with scrolls of parchment and writing materials—a strange contrast to the luxurious setting he had seen her in before. Suddenly it struck him that until now he had never seen her on her feet. She was smaller, actually, than he had imagined, and the dark blue dress, unrelieved but for the jeweled belt at her waist, made her face, framed by the shoulder-long black hair, look paler than ever.

"I'm acting as father's secretary," she smiled a little. "You didn't credit me with such filial piety, did you? But you see, fundamentally we agree with one another."

"But weren't you in Narbonne? It was safer there," he asked, bewildered.

She shook her head, laughing slightly. "I'm not quite such a sybarite as you imagine. When there was a chance of really doing something I went back to Béziers. Besides, you know, you'd interested me in the Cause."

Was she mocking? he thought furiously. But she was

292

looking at him gravely. "Tell me," she said again and, signing to him to be seated, perched herself on the edge of the table.

He remained standing. Desperately he began to tell her of Guiraut.

She listened, her face contracting with disgust. "Good God! But don't you see it's hopeless? Even if he could be moved, he hasn't a chance. At some of the places they've even been stripping the bandages off the wounded to see they don't smuggle anything through. Besides, why rob the poor wretch of a chance of getting out of his hell? After all, if they finish him off, it'll be a mercy."

"To leave him—to them?"

"You'll have to—it's all one can do," she paused a moment, "unless . . . Father knows a physician. The man's clever enough. He could send him down. It would be quite painless."

"No." He stared at her, aghast.

"Why?" She smiled bitterly. "Isn't it more humane?"

"You don't understand," he cried vehemently. "He was one of us." He might have known how she would take it.

"But don't you see something's got to be sacrificed?" she said. "He's not the only one, and there's nothing you can do."

Probably she was right. But still he must try. He turned to go.

"Wait. Don't you see it's useless to worry about the inevitable when you've enough to do besides? And tomorrow— By the way, I suppose you're going back to Foix?"

His hand was on the door. And then suddenly it became so clear that he couldn't understand why he hadn't seen it before. "No," he said roughly, "I'm not—I'm staying here."

"Are you mad?" For a moment there was silence. Slipping down from the table, she took a couple of steps toward him.

"I've got to stand by them," he said, facing her. "Guiraut, and all the others. Trencavel . . . I swore to go on." Now it had only one meaning.

"Go on—how can you, when you're dead? Don't you see they'll get you at once—you—his own squire? Why did you stay, except to plot? They'll draw conclusions and remove you nicely out of danger's way. Will that help him?"

"I must."

Fixedly her eyes lay on his white, set face. "If you *must* do something hazardous, let it at least be of use." She paused. "Perhaps after all I can help—only it's not easy—"

"What—what do you mean?"

"Come away from that door."

Half reluctant, he approached the table.

"Father was going to try," she said, lowering her voice. "He wouldn't trust anyone else. But he's far too old to take the chance."

"But what?"

"It's some things—documents, mostly—we've got to get them away."

"Documents?" he echoed dully. "But what has that to do with—"

"Trencavel?" she finished, laughing. "A lot. Bonds, foreign credits. They'll help toward the ransom."

"The ransom? But they haven't asked for one."

She shrugged. "They're out first for the plunder. They're rabid at having lost so much in the flames at Béziers. Afterward they'll start treating for *him*."

"Cab-Aret said something about it," he admitted.

"Naturally. He sees things black and white. And he's none too happy about them either. Who's going to pay? The Carcassais is drained dry. Your father will have enough to do financing his own affairs. Raymond?" she laughed, "or perhaps Aragon?"

"He offered to help before," he murmured.

"Yes. And what will he ask in return? Allegiance, naturally. And that would mean—the end of your new world. A military alliance is one thing. Even the overlord-ship's pretty nominal. But if Pedro buys his life—you know what Trencavel is."

|"And you mean," he asked excitedly, "if I rescue the things, he'll be freeing himself?"

"Exactly. And what's more, you'll be the means of his doing it—your first feat of knightly prowess. Why, I quite forgot, I haven't even congratulated you yet. Didn't I tell you long ago you might have to rescue us from the Franks?"

It stung. Yet was this not the chance for which he had prayed, and a way to prove himself?

"But how?" he asked feverishly. "How can I, when they won't let anything through?"

"That's just it. But there's one chance." She looked around as though to make sure no one was listening. "There's a subterranean passage from here right under the Aude. In the old days Roger Taillefer confided it to Father. No one knew except Saissac. If one could get through. The outposts are thin enough out there. Afterward it should be easy. The whole Crusade's camped here waiting for the kill. They've only a few stragglers between here and Narbonne. Once there, one's safe enough as long as one isn't a Cathar."

"But didn't Trencavel know about the passage?" he asked anxiously.

"Probably. But he wasn't trying to escape."

"And I?" Once more his face clouded. "If I leave them, it's like running off."

"When you're rescuing him? Besides"—she touched the sword hanging at his hip—"don't you want to rescue that?"

Only then did it rush home on him. He would have to leave it behind. "Unarmed, in breeches and shirt." And Trencavel had said, "Guard it till I come." He turned to her, his mind made up. "I'll go."

She glanced at his surcoat. "It's too light."

"I can change."

"There's no time." Turning, she took a dark blue cloak from a peg on the wall and handed it to him; then, unlocking the chest, drew out a packet. Returning to the table she wrote a few words on a piece of parchment and placed it beneath the candlestick.

"He'll fret a bit," she smiled. "But he's sensible enough to see it's the better way. By the time he finds it we'll probably be under the Aude."

"We?" he echoed uncomprehendingly.

"Of course. I'm coming, too. I know about such things." Taking up the packet, she thrust it into the bosom of her dress. "You don't believe I'm capable of it, do you?—a mere woman." She laughed softly. "Well, if you think I need protection, surely you can give it me better than Father?"

He did not reply, or help her as she wrapped herself in her cloak.

She had kept up with him all along, though the ground was rough and slippery. Often she was so close to him that he could feel her breath, panting a little, upon his neck. But he hurried on, ruthless, scarcely giving her time to keep within the glow of his torch.

"You never would believe I was serious—all these years," she had mocked, as though she were determined to avenge herself. But in his very self-accusation he hardened against her. It was his adventure, not hers—undertaken for Trencavel's sake. He had set out without leaving word with anyone. In vain he had pleaded at least to tell Ademar, but she had laughed scornfully.

"What, that old graybeard—he'd feel responsible for you to your father—in spite of the spurs. Cab-Aret? He's not very fond of you, is he?—a bit too revolutionary for his liking. He's hardly likely to approve of your meddling in plans of state. Incidentally, it would just about suit those old diehards to get Trencavel safely under Aragon's wing."

"But in the end," he had argued, "they're bound to find out."

She had shrugged. "Well, what does it matter—once we're gone? Leave Father to manage them."

And still there was Guiraut. . . . But it's for him too, so that the Cause can go on, he kept repeating to himself as he hurried forward.

Now the passage had narrowed so much that they had to wedge themselves through, almost bruising their heads on the overhanging rock. At one place moisture oozed through the stone, fell in a trickling fountain. "Water!" He halted then, stretched forward, his mouth avid to drink—but she dragged him back. "One can't be sure—wait—soon we ought to be out." Only then did he notice that her own lips were dry and split. Again they were struggling on. At last the ground grew steeper, till the rock seemed almost hewn to steps.

"We must be nearly through," she said at his back.

"We are," he answered a moment later, and stopped short. "It's the end."

For a moment, indeed, it really looked as if there were no way out, for before them the wall ended in an unbroken mass. His heart seemed to stop. Had they been led a wild-goose chase? Was it even some devilish trick of hers? To return all that way through the unending tunnel, through the labyrinthine corridors of the dungeon, the rank fetid air. Suddenly he seemed to suffocate, and leaned against the wall, but snatching the torch from his hands she raised it above her head.

"Look."

Just above them the rocky ceiling curved, domelike, to be crowned with what looked like a slab of stone. Spurred by new hope, he reached up.

"Push," she urged.

The stone did not move.

"Try again—it probably hasn't been touched for years." Bracing himself to another effort, he tried again. If now they should be frustrated, he thought desperately, and shoved with all his might. The stone gave a little, then stuck fast. But spurred on by hope, his efforts increased. Vaguely he became aware that she had thrust the torch into a crevice and was pushing with him. Suddenly a small shower of earth and stones rained down. With a smothered cry of triumph he sprang back. A moment later, thrusting his arm through the hole, he drew it back cursing. "Brambles!"

She laughed softly. "Brier rose. But the princess is on the wrong side, and, alas, she's wide awake."

Savagely he shoved at the stone. Now his shoulders were through. Thrusting his feet against the rock he swung himself up, and almost reeling under the impact of fresh air stood in the open.

"Is anything wrong?" Her voice came from below muffled, remote. She had extinguished the torch.

"No." Bending, he grasped her hands, her shoulders, and drew her up. For a moment she hung heavy in his arms. Then they stood silent, overpowered by the vastness of the night, breathing that indefinable fusion of a thousand scents, merged for them only to one dark and infinite coolness, unbelievably free from the stench of blood and fever and death.

"God! Think of living in catacombs!" Stirring, she signed to him to replace the stone. "Take care," she whispered as he made to go on.

They had emerged in the midst of a small wood. By what she had told him he guessed its whereabouts, and from his frequent rides through the district knew the lie of the land well enough to find their way across the surrounding countryside. The moon had not yet risen, but through the network of the branches the stars gave a faint light.

Not daring to speak, they moved carefully forward till the silhouette of tree trunks against a fainter darkness suggested they had reached the edge. A moment later they drew back, startled. Below them, hidden before by an overhanging bank, a man was sitting by the last smoldering embers of a campfire. His head lolled forward over his chest. For a time they watched him. He did not move.

Still they waited, hardly daring to breathe. No sound broke the silence but for the faint stir of a bird, the creak of wood. The night stifled like a blanket. Her breath seemed to singe his neck.

"He's alone. Are you ready?" she whispered.

He stiffened.

She drew the sword a little from the scabbard.

"With the hilt—close behind the ear—stun him before he can call out."

She felt him recoil.

"He's asleep—it's unfair."

"Did they care about fair play with Trencavel?"

Suddenly he snatched free his arm and moved carefully forward.

The next thing to be clear to him was that the man lay on the ground, stretched on his face. Miriam was already at his side.

"Quick," she whispered.

Already he had turned to go on, but she was pointing to the motionless form at her feet.

"Finish him. We can't take risks. If he wakes and calls the alarm—"

He stood inert, sick with horror.

"I can't—in cold blood."

"He'll never know." She pulled at his sword arm.

"No," he gasped hoarsely. "Never with that." Feeling beneath her cloak she drew out a small thin dagger.

"Well, then, if you won't, I suppose I must."

But he dragged it from her hand. As it struck, the body jerked up in a bow, then doubled up. For a second Miriam bent above it. The next moment they were fleeing into the night.

Hours later they were still pressing on through the darkness. At first every nerve had been strained to the sound of pursuit; later, when that fear had abated, to taking heed of the way. Now even that had grown mechanical. His limbs, scarce aware of weariness, responded to a force outside himself.

The moon had risen, a mere crescent merging wood and plain in a sea of uncertainty.

Flight, treachery, murder—they were phantasms vivid yet insubstantial as the fluctuant shadows beneath his feet, as the nightmare of the last twenty-four hours, the promise of triumph beyond—Trencavel. But even his image, suddenly, agonizingly sharp, escaped. "Only the present is ours": something echoed from far off. And the present would never end. They would go on fleeing forever under the spangled tent of the sky.

"It always ends up there among the stars." But what? Besides, it was long ago she had said that.

Suddenly he realized that his hand lay about her waist. It must have lain there since he had helped her across the ford.

They were standing on the brink of a wood. They must have come through it. Vaguely he remembered slashing at brambles and thorns. But she halted, drawing him back against a fallen trunk.

"When did you last sleep?"

Mechanically he tried to think and found himself tearing open his eyes.

Beyond the trees, the land swam cold and white. The moon, he thought, had never been so strong. Daybreak—yesterday at this very hour. . . .

"There isn't time. We've got to get on." He dragged at her arm; made an attempt to stumble forward, and found himself lying on the moss.

"Time . . ." murmured a voice huskily in his ear. "Why bother, considering the learned doctors say it doesn't exist?"

On the fifth day toward evening they at last came in sight of Narbonne—the promise of safety, of peace. At nightfall they would reach the house of her friends outside the walls. There would be little difficulty in entering the city. But as they stood looking down on the towered mass rising darkly from the brink of the plain against the shining foil of the sea, he turned his head, searching across the distance they had traversed—Carcassonne. It surged back on him with such violence that he almost cried aloud. Her hand was on his arm.

"Don't think of it now," she said softly. "That's past—it's the future we're going to build." And as he gazed down on her face, upturned to his, he was filled with sudden certainty, while all his anguish was drowned in the warmth of her lips.

BANQUETS AND BOREDOM

Because I cannot accurately conceive
Any ideal, even ideal Death,
My curses and my boasts are merely a waste of breath. . . .

Nostalgia for the breasts that never gave nor could
Give milk or even warmth has desolated me,
Clutching at shadows of my nullity
That slink and mutter through the leafless wood
Which thanks to me is dead, is dead for good.

(LOUIS MACNEICE, *Spring-Board*)

I

IN CARASSONNE THE FEVER HAD AT LAST BEGUN TO ABATE.
There was water, if not from the sky then at least from
the Aude. But still the wagons rumbled through the streets
bearing their human burden, no longer of the dead, but of
the living, as day by day the faggots were piled anew in
the market square and yet another batch of heretics was
led to the stake. Beside them, safely beyond the reach of
the flames, the stacks of loot mounted hourly, piled with
silver and gold and jewels, furniture and apparel, dragged
from the houses, heaped on high to the glory of God. For
the Abbot of Cîteaux had forbidden pillage. The fanatic
zeal that had reinforced the vandalism of the *ribauds* at
Béziers had, after all, proved too devastating to the
progress of the Crusade, and if, as the monk of Vaux-Cernay so aptly comments in his *Historia Albigensium*, the
same methods had been applied to Carcassonne, the prospective governor of the region would have been deprived
of the wherewithal to live and to maintain the soldiers indispensable for its tenure.

The installation of that governorship was in fact the reason for the celebrations that were even then being held in
the city.

In the great hall of the castle the noise of the banquet grew deafening—a fluctuating sea of sound, raucous, sibilant, guttural—a thousand voices uttering the confused gibberish of a dozen outlandish tongues.

The consummate restoration of the barbarian, thought Raymond of Toulouse, and, wincing, helped himself to another slice of capon *à sauce giroflée*. The food, at least, was excellent—a positive relief after the monotony of the camp cuisine, though he had brought with him his own chef. His eye wandering critically down the board, past the platters of glittering gold heaped with delicacies, was arrested by a bunch of grapes reposing in a shallow bowl of sea-green glass—so completely wasted on that brute of a Norman baron boasting jovially about the exploits of his hounds. True, to Raymond's myopic vision the outline remained somewhat blurred, but the effect was thereby, perhaps, enhanced rather than impaired. Divine fruit culled from Bacchus' own grove. Tyrian purple washed against aquamarine translucent as the wave from which Aphrodite sprang. Alas, that the poets had lost the delight in the miracle of the impression. Who since Fortunatus—the last of the pagans—had felt the wonder of textures? . . .

His reflections were rudely interrupted by the unmodulated tones of a female voice. Was it really necessary for the woman to rival the blast of a clarion? Then let her, instead of imperiling his eardrum, reserve it to proclaim her spouse's triumphs in the open field, and so save the man the cost of a herald. They said he was poor as a church mouse—Simon de Montfort l'Amaury, Simon, disinherited earl of some English fief (God, if he'd only run off to claim it!), Simon, by the grace of a just God lord of Carcassonne and the lands of the deposed Viscount Trencavel, for the Lord rewarded his servant; and, incidentally, my lords the Duke of Burgundy, the Courts of Nevers and St. Pol had scorned to accept the spoil—scorned or feared? So far, Raymond reflected, paralyzing the richness of the meat with a draught of wine, he had been correct in his prognostications. They doubtless had sense enough to realize the Carcassais might prove a thorn in the flesh, wedged in between Aragon and Toulouse and in the shadow of the incalculable mountains. Yes, in spite of all the humiliations heaped upon him, in spite of the machinations of that serpent Fulk, they were unsure of him still. Had he not cheated them of the fairest prize—Toulouse the sacred, the golden, the shrine of myth and legend, of fabulous wealth and ineffable seduction, of a *luxuria* to be irretrievably exterminated but first experienced in the name of the most holy Crusade? But already, the prize still unachieved, the hosts were breaking up; the leaders, dissatisfied, raking up old feuds, picking new quarrels, were broaching the question of returning home—Nevers, further down on Montfort's right, still liverish with rancor at the thought that the trap to catch the viscount had been laid in his own tent, and the shield of his august house smudged with dishonor, having learned, too late, that the ideals of chivalry do not always tally with ecclesiastic exigency; St. Pol, coldly disdainful as ever—no doubt he had coveted those lands, but, mused Raymond, he had proved right in guessing he would spurn Burgundy's and Nevers' leavings. He had reckoned with them all except that upstart Montfort. Probably the woman was behind it. He had always felt an aversion for that striding, tawny-haired type of female—the hectoring Hera in unadulterated Nordic form. What a pity, incidentally, that the full effect should be impoverished by the domestic coif. Only yesterday she had arrived at the head of a perfect cavalcade of Amazons to witness the investiture of her husband. (Really, Montfort ought to leave Jehovah out of it, but of course the Judaic conception reinforced so excellently all aggressive enterprise.) Frenchman, Norman, whatever he called himself, the blood of the barbarian ran undiluted in his veins. And in his own? The skeptic ever vigilant whispered in his ear. But centuries had passed since the Goths swooped upon Septimania—centuries in which to become civilized!

Gazing around him, he felt grateful that his impaired eyesight spared him too many a detail—these roistering gluttons, these bellowing hooligans. There were exceptions, of course, though to tell the truth he found their crudity actually preferable to the slick veneer of Philippe's court. There was even a certain amusement to be derived from the supercilious condescension the temporal leaders of the Crusade displayed toward their host, of which Montfort himself was evidently superbly oblivious. Crouched forward in the high seat, head thrust forward from the ponderous shoulders, the shaggy mustache trailing over the cup. . . . For a second the memory of the figure that by rights should be sitting there flashed across his mind—that godlike countenance, the lithe, slim limbs—but he pushed it from him. Christ, the voracity of the man! His gastric sensibility must be as obtuse as his conscience. How enviable that rudimentary arrogance, oblivious of the scorn of his peers as of their perfidy. Why not? The cause was sacred, the means therefore unimpeachable. Besides, he knew he was the best soldier of the lot. The fellow's self-esteem put in the shade the vainglory of Fulk himself, let alone the zeal of Cîteaux and the legates. What was it he had styled himself—the Chosen of God?—if that tale of the divine summons in the chapel of Rochefort were true and not one of those little emendations—*post festum*—with which that sly scribe Pierre de Vaux-Cernay intended artistically to embellish his history of the holy Crusade. Well, he would certainly need the aid of the Lord God of Hosts if he were going to hold the Carcassais. Did he imagine my lords were not going to leave him in the lurch?

"They left him high and dry." The unmusical voice insised, indignant. (Doubtless, and they would again.) "And so he set sail, alone, for Palestine." Launching out on the tale of her husband's prowess, Alys de Montmorency had begun to inveigh against the tardiness of the feudal princes in flocking to the liberation of the Sepulcher, with a pointedness that must have suggested definite malice had it not fitted in so completely with her general lack of grace. Moreover, despite the clumsiness of her tactics, she seemed curiously eager to ingratiate herself and had singled out Raymond among all the guests. She should not find him wanting in appreciation, he thought wryly. Palestine—the East. At last she had embarked on a subject on which he could pride himself to be an authority even if not through firsthand experience. Goaded by a sudden desire to pierce her imperturbable self-assurance, he was in the act of pondering what little anecdote relating to those sanctified but soul-imperiling expeditions might cause the unadulterated roses to flame upon that strong-boned, firm-fleshed cheek, when the general hubbub was broken a moment by a burst of applause. A particularly vulgar turn by one of those tumblers, he presumed, who were showing off their tricks lower down the hall. Bending forward, Burgundy threw him one of his wearying puns.

Tonight's entertainment had, alas, proved something of a disappointment to the duke, who had suggested a little dancer he had discovered. The girl had been found, half

starving, in the town. Hadn't left, it appeared, on the capitulation of the city, as she was down with the fever. She
had behaved like a little virago to her captors who had
dragged her along as a titbit for Montfort's feast. Her
resistance, however, had proved superfluous, for the suggestion had caused Simon to fly into one of his ungovern-
able rages—harlot, strumpet, Babylonian whore, the Lord
strike him before he let her perform under his roof. The
good duke had actually had some difficulty in saving the
girl from the stake, for which he had received scant reward. She'd scratched and spat like a cat—a procedure
that had only moved him to the laughing comment, "he
was used to taming young leopards." Whatever Eudes
might lack in more delicate qualities, Raymond reflected,
he certainly possessed humor and largess. It was a matter
of mood certainly, and dependent on the flow of his gastric juices, but the ducal stomach had been the cause of
saving more than one citizen of Carcassonne. That
woman, for instance, who had yesterday thrown herself at
Montfort's feet begging the life of her son. A widow,
formerly, it appeared, a pastry cook at the castle. The boy
had been hopelessly mutilated in the fighting. Soldiery—of
all themes it was one that was likely to soften Simon's
heart, but the Cistercian had forestalled him. "They are
confirmed heretics." At which, however, the woman had
broken out in new protestations. The youth, it seemed, had
seceded. He had refused the Cathar's consolation. For
months he had attended no heretic meeting, his leisure
hours devoted entirely to his duty in the viscount's new
guard. It might have been amusing, thought Raymond, to
see how far in the eyes of Montfort and the abbot Trencavel's flirtations with Apollo and Mars would have appeared preferable to Catharism, but at this point Burgundy
had intervened. God, he maintained, had surely determined on the woman's conversion, for the youth, maimed
as he was, was helpless without her. Let her show pen-
itence and be spared. Incidentally, he had winked in an
aside to Raymond, they might all profit by a good cook.
The thought of the menu Montfort was likely to offer was
hardly promising. Inevitably Raymond's gaze returned to
his plate. A pastry—the life of a man—interchangeable
values. But then what, according to the wisdom of the
East, was man but a grain of dust in the sight of Allah?

Appreciatively savoring the pie crust, he embarked on

the chosen anecdote of Palestine. How stolidly the woman responded to the delicacy of the theme. It had often served him as a test of feminine character. Before, however, he had reached the point, her attention was suddenly withdrawn and focused on the doorway.

"Your son?" she queried, with suddenly awakened interest.

Of course the boy would choose to arrive at that very moment. He had sent messengers to Toulouse at the special request of the nobles. Already many an eye was directed toward the door. Yes, after all, he was still Toulouse, and the entry of young Raymond was that of a prince. To give him his due, he did not fail in playing his part. There was no fear the son of Jeanne Plantagenet would shame him. After all, she had the blood of Eleanor of Guyenne in her veins.

For a moment the boy stood in the doorway a little in front of his tutor, then advanced. Indeed, the movement of the small slender figure was so unhesitating as it proceeded toward the high seat that Raymond was almost startled. Had he forgotten who should be sitting in that very place, who even now, in the dungeons of this very building. . . . Once more he thrust the rising image from him. What was Trencavel to the boy, anyway, but a name—the name of the man who in his priggish arrogance had insulted Toulouse, his father, and brought ruin and misery on the land? And yet, he reflected, would he himself, at that age, for all his precocious skepticism, have managed to make that obeisance with such ease, such almost indolent grace? Perhaps. Suddenly confronted with the ghost of his own childhood, a curious sense of fear swept over him. What! Was he beginning to develop a conscience? But no, he reflected, as young Raymond turned toward him with unfeigned affection, the boy was no cynic. Had he himself ever shown that filial loyalty? Respect, born of fear, perhaps, till skepticism had provided an armor against it. But this child of his was frankly loving and lovable enough. Was that at the root of the matter, an overwhelming desire to please, less in self-conceit than in a sensitive revulsion from the unpleasant and an irresistible craving for love? But in front of this upstart! For already the boy was beaming with delight at the notice bestowed on him by Alys and the nobles. And for the first time in the past months rage began to burn in Raymond's heart, as if, in the presence of his son, the shame and humiliation to which he had been subjected at last became really manifest. And yet, he reflected, sinking back into his characteristic detachment, might he not even now, secretly, be master of them all, he who, seeing further, had swallowed insult on insult smiling, would go on swallowing them while these usurpers, drunk with success, quarreled and squandered their gains, till this ruffian found himself wallowing in a sea red enough with his own blood, and no Jehovah to stem its flow?

Young Raymond was evidently getting on well with Burgundy. Wide-eyed, he was listening to the duke's description of his menagerie—panthers, leopards, not to mention his falcons. What, he was offering to send him one of his leopard cubs! The boy's face was radiant. Doubtless, Raymond considered, it would be politic to invite the duke to Toulouse on his return northward, and make up for the disappointments caused by Montfort's puritanical fervor. So with patience, with endurance, he smiled to himself, he had returned to his original plan. Step by step the circle closed. Seemingly fluctuant, he alone would remain. He had sacrificed heroics, yet he alone, maybe, would stand unbroken.

Alys de Montmorency was in the midst of delivering a homily on the rearing of children in a northern clime. "It is essential that they should be hardened. Existence is a battle."

No doubt. And yet it might turn out, he reflected, that water was stronger than rock.

"Of course," she was saying, "it is different for a girl. One can spend more time on the education of the mind. Our little Yolande is certainly not behindhand in intellectual attainments."

Bored, he had resigned himself to listen absent-mindedly, when the sound of a child's light treble recalled him to the palpable reality. So that was the little wench? His eyes narrowed to focus better the round rosy face, framed by the flaxen plaits as the child made her curtsy. Within a few moments she had become fast friends with young Raymond. Why, the boy, he thought, watching them, was already quite a gallant. Clasping the orange he had so gracefully presented her with, she had run to her father in triumph. "And he's promised to show me them

307

growing—actually growing down in their castle by the sea," she was crying in glee.

"Better teach him to grow Norman apples, especially on those pasty cheeks of his," Montfort retorted gruffly. But even if the gibe, delivered in broad dialect, had not been lost on the boy, the smile with which she attempted to redeem her parent's surliness would certainly have provided ample consolation.

"After all," Alys de Montmorency was saying, "one must allow the children a share in the festivities."

Alias the gloatings of the victor, he thought bitterly.

"Quite a charming picture, surely," she turned to him smiling.

He agreed, reflecting inwardly that the sight of a batch of heretics led to the stake that morning had more than likely aroused in her an equal satisfaction.

"How gratifying," she continued, "if the differences of the parents could be settled by the innocent children."

Was it a hint? Ever alert to the chance of diplomatic strategy, he gave pause. Incredible as it seemed, after the events of the last weeks anything was possible. Suddenly the woman's tactics throughout the banquet became clear. The special favors, those allusions earlier in the evening to the claims of the Montmorencys, the legendary royal lineage of Montfort. God, had it come to this? Did this braggadocio perhaps imagine that he was conferring an honor upon him in mingling his blood with that of the "decadent" south? Or did he not know? The fellow had certainly attempted no flattery. Was this *her* plot? Was this determined and outspoken woman actually ready to play at his own game? He laughed aloud and, pretending to have missed the allusion, discoursed sympathetically on the magnitude of paternal cares, while simultaneously the inevitable diplomatist within him silently pursued that more significant theme; for after all, betrothals were as easily broken as treaties. Yes, he thought, with mounting optimism, which was the trapper, which the trapped?

A sudden lull in the surrounding clamor interrupted the double thread of his consciousness. The Abbot of Cîteaux had risen. Speeches! Raymond groaned inwardly and, yawning behind a hand that despite the ardors of the campaign had remained immaculate as ever, returned to his former train of thought. Beyond the delicate mesh of his speculations the clichés grown familiar in the course of

308

the last weeks fell heavily on the atmosphere of abandoned triumph, of spiced wine and seasoned meat—the oft-reiterated miracles, manifestations of the infallibility of Divine Justice—"for the Lord shall guide the hand of His servant and bring ruin upon the heads of the iniquitous."

But what, pondered Raymond, if one day, and possibly before so very long, the Lord should transfer His allegiance and devour the conqueror as He now trampled on the victim? After all, did not the Judaic prophecies of Cîteaux's own quotation give the precedent? Was not, in his own turn, the oppressor threatened to perish like the oppressed? How incorrigible, despite the lessons of history, quite apart from all Christian teachings, was man, and how shortsighted, swept away in an orgy of violence and brutality to his own doom. What cruel irony, moreover, that only through perpetuation could despotism be rendered a benefit. Where was the world without Rome, and yet what blood had not flowed that civilization be spread over the earth?

His ruminations were interrupted once more as he became aware of another voice speaking. Resembling a growl rather than human intonation, it had burst into the room, arresting, compelling in its very bluntness. Montfort had risen and stood glowering from under his beetling brows—he was a mere soldier, not used to mincing words—curt, ungracious, careless of flattery or effect, he jerked out his appreciation of the honor bestowed on him by the leaders of the Crusade, oblivious of Nevers' disdain, of Burgundy's mocking asides.

He had not looked for reward. In faith alone he had taken the Cross, had sworn himself to the destruction of heresy. If for a moment he had hesitated, if after a life of toil and hardship in the service of God and of France the tempter had held out the lure of domestic peace, triumphantly he had been overcome, not only by himself, but thanks to her who now sat in honor at his side. A shining example to her compeers of France, she had set out to follow in his path, risking the arduous journey, the dangers of the road, to play her part in the sacred cause, where many a one of her sex would lie snugly at home, making her man cuckold the while.

Upon the haughty supercilious countenance of St. Pol the blood rose in a hot flush, but mastering himself he resumed his icy composure, while swerving from the pre-

309

carious brink of domestic intimacies Montfort began to inveigh against the corruption of the south—"this human canker, this pollution of the earth, this race of lechers and fornicators, poisoned by the vices of infidels and Jews." Inspired by hatred, the ruggedness of his address gained a power that put in the shade the abbot's oratory.

"To wipe the heretic pestilence from the soil of France, the holy soil of Charlemagne, we have set out. Shall we stop short in the work that the Lord has blessed? Even as Béziers is burned to cinders and ash shall the cities of Languedoc be consumed, one by one, in the fires of their own corruption."

Was, after all, the Cistercian behind all this eloquence? Raymond wondered, but he doubted it. The man's manner had an immediacy that he doubtless would claim inspired by God himself.

"For the beast has many heads. What though one be severed, another withered to a charred and blackened stump, if another remain? Still it will drag its mutilated body back to its lair and lick its wounds. But the venom oozing from the bleeding trunk will filter through the soil, poisoning not only the debased inhabitants of this God-forsaken realm but threatening the lifesprings of the whole world." He paused a moment, bent forward, menacing above the assembly.

"Victory has been ours. God has vouchsafed us His miracles. Will He not spurn us if we leave His command unfinished, if we falter before the end? For the serpent is slippery beneath the heel. Coward that he is, he will ever feign subservience. But we know his tricks, his honeyed tongue that cajoles with words where his sword arm quails. Mercy? Shall we show mercy to those who blasphemed and mocked, who have murdered the servants of the Church? Pity the kin, the children of those who have scorned the ties of matrimony, the holiness of the marriage bed? Shall we spare the palaces, the cities, the very dwellings of those who have desecrated the house of the Lord?" Once again he paused, and then still unmoving, as though tranced, his voice rose in imprecation. "Nay, I call God to witness that I shall persist untiring in the work to which in His grace He thought fit to choose me, even by signs and wonders in the chapel at Rochefort, that I flag not nor falter till my sword has wreaked vengeance and justice upon every heretic in the land, and all who succor and sustain them, yea, though it mean the extermination of the last of their cursed race—so help me God!"

For a moment, as he ceased, dead silence fell on the whole hall, till into that emptiness applause broke tumultuous, shattering, wave on wave, mingled with the clatter of weapons hammering on the board, steel on steel.

"Lechers—fornicators, God-revilers—followers of the Antichrist.

"Burn—destroy them—slaughter the swine."

The words were drowned in the clamor. Many had risen. Instinctively Raymond looked for his son. He was standing by Burgundy's side, rigid, white to the lips, oblivious of his playmate who was gazing rapturously at Montfort; and as the duke, good-humoredly, stretched out an arm toward him, Raymond was aware of the boy's hesitation, almost recoil. He had been a fool to bring him here. Still, he had better get inured to barbaric eloquence. After all, wasn't it probably less dangerous than the oily vituperation of Bishop Fulk? Signing to the boy's tutor, he indicated that he should be removed from the hall. Only the little girl made an attempt to stay him, but even she was too engrossed in her father for her disappointment to last long.

Turning toward him, Alys de Montmorency suggested that the boy appeared somewhat delicate. The journey, followed by the excitement, had doubtless proved something of a strain, but tomorrow the children must resume their acquaintanceship. Mumbling a polite but evasive reply, Raymond rose from his seat, his action passing unnoticed, for already a crowd had risen and, rallying round Simon, were ardently swearing allegiance to his cause. Vaguely he became aware of Nevers standing apart from the ring, silent and grim; of St. Pol joining him with a supercilious shrug. Burgundy, calling to a page to refill his platter with new delicacies, threw him a wink and returned to share some luscious anecdote with his neighbor. Unnoticed except by a couple of his own knights and retainers who hastened to escort him, he made his way through the throng—Toulouse, whose coming and going was elsewhere attended by the proclamation of heralds, the sounding of fanfares. Waving aside all but one of his followers, he signed to him to light his way.

Behind him the doors closed. Shouts, suddenly muffled,

truncated, faded to a dull roar, anonymous and already half meaningless.

Following in the path of the torch he passed along vaulted corridors, up winding steps. Deserted (all had gathered in the hall), the place seemed like a tomb, arched with hollowness, engulfing bottomless silence, long-buried history, lust, and crime. Above the massive piers vulture heads leered from carved capitals. Distorted, his shadow loomed on the walls. Silent, he moved on, suspended, it seemed to him now, between the double abyss of barbarism past and future, while still he clung to a tenuous present already dead.

He stood on the threshold of the room allotted, or rather appropriated by him. The larger apartments had been commissioned for the leaders, but with characteristic circumspection he had arranged for this one to be reserved for him; though not till today, shunning the risk of fever, had he actually lodged within the city gates. Certainly the small, almost ascetic room was a strange setting for one of his pampered habits, and the bewilderment on the face of his squire told as much; but dismissing him with a command to let none disturb him, his gaze wandered curiously round the walls. It had been Trencavel's sanctum, he had gathered. Speculating as to the treasures it might contain, and moved besides by a more generous impulse to rescue it from invasion, he had waived the point of its humble dimensions.

No wonder, he thought, peering round him, that, in contrast to this affectation of Spartan simplicity, the youth had found Toulouse somewhat overwhelming. Still, one must admit, it had a certain style. Too austere for his taste but not without elegance, and today it appeared almost an oasis amid barbaric chaos. Even now his unquenchable curiosity was beginning to conquer his melancholy. . . .

To savor every nuance of the present, to gauge, dissect every detail of life's infinite phenomena, watching disinterested the very spectacle of his own decadence, had that not been his strength? To stand apart where others were engulfed in the vortex of their own emotions that he might rescue the last shred of the civilization they in their passion of lust and ambition or blinded idealism had wrecked? Little enough, certainly, had he appeared to rescue today, yet if he waited. . . . In the meantime, he pondered ironically, his eye roving to the books and parchments strewn about the room, at least he might rescue these. Shifting the great candlestick of wrought bronze (of consummate workmanship, he noticed), his eye was arrested by a carving over the hearth. Where, he wondered, had Trencavel picked it up? He peered closer. Ah, no, not quite the golden age of classic harmony. After all, the thing was a little crude, stylized, primitive almost. But still, what power in those swelling flanks, that forward urge of the riders—young athletes—horse leashers, maybe—training their steeds upon the Attic shore. And suddenly the other image was there—that first discovery of the antique, upon some old sarcophagus, long ago in the days of his childhood—the rearing stallions, the panic-stricken youths, and there beneath the beating hoofs those supple limbs, the godlike countenance—shattered, prostrate in the dust—the devotee of Artemis dragged from the pedestal of his arrogant chastity. . . .

Through the unshuttered window the moonlight streamed, cold, immitigable. From far below, the sound of cheering broke like the waves of the sea. Did Trencavel hear it too? The light quivered in his hand. Tomorrow he would approach Burgundy again. They had promised to treat the viscount with consideration, but who could be sure? While Nevers was still here, perhaps; but now all they cared about was seemingly to wash their hands of the whole business, and since that madman Montfort ruled the roost—God, would he have to see for himself? If they let him. Toulouse, beg a boon of that upstart? . . . They said the dungeons were often deep in water and the clinging miasma of the pestilence must still linger. . . . Vainly he struggled to change his thoughts, but now the image dispelled so often during the course of the last days and weeks would not recede. Hippolytos—it was fixed—crystallized to form with all the lines of fate converging upon it. And he had held them in his hands—that day at Toulouse—that little discussion upon the lunar goddess so nicely planned and never entered on. And if they had? Might the whole catastrophe have been avoided, the implacable Cyprian been robbed of her revenge? Ah, was she ever placated? Sighing, as at last his thoughts glided away at a new tangent, he sank wearily upon the couch.

After a time he drew a couple of books toward him, opened one and put it aside. Then, desultorily glancing at the other, he uttered a little exclamation of delight and settled himself more comfortably upon the cushions. The book had fallen open as if habitually bent back at a certain place. Between the pages lay flecks of ash—a blackened wisp of parchment. Careless, he brushed them aside and, bending, peered over the Latin letters inscribed in black and crimson on the page.

"Sadly though, he: yet still to your hills you'll be singing,
    Arcadians.
None but Arcadians are skilled to sing. Oh, how softly
    may then my
Bones repose if your reed should tell of my loves . . ."

A drop of wax, long since hardened, lay on the page, obscuring the script. Absent-mindedly he scratched it off with his nail.

                      ". . . Had I only
Been one of you or yours been the flock that I pastured,
    the ripening
Grapes of the vintage . . ."

Had Trencavel, too, feasted on Vergil? What had he sought in the melodious graces of these idyllic rhapsodies—an escape? Raymond reflected on society, the trammels of a morne and inhibiting faith. Curious, his eyes roved over the half-forgotten lines. But the scene darkened, the vales of Arcady yielded to yawning chasms, precipitous crags.

"Now through echoing woods, over rocks I see myself
    speeding,
Rapturously shooting Cydonian darts from the Parthian
    bow. Ah
No, as if ever a cure could be found for my frenzy, or
    ever
That god learn to look down with pity on mortal
    affliction . . ."

Had the torment that once had consumed Gallus at last stricken Trencavel, the too-ardent devotee of Artemis, himself?

"Now nor nymphs of the wood nor even songs can delight us.
Once more, forests, farewell. No toil of ours can unbend him.
Not though in sharpest cold, we drink of the waters of Hebrus,
Suffer the lashing snows of a Scythian winter; nor even
There where the withering bark is scorched from the towering elm tree
Drive Aethiopian flocks far under the tropic of Cancer.
All is conquered by Love. To Love, then, let us surrender."

But where? Surely Agnes could never wake that depth of anguish. And why had Trencavel sought release, not in the outpourings of courtly love but in these idyllic artifices and the remorseless passions of a loftier and freer age?

Once more his gaze traveled to the riders on the frieze. Were they, too, but symbols of a hopeless yearning to break the doom of a despairing solitude? Had he not been able to find true comradeship in his companions of the tilting field and the chase, in the New Guard? He smiled a little skeptically. But what of the devotion of that young squire they spoke of . . . ?

Hippolytos . . . Vergil . . . Amyntas . . . How many points of contact missed? Perhaps even yet, Raymond pondered, on some happier day, they might enter that fruitful field of discussion. Shrouded in melancholy, his eye returned to the page.

But already all else was growing remote. From somewhere far below, the din of revelry echoed faintly, no more than the murmur of those distant seas. Held secure in the tempered measure of those cadences, he abandoned himself to the luxury of an anguish rendered divinely innocuous through art.

II

"Love," mocked Hugo d'Alfaro, drawing nearer the fire, "only one of a countless variety of narcotics—drink, drugs, religion, love—romantic, ideal, disembodied love— all the blessed claptrap of the troubadours. Just another hopeless attempt to free oneself from the burden of the ego. Drown it in a vast nebulous ocean of the impersonal."

"And if the ocean turns out no more than a soup plate?" Miriam Caravita shrugged, coiled on a pile of cushions before the hearth.

"It inevitably does." He kicked at the logs. Falling asunder, the flames shot up with a shower of sparks. "A nice plateful of soup, spiced and steaming, and you go bearing it on high as though it were the Grail."

Laughing, she stretched her hands to the blaze.

"Hugo, you can hardly pretend that's quite my style."

"Because you sanctify the intellect in place of the soul?"

"Your soul," she echoed triumphantly. "What! You're actually coming to believe in a soul?"

Lazily yielding to the warmth and the Orientalized luxury of her surroundings, she lay back and, blinking, gazed at the leaping flames.

"I've never denied it," he retorted. "All I object to is the confounded sanctimonious fuss they kick up over a pitiable compound of heart, conscience, and biliary excretions. There's no chance of love being anything but a mess except on two unreachable levels, that of the animal and the divine—pure functional organism or pure spirit—and we can't attain either."

"Spirit! Heavens, Hugo, you're ripe to become a Cathar, or has grace actually descended upon you already? Of course, Esther always insists you'll end as a saint."

"God spare me!" His features twisted in a gargoyle-like grimace. "Fancy having to face the hordes of God-worrying humanity dripping wax."

"You wouldn't have to. You've forgotten canonization comes after martyrdom."

"I feel more like murder."

"Poor Hugo. Wouldn't you love to wipe humanity off the face of the earth? You're missing your chance. Why don't you go and join Montfort? After all, he's begun the job pretty efficiently."

"Hm—unfortunately some are sure to be left—inevitably the least desirable."

"So there's no way but to join the Cathars. If only the growing pains aren't too bad. You've got to sprout a double set of wings—a spirit as well as a soul. A spirit—but of course, that's exactly what you want—better than the biliary excretions, only unfortunately, as you said yourself, unattainable. Caught you again, Hugo. At heart you're a pure romantic."

"You confounded little word-twister. What about you, all the stuff you've been dishing up to that wretched boy? Better homes, nice clean world to rise phoenix-like from the ruins of the old. Progress with a great big P, like Love with a big L, beautifully illuminated in best gold leaf."

"Well, surely we've improved a bit since Adam."

"By building a series of new Babels?"

"Why not? After all, one must keep hoping that man's intelligence may now and again rise above the muck. The only trouble is, of course, that he keeps on smashing them before they even fall down of themselves."

Amused at her characteristic anticlimax he broke out in laughter. "You mean he actually couldn't bear to see them a success. What he really wants are ideals, not reality, while as far as you're concerned," he glanced at her appraisingly, "the trouble is, as you'd say, that without a realistic basis ideals become too boring. Come now, isn't that the whole truth? Well, why don't you enlighten young Foix on the subject?"

"He doesn't believe me."

"What, that ideals can be compatible with a profit of ten per cent? Good God! So he still believes it was only ideals you rescued that night—and you're an angel incarnate."

"Goddess, Hugo. Neopaganism hardly admits of angels."

"Goddess then, all the more appropriate. Perched on a pedestal and there you'll stick. And you're beginning to find it dull, naturally—white marble, shiny and veined, but the veins don't come in the right place. No hope of Pygmalion. The only thing is a crash."

"But why?" she drawled. "I do hate messes, and he's sure to be hysterical."

"Quite. Moreover," he retorted, "the statue has its points. First, part of you, at any rate, finds it flattering. Secondly, the portrait's not altogether untrue. The truth is, you've got plenty of virtues as well as vices, however much you like to disguise them under that mask of hard-boiled cynicism—brains, wit, courage, tenacity (as long as you're interested), even self-sacrifice—heaps of them, all mixed up with their opposites. It's one of the besetting sins

317

of humanity to see things white *or* black. Man's an inveterate magpie. Even virtue's a questionable factor. Besides, everything depends on its application. It's capable every minute of turning into vice."

"While vice may equally turn into virtue, mayn't it?" Leaning on her elbow, she gazed reflectively into the flames. "Of course you won't believe me," she turned to him suddenly, "really, I am rather fond of him: if only he'd stop worrying."

"Well, can you be surprised? After all, statues are breakable objects. Besides, we're hardly living in the midst of a festival even if you've managed to preserve the trappings." He glanced round the lavishly furnished room. "After Carcassonne. . . ."

She gave a little shudder. "I went through it myself."

"My dear, not everyone possesses your power of acclimatization."

"One would think he'd be glad to get out of it."

"Trencavel isn't out of it—and since old Foix made terms with Montfort—"

"But when nothing can be done?"

"Inaction isn't the best remedy for nightmares, however voluptuous the couch. I've told you already, love's a good narcotic, but the horror reasserts itself unpleasantly between the doses, especially when one's vowed oneself to the quest of the Grail."

"Montségur?" she laughed. "At least I think he's cured of that."

"Cured? The malady may have complications, but it's the same disease. Montségur, Trencavel, the people, even you yourself, my dear—variations on the same theme—clasping the infinite in the terms of the finite. I suppose you're actually flattered. What you women are really after is to be treated as a wraith."

"A wraith?" She yawned slightly. "It's he who does the haunting. If only he'd leave me in peace."

> *"So claws and cleaves like a talon*
> *My flesh to her,"*

Hugo sang, mocking. "Exactly—claws and cleaves to his ideal, and he won't let you budge. Whether Arnaut Daniel was indulging in allegory or not, he's hit the nail on the head."

318

"Really, Hugo, you're hard on the poor boy. He *has* grown up a bit."

He shrugged. "I take it for granted he's got a body as well as an intellect. But they've got hopelessly mixed up, so ashamed of each other they daren't be themselves."

"But what can you expect? He's even in the dark as to what he is himself."

"Who isn't?"

"Metaphysically?" She laughed, and stretching out her hand took a sweet from the casket at her side. "Still, most of us are pretty clear as to our parental origins. But he's never even found out who was his mother."

He laughed. "A bit of an ordeal to tackle old Foix on the subject."

"Quite. But it's more than that. The truth is," she paused significantly, "he didn't want to find out."

"In case it shatters the illusion?"

"Exactly." Nibbling fastidiously at the sweet, she pushed the box toward him. "Have one? You know, Hugo, I'm discovering more and more about human nature."

"Thanks to the menagerie? You ought to, considering the range of your specimens. Well, what's the latest discovery?"

"Don't mock till you've heard the end. The thing is, he'd fixed his mind on the idea that his mother was a peasant."

He laughed aloud. "Good for him. For once, at any rate, he's got near bedrock."

"But supposing she wasn't? Supposing he's blue blood throughout, just as exalted and rotten as yourself?" she mocked, regarding him through narrowed lids.

"Lucky for him it isn't proved."

"But it might be. Put two and two together: there was a little story, you know, how Ramon-Roger of Foix went hunting the wolves right to the door of Salenques. . . ."

"And the Count had his fun with the little nuns?"

"So it goes. But one must allow for some exaggeration. The singular, after all, might be enough. It seems the abbess had a little sister, Ermengarda. Whether she was actually a novice or just paid visits to the convent isn't clear. It's a bit complicated to get hold of details under present conditions. Anyhow, it's pretty irrelevant. The thing is, that about the date of Wolf's birth she sickened—not at Salenques but safe home at Telho. The physician they called in was a friend of Father's. There was a little financial business attached to the case; that's how he heard—purely confidential, of course. The girl died; ostensibly of some female complaint, but it seems something else remained."

"As legacy of the conventual tryst?"

"And the rapturous bliss of Ramon-Roger's safe return from Acre. It's pretty certain, from what we've gathered, that the babe was identical with the little boy delivered to the good monks at Bolbona. Certainly Ramon worshiped at the feet of Ermengarda (at whose didn't he?) till his father forced him into a politic marriage. Old Telho, maybe, was advised to keep his daughter safely out of temptation's way. Salenques proved handy, naturally, but in more ways than one, and so romantic a setting."

"And story," d'Alfaro concluded.

"Yes, but actually more credible than Wolf's little fiction."

"And you imagine," he burst out laughing, "it's going to cure his sense of inferiority? Is it necessary? He seems to have got over it pretty well already, thanks to Trencavel."

"But don't you see, he's building his life on a complete fallacy: all this reform business, this obsession in the people."

"By the way you talk to him one would believe that you at least shared his enthusiasms."

"I do, as long as they're sanely capable of realization, but when he's fixed his mind on a mad dream till he kills himself over it, isn't the only way to save him to prove that he's built the whole thing out of himself—out of his sense of insecurity, because being, at root, ashamed of his mother he tried to compensate himself with a fetish, the rights of the people, and so on?"

Uninvited, d'Alfaro helped himself to another sweet.

"My dear, one must admit you'd make a first-rate assistant to Domingo. Talk of ransacking men's souls!"

"But he's really rather pathetic. He's just consuming himself. I *had* to try and make him see daylight."

"Christ! You don't mean you told him! When?"

"Shortly before you came."

"And how did he take it?"

She shrugged. "I haven't seen him since."

He looked at her hard and broke into mirthless laughter.

"A delightful little experiment in the alchemy of the mind. So you reckoned the undermining of the foundation would wreck the whole edifice of dreams; but there's a little flaw in the formula, my dear. Didn't it strike you he might try a bit of underpinning first? Ten to one he'll argue that, having deluded himself, he'd cheated the people, and start the expiation stunt—à la Trencavel."

"Oh, God! As if it wasn't bad enough already. Look how he goes on about that Guiraut—thinks he's betrayed him, left him in the lurch."

"Well, didn't he? It's an unfortunate paradox that loyalty to the cause of humanity inevitably involves the sacrifice of the individual. He's learning the lesson pretty painfully and you're hardly being very helpful about it in spite of your subtle lessons in enlightenment. No, my dear; the fact is, you're bored and ripe to behave like a little beast, a thoroughly human one, mind you, with all your cursed intelligence and your own repressed and perverted idealism brought into play to assist in the process of slow torture."

"But Hugo," she drawled, "considering it's you who've been egging me on to enlighten him, you might really be a bit more helpful."

He rose abruptly, and leaning against the mantelpiece stood looking down on her scathingly.

"I—you confounded little Circe! If you think I'm going to provide the antidote for your potions and enact the transformation scene in your menagerie, you're mistaken. You've got to do the disenchanting yourself. And having picked *him* to pieces, it's high time you cleared him up as to your own failings, so that he sees you for what you are—a walking bundle of atrophied emotions, a damned little prostitute of the intellect."

"In short," she interrupted, unperturbed, "a typical product of the age—a victim of the sickness of hypercivilization: isn't that it?" For a moment she regarded him through half-closed lids, then with a sudden movement leaned forward a little on her knees. "Hasn't it struck you, Hugo," her voice, low and husky, came with a little intake of the breath, "that I might want to be cured?"

"It's incurable," he muttered.

Suddenly, before either could say more, the door was thrown open. Breathless and plump, Esther Calonymos burst into the room.

"Oh! it's too utterly—" Too excited or out of breath for speech, she gesticulated to the figure that appeared immediately behind her on the threshold.

"Heavens, Peire!" Miriam sat up on her knees. "We thought you were in Mont Salvat."

"He's evidently descended to the mortal sphere," d'Alfaro laughed as Mirepoix advanced across the room, "and in the nick of time to the rescue of Elsa."

"But where's the swan?" Critically her eyes rested on the dark blue cloak, strikingly simple but for the elegance of its cut. "What a pity you grudged us the full effect. Do you realize we've never seen it?"

"My dear, one daren't be spectacular, even if old Foix *has* made his peace with Montfort. After all, I had to come through the Carcassais. The forest perilous wasn't in it." Approaching with an air of studied fatigue that did nothing to detract from his inborn grace, he bent above her hand and sank upon the cushions at her side. "Still, here I am, and in time, as Hugo says." He shot him a questioning glance. "Well, so far, at any rate, the trouble doesn't appear to have been too devastating." Impudently, his emerald eyes roved over her face. "As beautiful as ever. What's the matter, darling?"

"Boredom," d'Alfaro commented sardonically.

"Boredom—if that's it, it's mutual. I must have felt it. Heart spoke to desolate heart across the arid waste. I heard, I spurred my trusted steed, I came." Bending nearer, Mirepoix regarded her quizzically. "You must admire my sensibility, considering I'd gathered you were completely absorbed in the New Life. Alas, I'm afraid it's defunct already." He paused. "At any rate, if you're feeling like this," he smiled a little ironically, "it won't be such a blow."

"Oh, it's too fearful," Esther having recovered her breath broke in vehemently. "Trencavel—"

"It seems I'm the first to bring the news," Mirepoix went on. "I was on the way through Carcassonne when it came out. Needless to say, I didn't linger. Yes, my dear, I'm afraid it's all up with the great cause. Trencavel died last night."

"Trencavel?" For a long moment there was silence.

"They're saying it was poison," Esther began sensationally.

322

"Not officially." Peire-Roger gave a smothered laugh. "It was given out as dysentery."

"But the epidemic had died out," the younger girl insisted.

He shrugged. "In those dungeons. . . . Personally, I'd prefer the poison."

Miriam shuddered.

Leaning toward her, his fingers lightly stroked her hand. "Don't think of it, my love. Reality unadulterated never bears contemplation."

"Until it's turned into artistic phrases," muttered d'Alfaro in the background.

"Don't fret," Mirepoix was saying. "After all, as things were, he's best out of it all. Incidentally, one might question whether he was ever *in*. What was it we called him once? A wraith suspended between past and future; only the present he cannot reach."

"But he was always talking about it," Esther insisted. "Why, Wolf's continually quoting him. 'Only the present is real.' "

"Naturally, because he couldn't get there. The man was a walking illusion."

"Which doesn't mean," d'Alfaro muttered, "that it mightn't be real enough to him—a regular nightmare."

"And it might go on." Once more Miriam gave a little shudder. "Who knows?"

"No one. Therefore, my dear, why worry?" Rhythmically, soothingly, Peire-Roger's fingers, wandering over her wrist, stroked up her sleeve. "I never realized you took it so seriously. After all, the whole thing was a sort of myth. Of course, to young Foix . . . I suppose he'll be fearfully shattered."

"But where is he?" Esther looked round anxiously. "I thought he'd be sure to be here. Miriam, you really ought to break it to him. Think, if he finds out in the town. You know he's frightfully overstrung already."

"In that case," Mirepoix laughed lightly, "why not run along and try and find him. Only I shouldn't advise you to bring him here. Best take him along to Reuben or Uncle Moses. They've got philosophy—each of their own kind."

"And hold your own tongue," d'Alfaro called after her.

"I'm afraid," Mirepoix remarked as the door closed behind her, "it's going to be pretty hellish for him." His eyes rested on her inquiringly. "Your father was quite paternal about him. I swore to break the news most delicately. He thought, you know, he'd be here. Incidentally, the old man's aged quite a lot. Of course the whole business must have been terribly trying. Still, he must have made quite a little pile in Carcassonne. Is this one of the results?" His fingers, pausing in their sedative ministrations, twirled the bracelet on her arm. "Nice. The affectation of the barbaric suits you." Appreciatively he contemplated the dragon heads clasping the deep-red stones. "To think they'll be getting quite excited about this long after they've forgotten about Trencavel's, let alone Alarac's agonies. Worlds crumble, art endures."

"All very well," d'Alfaro retorted, "as long as you aren't under the rubble. And it looks as though your aesthetic world were going to pieces pretty soon."

"Well, then, for God's sake, let's enjoy it while we can." Yawning, Mirepoix leaned back upon the cushions. "If you knew what it means to be in the midst of civilization, after those barbarous mountains and what I came through—not much better than Béziers."

"We may still be victims," Miriam reflected. "After all, we're on the brink of a volcano."

"Hardly, at the moment. Montfort's too busy." Mirepoix stretched his legs to the blaze. "True, the exalted ones have deserted him, but he's sent for reinforcements. In the meantime, however, what's Aragon going to say about Trencavel? Whether it was poison or not, he was a hostage, not a prisoner, and to fling him in those dungeons . . . besides, he knows well enough trouble's brewing in Andorra, and in spite of the treaty old Foix's only waiting. No, I fancy Narbonne can sleep quiet for the present, snuggled comfortably against the bosom of the Church."

"Quite," d'Alfaro commented. "And Arnaud-Amelric will doubtless see that he keeps her warm. He's had his eye on Narbonne for a long time. Even fanaticism is worth curbing when it interferes with personal ambition (not that even Cîteaux has ever quite managed to emulate the criterion of Fulk). But the danger is that once ambition's satisfied, ideals come cropping up again. The abbot's vision of Christian society, my friends, hardly corresponds with life in this blessed city. And once he's installed here in glory, you'll probably find him advocating a wholesale purge."

"Possibly," Mirepoix shrugged. His hand, abandoning its

324

interest in the bracelet, transferred it to her girdle. "Well, let's hope you'll be spared another migration. I daresay the old man feels it badly enough. He was attached to the patriarchal home. To give him his due, I believe he's really cut up. After all, he's been with the Trencavels for a lifetime. But even if Carcassonne were restored you couldn't count on fair Agnes. She's only waiting for the first possible chance to make her peace with the Church—writing nice little letters to Bishop Fulk. God! If she doesn't strangle Gogo in her joy when she hears the news. She's probably on her way to Montpellier already."

"What a pity," d'Alfaro put in. "You're just a day or two too early. You might have acted as courier."

"Exactly. As if I hadn't had my fill up there. She's driven the whole place mad—wandering from Roccafissada to Perelha's and back to Lavelanet—twittering and bickering all the time. What she'd do up on the top of Mont Salvat God alone knows."

"Feed the sacred pigeons," Miriam drawled. "After all, it would be such a pretty sight."

"But a bit too cold for those tiny feet. We've had a snowfall already—wait till midwinter. In summer, of course, it might turn out quite Arcadian, but Chloë might be sweeter for a bath, and the cheese is all too definitely goat. Besides, the herd is painfully human. The place is swarming already. The whole slope's covered with wattle huts. They'll have to crowd in like cattle. Phew!" Fastidiously he wrinkled his delicate but slightly tilted nose. "How the Luminous One can stand it, God knows, but she's grown used to castigating herself in Pamiers. Heavens, what waste! One could do something about it if it weren't for that black beetle of a Guihalbert—the slightest bit of symbolism makes him go green."

"Poor Peire," Miriam sympathized, "so the grand scheme's fallen through?"

"Oh no," he smiled, eternally resilient. "There's still hope. After all, they're not all as stringent as the Beetle. Besides, she's really craving for it. Do you know, I never realized till Jordan accidentally put me up to it—"

"Jordan?" d'Alfaro interposed. "By the way, what's he up to now?"

Mirepoix shrugged. "Marking time. Still, I managed to rouse him out of his apathy for once. That's how I first

325

really got on the scent. I couldn't resist letting him have a glimpse of the getup. He turned absolutely livid."

"Too blasphemous?"

"Probably. Anyhow, I believe I hit on the possible root of Jordan's piety. Always thought there was something more than orthodox tradition behind it. Right enough, it seems the pride of the house of Jordan was jeopardized in other ways than by the lovely Esclarmonde's flirtation with heresy. A singer from the Asian wilderness—a mystic song, about some Eastern Grail . . ."

"Good God!" d'Alfaro growled and kicked again at the logs. "Have you started soul-scrounging too? I shouldn't advise you to go too far—the human mind is all too redolent of the cesspool."

"Exactly," Mirepoix laughed; "and so I prefer to leave something to fantasy. It's so much more capable of artistic development. Think of the Luminous One inspiring the beatific vision in the little singer's heart—Esclarmonde, guardian of the Grail—the apotheosis of the unfulfillable—ideal romantic Love. Why, it seems almost as though I'm fated to realize her frustrated dreams. And since Galahad's deserted . . ."

"Let's hope you win the quest." Miriam gave a husky laugh. "After all, you have a chance. Originally, you know, it *was* Gawaine's."

"Before he became too civilized," d'Alfaro commented acridly, "and they invented the guileless fool."

"Young Perceval?"

Lightly evading the thrust, Peire-Roger regarded Miriam quizzically. "So that's what you call the Wolfling now, since Galahad's evidently grown too earthly? Well, shall I take him back to Mont Salvat?" He smiled, curling his finger in a tress of her hair. "After all, what hope's left for him—or is there?"

She ignored his question. "What really brought you to Narbonne?"

"I've told you—boredom. I pined for sympathy. Besides, do you know I've become interested in astrology? Staring up at the firmament from that height, one begins to wonder." He turned to d'Alfaro. "It made me think of that fellow you brought along once—a semi-Arab. Well, I thought I might look him up. You remember, he had a most interesting theory—that all things are based on a secret law of proportion hidden in the stars. It's the job of the artist to find it out—to re-create the ideal relationships inherent in the stellar system. One of the masons working up at Montségur is frightfully interested in the technical side of the question. It seems architecture's becoming a mathematical science. It struck me one might work something of the sort into the building up there. A mathematical *mystique* reflecting the stellar harmonies. Why, it would be so subtle that even old Guihalbert couldn't cavil."

"Heavens, Peire, so that's the latest craze. At any rate your flights of fancy reach higher and higher."

"My dear, don't you see the marvelous possibilities, for if the thing's true of form, why not of the spirit? What vistas open before the imagination, what vision of a new world, of society reborn! You must admit Trencavel's wasn't in it—the golden age restored—on earth as it is in heaven, and the whole secret contained in a simple law of proportion."

"Excellent," d'Alfaro chimed in. "Euclid applied to human relationships. Well, I'll leave you to solve the problem." Pulling himself upright, he turned to go. "Good-by. If you want Hassan, you'll find him down by the docks, the street behind my lodging—anyone will tell you. I'm afraid I can't take you along as I'm leaving tomorrow."

"Leaving?" Startled, Miriam rolled over on her elbow.

"I'm going on a little journey. Shan't be back for some time, I fear."

"But, Hugo, it's so sudden—when on earth did you decide?"

He shrugged. "My dear, I've been contemplating the likelihood for the last four months—the last hour has decided me."

"But where? Surely not to the land of your fathers?"

"Hardly." He laughed harshly. "Possibly Andorra."

"What! Oh, I see, the last refuge of freedom, is that it?"

"But why go so far?" Mirepoix smiled. "Why not join us?"

"Hugo!" Miriam echoed incredulously. "Hugo going to resist the barbarian invasion! But why trouble if it's only preserving the rotting carcass, as he calls it."

"Because," he answered, "there's still just a possibility that the rot's gone far enough to manure the new seed. Good-by." Turning abruptly, he strode from the room.

"What on earth's come over him?" Mirepoix shrugged

as the door closed behind him. "Why, one would almost think he was jealous."

"Hugo?" She laughed. "He's incurable. Do you think he'd risk losing a shred of that precious personality of his to allow himself the luxury of what he calls amorous escape? He's been haranguing me about it half the afternoon."

"Has he? Well, perhaps it was necessary." Leaning on his elbow, he twisted his finger further into the curl of her hair. "You know, I don't think you're being very kind to young Perceval. What's going to happen to him now?"

"My dear Peire, I'm not his guardian angel."

"No? Still, you seem to have taken quite an interest in his education. Hasn't he proved an adept pupil, as Hugo thought you needed a course of instruction yourself—a little lesson in morality, perhaps? Well, supposing we try a few mathematics instead?" Disengaging themselves from her locks, his fingers slipped, cool, caressing, beneath the nape of her neck. "Only consider; supposing we discovered a formula for the ideal relationship between man and woman. To begin with, of course, we must ascertain—is it to be based on the triangle or the equilibrium of two forces?" Mocking, tantalizing, his sea-green eyes swam above hers. "Eternal withdrawal, eternal renewal—like the tide and the moon? Is that it?" he whispered, but even as his lips bent toward hers they were held suspended by the sudden mockery in her eyes.

"But surely, Peire—since you're becoming such an authority on architecture, you ought to know—tension—thrust and counterthrust!" Laughing, she loosed herself, supply, sinuously from his embrace.

THE WASTE LAND

Ai! Tolosa e Provensa!
E la terra d'Agensa!
Bezers e Carsassey!
Quo vos vi! quo vos vey!

(BERNARD SICARD DE MARJEVOLS)

I

IN THE MEANTIME, IN THE GATHERING MIST OF THAT
November afternoon, Wolf of Foix was roaming blindly
through the streets of Narbonne. Where exactly he had
been, or what was his goal, he neither knew nor cared.

The raw fog seeping up from the lagoons hemmed him
in, accentuating the sense of unreality. Outside it lay the
world—a world bathed in blood and horror—a waste of
human misery and wretchedness. He was marooned on an
island, held fast in an enchantment from which there was
no escape. For days, months, years perhaps, it seemed to
him, he had been roaming these streets—time had ceased.
At first he had made a habit of wandering up to the castle,
urged by an unquenchable hope for news. As though any
good could come from that quarter! In any case the Viscount of Narbonne had made his total submission to
Montfort. There was even talk of his marrying Marly's
daughter to seal the pact. With waning spirits he would
wander back to the city square, though the news he could
pick up there would be, at the best, he knew, what old
Caravita would bring within a few hours, and more likely
what he had already brought. So it had gone on, from day
to day, week to week, an endless tale of new violence, new
surrender. News of the crusaders' entry of Carcassonne, of
Montfort's investiture. Pillage, massacre, death on the gib-
bet, death at the stake, till horror that had staggered at
first became part of the day's expected routine. He had
given up the useless quest for tidings. But the tale went on,

fresh sieges, further capitulations; a vain attempt at revolt and yet more brutal reprisals. Then, suddenly, one day the tide seemed to change. Cab-Aret had made a stand in the Black Mountains, had actually taken Bouchard de Marly prisoner—Montfort's own kinsman. For a brief moment hopes had risen wildly, only to be dashed by the tidings of fresh disaster. Fanjeaux, Castres, Lombers had already fallen. Now Limoux and Saissac followed suit. In spite of the fact that Burgundy and Nevers, indeed the bulk of the crusading forces, had returned home and Montfort was left with a mere remnant, his tenacity increased. Often incredible enough, his successes won the fame of miracles. "God is with me—what matter numbers?" Where he moved, walls and fortress fell. Besides, he had established himself in Carcassonne, the gate to the mountains, the gate to Toulouse. Carcassonne and no drought. And then came the worst blow of all—the Count of Foix had made terms with Montfort. Rage had swept over Wolf—rage and misery and shame, only redoubled by the consciousness of his own impotence. Vainly Miriam would argue that resistance would have been mere suicide, that his father was doubtlessly only preparing a new front, awaiting the right moment to strike—a suggestion that made him feel that he should not have come here but have gone to Foix; that then he might have persuaded his father to immediate action—reasoning that she soon enough put to scorn. He had received a message from him since his arrival—"It has been brought to my knowledge that your conduct at Carcassonne, though demented, was at least not without valor. When you have returned to your senses, I shall expect you at Foix!" It was evident enough what "senses" would entail. Swear loyalty, even if only temporarily, to Montfort—to the man who had massacred his friends, had been party to, if he had not actually engineered, a foul plot, had broken his own promise and held Trencavel prisoner in the dungeons of Carcassonne. Anguish swept over him again. If, as Caravita said, negotiations for Trencavel's release were still in progress, it had seemed to him that, staying here, he could at least see that the old financier's efforts did not flag. So, after all, he would have played some part in freeing him, and might be the first to welcome him on his release. New hopes of a satisfactory transaction had arisen through Marly's capture. Montfort valued his kinsman deeply. Even so, he remained adamant

330

while Caravita had put out new feelers. "Impossible for the old man to believe that someone is proof against lucre," d'Alfaro mocked. Certainly if one lived in this atmosphere, Wolf meditated, Caravita's attitude was scarcely surprising. Even now, after three months in Narbonne, he reeled under the impact of his strange surroundings, this world built upon finance, this towering edifice of dizzying loans, payments, and credits, as precarious, dazzling and intricate as the architectural fantasies that encompassed them.

"But isn't it a fact?" Miriam would insist when, staggered and helpless, he raged against the vast ascendancy of property. "Fundamentally the world's rooted in it. The Church, the State, the feudal system."

"Tyranny," he retorted.

She smiled. "But even your dream city, your new world."

"You believed in it," he cried bitterly.

"I do. Only I don't deny its foundation. It's merely a case of shifting the ownership from the individual to the community. The basis still remains the same—property."

"But the idea's completely different," he persisted; "if property really represents men's labor."

"It's still property."

"But not money for money's sake."

She laughed. "You're so horrified of it, Wolf. I believe you'd recommend our returning to simple barter. So many cows, women, and sacks of flour. Anyway, all these magnificent projects, better homes, education for the workers, emancipation and spiritual liberty, they're all the result of civilization, at rock bottom—wealth." And before he could argue more she would start to paint the benefits of the future world with such brilliance that all his misgivings would fade. After all, she was the Miriam that he had learned to know the night of their flight from Carcassonne, the real Miriam he had so long denied. If she hid herself continually beneath a veil of cynicism, he had done little enough in these years to help her to free herself. If only, he thought desperately, he could get her away from the poisonous, enervating atmosphere of this fearful city that spun its enchantment round her, that if he stayed much longer would even begin to threaten him—smothering, paralyzing like some subtle soporific. Sometimes it appeared to him that he was caught already, and he would seem to wake with terror wondering whether, for a moment, enwoven in the magic of her beauty, the acrid brilliance of her conversation with her intellectual friends, he had not even ceased to want to escape, till the memory of the outside world swept over him again. Sometimes it seemed that even if he got back it could not be the same. Once, he remembered, he had been afraid that even Sicard might have got between his friendship with Trencavel. How much more, then, would Miriam! But the fear was as soon dispelled. The two emotions that controlled his life were on altogether different levels: of course they could exist side by side, enriching each other. Only then would they be quite fulfilled, for no secret remnant of a frustrated passion for Miriam, which after all must have existed all these years, could cloud his friendship, while she on her part would no longer have to see his love torn by his feverish unrest. Once removed from these surroundings she would find her real self. Had she not been the means of rescuing their cause in the hour of its peril? Then how brilliantly she would devote herself to its triumphant realization. But the thought only increased his impatience. At all costs they must get away from here. It had struck him that they might go to Durban. Sicard, of all people, would be sympathetic. But the plan was soon shattered by her reasonableness. Durban was Foix's fief and as such sworn to the treaty. Of what use was the revolt of the petty baronage when the mightiest fortress in the land had fallen? The project was no better than suicide, and in the meantime the ransom might even have been effected. For Montfort was definitely short of funds. Philippe Auguste was not going to subsidize the frenzied adventures of a fanatic, and the reinforcements expected from Flanders and Germany were still a myth. It was significant, moreover, that Montfort, in spite of his threats, had not actually dared attack Toulouse. Once more Wolf was cast back into fevered inactivity. "But even death would be better than this," he cried wildly.

"What, when it's completely useless?"

"But at least it's making a stand, defending one's ideals."

"Ideals, ideals, you're incapable of bearing anything that's tangible," she would start mocking; "You're really terrified of touching *me*." And as, tentatively, never yet able to get over the wonder of that first encounter, his lips sought her wrist, the white curve of her throat, she would laugh softly.

"At heart, Wolf, you're a complete Cathar—absolutely terrified of adulterating your ideals with anything that isn't pure as ice. But what are ideals anyway?" Drawing her fingers through his hair, she would look at him with her old tantalizing mixture of irony and mournful seriousness. "Do you know what Hugo calls them—vapors risen from the cesspool of the ego. My dear, probably he's about right. Just look at the secret cravings, perversions and nightmarish obsessions that ferment in people's minds." As a palpable proof of her argument, she began to probe the characters of their acquaintances. "Look at Hugo, living like a sort of hermit in noble squalor, cutting himself off from every human emotion because he must convince himself of his superiority to the world; look at Trencavel, obsessed by his sense of paternal guilt and raving about life because he's really craving for death."

But he would not let her continue. "You don't know him," he insisted.

"Well then," she smiled, regarding him fixedly, "look at yourself."

Himself. . . . Was everything, then, reducible to a conglomeration of chances and circumstance; every ideal, every belief and faith no better than any crime, the inevitable reaction of one's personal make-up, itself determined by all the preceding circumstances that had gone to make it what it was? Was there then no such thing as free will? The terror experienced by the frantic gropings of his spirit in those long-past days of the monastery clutched at him anew, but now the way of flight, of adventure, of unknown life, that had held out the promise of an answer and ultimate illumination was closed. He was hedged in, chased round the alleys of his own emotions as in a labyrinth, incapable of discovering the center as he was of finding the way out.

Hours had passed. Still he must have wandered on through the alien streets grown familiar in the hopeless peregrinations of the last months. But today he was heedless of his surroundings as he was hopeless of news. Once more before him the silhouette of the castle towered out of the mist. Perhaps he had wandered in a circle.

What else could he do anyway? He swerved aside to avoid a group of youths turning out of a high arched doorway. Voices, faintly foreign, drifted past; features, a little exotic yet by now grown too familiar to arouse his attention, hovered an instant and were gone—students leaving the college of law. Instinctively he hastened his steps, afraid that he might by chance run into Reuben Calonymos or Hugo d'Alfaro.

In his imagination the long narrow face of the rabbi's son floated up out of the mist, the delicate, almost too refined features, the heavy-lidded eyes—so reminiscent of Miriam's but lacking her sudden flashes of passionate brilliance—lifted a moment from brooding over the intricacies of the law; the soft contour of the lips that always seemed to hover on the brink of sorrowful skepticism like the smile upon the faces of the strange images that gazed out, wrapped in an impenetrable aura of detachment, from the walls of his study.

Was there then, after all, a sense beyond the mechanical inevitability to which Miriam's theories seemed to reduce existence? Had those carven images, had Reuben himself found the answer? But what? What if it were nothingness, or a philosophy in which felicity and sorrow, good and evil themselves were transfused to an equation so complete that it seemed no better than nothingness? What if, after all, as Reuben (whether seriously or with gentle irony, he was never quite sure) would suggest, the world were but an illusion? Perhaps, he thought, plunging on, it was all a dream, a nightmare from which he must wake.

Figures brushed by him, faces urbane and arrogant, preoccupied, bemused, surly, coarsened, wizened and haggard with starvation or misery, hovered an instant before him and passed, swallowed up in the mist, alien, remote, each shut in with his own private rapture or agony or weariness—nothing but their own imagining. . . . Their own, or his—if everything were but the illusory projection of his own dream? To convince himself of their reality he stretched out his hand, but withdrew it again.

Somewhere a voice began to sing—absurdly—of spring, till the words echoing out in their reiterate rhyme modulated into a ringing plaint:

Tal via
Faria

Qu'om ja mais no'm veiria;
selh dia
morria
Domna pros, qu'ie us perdria.

"The same old insatiable craving for self-destruction,"
Miriam would laugh—"passion—war—it's all the same."

Haunting, persistent, the voice rose again, tearing at all
his fibers. Oblivious of where he went, he stumbled on.

Later he became aware that he had reached the docks.
At his feet the water lay dark and heavy as liquid lead,
shrouded in mist that had turned to a fine, almost invisible, rain. The quay was almost deserted. On the top of a
half-demolished wall the shapeless figures of some workmen, muffled against the fog, moved with uncouth and
meaningless gestures, as though suspended on the edge of
a fathomless abyss. Now and again, from beyond the
sound of sliding rubble, the clang of a pickax on stone fell
blunted, without resonance.

Yesterday, it swept over him bitterly, would he still, as
Miriam made out, have cheated himself with a fiction of
brotherhood? Was his whole dream of social justice really
worth no more than the expression of a personal mania,
the long-harbored vengeance for his mother's imagined
wrongs? But if the wrong turned out an illusion, must the
whole project fall with it? What—she would of course argue—were these loutish men to him, what the heaving
masses with whom he had often rubbed shoulders, roused
by their undeniably unsavory proximity to a strange elation? She would strip him to the soul, lay bare the false
exhilaration, the mawkish emotions on which he had nourished himself, hiding before the truth, even after he
guessed it well enough—hiding, till he knew not that he
hid, while he built dream-castles with Trencavel, worked
himself into a fierce comradeship with Guiraut. If he had
not, it swept over him with new horror, might they even
have been saved? Again the faceless bandaged head floated
before him. "Another victim of maternal possessiveness,"
d'Alfaro had commented on the day when at last by repeated efforts he had got news of the youth. "Why
couldn't she let the poor wretch get out of his hell?" and
he had launched out on another invective against humanitarianism. "A downright massacre of the unfit would be a
335

blessing compared to the perpetuation of agony inflicted in the name of humanity."

Easy enough for him to voice his glibly cynical comments. He hadn't been there. But Miriam had been through it. Oh, he knew well enough what was said against the Jews for the profit they had made out of the siege, because they had escaped from Béziers as they had escaped that massacre years ago. But what of Cab-Aret and the others? Which of them wasn't out to hang on to his property? Look how they treated the serfs. Speculating with human coinage instead of ducats! "There's no conquering the anti-Semite bogey," d'Alfaro would mock. "People will always shy, face to face with the flagrantly picturesque representation of their own vices." And which of them, after all, thought Wolf, had shown Caravita's devotion toward Trencavel? Old Ademar and Pons perhaps, but what was the use? None of them possessed Caravita's *nous*. Once more the memory of Trencavel surged back with redoubled violence. Was he to believe that all they had dreamed and striven for was nothing but the outcome of their own tormented obsessions?

He stared out across the quay. At his feet the water heaved darkly, strewn with scum and pieces of offal. Shrouded in misted rain, the prow of a ship loomed dark, amorphous and forsaken but for a gull swooping for garbage. Somewhere a bell began to toll with a thin fretful clang, until the senseless reiteration tore the laughter from his throat. If all things were an illusion, then the very shattering of a delusion was an illusion itself. What if, after all, there existed beyond the chaos an ultimate truth against which human reason was as nothing—reason that reduced every ideal so glibly to perverted egoism and ulterior motives? Then Miriam might be right, but only in part, not in the whole.

A ray of hope began to break through his despairing inertia. In any case her story was not proved. Suddenly it seemed almost irrelevant whether it was or not, if the Cause existed for its own sake, for the sake of something bigger than themselves, something that included their own dreams and delusions but was infinitely greater.

Fortified a little, he turned and began to retrace his steps along the quay. He would prove it to her. If he could only get her away from this cursed city, from her cynical friends. For even now, at heart, he convinced himself, she believed. "It's the new world we're going to build." Oh, she could not have lied. That night he had seen her as she really was. Only she hated confusion. After all, it had needed her sting to wake him to clear-sightedness. How intolerably puerile she must have found him, woolly-minded in his ideas as he was inexperienced in his love. But that, too, would change. Sure within himself, he could be bolder in his claims.

Borne forward on a new wave of confidence, he had wandered blindly through the rain when he almost collided with a figure just emerging from round a block of warehouses. Unheeding, he was moving on when he felt himself gripped by the shoulder.

"Christ! What are you doing down here?"

Turning reluctantly at the sound of the familiar voice, he found himself face to face with d'Alfaro.

He's heard, had been Hugo's first thought, his mind leaping to the dark water.

"Oh, just a stroll. I'm going back." The little smile, almost triumphant, that quivered on Wolf's wan face belied the other's fear.

"You're soaked through," he muttered; "you'd better come to my place and dry. It's quite near."

He was about the last person Wolf had wanted to meet just then, but mazed as he still was by the despairing thoughts of that afternoon, and discovering moreover that he was really shivering with cold, he let d'Alfaro lead him off.

Curse him, Hugo thought. Of all the devil's luck to run into him now. It would fall upon him to break the news. Of course he could take him back to the Calonymos mansion and hand him over to old Caravita or Reuben. What was the young fool of a dreamer to him? He glanced at the youth's white face, plastered with limp, rain-soaked hair, and remembered him as he'd arrived in Narbonne, desperate enough but full of feverish activity. God knows what he's heading for, and with Mirepoix to cap it, he laughed to himself bitterly. The only hope was to make it final. "Come on," he muttered, towing him by the arm.

They traversed a piece of the quay, then, diving suddenly into an alley, d'Alfaro pushed open a door. It belonged to a biggish building that fronted the water and which, though it now looked like a derelict warehouse, might once have boasted some pretensions. The foreroom was filled with tools and timber that suggested the business of a ship's carpenter, while the further quarters evidently served as living room and kitchen. As they entered, a savory smell rose from the pots on the hearth. The woman, he gathered, had once been in the service of Hugo's family.

"Pilar's no bad cook," laughed d'Alfaro. "Mother out?" he called good-humoredly to a black-haired girl who sat rocking a cradle by the hearth.

"Shopping," the child nodded.

Or gossiping. Well, she's likely to find enough to keep her tonight, he thought, as, throwing back the sackcloth that covered an arch in the further wall, he led the way up some steps. At the top he thrust open a door. The room was barely enough furnished, except for the low bed in the corner, a table, and a couple of chairs. Nevertheless, despite the rotting timbers and moldering walls, the fire burning in the hearth gave it sufficient comfort.

"For God's sake, go and dry," d'Alfaro said. "You'd better strip," he added, as Wolf desultorily pulled off his cloak.

"I'm all right. I can't stay very long," he answered.

Pouring wine from a pitcher, Hugo handed him a goblet.

"One of the few good things that Spain still produces," he commented.

The thick, oily liquid ran like fire through Wolf's veins. "Your Pilar makes you pretty comfortable."

"A bit too comfortable." Hugo grimaced. "She's set her heart on letting the old man hack out the family arms over the mantelpiece." He pointed to some notches in the stone. "Luckily I found out in time. Three hundred years of rot's enough to live with," he laughed, indicating the worm-eaten timbers. "No need to make it half a dozen. I only pacified her by saying he should put them up when I'd won my own. I suppose she still harbors a last hope I'll exchange the pen for the sword. Well, *they're* going to have a little rest, anyhow," he said, nodding toward the books that littered the table. Then, hanging his cloak before the fire, he pulled off his tunic. "The fact is I'm leaving Narbonne. I'm afraid I'll have to start packing now. Do you mind? Nearly all of it's staying here, of course, but I'll have to sort it out. Make yourself comfortable," he added, pulling a chair to the fire as Wolf stood looking at him blankly.

"You're leaving?" So *he's* getting out of it, he thought with a pang of jealousy. "To Spain?" he added bitterly.

"Spain?" d'Alfaro laughed. "Not quite." His eyes roamed over a sheaf of parchments covered, it seemed, with a curious script. Arabic perhaps, thought Wolf. They said he knew it.

Gathering together the parchments, Hugo began to tie them in a roll. "If you want to know," he said suddenly, "I'm probably off to Andorra. You've a brother there, haven't you?"

"Yes." Roger, thought Wolf, Roger whom he had scarcely seen. Of course, he'd be following in his father's footsteps.

"Something," Hugo continued, "is likely to happen soon. If one leaves it too late, one might find the way cut off."

But Wolf had sprung to his feet. His face had suddenly come to life. "You mean—they're going to resist?"

"There's a limit to what one can put up with."

"But—you don't believe in causes." It broke from him wild and bitter, all the pent-up fury gathered in the argument of months.

"I don't."

"Then why—"

"Resist?" d'Alfaro completed. "Resist for the sake of the Cause, resist for the sake of honor, resist for the sake of resistance. . . ."

Of course, Wolf told himself, it was only another bit of the man's devilish mockery. Nevertheless, he was burning with an unbearable excitement.

For a moment d'Alfaro glanced at him. "Well, do you feel like coming?" he asked, and cursed himself.

"I?" Then Hugo was really serious. How he had come by the news Wolf hardly waited to ask, conscious only that escape had offered itself at last. Miriam—it flashed through his mind. But wasn't she always saying, "Only wait for the right moment?" Of course she would come. "When are you starting?" he asked.

"At dawn."

It hardly gave them a chance to prepare. But she had been quick enough to act that night in Carcassonne. Surely she would now. Tomorrow they would be gone. Narbonne would be left behind them forever. She would be as she had been that night. Oh, he would prove to her he was no longer the green fool she believed him. It would have been better without d'Alfaro, he thought, but as he suggested it they could hardly leave him in the lurch.

"Does Miriam know?" he asked, his heart beating violently.

D'Alfaro had crossed over to a chest against the wall. Lighting a candle and setting it in the corner, he had begun to fit in a pile of books. "Yes," came out of the depths of the chest.

A pang of jealousy swept over Wolf. Intellectual rather than physical, for he no longer had qualms as to d'Alfaro's sentiments toward Miriam, it was nevertheless sharp enough. Had they arranged it together? Why was he then left out, or had it all taken place within the last few hours? Had she known already, would she have told him, if, overcome by her revelations, he had not fled? He could not bear to ask. One thing only was certain. He must go to her at once. He snatched up his cloak. He would return with her. After all, it would be his triumph.

"I'll be back soon," he said, already halfway across the room.

D'Alfaro swung round. "Where the deuce are you going?" he asked roughly.

"To Caravita's." His hand was already on the latch of the door, but Hugo had got to his feet.

"Wait."

Lifting the candle, he replaced it on the table. "I'd advise you not to," he muttered. Standing there, in shirt and breeches, his bony features illuminated by the light of the candle, he had even a sort of brigandish handsomeness. "Are you going to ask Miriam?" he gave his sardonic laugh.

"Of course—after all," Wolf retorted, only wishing that they need not accompany him, "she's in it too."

"In it? You young fool—she may have been."

"She is." Fury and jealousy combined to conquer the icy fear that rose within him. "You don't know her."

"Don't I?" Indifferent, d'Alfaro began to turn the pages of a book. "My friend, I've known Miriam Caravita long enough not only to appreciate her exceptional qualities— and you can imagine that but for them I would scarce have been likely to waste a moment upon her—but to know also, by experience, that, fortunately for her, she's

340

more interested in the reality of the present than in the phantom past."

"And she's right." Dropping the latch, Wolf turned on him vehemently. "We've finished with the past. Aren't you always mocking at it yourself—the rot of ages—the blight of the centuries?"

"Exactly," d'Alfaro smiled, "only unfortunately it's impossible to throw them off."

"With words, of course. But that's what we were fighting for up there—Trencavel—while you—'resistance for resistance sake. . . .'" It broke from him furiously. "You don't believe in anything, and so you don't imagine anyone else can—and just because she's reasonable, and wants things founded on fact, you think she's as cynical as yourself. But when it's a reality—you—you'll see . . ."

"I happen to have seen already."

"You . . ." But something in the piercing, sardonic gaze withered the rising retort. "What—what do you mean?"

"Just what I said." Shrugging, d'Alfaro laid down the book. "Well, if you don't believe me, go and see for yourself. But on the way I'd advise you to cultivate an aesthetic sense to help you to appreciate what Mirepoix no doubt calls a little work of art—a discourse on the mathematics of love."

"Mirepoix?" The heightened color drained from Wolf's face. He clutched at the door handle. D'Alfaro was coming toward him.

"He arrived this afternoon. Look here." As Wolf made a convulsive movement to open the door, he thrust himself between. "You're going to clear all that off your mind. After all, it's pretty irrelevant." His hand was on his arm. Suddenly all the cynicism had gone out of his voice. "Trencavel died last night."

There was an interminable silence. And then, at last, out of Wolf's white staring face broke a strangled sound, hardly even a cry, but torn terribly from the depth of his being. He swayed a little. Then his body sagged. Catching him in his arms, d'Alfaro lifted him and laid him upon the bed.

And the streams thereof shall be turned into pitch, and the dust thereof into brimstone, and the land thereof shall become burning pitch.

. . . From generation to generation it shall lie waste; none shall pass through it for ever and ever.

But the cormorant and the bittern shall possess it, the owl also and the raven shall dwell in it: and he shall stretch out upon it the line of confusion and the stones of emptiness.

They shall call the nobles thereof to the kingdom but none shall be there; and her princes shall be as nothing.

ISAIAH XXXIV

It was no longer human—an empty waste pitted and scarred with rubble and ash. They had journeyed beyond time into a country of the unknown, petrified, oscillated, a landscape of the moon.

And then, incredibly, a house, doored, shuttered, seemingly intact. They climbed the stairs, wondering that they did not dissolve beneath them. Hollow, their tread echoed from the empty walls. By silent consent they passed the night in the barn.

Later—it might have been centuries—they met a living creature. For a moment they stared at each other—ghosts from an obsolete world.

All at once there were more—a trickle of humanity creeping back, furtive but indomitable, trailing their remnant of salvaged goods. Somewhere a thin spiral of smoke rose from the broken chimney of a roofless cot. In a field an old man was plowing. Deprived of oxen, he had harnessed himself to the plow. Behind, her wispy hair blown on the wind, an aging woman trudged through the deepening furrows.

After all, it was still the earth. Beneath the hard-caked crust the soil waited, secret and dark. Cities crumbled—a heap of blackened timbers and fallen rubble—Béziers, Monreal, Fanjeaux, Castres. The earth went on.

Once more there was day and night. The seasons would pass—the rotation of the years. "The king," a voice echoed through Wolf's throbbing brain, "had also to be priest—the worker of magic—safeguarding the seasons—

till he became their sacrifice." In the firelight the riders rode on, unflinching.

But the slopes were studded with stumps of vine, the knotted trunks of the olives. Behind them the Aude flowed down to Carcassonne. Pricking their horses, they galloped over the frostbitten soil. "The earth . . ." challenging, it was flung back from Trencavel's lips, "the earth—isn't she enough?"

But dark, mocking Miriam's eyes were fixed upon his. "Life? Of course he's always raving about it, because what he's really craving for is death."

The hills grew higher, forests choked. Icy rain beat on Wolf's face, ran down his spine. Little daggers of fire shot through his limbs. Inside his head a hammer had begun to beat ceaselessly.

The forests were walls of stone, alleys foul with stench. Suddenly an archway gaped ravenous, swallowed them up. They had never come through, and yet hours later, it seemed, he was on his feet. A cobbled courtyard, the hiss of flaring torches. A room heavy with smoke. And faces, crowding, haggard, ravaged with hate, above the ceaseless mutter, senseless but for the one reiterated word: "Montfort—Montfort—Montfort." Or was it only the fiery hammers pounding on the anvil of his brain?

III

Hatred, thought Hugo d'Alfaro, glancing at the youth riding beside him. Next to love, doubtless the best means of escape. Probably it excelled it.

Only find a scapegoat, and the worst ills became bearable.

"Dysentery; personally," Mirepoix had shrugged, "I'd prefer the poison." Like many ribald remarks it was capable of deeper interpretation. Poison, murder, human violence—the wrong that could be got hold of, branded, avenged, the sensation offering the incomparable dope. It was the drab, sordid reality that Peire-Roger had called intolerable, but worse still, surely, was that vast impersonal malice of—what—fate?—the imponderable something that

343

man invented to cover the annihilating veracity of cause and effect, the Gorgon image of his own self-implication.

Well, since it was often enough the means of saving his reason, let him wallow in his hate. In the weeks during which Wolf had lain racked with fever in the little mountain town it had probably been the cause of saving his life. Certainly the news of Montfort's breach of the treaty with Foix had acted on him like a tonic. During the count's absence in Andorra, Montfort, it appeared, acting on a mysterious invitation, had swooped boldly upon Pamiers. Triumphant at the success of his ruse, the Abbot of St. Anthony delivered the castellar, that stronghold of heresy, into the devout hands of a true son of the Church. The saint was avenged. Another prophecy fulfilled.

In the twinkling of an eye, Mirepoix, Saverdun, the whole of the lower country were in Montfort's hands. Raging, Ramon-Roger had sped back to Foix. With a last hope of pacific reconciliation, Raymond of Toulouse had set out for Rome.

Whatever the ultimate hopes of that colloquy, Simon's next step might call for action any moment, no longer as a question of ideals or strategic exigency, but of sheer self-preservation. After all, thought d'Alfaro wryly, glancing once more at Wolf, old Foix might at last find satisfaction in this son of his. It looked as though for the first time in their lives the two might really understand each other. But, still unable to resign himself to the set hardness of the thin stark face, he turned away.

At the junction of the roads, where the valley, dividing, opened up a narrower gorge leading over the pass to Andorra, they parted. A few weeks ago they would have journeyed on together. Instead, Wolf rode on alone, bound westward along the highway to Foix.

The sun had vanished. The sky hung like a leaden pall. With luck he would reach Foix before the next fall of snow. Around him the mountains closed—a world of rock and snow and icebound peaks. He passed through Lavelanet. To his left Montségur stuck out blunted from the white rump of the Tabor.

Still he rode on without turning. The rock was metal. In the rifts the snow reached down to the road. The air had the thin, acrid smell of iron.

Somewhere on the way he had struck back a branch

from an overhanging tree. A twig had remained clinging to his cloak. Mechanically he pulled it off. After a while, discovering it still in his hand, he began to gnaw at the bark. It was sticky sweet under the frozen rind.

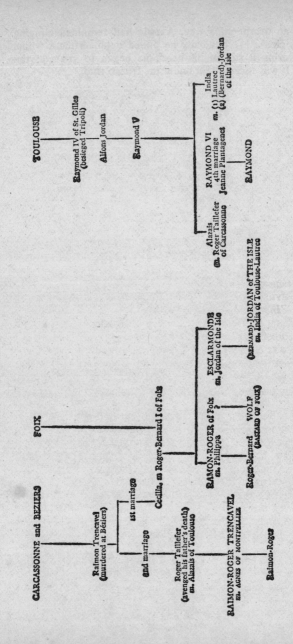

SOME BOOKS
BEARING ON THE SUBJECT

P. MEYER: *La Chanson de la Croisade contre les Albigeois.* Paris. 1875–79.

DOMS VIC ET VAISÈTTE: *Histoire générale de Languedoc.* Toulouse. 1872 ff.

N. PEYRAT: *Histoire des Albigeois (La Civilisation Romane; La Croisade).*

N. PEYRAT: *Histoire des Albigeois (Les Albigeois et L'Inquisition).* Paris. 1870.

DENIS DE ROUGEMONT: *Passion and Society;* tr. by M. BELGION. Faber and Faber. 1940.

O. RAHN: *Kreuzzug gegen den Gral.* Freiburg i. B. 1933.

F. v. SUHTSCHEK: *Wolframs von Eschenbach Pârsîwal-nâmâ-Übersetzung.* F. u. F. 1931.

PIERRE DE VAUX-CERNAY: *Histoire Albigensium et sacri belli in eos anno M.CC.IX. . . .*

PIERRE BELPERRON: *La Croisade contre les Albigeois et l'union du Languedoc à la France* 1209–1249. Paris.

DEODAT ROCHE: *Le Catharisme.* Toulouse. 1947.

HANNAH CLOSS: *Courtly Love in Literature and Art.* (Symposium. Syracuse University, Syracuse, N.Y. November, 1947.)

HANNAH CLOSS: *The Meeting of the Waters: An Enquiry into the Interrelationships of East and West in the Mystery of the Grail.* (The Aryan Path, May and June, 1948. Bombay, India.)

Since the completion of this volume I have come across this passage in *Horizon,* vol. xi, February 1945:

"Rebels just as much as the insurgents of Spartacus

were the heroic Manichæans, massacred in hundreds of thousands, during eight hundred years . . . and whose torment was to . . . burst into brightest flame in the Catharist quest for the Grail."

(JACQUES B. BRUNIUS: *Neither God Nor Devil*.)

ALL TIME BESTSELLERS
FROM POPULAR LIBRARY

☐ THE BERLIN CONNECTION—Simmel	08607-6	1.95
☐ THE BEST PEOPLE—Van Slyke	08456-1	1.75
☐ A BRIDGE TOO FAR—Ryan	08373-5	2.50
☐ THE CAESAR CODE—Simmel	08413-8	1.95
☐ DO BLACK PATENT LEATHER SHOES REALLY REFLECT UP?—Powers	08490-1	1.75
☐ ELIZABETH—Hamilton	04013-0	1.75
☐ THE FURY—Farris	08620-3	2.25
☐ THE HAB THEORY—Eckerty	08597-5	2.50
☐ HARDACRE—Skelton	04026-2	2.25
☐ THE HEART LISTENS—Van Slyke	08520-7	1.95
☐ TO KILL A MOCKINGBIRD—Lee	08376-X	1.50
☐ THE LAST BATTLE—Ryan	08381-6	2.25
☐ THE LAST CATHOLIC IN AMERICA—Powers	08528-2	1.50
☐ THE LONGEST DAY—Ryan	08380-8	1.95
☐ LOVE'S WILD DESIRE—Blake	08616-5	1.95
☐ THE MIXED BLESSING—Van Slyke	08491-X	1.95
☐ MORWENNA—Goring	08604-1	1.95
☐ THE RICH AND THE RIGHTEOUS —Van Slyke	08585-1	1.95

Buy them at your local bookstores or use this handy coupon for ordering: